GATE OF SOULS

BOOK ONE: A FAMILIAR'S TALE
Verna McKinnon

WolfSinger Publications ◖ Brackettville, Texas

DEDICATION

I dedicate my novels to my loving husband, Rick Hipps,
who always supported my writing and believed in me.

PROLOGUE

Belwyn was agitated by the dry heat and sand. A gray mountain owl, Belwyn was bred for cooler climates, and the constant grit and hot sun of arid deserts made him cranky. His magical nature as a sorcerer's familiar broadened his adaptability, but that didn't mean he liked it.

"My feathers itch," Belwyn groused.

The shrill whistling wind outside their tent only added to his frustration—one born of helplessness as he watched over his sorcerer, Cathal. Cathal sat in mute misery on the dusty rug, dark hair sweaty and matted, gray eyes cast in a blank stare. Not even his rage remained, only a sorrow that devoured his heart.

The oil lamps smoked and sputtered out, casting more gloom in the shelter.

"Bloody hell," Belwyn grumbled.

Caliste entered the tent. "The storm is finally abating. We should be able to leave tomorrow," she said in a weary voice, shaking red dust from her hair and clothes.

"Good. I hate being blasted by sand," Belwyn said.

"Why is it so dark in here?"

"It reflects my mood," Belwyn said.

"How's Cathal?" she asked. "Any change at all?"

"You needn't whisper, my dear. He's a statue of flesh, closed off to everything…including me."

Caliste sparked the lamps to flame with a nimble turn of her hand. "That's better. There has been enough darkness." She sat next to Belwyn; her beautiful black face pinched with concern. "I wish we could do something. He can't go on like this."

"The Sorcerer War is over," Belwyn said. "But for some of us, it will never be finished. The death of his family was the final blow that broke his spirit." Belwyn fought down raging emotions that threatened to erupt. Nothing could excise this pain, but Belwyn would not retreat into his own mourning until Cathal could at least weep for his loss.

"Cathal once called Ashur son, when he married his daughter," Caliste said with bitterness. "I still can't fathom how he became such a monster. How he could—"

"I know," Belwyn whispered. "None of us will ever understand why."

Belwyn winced as memories of Cathal's wife and daughter rose like ghosts. "So many lost. Yllia, Rualla, even Rualla's familiar, Striker, all dead, along with so many others, because of a sorcerer's madness. The worst blow was Runa."

The thought of Ashur murdering his own daughter tormented Belwyn. Talons dug deeper into the ragged carpet as more memories were unleashed. The fateful meeting on the battlefield in Thill and Ashur's gruesome gift—a silver urn filled with the ashes of Cathal's wife and daughter—and his granddaughter, Runa. Tied to the urn were the women's silver and amber wedding rings, and Runa's tiny rattle.

That confrontation led to a mad chase across the continent and several battles, ending here in Mowad, in the middle of this damned desert. The forbidden magic they used to defeat Ashur would give Belwyn nightmares for years to come. There wasn't enough ale in the world to make him forget, but he learned a long time ago that to fight evil you had to get your talons bloody.

Ashur was dead. The fight for Cathal's salvation would be harder.

"Any word on Ashur's forces?" he asked.

"Fled or surrendered, all over the continent. Even Ashur's demons are vanishing like phantoms, or crawling back into the foul pits they slithered out of. It's like they know Ashur is dead."

"What of Koll?" Belwyn asked with grim interest.

"That evil sorcerer has disappeared," Caliste replied. Her voice was sharp with anger. "He's not among the dead or captured."

Belwyn's feathers bristled. "Pity. I wanted to stain my claws with the blood of Ashur's Chief Warlord."

"Don't upset yourself further. You should rest. It's been two days, and you haven't slept or eaten. If I bring some fresh food and water, would you at least pretend to eat?" Caliste asked.

"Maybe later. For now, just tell the others Cathal is resting," Belwyn suggested. "Let's not add to their concern. They've all been through enough already."

"Very well," she agreed. She kissed Belwyn, then Cathal, on the head, and departed.

Alone with Cathal again, the owl pondered on how to reach his sorcerer. He couldn't remain like this. The dangers of his emotional retreat could be permanent if he didn't do something soon. He shouted, cursed, and begged. He nudged Cathal with his beak again and again without response. Desperate, he bit him on the shoulder, drawing blood. Nothing. Belwyn finally used the bonding to telepathically slip into his mind. He had not intruded before, since he wanted to allow Cathal his private mourning. But enough was enough.

Cathal…Cathal! Can you even hear me? It's Belwyn. Remember me?

There was a stubborn wall shielding Cathal's thoughts. At least it wasn't an empty void.

Cathal!

Leave me alone, Belwyn.

His response was hollow, barely a whisper. But it was something.

Not a chance. You should know me better than that.

They're dead. There's nothing left.

I know, Belwyn answered. *The sorcerers need your leadership. I need you.*

I'm not strong enough…not anymore.

"I need you," Belwyn wept aloud. "I will be strong…strong enough for both of us. Come back to me."

Loud voices outside disrupted Belwyn's concentration. "Damn it! Now what?" he snapped.

"Belwyn," Caliste shouted, "you better come see this!"

He relented and poked his head out of the tent to see what the commotion was about. The glaring sun *still* scorched the earth. The people were *still* dirty and smelly from lack of water.

And above, in the hot, cloudless firmament of this unbearable desert, Belwyn spotted some new, unexpected arrivals.

In the sky a cavalry of Ilyrran rangers riding perytons descended to earth with powerful grace. Perytons, the magnificent, winged deer native only to the lands of Ilyrra, were a rare sight in this bleak land. The stunned soldiers and sorcerers gave them a respectful welcome as they rode into the camp.

What the blazes are they doing here, Belwyn wondered.

Belwyn's feathers raised on his back when he recognized the lead ranger in the dark green and black of his command. As he dismounted a silver peryton, the desert gusts exposed a resolute windburned face, long black hair, and the upswept ears that marked the Ilyrran race.

It was Ryen.

The gathering crowd parted with solemn silence at his determined stride as he marched toward their tent.

Belwyn winged to Cathal's side. "Our friend Ryen is here. Cathal please, this must be important!"

Caliste lifted the flap and led Ryen into their small tent. Ryen looked weary and filthy, but it lifted Belwyn's heart to see him.

"Light's Blessing, Belwyn," Ryen bowed, giving the traditional Ilyrran greeting.

"No blessings or light here. We're a bit short on those now," Belwyn said with grim humor. "But I am glad you're alive, Ryen. Is your family safe?"

"Yes, thank be the Gods," Ryen replied. "I've been hunting you for days." He looked at Cathal, brow furrowed with worry. "How bad is he?"

"I wish I could say he's been worse, but that would be a lie," Belwyn confessed.

"Perhaps I can lighten his burden," Ryen said, kneeling before Cathal. Ryen gazed into Cathal's face "I'm sorry for your loss, my friend. Yllia was of our people. We mourn her and Rualla. But I have someone you need to see, Cathal. Someone who needs you."

Ryen opened his heavy cloak, revealing a small bundle wrapped in a blanket that began to cry. Belwyn sucked in his breath when he saw the treasure he held was Runa.

Cathal stirred and gasped in a weak voice, "Runa."

"Yes—it's Runa," Ryen nodded. "Your granddaughter."

Cathal opened his arms and Ryen placed the weeping infant in them. In the span of three breaths, Runa ceased crying and gazed with innocent trust at the man who held her. "How?" he whispered.

"We were fighting in the north, near Thill, where Ashur's forces crossed into our borders. While camped by the river, a red panther staggered into our midst."

"Striker?" Belwyn cried. "You found him!"

"Yes." Ryen nodded. "He was carrying a ragged cloth in his mouth. We recognized Rualla's familiar and ran to his aid. Striker's wounds were beyond our skill and he had lost a great deal of blood. Striker gazed at me with relief and laid his precious prize at my feet. He collapsed, and, in that fragile moment, he died in my arms. A cry issued from the rags he protected. We opened the scraps of cloth and found Runa. She had been content in the jaws of the panther and cried when we took her from him. Striker died before he could tell us how he rescued Runa from Ashur's wrath. He paid for his last act of bravery with his life. I'm sorry, old friends, for Striker. But I return Runa to your loving care, Cathal."

Runa's crystal green eyes, reminiscent of Rualla and Yllia, lit up the dim shelter. Tenderness softened Cathal's features as he cradled the baby. Hope seemed possible again.

Weary but relieved, Ryen stood. "We carried Striker's body back to Moonthorne. The Raven Wing honored him with the funeral of fallen heroes and buried him in the sacred grove beneath an old willow oak. When word reached us the war was over, and you were here, we came as fast as we could."

"Thank you, Ryen," Cathal said, his voice choked with emotion.

Cathal rocked Runa in his arms, until finally, blessedly, he wept.

CHAPTER 1

Mellypip crouched behind his siblings in the nest, trying not to sneeze as rough twigs scratched his sensitive nose. Sneezing would make him visible to the strange silver-haired human floating before their tree hole, and he did not want that. Sweet, warm grasses and leaves of the wampu's lair did not stop Mellypip's shivering, and the excited chirps of his siblings only added to his discontentment.

"Now children, stop fussing," his mother warned. "Sorcerer Cathal is here to honor us! Behave like good little kits, or there'll be no cherries for dessert!"

"Cherries! Oh, if only I had some juicy red cherries to comfort me," Mellypip whispered. "Or gooseberries or hazelnuts, even." Eating was a favorite pastime and deflected his nervous thoughts for a moment as he sucked his paw.

Cathal levitated with apparent ease, holding a long, strange stick of smooth wood in his hand that gleamed with polish. The top was carved into the shape of an owl's head. Owls were predators, his mother taught him. Predators eat wampu.

"Now, now, young kits," Cathal said gently, "I'll need your attention for only a moment. I'm here for an important test. I have some sugared walnuts as a treat for your cooperation."

Cathal's voice, despite his knowledge of the wampu speak, was full of terrifying echoes. Humans were dangerous, after all. All forest creatures know this. And what was a *sorcerer* anyway? It couldn't be good.

Cathal reached into the hole with a strange rock, blotting out the beams of sunlight. Mellypip covered his face with chubby paws but could not resist peeking to see what the human was doing. The rock was a blue crystal and quite pretty. He waved the crystal over the heads of his more curious siblings. They chirped and sniffed as it passed over their fuzzy heads. It did nothing.

Silly. Was that all? Mellypip sighed, until the sorcerer made another pass, this time over Mellypip's head.

The crystal glowed with blue light and a melodic hum filled the air.

"Ah, Belwyn was right!" Cathal said. "One of your kits is blessed. He is a familiar."

"Gracious, my Mellypip a familiar!".

"What's a *familiar*, Mama?" his sister asked, round eyes studying Mellypip with more than the usual annoyance.

"It means you are magical. No one will hunt you or eat you. Familiars live with wizards and sorcerers."

"Yes," Cathal nodded. "Mellypip will learn many things, and I promise you he will have an excellent home."

"I'll miss my Mellypip," his mother cried.

"Miss me?" Mellypip squeaked. "Where am I going?" He waddled over the humphs and ouches of his siblings, and buried his head in her furry tummy. "I don't wanna go anywhere!"

His mother sighed, patting her plump little son with gentle paws. "You must go, Mellypip. The Sorcerer will take good care of you. He's a good magic human. I will miss you." Mellypip's brown eyes glazed with tears. "Don't cry. Life will be an adventure. And humans have lots of food. You won't have to pick and gather, or build a tree nest."

"Your mother is right," Cathal said. "We will keep you warm and protected. I know you're confused now, but soon you will see it's for the best. A familiar born in the wild these days is a rare thing, so you are very special." He gave his mother a large pouch of sugared nuts. Mellypip was so upset he couldn't even eat one.

She hugged Mellypip one last time. He waved goodbye to his brother and sister, who for once were sad to see him go.

"Come, Mellypip, it's time to go to your new home," Cathal said.

Mellypip allowed Cathal to pick him up.

"Goodbye, Mellypip," his family said sadly.

"Thank you, Mother Wampu. I'll see a season of berries and nuts are provided for your family." He gently rubbed Mellypip's head with his finger. "Now, my little friend, time to go." He held him close as they descended the many branch levels to the forest floor. Magic was indeed a wondrous thing—and nerve-racking!

Mellypip curled up into a furry ball like a stubborn hedgehog in Cathal's palm to hide his tears. As they traveled through the woods, Mellypip's keen sense of smell and sharp ears also alerted him to other woodland creatures, squirrels, raccoons, robins, and others not so friendly—wolves, lynxes, and the grumble of bears awakened from their winter slumber. It was dangerous to be so small in such a big, scary world. New, exotic odors of wood smoke and cooked food assailed his nostrils.

"We're home," Cathal said. "Don't you want to look?"

Mellypip unrolled his body and opened his eyes. He gasped at the sight before him. "That is the biggest tree I ever saw."

An enormous ancient tree loomed before him, decorated with windows on several levels and at the base a large door with a brass dragon knocker. "It must be the span of a dozen trees at least! I can't even see where the tree's top is!" Mellypip exclaimed. "You live in a tree too? Is this a magic tree?"

"Well, it's not exactly a cozy wampu nest, but I like it. You will grow to love it here too."

"Are you sure I'm magical?" Mellypip asked.

"Positive. The crystal confirmed it. Plus you can understand me. Without the gift of magic you would not understand human tongue. Your wampu family understood me because I used a spell to communicate with them," he explained.

He looked at Cathal, noting the crinkles around his gray eyes, and the curve of his smile in his close-trimmed beard. He was a nice human—so far.

"Did you make the tree?"

"No. It's a very old, but extraordinary tree, planted from an Ilyrran seed centuries ago. I have lived here for a long time. Let's go inside," Cathal said. "There's someone special I want you to meet."

They entered the sorcerer's lair. Mellypip noticed many bizarre things in the tree house. Objects he had no name for yet, but would come to learn them as chairs, stove, tables, chests, vials, pots, and beds. Fire (which terrified him at first) burned in the stove and in the round brick hearth. Stacks upon stacks of books and scrolls musty with age cluttered the living area on tables and bookcases, along with colorful maps and pictures of things ancient and mysterious. Several rocks that glowed like the sun captivated him.

"What are those?" he asked shyly. "They shine so bright."

"Light crystals. They are grown in Ironia by the Dwarven folk. It's their chief export."

"What are Dwarvens?"

Cathal laughed. "Dwarves. They're people; a race of little folk—though only in stature. They are big in battle and heart. I have a few Dwarven relations, as a matter of fact. They have magical folk too. They call them wizards."

They passed through the cramped surroundings of the human

nest to walk up a long, curved staircase. The steps seemed to go on for many levels, but they stopped at the second floor and walked down a short hallway where there were more doors. Cathal stopped before a blue painted door and knocked.

"Runa? Sweetheart? Are you in there?"

"Go away," answered a small voice.

He sighed. "Now, don't be upset. Let me in."

Magic opened the door. They stepped into a small, round room. At the far end of the cluttered chamber, curled up on a narrow bed, a young girl was weeping. She was barefoot, wore a blue dress, and had masses of shiny brown hair that curled around her face and touched the floor. Mellypip lifted his delicate nose toward her. His little heart filled with pity for the human girl. Was she taken from her family too?

"There, there, Runa," Cathal said gently, sitting on the edge of the bed. "Don't cry. It's going to be all right."

She sniffled, face puffy and red from crying. But when she looked up, her eyes were a startling shade of bright green. "Then…you're not mad about the potion?"

"Of course not. Explosions are a frequent danger in the art of potion making. Especially for an apprentice. I blew up a few myself at your age." He lifted Mellypip in his hand. "See whom I have brought to live with us."

Her face softened. "Oh, Grandpa, it's a baby wampu! Did he fall out of his nest?" She tickled his chin.

"No." Mellypip giggled. "He picked me. He floats too."

"He's a familiar!" Runa said surprised.

"His name is Mellypip." Cathal grinned. "He will be yours, if you bond."

"He's adorable, and so tiny!" she exclaimed. "You really think I'm old enough? I thought I had to be eighteen before I earned the privilege."

Cathal shrugged. "You'll be fifteen next month. I was lucky and received Belwyn when I was sixteen. And you are my best student."

"I'm your only student," Runa said. "May I hold you, Mellypip?"

"Oh, yes, please," Mellypip answered.

She scooped him into her small soft hands. "Is he old enough to be away from his family? He's so small he fits into the palm of my hand."

"He is about eight weeks, I think. He'll grow fast though. Wampu only grow to the size of a housecat. Good thing, considering their appetites. His golden-brown fur will be like velvet, his large round ears make for excellent hearing. They also have a keen sense of smell. His dexterous paws will enable him to turn pages of books and hold small objects with ease. They are also very curious, when not rolled up into a ball of fur, that is. But remember, you must bond."

"Oh, we will! I just know it! Thank you, Grandpa," she gushed, and hugged the old sorcerer. Mellypip, sandwiched between them, squeaked.

"Oh, I'm sorry Mellypip!" she cried. "I'm hungry. How about you?"

The mention of food made his tummy rumble. "Oh yes! I am famished for food."

"Well, let's go and make tea," Cathal said. "Belwyn should be back soon."

Runa put Mellypip on her shoulder. "Oh dear. I hope he's not angry with me."

"He'll get over it," Cathal sighed. "It's not the first time his butt feathers got singed."

"Who is Belwyn?" Mellypip asked as they went downstairs.

"My familiar," Cathal replied. "And your teacher too."

Mellypip pondered this. He thought just being magical was enough. In the living room, as they called it, Runa fashioned a make-shift bed with a blanket of flannel in a small wicker basket. "Rest here, Mellypip, while I make the afternoon tea."

He jumped into the soft material and curled up, quite comfortable and content until tea was ready.

The tea was quite marvelous. Mellypip licked his plate clean. He was content with a tummy full of fresh bread, blackberry jam, and hearty vegetable pie. Perhaps being a familiar was not so bad after all.

Then a dangerous smell assaulted Mellypip's nose. A flurry of gray and white wings flew through the open casement window, and an intimidating owl landed on the back of Cathal's wooden chair. Mellypip panicked and stumbled into a dish of cream. The regal owl was not perturbed by the ruckus he caused. Large golden eyes glanced at Mellypip with indifference. He sniffed the remains of the feast.

"Belwyn, you scared him!" Runa scolded, picking Mellypip up with one hand and wiping up the spilt cream with the other.

"Late for tea again," the owl lamented. "I see. Did you at least save me some jam and bread?"

"Of course Belwyn," Runa replied. "Would I let you do without?"

"How are your feathers?" Cathal asked.

"Burnt and raw, thanks to certain potions mishandled by adolescent females." He studied the wampu. "Plump little morsel, isn't he?"

Mellypip dove into Runa's apron pocket for protection.

"Belwyn!" Cathal warned. "Don't tease the poor little fellow. He's new to this. This is the wampu you told me about—remember?"

"Ah, I don't mean any harm to the furball," Belwyn said. He swiveled his head around to Cathal. "I told you I was right. I sensed him right off when I was getting my exercise a few weeks back." He turned back to Runa and Mellypip. "Let's see the little runt."

"Mellypip, come out of Runa's smock and meet Belwyn properly. He is a great familiar, with additional qualities of rudeness and sarcasm, but we love him just the same," Cathal said.

"You forgot to mention my charm," the owl added.

"Come out, Mellypip. He won't hurt you," Runa begged.

"No."

"Please. I'll give you a hazelnut if you do," Runa whispered.

Mellypip sighed and poked his head out.

"Say hello to Belwyn," Runa encouraged. "And Belwyn, be nice!"

"Hello," Mellypip said nervously. He looked at Runa. "Can I have my hazelnut now?"

"Belwyn won't hurt you, Melly." Runa smiled. "He's just being a cranky head."

Mellypip decided to be brave, and wiggled out of her pocket back onto the wooden table. He brushed crumbs off his fur. "I am Mellypip, the familiar."

Belwyn looked down at him with sharp golden eyes. "And I am your teacher, Furball."

"My name is Mellypip!" he chirped. *Please don't eat me*, Mellypip thought.

Runa gave him a hazelnut and he nibbled it with dainty ferocity, never taking his eyes off the owl.

The large owl waddled over to Mellypip. He towered over the wampu's tiny form. "Don't worry, Furball. We are brothers now in the clan of magic. Familiars don't eat each other...unless they are enemies." The owl hooted a chuckle and snatched a bit of jam covered bread Runa put before him. The playful glint in his hoop-like eyes allowed Mellypip to relax a bit.

"Tomorrow you will begin to learn things," Runa said, picking him up and stroking him. "We understand each other because of the magic born to us. But there is a lot more."

"Because that is where the free ride ends," Cathal said. "You will learn a familiar's magic, but also how to read and write languages; understand the power of runes, crystals and spells. There will be a great deal of study."

"Welcome to my world," Runa sighed.

"Can anyone learn magic?" Mellypip asked.

"No," Cathal answered. "You must be born to it. That is what makes our caste special."

"And why we spend so much time with our nose in a book," Runa said.

"Can I call you Grandpa too?" Mellypip asked.

"Yes," the sorcerer said with a laugh.

Between the wonderful food that stuffed his belly and the overwhelming events of the day, all energy drained out of Mellypip. "I'm pooped," he sighed.

"It's been a big day," Runa said. "We have to bond too, and until we do, you're not really my familiar. I hope we can soon."

Mellypip remembered Cathal mentioning that before. "What's bonding?"

"When a mage and familiar telepathically communicate."

"Huh?"

"Oh, sorry," she said. "That was a bit much to say."

"I don't think the big words are a good idea yet," Belwyn suggested. "Think monosyllabic communication for now."

"Belwyn, that's not nice!" Runa said. She turned to Mellypip and explained. "When we can read each other's thoughts and feelings is bonding."

"That is hugely magical," Mellypip agreed.

"Until that momentous occasion, it's time for class," Belwyn said. "Do you know what an alphabet is, Furball?"

"I'm about to find out, aren't I?" Mellypip replied.

"That's a smart little wampu," the owl said.

~ * ~

The sorcerer's tree tower was a wondrous place. There were many levels. The main floor of the tree was the kitchen and living room. A bathing chamber and a separate privy were amazing! The large copper tub could be filled with water at the turn of a tap, and

Runa often sprinkled sweet smelling lilac powder into her bath that made bubbles. He liked bubbles. The privy confused him. Why not go outside to do your business? But people were indeed different and strange from the animal clans.

On the second floor were the bedrooms. Runa and Cathal each had their own room. The third floor was the magic room. He liked that chamber the best of all. The fourth level was storage, where there were many boxes and trunks filled with books and old clothes.

He had been living with Runa for about three weeks. The days had gone by so fast, but they still had not bonded. It worried him a little. But he loved Runa and tried to not let it darken his mood. He woke up one morning, rubbed his face with his paws. Sunbeams poured through the window. He leaned over his sleeping basket next to the bed. Runa was just waking, her cotton shift rumpled and braids unraveled.

She stretched and smiled. "Morning Melly," she yawned.

"Morning Runa," he said, swishing his fluffy tail.

"Want some breakfast?"

"Oh yes, please!" he replied, leaping out and greeting her with a playful lick on the nose. He patted his tummy. "Surely my growls of hunger must be very loud."

"They are echoing through the tree house," she said with a laugh.

She dressed in an oatmeal-colored tunic and black trousers. "I wonder what Grandfather wants to do today?" she asked, opening her window. "It's so nice outside. I wonder if we could skip study and go swimming."

"I like swimming," he agreed.

They went downstairs, and Cathal was already up, cooking porridge and toasting bread.

"Morning," Runa said, giving him a kiss on the cheek.

"Morning. Are you ready for a little potion making today?" he asked, flipping the toast on the hearth magically.

Runa hung her head. "Can't I try a new spell or something? Potions hate me."

He spooned porridge into bowls, and they sat down together. Runa added generous amounts of honey and cinnamon to her cereal.

"They don't hate you. You simply need to focus," he insisted.

Belwyn flew down the stairs and perched on a chair. "Speaking of focus," Belwyn said, "we have more book learning this morning."

"But it's nice outside," Mellypip groaned. "The clouds are fluffy, and the sky is blue."

"If you desist from whining we can study in the yard. Will that suffice?"

"I thought being a familiar would be more fun," Mellypip grumbled, stirring his porridge with his tiny spoon.

"Time for play later," Belwyn insisted.

Runa and Mellypip exchanged martyred glances and knew there would be no fun at the river today.

After breakfast, Cathal set up his primer outside on the wicker table. It was large, on glossy paper with bright pictures, and Mellypip enjoyed looking at.

Belwyn pointed to the first page with his wing. "Read the first page, Furball."

Mellypip looked at the words, and slowly sounded them out. "See the sorcerer run…run, sorcerer run."

"Excellent," Belwyn said, and turned the page magically. "Now, read the next page."

Mellypip became distracted by a ripe yellow dandelion and nibbled it.

"Furball!" Belwyn shouted. "Pay attention."

"Yes, Belwyn," he said. "I'm sorry."

"Don't be sorry. Be better."

A muffled crash startled them. They looked up to see a stream of pink smoke floating out of the third-floor window.

"Oh dear," Belwyn said, and flew up to the sorcery chamber.

"Hey, wait for me!" cried Mellypip. He ran into the house and up the stairs, his heart racing. He rushed into the room, to find Cathal and Runa both covered with pink dust, coughing and laughing uncontrollably.

"The laughter potion was a tad overdone dear."

"It's a lethal weapon," Belwyn said.

Runa, you scared me, he thought.

"I'm sorry I scared you, Melly," she replied. She stopped and a smile lit up her lovely face. "Melly, think that again."

You scared me, he thought toward her.

She sent a thought back, *Can you hear this?*

"Yes," he replied. "Of course I heard—"

"She spoke in my head!" Mellypip announced, bouncing into her arms, pink dust powdering his fur.

Cathal hugged Runa. "You bonded! I'm so happy for you. I knew you too were right for each other."

"Yeah, like there's a lot of choice out here in the sticks," Belwyn hooted.

"We're finally bonded!" she said happily.

"I think this calls for a celebration," Cathal said, beaming with pride.

"I vote for ale," Belwyn suggested.

"Belwyn, they're children," Cathal said. "Cookies and lemonade."

"Goody," Mellypip said.

They had a wonderful day, full of fresh baked cookies and icy drinks. That night, Runa crawled into bed, tired but elated. Mellypip curled up on Runa's pillow and went to sleep. In the cradle of slumber, his dreams interwove with Runa's. He floated in her dreamscape, the strange ethereal bond pulling him along, which was fun, until a dark vision made her weep in her sleep. Her dream state flowed into Mellypip's mind, tethering him to its images of a dark red crystal cracking and a man cloaked in black fire that made Mellypip whimper. He pulled himself out of sleep, shaken. Runa was crying, bound by her nightmare. He called to her, both in voice and bonding. "Wake up!"

She woke with a cry, damp with sweat.

"What was that, Runa?"

"I don't know," she said weeping. "A bad dream."

"Have you ever had that dream before?" he asked.

"I've had bad dreams, but never anything like this."

"Maybe you had too much sugar?" he said. "Belwyn says that's my problem."

"Perhaps." She shivered.

He crawled into the nook of her arm and cuddled. "It's all right Runa," he said softly. "Go to sleep. I'm your guardian, so I'll protect you."

They huddled together for several sleepless hours. Mellypip would be brave. He would always protect Runa, no matter how scared he was.

CHAPTER 2

Mellypip loved the sorcery chamber. It smelled of potent magic and mystery. The deep blue ceiling was decorated with silver stars and moons that drifted above him with sorcerous motion. The large, oval window was open and fresh spring breeze filled the room. Mellypip relaxed on his back, snuggled into the soft rug, watching the stars dance.

The owl leaned over him, blocking his starry view with impatient golden eyes. "Wake up, Furball."

"I'm awake, Belwyn. I'm studying the constellations."

"It's a ceiling." He nudged him with his beak. "Time for a quiz."

Runa worked at the potion table, carefully adding drops to her bottle. The small copper cauldron simmered over a blue flame. Dozens of glass vials were scattered on the table, the vivid colors sparkling.

"I hope your latest concoction doesn't go boom," Mellypip said, investigating the collection of ornate spell boxes, scrolls, volumes of enchantments, and crystal tomes lining cedar shelves that covered the opposite wall from floor to ceiling. In front of that sat Cathal's enormous desk of pale golden oak, intricately etched with rune symbols. He whiffed several of the magic boxes, charmed by their mystical scent.

Runa sighed. "It won't—and you can take that look of fear off your face, Belwyn."

"I'm not afraid," Belwyn replied. "Just cautious. My tail feathers are just now growing back in."

She stuck out her tongue and resumed her sorcerous chemistry. "Spells and incantations are easy for me. Why are potions such a torment?"

"We all have obstacles to overcome," Belwyn said. "That's why Cathal insists you master them. Potions are a great asset to any mage."

"Where did Grandpa Cathal go this morning?" Mellypip asked, toying with the forbidden spell boxes. "He was gone when we woke up."

"He went to the village to do a little shopping," Belwyn said. His head swiveled around to Mellypip. "And put down that box,

Furball."

Mellypip snapped to attention, paws frozen—until Belwyn looked away again.

"For my birthday?" Runa asked excitedly. "What am I getting?"

"None of your business," Belwyn said. "But yes, he is getting
your presents, plus supplies for the party. It's school time now, so
back to work."

A delicate round box made of smooth jade intrigued Mellypip.
The salty smell urged him to peek, just a little. He lifted the lid and a
whoosh of enchantment sent him high into the air, where he floated
around the room. "Help! I can't get down!" He waved his little arms
and legs desperately.

Belwyn groaned. "I told you not to touch the spell boxes. Does
anyone ever listen to the wise old owl? No...never. Why am I even
here?"

Runa chased after Mellypip, trying to catch her flying familiar,
but he was above her reach.

"I should let you bobble in the air all day," Belwyn threatened.

"Please don't," Mellypip begged. "I think I need to piddle."

Belwyn flew over to the jade box and snapped the lid closed.
The tug of magic that pulled Mellypip was severed, and he dropped
into Runa's waiting arms. She set him on the rug.

"Are you all right?" she asked, concerned.

"That was fun," Mellypip said.

"Enough nonsense! This is study time. We must be serious,"
Belwyn boomed.

"Sorry, Belwyn," Mellypip said. He jumped on the large oak
desk. Belwyn propped up a large colorful text, turning the page to a
brilliant painting of a creature. "What is this?" he asked.

"A gryphon."

"And what are they?"

"Magical creatures, but serve no purpose as familiars, since
they're not very smart. Many folk use them as flying mounts."

"Excellent," Belwyn said, and a candied nut bounced from the
dish into Mellypip's mouth.

The page turned. "And this elegant creature?"

"A peryton, which is a winged deer. They live in Ilyrra and are
the mounts of the Ilyrran rangers, called Raven Wing. They are smart
and come in many pretty colors. They are fierce fighters."

"Good," Belwyn said. Another nut magically flew toward

Mellypip, who caught it with unerring precision. "Now what about this picture?"

Mellypip stopped chewing when he saw the fearsome drawing. It was a hideous creature with bulbous black eyes and grayish green skin. "That's a goblin. I don't like them. They are ugly and evil."

"Very good. Now, what are the three castes of mages?"

Mellypip crunched the yummy treat. "The Sorcerers of the human folk, The Wizards of the Dwarven folk, and the Drusai of the Ilyrrans."

"Very good," the owl complimented him. "And what are their leaders called?"

Mellypip thought for a moment. "The Archon is the Sorcerer's leader, the Mage Chieftain for the Dwarven Wizards, and Drusane for the Ilyrran Drusai."

"Excellent!" Belwyn said. Another nut bounced from the dish to Mellypip's mouth.

"Are you sure that's a good idea?" Runa asked. "He needs to learn, but that incentive could backfire."

"Hey, it works," Belwyn said. "How's the potion coming?"

She whispered a magical phrase, and the bottle of liquid turned a soft pink and fizzled. "It's done."

"At least it didn't blow up," Mellypip encouraged.

"Well, time to test it," she said, and sipped the potion.

They all waited for her to laugh, since it was a laughing potion and a simple thing to fashion usually. Instead, she began to hiccup. A lot.

"Oh, the mixture…of potions…is so delicate!" she said through the hiccups.

Runa continued hiccupping in musical spurts, leafing through her notes for the reversal spell until she found it. She read it aloud and the hiccupping ceased.

Outside, rain began to fall and thunder resonated.

"Drats, I better go through the tower and shut all the windows," Belwyn said. He spun his head around, and the large casement window closed and latched with sorcerous speed. "Don't blow anything up until I get back," he said as he winged out of the chamber.

"Show off!" Mellypip shouted. He bounced over to Runa. "I know Belwyn's special ability is moving things with his mind, but when am I going to get my special ability? I thought all familiars had a unique magic inborn to them?"

"When you're older," Runa assured him. "Belwyn didn't develop the telekinesis until he was several months old."

"I'm three months old. That's several."

"I know, Melly. Be patient. I wonder what Grandpa is planning this year?"

"Don't ask me. I'm out of the loop," Mellypip said. "Belwyn says I need to be surprised too."

She sat on the large desk and hugged her knees. "I hope all of my aunts and uncles make it this year."

"Grandpa Cathal said we would have guests, but he didn't mention he had any siblings?"

"Well, he doesn't…but they're all good friends. They are my honorary aunts and uncles. They visit once a year on my birthday. Aunt Caliste and her familiar, Sanura, always come. So does Liat and Dabiro, Myrsalian and Felisia, and Riva and Buzzy. There are more, but you will meet them soon. The tower gets terribly crowded, but we have so much fun."

Mellypip sniffed the mystical items, his nimble paws examining a small glass ball of sapphire blue. Runa opened one of the heavy desk drawers and took out a small black velvet box.

"I want to show you something, Melly."

He curled up in her lap and she flipped open the lid. Inside there was a silver locket on a chain.

"It's very pretty," he said. "What are those symbols engraved on it?"

"It's Ilyrran. I learned Ilyrran when I was small. It says, 'forever beloved.'"

"Belwyn hasn't taught me languages yet. I'm just now beginning to understand those strange shapes called words."

She opened the locket, and inside there were two tiny portraits, one for each half of the locket. The two women were almost identical, except one had blonde hair and the other dark brown. Both had pointed ears. He saw much of Runa in those pictures, especially the same vibrant green eyes.

"The ladies are so pretty," Mellypip whispered.

"They were beautiful," she said wistfully. "The fair one is my Grandmother Yllia. The darker is my mother Rualla. I love looking at their pictures. It's all I have of them. Grandpa doesn't mind, but I know it upsets him. They died when I was a baby. So did my father, a sorcerer named Ashur. There was a tragic accident. It hurts Grandpa to talk about that too, but he promises one day we can visit my grandmother's homeland of Ilyrra." She closed the locket and returned it to the velvet box and placed it back on the shelf.

"That's very sad, Runa. I'm sorry."

"I wish I had known them." Her voice was heavy with sorrow.

"But you have Grandpa Cathal, Belwyn, and me."

She laughed. "I know, Melly. I love all of you too. I love it here —but it's so peaceful here sometimes I could scream. I want to travel someday and have adventures. Nothing ever happens here, except for pumpkin festivals in the village. I want to explore the world. Go to a real city, like Aybarr or Tiamet."

"The world is a big place," Mellypip said.

"Caliste has told me many tales of Tiamet. They call it the 'White Dragon City,' and thousands of people live inside its walls."

"Thousands? Sounds crowded and nasty to me."

"Now you sound like Belwyn and Grandfather," she teased.

"Do dragons really live there?" he asked shakily.

"Oh no. Dragons don't like cities. They have their own continent, called Rapiveshta. Tiamet is the capitol city of the Ivory Kingdoms. An Emperor rules there, and the buildings are constructed of white and gold stone."

"Sounds hot," Mellypip remarked, snatching a few more nuts from the glass dish.

"All great cities have Sorcerer Houses too. They are centers where other mages can live and learn."

She went to the maps and pictures, painted with rich colors and elegant script, that covered a whole wall. Mellypip liked looking at them, even though it was educational. "See, there are the countries that make up the Ivory Kingdoms, here on the southwestern coast. They include Orlion, where we live, Talreja, Calmeria, Paramys, and Silturen, where Tiamet is. In the north above us is Ironia. That's Dwarven country. The great Thill Empire is here in the north, toward the middle of the continent. Of course there are so many exotic lands, Thema, Urgonclaw, and Narunia."

What's that big gray patch on the map?" he asked, cheeks puffy with nuts.

"Oh, that is *The Wasteland*. No one lives there. It's all black desert and harsh territory. It's also called Skarros. There are legends great evil once ruled there and the land is cursed. A war of darkness left it barren and lifeless a thousand years ago."

"That's too scary."

"Sorry, Melly," she said. "But the world has many dark mysteries."

They went back to the desk, where Cathal's silver casket of crystal tomes enchanted Runa. She opened the case and sighed. "See how the crystals glow with powerful magic! Aren't they dazzling, Melly? And the colors—red, blue, orange, green, and black."

"They do vibrate with powerful magic," Mellypip agreed. "But Belwyn will know we've been snooping."

"Grandfather says they hold powerful spells and can be called upon at will. Someday I will have my own collection of powerful stones, and a staff forged by my own hands, just like him." She touched one of the small stones.

Mellypip slapped her hand with his paw. "No. Bad Runa! Belwyn will have our behinds if he knew we were poking about those tomes, Runa. We aren't supposed to touch, remember? Belwyn is already mad at me about the box. I like my hide unpecked, thank you very much."

Belwyn suddenly flew into the chamber. Runa and Mellypip quickly slammed the casket shut and pretended to look at a scroll.

Belwyn landed on the desk, tapping his talons and quite suspicious. "Peering away at Cathal's crystal tomes again?"

They both lowered their eyes in penance.

"I'm not four years old anymore, Belwyn," Runa said. "How did you know?"

"I'm a sorcerer's guardian. You figure it out."

The storm pressed its virulence. Mellypip looked out the window. Flashes of lightning burst through red and black clouds. The booming thunder shook the tree tower too its core. Mellypip jumped from the windowsill and hid under the desk. He hated thunderstorms. He sucked his paw, wishing the sunshine would return and blow it all away.

"I think Furball needs a cuddle," Belwyn said, looking at the shaking wampu. "Stop sucking your paw, Furball. We are quite safe."

Runa stroked Mellypip to calm him down. "He hates storms, Belwyn. You know they upset him. Maybe we should take a break."

"Well, let's make some tea," Belwyn suggested. "I'm getting worried about Cathal too."

They went down to the kitchen. Runa put the kettle on and toasted the bread. "Butter or jam for your toast?"

"Both please," Mellypip said.

"I'll take butter," Belwyn requested. "Don't burn it."

They enjoyed their snacks, but the heavy rolls of thunder that shook their tree dwelling upset Mellypip, who ate extra jam to calm his nerves.

"I think I'll fly out and make sure Cathal hasn't floated away," Belwyn said. "You two stay here."

"Not a problem," Mellypip squeaked as Belwyn winged away.

"Come on, Melly. Let's practice my light weaving. It'll keep our minds off this dreadful weather."

"Yes, yes! But the sun is hidden by clouds and water."

"Light is light. We can use candles."

They gathered some pewter candlestick holders and thick beeswax candles from the cabinet and placed them in the middle of the table. She lit the candles with a snap of her fingers. Mellypip sat on the round kitchen table, upright with his paws resting on his tummy and long fluffy tail arched over his head like an umbrella. Runa closed her eyes and whispered the incantation, her hands moving with grace and control while she conjured. Mellypip swayed, feeling a subtle hum inside his body. The candlelight became ethereal, and from the hot, dripping wicks trails of light spun into colors on the air, dancing and coiling in elaborate patterns. The mystical radiance sparked the air with sorcery. The spell had no practical use of course. But it was fun and helped with concentration.

The enchanted moment burst when the front door opened, bringing in the rain and wind. Cathal staggered in, laden with packages and grinning, despite being soaked to the skin. Belwyn flew to his perch, feathers dripping and leaving a trail of water everywhere.

"Grandpa, what did you do? Buy out the village?" Runa said, rushing to help Cathal with the parcels and shut the door.

"Nearly, my dear. You'll be fifteen in two days. It's a special time," he said with a laugh. "I refuse to let the elements put a damper on our party!"

Mellypip gingerly sniffed the wrapped parcels, noting the aroma of food inside some of them.

"Don't peek!" Cathal warned.

Belwyn flapped his wings and shook his wet body, and Mellypip scuttled away from his weeping feathers, scrupulously wiping his golden-brown fur. "Hey, watch where you dribble!" he said, giving the owl a nasty look.

"How about until the big day, we make do with a batch of drobba chip cookies?" Cathal suggested.

Runa clapped her hands. "Oh, you bought drobba at the village!"

"What's drobba?" Mellypip asked.

"Oh, a heavenly treat! You'll love it," Runa said. "The village markets hardly ever get any in stock. It's usually a special order through the local merchants. You can make cookies, cakes, puddings, hot drinks, and lots of other things with it."

"Drobba is a bean grown in the southern continent of Zeli," Belwyn added, "because it requires a tropical environment. Most folks like the stuff."

"Get washed up, and I'll heat up the stew for supper later. Then we can make cookies and relax," Cathal said.

Later, when Cathal placed the platter of freshly baked cookies on the table, the smell alone made Mellypip dizzy with ecstasy. But the taste! It transported him with heavenly, gooey pleasure. The dark brown sweet chips in the cookies were ambrosia, and Mellypip was sure some wise mage invented the drobba bean. He held out his little dish. "More drobba cookies please!"

"You're going to get fat if you don't stop eating!" Belwyn said.

"Need drobba energy to make big magic," Mellypip replied seriously.

Belwyn shook his head. "I think we created an addict,"

"I think drobba-chip cookies and a nice cup of chilled milk made for the perfect bedtime snack," Mellypip announced. After he ate his fill, he lay on the table, his whiskers coated with crumbs, and patted his round belly. Drobba made the nasty storm seem so far away.

"Time for bed now, children," Cathal said, clearing away the dishes.

"Have you heard from anyone yet?" Runa asked with concern. "Usually they have arrived by now."

"Perhaps the rain has delayed them. They all come from very far away you know. They have never missed your birthday," Cathal said. He kissed Runa on the forehead. "Now get some sleep, like a good girl."

A resounding knock on the door startled them. It was followed by a feminine voice calling, "Cathal! It's Caliste. Let me in before I drown on your doorstep!"

Cathal opened the door. A tall woman rushed in, her gray cloak soggy. She threw back her hood, revealing a beautiful, exotic woman with black skin and long black hair coiled into an elaborate braided hairdo. She held a long staff in her hand, the top carved into the likeness of a cat's head. She laid it against the wall. Cathal took her wet cloak and tossed it on a chair. They hugged warmly, until an annoyed voice interrupted. "I need to breathe, you know."

They parted and laughed. In Caliste's other arm a plump cat with bronze fur shook her fuzzy head. Her blue eyes blinked up at Cathal. "Nice to see you too."

"Hello, Sanura. How are you?" Cathal greeted her with a scratch behind her ears.

She purred contently. "Soaked and tired," she replied, "but better now."

"I was getting worried about you two," Cathal said.

"The weather has been dreadful everywhere, Cathal," Caliste wearily replied. "Sanura and I shapeshifted into hawks and flew most of the way here, until the storm made it impossible to fly straight. Now where's my girl?" she asked, putting the chubby feline on the table. The cat immediately began to preen her glossy, wet fur.

"I'm right here," Runa cried, running to her embrace.

"Let me look at you," Caliste said. "Goodness, Runa you are a woman now."

"I wouldn't go that far," Cathal said.

"She's turning fifteen, Cathal. Open your eyes."

"Men never notice such things," Sanura commented.

"Hey! Remember me?" Belwyn hooted. "I just helped raise you, that's all!"

"How can I forget my favorite owl and Sanura's teacher?" Caliste said sincerely. "Foolish, noble Belwyn." She kissed him on the beak and Mellypip could swear Belwyn blushed beneath his feathers.

"It's rude to stare," the cat said.

"What? Excuse me?" Mellypip asked, startled.

The cat's lazy blue eyes peered up at Mellypip. "Stare. As in ogle, gawk, blatantly rest one's eyes upon another."

"Sanura, you're being rude," Caliste scolded her. "And who is this charming little wampu?"

"I'm Mellypip. I'm Runa's familiar," he said proudly.

Caliste swept him up in her arms. "Such an adorable creature." She turned to Cathal. "You spoil her you know. I wasn't allowed a familiar until I was eighteen. You were very strict."

"Grandpa Cathal was your teacher?" Mellypip asked.

"He and Yllia were my foster parents after my own family died when I was thirteen. I lived with them for years. We won't say how long ago that was, will we Cathal?" she grinned.

"A gentleman never tells," Cathal assured her.

"I'll make some hot tea," Runa offered. "You must be cold."

"Yes, I better do something about that," Caliste said and with a gesture of her elegant hand she and Sanura were dry again. "I do love being an enchantress."

"As I recall, you were supposed to bond with Buzzy." Cathal said. "Riva was going to bond with Sanura."

Caliste took off her boots and sat down with a relieved sigh. "There. That's better. It feels so good to rest. Yes, the situation with Buzzy was amusing. They brought Buzzy all the way from Zeli, since that was my homeland. But Buzzy didn't want me, and Sanura didn't want Riva. Sanura bonded with me, and Riva bonded with Buzzy."

"A prime example of the quirkiness of fate," Belwyn said. "How some mages and familiars end up together is often strange."

Cathal handed Caliste a steaming cup of tea. "Yes, Belwyn. I remember how you made me suffer for weeks until you bonded with me. They were going to send you to another apprentice because they thought it was hopeless."

"Don't be petulant, Cathal. I relented eventually. I wouldn't have any other sorcerer but you anyway," Belwyn said.

"What kind of familiar is Buzzy?" Mellypip asked.

"A sloth," Caliste answered simply, sipping the fragrant tea.

Confusion knotted Mellypip's face. "What's that?"

Belwyn chuckled. "A lethargic, odd-looking mammal that sleeps most of the time hanging from a tree, shedding fur into his sorcerer's experiments."

"Ah, do I smell drobba-chip cookies?" Caliste asked.

"Yes. We just made some. I'll bring us a fresh plate," Runa said. "And some milk for Sanura."

"Thank you," Sanura said. "I could do with some nourishment."

"Mellypip ate most of them though," Belwyn said.

"Hey!" Mellypip chirped.

"I'm so glad you finally made it!" Runa said. "Have you heard from the others?"

"I would never miss your birthday, Runa," Caliste said. "I am surprised no one else is here. But, they should be here soon."

"I hope so," Runa said. "I want them to meet Mellypip too."

"They will adore him," Caliste agreed.

"Sure, fawn over the furball and ignore me," Belwyn groaned.

"But I'm adorable," Mellypip said proudly.

"Of course you are," Belwyn said dryly.

CHAPTER 3

The sun shone again. Cobalt sky and white clouds graced the warm morning as Belwyn glided to the ledge outside Runa's bedroom window. A magic nudge opened it, and he flew to the bedpost. Runa snored, curled up with her night shift bunched around her knees, and her long hair trailing to the floor. Furball slept on his back, nestled on a thick, snowy pillow, sucking his paw with a steady rhythm, lush tail draped over his face.

Belwyn hopped off the bedpost, quietly waddling across the mattress until he stood over the sleeping children…waiting. He nudged his beak right up to Runa's nose. Runa's eyes fluttered open, crusty with slumber, blinked sleepily…and screamed. She fell off the bed, landing with a thud.

Runa's screams startled Mellypip awake. Mellypip yelped in terror and rolled off the pillow a heaving, wild-eyed wad of bristled fur.

"Happy Birthday!" Belwyn shouted.

Runa poked her head up over the bed. "Belwyn! I could have broken something!"

"Tosh!" he said with a snicker. "The young have strong bones. It's breakfast time, kids, then out of the tower!"

Runa, still in a crumbled heap on the floor, muttered, "I'm gonna start sleeping with a stick."

"A big one!" Mellypip agreed.

"Don't forget to wash behind your ears," Belwyn hooted as he flew out of the window.

"My butt hurts," Runa moaned.

"Food will make it better. Happy birthday, Runa," Mellypip said, licking her nose until she giggled.

After a quick wash and breakfast, Runa and Mellypip were banished outside. Mellypip managed to snatch the last drobba chip cookie and made a mad dash out the door as Belwyn chased him through the tree tower, raving about too many sweets and nobody loving a fat wampu.

Outside, the ripe earth burst with raw smells awakened by heavy rains that stimulated his senses, while cake baking inside whetted his hearty appetite. He climbed the enormous tree tower with nimble paws, the cookie clenched in his little teeth. He settled on a leafy branch and ate the sugary goodness with gusto. The sweet snack boosted his exuberant mood, and he ran up and down the tree again and again to burn off the excess energy. The various inhabitants of the tree; robins, bluebirds, and swallows that lived on the higher branches chattered and screeched at his intrusive acrobatics as he buzzed past them, a lightning streak of fur. He flipped his long soft tail and waved when he stopped. Not amused, the birds chastised him with every lap near their nests.

Sanura the cat did not feel like playing, preferring to doze in a warm sunspot. Belwyn acted as sentinel while Cathal baked. Mellypip peeked in the kitchen window to check on Grandpa Cathal's progress but met only Belwyn's baleful glare. Cathal dispensed with the usual method of baking and prepared the goodies magically. Bowls of batter stirred themselves, eggs danced along the table, and layers of cake rose to fluffy mounds without hot ovens.

"Come down now, Melly," Runa called. "It's almost ready."

Have you seen it yet, he thought back, racing along the bark of the ancient tree.

No. Belwyn is on watch.

He scurried down and joined Runa and Caliste on the lawn. Sanura, revived from her nap, helped supervise the ladies. Caliste spread a white linen cloth over the old wicker table. Runa set out chairs of twisted wood, decorated with flower garlands they had spent the morning gathering. Runa's beautiful hair was twined with blossoms into a single thick braid that almost touched her ankles. Mellypip loved her hair! Her soft and shiny mane made a great bed to sleep in, and smelled of lilacs, which he found comforting.

Mellypip jumped up on a chair next to Sanura. Caliste wore a caftan of flowing ivory silk and matching slippers, which enhanced her ebony skin. Runa's short-sleeved frock of rust-colored cotton, with saffron and green embroidered neckline, suited her fair complexion, though the hem was soaked from walking on dew saturated ground.

Curious, Mellypip tasted a petal from the lush flowers that decorated the chairs.

"Please refrain from eating the decorations," Sanura scolded. "We spent all morning gathering them."

"Runa, you should put on some shoes," Caliste said. "The ground is still soaking wet."

"But it's not winter," Runa said with a shrug.

"Runa, my love," Caliste said with a laugh, "you're growing up a wild child."

Runa kept glancing around excitedly. The other expected guests had not arrived yet, which put a damper on the festivities. Mellypip was disappointed too. He wanted to meet more familiars.

"Don't worry, Runa," Caliste comforted her. "I'm sure this inclement weather has delayed them; that's all."

She nodded. "I know. I don't care about presents or anything. I just miss them. I only get to see them once a year."

Belwyn flew out of the tower and landed on a chair. "The birthday party may now officially begin," he announced. "Ladies and familiars, take your seats!"

Runa and Caliste sat down, brimming with smiles and anticipation. At last, Cathal emerged, the cake floated before him like a cloud; two tiers high, puffed with swirls and peaks of majestic blue and white icing. The cake gently landed in the middle of the table. Everyone applauded Cathal's success.

"Oh, Grandfather, it's beautiful!" she cried.

"A masterpiece!" Caliste complimented him. "But so much! The others—"

"Now, let's not fret. Remember things have come up before," Cathal said. "One year Liat and Dabiro were late because Liat left the cooking fire on, and they had to return to make sure their house didn't burn down." Cathal lit the candles with a gesture. "Now Runa, make a wish," he said.

Runa closed her eyes, her smile making her dimples deeper.

What are you wishing? Mellypip asked.

It's a secret, Melly, she sent back.

She blew out the candles. Cathal cut generous slices of confection, which was golden, marbled with drobba and creamy frosting made with sugar and butter. It was delicious. Runa and Caliste ate two healthy helpings. Mellypip devoured his with zest.

"Melly, you're a mass of icing." Runa laughed as she wiped his face clean with a napkin.

Belwyn raised his beak from his strawberry cordial. "There's still blue frosting on his whiskers, Runa."

"He's young and messy, like most of the male clan," Sanura said, licking her paws daintily. "Cathal has flour on his trousers and your beak is dripping cordial."

"Oh…sorry," Belwyn said.

Runa washed Mellypip's muzzle and tied a fresh napkin around his neck. Mellypip purred under her attentive hands. Cathal dusted off his pants and poured more cordial for everyone.

"You can open your presents now," Cathal said. "Oh, they are inside!" he teased. He returned to the tree. Endless seconds passed until Cathal reappeared with gifts wrapped in bright-colored cloth and ribbons. Cathal gave two packages to Runa and two to Mellypip.

"I get gifts too!" Mellypip exclaimed.

"Of course. We never got to celebrate your birthday when you were born. Now you are family."

"That is lovely, Cathal," Caliste agreed. "And this is our present for Runa." She handed her a small, wrapped package. "But open Cathal's first, before he bursts."

Runa chose the large one to start with, undoing the dark blue ribbons, quickly, but carefully, to reveal a new cloak of dark teal wool, with a braided border and hood. "Oh, I love it!" she exclaimed, throwing it around her shoulders.

"Pretty!" Mellypip said. He opened his gifts, his agile paws easily undoing the bows. Inside, he found a blue flannel blanket so soft it felt like rose petals, and a tiny matching pillow. The other package was a yummy basket of treats. He sniffed the bouquet of apples, pears, cinnamon sticks, honey bars, walnuts, and hazelnuts. "Thank you, Grandpa Cathal and Belwyn."

"You're welcome, Mellypip," Cathal said with a nod.

"Don't eat them all at once," Belwyn advised.

The next gift Runa unwrapped was a small velvet box. Runa's lips quivered as she opened it, and touched the silver locket, tears welling in her eyes. It was the one she had shown him, with her mother and grandmother's portraits inside. The elegant Ilyrran script gleamed in the sunlight.

"Oh, Grandfather," she whispered.

"I thought it was time to pass it on to you," Cathal said, gently taking the locket and putting it around her neck. "I have real memories of them, but you never had that joy. Now they will always be with you."

Runa threw her arms around him. "Thank you. I will treasure it always."

Cathal hugged her and wiped away her tears. "No sadness now! This is a happy day."

Caliste dabbed a stray tear with a napkin and sipped her cordial.

Runa opened Caliste's gift, a collection of small crystals in a variety of colors. "My first tome crystals!"

"Yes, they are for simple spells only,' she insisted. "But still good practice for you."

Runa embraced Caliste and Sanura. "This is the best birthday—"

The sky clouded over. Strange sorcerous odors made Mellypip's nose twitch. "Something bad is in the air. Smell horrid," Mellypip gasped. "Nasty energy makes me itchy."

Runa gathered Mellypip in her arms. "I sense sorcery too. Why is the sky suddenly so dark?"

The owl snapped to attention. "Furball's right. There's a wave of conjury in the air that's not our own."

Above them, the nebulous matter spread, blotting out the pristine blue of a moment ago. Swirling with black and red energy; it roiled with power; growing larger with each breath, casting longer shadows over their heads.

"Get into the house…now!" Cathal ordered. "Caliste, protect Runa!"

Caliste grabbed Runa with one hand and Sanura with the other then ran toward the tower. Shrill cries echoed in the air. From the violent vapors burst two giant ravens, twice the size of a full-grown horse. Black wings wide, their garnet eyes glittered with malice. They wheeled overhead, descending rapidly, talons extended. Runa stared back over her shoulder, breathless at the strange sight, unable to look away, until Caliste yanked her about. "Come on, Runa! Move!" she cried, pushing her through the doorway. "Move!"

One of the ravens dove straight for Caliste and Runa, its eyes narrowed in deadly pursuit. Caliste stumbled inside after Runa, just as the great predator impacted against the tree. A shield of mystical green energy glowed around the bark just as the raven struck the tree. Sorcery crisped the air as the giant bird bounced off the magical shield.

"What happened?" Runa gasped.

"A protective ward," Caliste said quickly. "Cathal always kept one activated around the tower. I guess old habits never die, thank the gods."

"Now you tell me!" Runa cried.

The power of the shield flung the raven backward painfully, and it crashed into the party table, tumbling tail over beak. Birthday cake, place settings and cordial filled the air as the creature skidded across the ground, tearing up grass and dirt in its wake. Disoriented, the monstrous raven cawed and beat its wings, lifting into the air once more.

"Where are Grandpa and Belwyn?" Runa cried. "Aren't they coming inside?"

"They have other plans, dear," Caliste whispered. "Cathal doesn't run from a fight."

"What! Why, if the tower is safe—"

"We also can't stay in the tower forever, Runa. These creatures must be stopped—now!"

Cathal levitated high in the air, drawing the second attacker's attention. A flash of blue-gray energy sprung from his hand, as the bird met him. Too late to avoid it, the creature took the force of the spell full in the breast, as if striking a stone wall. Redoubling his effort, Cathal flung the predator backward, several hundred feet into the forest canopy, where it smashed into an ancient, thick-boled tree.

"Grandfather!" Runa cried.

Cathal heard Runa scream, but before he could turn, the second raven, frustrated in its attempt to breach the tree-tower's defenses, fell upon Cathal with an ear-splitting caw. Its massive talons closed tight about the sorcerer, pinning his arms. It lifted into the air; whether meaning to either crush its prey, or drop him from a height even Cathal could not survive, he did not wait to find out.

His body began to shimmer; a pale-blue glow engulfing man and bird, as he shapeshifted into the form of a gray owl. Before the raven could react, Cathal slipped from its talons, and sped clear of the giant raven like an arrow loosed from a bow.

"That was *too* close," Runa breathed heavily.

"There's Belwyn!" Mellypip shouted. "He's attacking the raven! Is he crazy?"

"Crazy or drunk," Sanura answered. "Take your pick."

Belwyn flew straight toward the slowing raven, which had only just become aware of his prey's escape. His own talons extended, Belwyn struck hard, tearing both feather and flesh from his enemy's right wing. The monster raged, thrashing wildly as it lost momentum and plummeted. The familiar pursued the raven, careful to keep clear of its razored claws and snapping beak. Seeking another opening, another chance to cripple it further, he attacked areas the massive bird could not easily defend; like its back and flanks.

Suddenly, the first raven, having recovered from Cathal's mystical assault, erupted from the forest canopy with a renewed fury.

"We need to help them!" Runa cried. "Come on," she said to Mellypip. She hiked up her skirts and ran toward the stairs.

Sanura chased after them. "Wait! Where are you going, young lady?"

"Runa, come back here this instant," Caliste shouted, trailing after them. "Cathal will never forgive me if anything happens to you!"

Runa ran up to the sorcery chamber, Caliste and Sanura at her heels. "Get Cathal's special crystals!" Runa said. "They need all the help they can get!"

"Yes!" Caliste smiled, nodding her approval. "That's a marvelous idea! I wish I had brought my own!" She opened the silver casket and chose two stones. Runa gathered two potion bottles, mixing quickly but carefully.

Mellypip craned his furry neck from the tower window, clutching his tail anxiously. "I don't see Belwyn or Cathal anywhere!" he cried.

"That's because I'm right here!" Belwyn suddenly flashed through the window, knocking Mellypip on his bottom. The wampu squeaked in alarm.

"As am I." Cathal, still in owl form, slipped past the confused wampu like a gray shadow.

Both owls hovered above Caliste. She tossed each one a crystal, red to Cathal and a black to Belwyn. They caught the stones easily in their talons.

"Thanks!" both said in unison.

"Be careful, you two!" Caliste begged.

"We will," Cathal replied as he shot out through the casement window again, close behind Belwyn. "Runa!" he called. "Stay back from the window!"

Runa bolted for the window, before her grandfather's words even dispersed on the wind, gripping a potion bottle in each hand.

"Runa!" Caliste shouted. "Cathal said to keep away. What are you doing?"

"Putting my mistakes to good use," she replied, leaning out the window as one of the ravens flew past. "Hey! You molting bag of feathers!"

The confused raven whirled about just as Runa hurled one of the potions at it. Sorcery amplifying both the distance and accuracy of her throw, the bottle shattered against the bird's inky feathers, exploding upon impact. It rolled away into a dive, dusted with pink powder and laughing uncontrollably. The other raven, alerted to Runa's actions, flew too close and struck the tower shield. Runa hurled the second potion. Another explosive burst, and the momentarily stunned raven, like his companion, wore a dusting of pink powder; all but crippled with laughter.

"Belwyn was right," Runa said. "Potions are a great asset."

Belwyn and Cathal pressed their unexpected advantage. Side-by-side, they dove for the ravens, the red crystal tome in Cathal's talons pulsating angrily. Despite the potions' effects, the giant birds fought back savagely with thrashing wings and raking claws. Belwyn took a terrible blow to the head and came dangerously close to losing a leg to one of the predator's snapping beaks. Thin ribbons of crimson blossomed from Cathal's feathered chest from a flaying claw.

Without warning, a shaft of scarlet magic erupted from the red crystal, striking both ravens, stunning them. The next moment, wraith-like streams of energy shot out from the black crystal in Belwyn's grip, roping about the raven's wings and talons. They plummeted helplessly to earth.

Runa scooped Mellypip up and ran back down the stairs, ignoring Caliste's pleas to stay put. Mellypip's heart beat so rapidly with terror he thought he would faint.

"Grandpa!" she cried, running out the door. "Are you all right?"

Cathal held out his arms, and she fell into them. He stroked her hair gently. "There, there, you are safe now." He glanced at the tethered ravens. "More or less."

Panting, Caliste joined them. "Sorry, Cathal," she gasped. "She never listens, you know. I'm getting too old for this!"

"Your temperamental potions helped us," Cathal added. "They stunned the ravens long enough to enable me to use the tomes." His expression and voice became stern. "But, if you ever do anything like that again young lady, you are grounded for a year."

"I'm all right too." Belwyn swooped down onto a nearby tree limb. "In case anyone's interested."

"Those raven feathers are large enough to sweep with." Sanura shivered as stray ones showered them from the air. "And of course you're all right. How could you not have avoided anything *that* big!"

Several yards away, the immense birds cried out, still thrashing; struggling futilely against their mystical bonds. Suddenly, a dark flash, like a brief taste of midnight, shocked them into silence. The creatures began to shrink rapidly, dwindling to normal size. The raven's fierce nature fought the transformation, ripping stalks of grass, angry caws issuing from their clacking beaks. Black feathers, which were shiny only a moment before, turned to decaying dust, their garnet eyes faded to milky white. The screaming ravens smoked and crumbled into two unrecognizable mounds; the winds scattering their ashy remains, leaving nothing.

"Horrible!" Runa cried. "Grandpa, that wasn't your magic."

"No. My magic only bound them. The same foul sorcery that made those creatures destroyed them as well. It wasn't the return of their natural state that killed them. They failed—and were punished."

"They were innocent creatures," Runa said, then burst into tears. "Oh, it's all my fault!" she cried.

"What do you mean?" Cathal said.

"My fault," she said with shaking sobs.

"Sweetheart, you're not making sense," Cathal said.

"My birthday wish," she sobbed. "I wished for an adventure!"

"Nonsense! That had nothing to do with this chaos!" he assured her, holding her close. "An unforeseen coincidence, that's all."

"I would like to know who did this, however," Belwyn added. "It was a deliberate attack on us using dark magic. Whoever used it must be nearby, too."

"I know, Belwyn," Cathal nodded. "We'll talk of it later."

"Bad magic," Mellypip said, burrowing his head into Runa's shoulder and sucking his paw.

"No, Melly," Cathal said ominously. "They don't know what bad is until they have dealt with me."

~ * ~

Panthara's screams of rage disrupted Azmadu from his nap. "Now what!" he grumbled. He lifted his head from the warm stone he rested upon, magically heated, of course, for his pleasure, and stretched, unfolding his azure blue and dusky green wings. He sluggishly slid off the rock and shuffled to the next room.

Panthara paced in front of the massive crystal, silver-ringed hands pulling at the glossy mane of black hair that fell to her waist, blue eyes smoldering with anger.

"What's wrong, my Panthara?" Azmadu asked.

"That imbecile failed!" she said hotly. "Let me show you." Picking Azmadu up, she swept her hand across the clear crystal until it throbbed with magic, revealing the dramatic images of two giant ravens battling Cathal and Caliste. The great birds were defeated by the sorcerers.

"Gorvanus failed us," Azmadu agreed.

In the vision, Azmadu noticed a short girl with eyes like green ice and long brown hair, carrying a fat, furry creature. "Who is the strange girl with the wampu, Panthara?"

"Runa—Cathal's precious granddaughter. Drab little thing—isn't she?" She put him on a silken pillow. "I told Gorvanus using wild ravens for this magic would be dangerous."

"Gryphons might have been a better choice, though they are stupid creatures," Azmadu agreed. "Gorvanus is like a gryphon—he's stupid too."

"My mother insisted Gorvanus be involved," Panthara said. "He was not only Koll's apprentice; but served our house for many years. Gorvanus was useful in helping me attain the throne with his clever poisons and disguises."

"Maybe he should not have gone after Caliste *and* Cathal," Azmadu said. "Cathal is the most powerful of the circle. Koll should have done that!"

"Perhaps. It's no wonder no familiar would ever bond with Gorvanus! His flashes of brilliance are short-lived. Koll was right. We shouldn't have attacked Cathal in his home territory," Panthara said. "Now he knows someone hunts him." She resumed her pacing, red silk whipping the floor, blue eyes clouded with anger.

"My Queen," a deep voice said. "You are distressed?"

Koll the Sorcerer entered, his flowing black robes trailing the floor, Xabral, his red and black scorpion snake, coiled around his body like a lover's caress.

Azmadu lowered his head and mumbled, "Hello, Koll."

"No greetings for me," his familiar, Xabral, hissed.

Azmadu avoided the scorpion snake's gaze. "Hello, Xabral."

"You are not very sincere," the snake replied with menace.

Panthara stomped her foot. "Stop scaring him, Xabral! And Koll, your minion failed me!"

Koll unwound Xabral from his shoulders and laid him on the silken couch. "You worry too much, my dear." The sorcerer gently stroked Panthara's shoulders. "However, I have something that should brighten your day," he whispered.

"What is it?" she demanded.

"Bring in the prisoners," Koll commanded.

Through the wide doors, several Rashurkeen warriors, clad in black, red scarves masking their faces, dragged in two men. Heavily chained, they also had rust-colored metal bands—sorcerer locks—bolted around their necks to prevent them from using magic. One man was red-haired, and the other a thin, wiry fellow with brown hair.

Panthara brightened. "Myrsalian and Riva! This pleases me Koll."

She stood over the prisoners and kicked each one. They fell over, groaning, eyes glazed. "They don't seem very upset. Drugged?" she asked.

"Of course," Koll replied. "They were difficult to subdue. The use of paid assassins is useful in such ventures. They are very aggressive and have no scruples about cruelty."

"What of their familiars?" Panthara asked.

"We didn't capture them, but they won't interfere with our plans. It adds to the cruelty too, to separate a sorcerer from their familiar. I have also been careful to keep myself…inconspicuous."

"I would hope so. There is a price on your head in every kingdom," Panthara said.

Riva roused, pulling at the metal band around his neck. He stared up at Panthara and then Koll, and his face twisted with hatred. "Koll! You think you can hold me with this?"

"Though it makes using magic on you a problem, you cannot use your sorcery at all," Koll said, and gestured to the Rashurkeen. "Take them to the dungeon."

They carried them away.

"We have five of the seven in our grasp. It is only a question of time until the last two are added," Koll assured her. "I also have set other things in motion that will force Cathal to leave his home."

"What about Gorvanus?" Panthara cried.

"He still serves our purpose," Koll replied with calm, pouring honey wine into gold goblets and handing her one. "He is performing other duties for us that are useful."

"Perhaps," she pouted. "He's just so…slimy. He thinks I love him."

"A ruse that ensures his devoted service. And devotion is the key, Panthara. For some it is power and gold. For Gorvanus, it's you. His desire for you will keep him with us, until we are done with him."

"But why do we need him?" Panthara asked. "He just failed in trying to capture Cathal and Caliste."

"Because he is expendable," Koll replied. "I knew he would not succeed in bringing us Cathal."

"But why allow it, then?" Panthara demanded.

"This puts in motion events I will complete in Tiamet. This will bring others into our web, and draw Cathal out, where he is vulnerable. It may take time, but I have several options planned. Gorvanus will serve us in those, when it is expedient." Koll sighed, and stroked Panthara's cheek. "Don't fret about these little obstacles, Panthara. You are Queen of Mowad now, and soon, with my help, you will be Queen of the world. Cathal no longer feels safe in his tower and will seek out allies where he will be vulnerable—to us."

The nine-foot scorpion snake lifted its heavy head. "I'm hungry, Koll."

"I will attend to your supper soon, my sweet," he said, stroking Xabral's glistening scales.

Bored with their talk, Azmadu also felt ignored and didn't like that at all. He grunted and went back to his heated rock to sulk.

Koll downed his wine and picked up his scorpion snake. "Xabral needs to be fed. I will meet you for dinner later, Panthara."

"Yes, Koll," she said.

They departed and Azmadu felt relieved. He hated the scorpion snake that was his teacher. He always looked at him like he was a meal. Panthara reclined on a couch of black and crimson silk, fingers tapping her cup with new ideas.

Azmadu, she called into his mind, *I have a new plan.*

Of course you do, my Panthara. You always do.

She laughed. "Come here, my sweet."

He slid off the rock and ran to her. She picked him up, stroking his crested head, and his long color-ringed tail swept the floor with pleasure. "Poor Azmadu, you want your dinner, don't you?"

He flicked his blue-black tongue and swished his tail excitedly. "Yes, my Panthara. Azmadu hungry."

"How do you want it, my sweet? Cooked or raw?"

He thought for a moment. "Raw."

CHAPTER 4

Runa opened the window in the sorcery chamber, letting light and fresh air wash over her. She sighed mournfully. "I wish we could go outside. If we have to stay indoors much longer, I'll go nuts!"

Caliste nodded. "I know it's misery, dear. But we have no idea what is happening now. Cathal knows what he is doing."

"Has Grandfather found out anything else?"

"No, just that pile of burnt and blackened crystals two miles from here. Cathal's been trying to contact our friends, but he cannot reach anyone. He's very worried. So am I. The others should have been here days ago. Cathal has even contacted the various Sorcerer Houses in the lands they live in. No one knows anything."

"I'm worried about them too," Runa said. "We have no idea why this is happening, and that scares me. I would like a face to put to my troubles, so I can focus on smashing it."

"Now you sound like Belwyn," Mellypip said grimly, curled up on Cathal's large desk, not even peeking at the spell boxes or stones in his lethargy. The stress of the attack and being cooped up sapped his energy. The tower had lost its joyful mystery and not even the magic room was fun anymore.

"I'll make some tea and sandwiches," Caliste said. "Come down and join me later?"

"I will." Runa nodded, staring out the window.

Mellypip rested his chin on his paws and wondered about the danger they faced. Belwyn taught him familiars were guardians, but he was too little to do anything brave or noble. His whiskers and large round ears drooped. The desolation that Mellypip would never be a proper familiar to his beloved Runa tormented him. He fought the urge to cry.

He sensed Runa's frustration too. They missed their walks under the open sky, the gathering of nuts and berries in the woods, the fun they had swimming in the lake; he even missed her exploding potions. The last seven days were a dull incarceration where Cathal had forbidden Runa and Mellypip to leave the tower because of danger.

Stupid ravens, he thought. It was their fault.

What worried Mellypip most was that he could not even protect his own sorceress. He looked at his reflection in the small hand mirror on the desk. His round brown eyes and big fluffy ears were unimposing—a fuzzy body with a tail, not at all terrifying.

"I wish I were anything but a wampu. I've no fierce qualities, not like a bear, owl, dragon, or even a sparrow would have. I climb trees and eat, that's what I do." A single tear fell on the reflective glass. Wiping his face with his paw, he hung his head.

Then Runa's soft hands stroked his forehead, her voice a gentle whisper. "Melly, you're still a baby. I wouldn't want anyone else as my familiar. I love you. We all do."

"I still wish I were big and scary."

"I know, Melly, but you are brave and valiant. I feel the same way, you know. My sorcery is still growing, but my experiments still go boom."

She cuddled him for a time. He always felt safe with Runa. He wanted her to feel safe with him. Mellypip wanted to be a good familiar.

Belwyn was right—he needed to study harder and be more serious about his duties. Mellypip carried her thin volume of spells to his new blanket. He dropped the tome and sat on it. Guarding it would be his new vocation.

Runa attempted to study her history, but after an hour flipping through pages in abject boredom, Runa dropped her head on the table and moaned. "Come on, I'm so tired of study. I want a bath."

"I'll guard the magic," Mellypip announced proudly.

"But I'm making a bubble bath," she added. "You can guard the door. I think my little tome should be safe," she suggested.

He buried her tome under the pillow, just in case, and bounced after her. Mellypip never understood the human obsession with soap and water, but baths were fun, and he liked the lilac-scented oils and soaps she used. They went down to the main floor. In the bath chamber, she turned on the taps, filling the copper tub, sprinkled bubble crystals into the steaming water, and pinned up her mass of hair.

"Where are Grandpa Cathal and Belwyn now?" he asked, sitting on the rim of the tub as she sank into the wave of foam with a contented sigh. His nose tickled from the suds and he sneezed.

"Searching the woods again, I think. Grandpa also mentioned something about extending the wards," she said, scrubbing her feet.

"I wish I knew some real magic," Mellypip said with a sigh. "Belwyn says I need to learn more reading and writing first."

Caliste knocked on the door, and peeked in. "Runa, get dressed. We have visitors."

"Is it our friends?" Runa asked with hopeful joy, jumping out of the tub, dripping water on the rug.

"No, sorry," she replied. "Have you seen Cathal?"

"Not since this morning," Runa answered, drying off with haste.

Caliste left them alone. Runa pulled her white tunic and green trousers on. "I wonder who it is."

"If it's an enemy, I will protect you," Mellypip announced, puffing his little chest out.

They ran to the front door, Runa's hair tumbling down around her ankles. Caliste was already outside, with Sanura at her feet.

But Runa stopped when she did not see their missing friends.

Instead, there were red-cloaked soldiers on horseback. Caliste was talking to one of them.

"Who are they?" Mellypip asked. "They look tough."

"I don't know," Runa whispered, peering out the front door. "They're wearing imperial uniforms though, just like in the books."

"I count five of them," he said. He could count very well now. "They look very stern. Horses are stinky though."

The leader of the group, in a long red cloak and thick leather armor, dismounted his horse. He removed his concealing plumed helmet. He had shaggy brown hair, which needed grooming, and a jagged scar over his left eye. The strange soldier and Caliste were talking too low for Runa to hear anything.

"Should we go and meet them?" Runa asked. "Caliste seemed to want us to. She is with them, so there shouldn't be any danger."

"Wait, there's Grandpa Cathal. Uh-oh, he looks grumpy, and Belwyn isn't any better." He pulled a lock of Runa's hair. "Maybe we should stay here."

Cathal was walking up the path with Belwyn on his shoulder, looking very ill-tempered. He approached the leader, waving his oaken staff, and a glimmer of light issued from the wood. "This is my land! Go away!" Cathal shouted.

Unimpressed, the man with the scar boldly walked toward him. "Get off your tricks, Sorcerer! Don't you remember a fellow comrade or has living in the backwoods turned your brain to moss? I know that old owl must remember me."

Cathal stared at the stranger. Runa could no longer bear the suspense and stepped outside. Mellypip perched on her shoulder, clinging to her head. With hesitation, Runa walked toward the cluster of people and horses.

"It's Darcus!" Belwyn hooted. "You get to live, you scruffy human! How are you?"

Cathal laughed for the first time in days. "Darcus, you ragged old warhorse!"

To their surprise the two men embraced and proceeded with a strange ritual of back slapping.

"Cathal, when did you go gray?" Darcus asked.

"A while back," Cathal answered.

"I blame raising Runa," Belwyn said dryly.

Sanura rolled her eyes. "Males are so odd in their greeting rituals. It's all right, Runa and Mellypip. There will be no territorial head-butting today."

Runa and Mellypip approached the group, though the massive horses and their nervous stepping and snorting unnerved Mellypip.

Darcus stood, hands folded across his broad chest, but his dark brown eyes were warm, and his tanned, weathered face friendly when he smiled at them. Cathal put his arm around Runa. "Darcus, you have not seen my granddaughter Runa since she was a baby. This is an old friend, Commander Darcus."

"I'm a Captain now, Cathal." The warrior's expression softened. "My, she's almost a grown woman. How old are you now, child?"

"Fifteen, sir," she said. "I'm pleased to meet you."

"She just had a birthday," Mellypip added.

"Happy birthday, Runa," he said, giving her a kiss on the cheek. He smelled of leather, horses, and sweat. "She's beautiful, Cathal." He looked at Mellypip. "Is this furry wampu her pet or her familiar?"

"Oh, I'm a familiar," he answered. "My name is Mellypip!"

Darcus reached out with a callused hand and scratched Mellypip under the chin. "Cute little fellow. He's still a kit too. Wampu are adorable, but can be very fierce when protecting their own, so you have a good one there."

Mellypip decided he liked Darcus.

"Runa, you were in diapers when I last saw you, so I don't expect you would remember me. Cathal and I are old war companions, you might say."

"You fought in a war, Grandpa?" Runa said, surprised.

"I'll explain later, Runa." He turned back to Darcus. "Don't think I'm not overjoyed to see you, but why are you in the 'backwoods,' as you call it."

"To see you, old man." Darcus shoved his hands in his belt and glanced at Runa. "I think I should speak to you and Caliste alone though."

"Runa, go back into the house for now," Sanura said. "The men need to head-butt after all."

"Cathal, my instinct tells me something bad has happened. What's going on?" Darcus insisted.

Cathal sighed. "Go into the house, Runa," he begged.

"No. I will not leave," Runa answered in a bold voice.

Mellypip's ear perked up. He gasped at Runa with his little mouth open.

"Grandfather, the last week has been turmoil. Our friends are missing. We've been attacked by giant ravens. Now a stranger, at least to me, who's an Imperial Officer, shows up on our doorstep with armed backup. Maybe he can help us!"

"What attack? What ravens?" Darcus interjected. "Caliste… Cathal, talk to me! Who—"

"Grandfather, you must not keep secrets. Not from me."

Darcus threw his hands up in frustration, his neck muscles corded with stress. His soldiers remained mute and nervous on their horses; eyes averted. Darcus tossed back his cloak. "Cathal! Caliste! Listen to me! There's trouble. The Emperor has sent me to escort you to Tiamet!"

"I'm not the Archon anymore."

"You were the Archon?" Runa asked, stunned. "That is the highest honor for a sorcerer to achieve among his caste. How come you never told me?"

"Slipped his mind. Brain being mossy and all," Belwyn replied.

"I see your owl hasn't changed," Darcus said.

Cathal shook his staff at Darcus. "Look. I don't answer to the Emperor. I never did. Ramirez is the Archon now. He can deal with him, not me. I have nothing to say to Emperor Tarsicius."

"Ramirez is dead," Darcus stated bluntly. "He was murdered."

They halted their verbal exchange, nose to nose, like two stags ready to butt antlers. Everything became very quiet.

Caliste broke down and sobbed. "Dead! I just saw him before I came here. How did this happen?"

Runa comforted Caliste, stunned by the news someone so close to her friend was murdered.

"I'm sorry to burst out like that, Caliste. Ramirez was a good man," Darcus said. He turned to Cathal. "Now explain what's been happening here."

"Let's all go into the house," Cathal said with a sigh. "Tell your men they are welcome too."

"Come, soldiers, but take care of your mounts first," Darcus ordered. "For now, all of you stand guard around the tower. Behave like proper knights or I'll have your hides for a saddle."

"Yes, sir," they responded with fervor and saluted.

Darcus walked by Cathal's side. Inside, Cathal retrieved a jug of ale and some cups from the kitchen. Cathal and Caliste related the strange raven attack, and about the strangeness of their friends not showing up like they did each year, except for Caliste. Runa and Mellypip sat in silence, praying they would not be sent away.

"Who comes each year, Cathal?" Darcus asked.

"Caliste and Sanura, of course, and Myrsalian and his elf owl familiar, Felisia, they come from Thill. Jiana and her familiar Jasper travel from Thema."

"Isn't that the wild woman with the tiger hare?" Darcus asked.

"Yes, that's her," Cathal said with a laugh. "Then there's Liat and Dabiro the badger, Riva and his sloth, Buzzy, and finally Ulan and his little hedgehog, Rosepetal."

Darcus leaned back as he absorbed the details of the tale with a solemn expression. When it was over, Darcus poured more dark ale into his cup. "That was a nasty birthday surprise. I'm sorry, Runa, your celebration was spoiled by such horror."

"Thank you, Captain Darcus," she said.

"What happened to Ramirez?" Caliste asked.

"He was found dead at the Sorcerer House in Tiamet. He normally doesn't reside there, so I was surprised to learn he was even in the city. The local watch alerted the Emperor. I was sent to investigate. When I arrived, he had been—" He looked at Runa. "Girl, you better not hear this."

"Darcus is right. Runa, you shouldn't hear such things," Cathal said.

"I think I must," Runa insisted.

"Well, I rushed over there. The place was shambles. Some magical battle had gone down. You could smell it. I found Ramirez on the second floor in his room. He was dead—gutted by a sword, which is not very mystical, but several people were involved I think. Some witnesses in the area complained about strange folk in turbans and dark robes. What got the Tarsicius involved is when I found Ramirez, his hand was stretched out, where he had written a message in his own blood before he died."

"What message?" Cathal asked.

"Just one word—Koll."

"Koll!" Cathal erupted.

Mellypip and Runa watched the shocked expressions on everyone's faces. Belwyn looked like he was about to spit flames. Cathal raked his hair back. "This is worse than we thought. Koll the Sorcerer slithers out from under some rock after fifteen years to openly murder the Archon. Now with our friends missing too, I'm even more concerned."

"Who is this Koll?" Runa asked. "He sounds evil."

"Evil is an understatement," Sanura said.

"Ahridum himself would be afraid of this monster!" Caliste spat; her elegant face twisted with hatred.

Mellypip shivered. Ahridum was a god of darkness and chaos. This horrible man must be terrible indeed.

"He's a vicious sorcerer. He committed crimes, horrible crimes, in the Sorcerer War," Darcus said, pouring more ale. "You were only a baby, Runa. The war ended when…" Darcus stopped and looked at Cathal. "She doesn't know anything at all about this…does she?"

"No, and I hoped to keep it that way," Cathal replied with exasperation.

"It's all moot now," Belwyn added.

"That explains the Emperor's interest," Caliste said. "He wants Cathal to come to Tiamet to help hunt him down. I fear for the fate of our friends too. These two incidents are not a coincidence, Cathal. I know there's bad history between you and Tarsicius, but if he is so desperate to summon you, we need to help. It could lead us to finding the others."

Belwyn jumped off Cathal's chair and took a drink from the ale cup. "I hate to say this Cathal, but Darcus is right. With Ramirez dead, the whole community of mages is going to be in an uproar—and scared. Koll is involved, and that means trouble. I know I'm not the only one who wants to dip Koll in a vat of fire and watch him sizzle. I don't like Tarsicius either, but we don't have much of a choice. I'm not saying I like it—I hate it. But we must go."

"Is he always like this?" Darcus asked in a low voice to Cathal.

"It's an owl thing," Cathal answered.

"Well, better to deal with the Emperor than his son," Darcus commented.

"Which one?" Cathal asked.

"Oh, you don't know. Young Prince Taran died four years ago, when he was only twelve. A riding accident—that's what they say at least. There were rumors, but everything was hushed. His twin sister, Princess Opaline, was inconsolable, but she has no claim to the throne as long as there's a male heir. Shame, she's a smart young woman. Levandius is a pitiful excuse for a prince, but the only heir to the White Dragon Throne now, which might be sooner than later."

"Why?" Cathal asked. "Tarsicius is only fifty-five. He was always a robust man."

"He's dying," Darcus replied.

"Tarsicius is dying? Caliste you never mentioned that," Cathal said, surprised.

"I knew any mention of his name would upset you, Cathal. His daughter, Opaline, is my friend. She has no fear of magic like the rest of her family. About two months ago, the Emperor fell very ill. None of the physicians can help him. He grows weaker each day. He can't even walk now. His son, Levandius, is not so honorable and drinks quite heavily too when not—" Caliste paused, looking at Runa. "Doing unseemly things," she finally said.

"This puts me in a foul mood, Darcus," Cathal said darkly.

"You're coming then?" Darcus asked.

"Yes, yes…I don't have a choice now," Cathal said.

"We should leave in the morning then. I have arrangements made in Sea Haven for us to travel by ship. It will be quicker and safer," Darcus said.

"That was presumptive of you," Cathal remarked.

"I prefer to view it as 'efficient and prepared,'" Darcus replied. "In the meantime, pack your things and get a good night's sleep. We will leave at dawn. It'll take about a week to reach Sea Haven by horse. Does the local village have a stable? You will need horses to travel, unless you care to fly?" Darcus asked playfully.

"Yes, there is. A man named Garret can help us. I'll go make the arrangements to secure three horses for us."

"I'm not flying," Belwyn stated. "I'm going, but only because I have to. You can fashion a perch and attach it to the saddle."

"Save your gold, Cathal. This is courtesy of the Emperor. I'll take care of the horses and the perch for Belwyn," Darcus said. He turned to Runa. "Have you ever ridden before?"

"No," she said. "I've never been anywhere that required a horse to take me. It looks fun, though."

He laughed. "Yeah…it's fun after your riding seat gets broken in. Expect to be stiff and sore for several days."

"Your men must be hungry. I'll be happy to make some stew and bread for them, Captain Darcus," Runa offered.

"Nothing like fresh hot bread and real butter to make you feel better," Mellypip said.

Darcus grinned. "Thank you, Runa. We would be most appreciative of a real, hot meal. We've been living on hard bread and dried meat for days."

Cathal walked Darcus outside, where they spoke in hushed tones before parting. Not even Mellypip's acute hearing could make out their words.

"I'll fix supper, Grandpa," she said when he came back, putting her hand on his shoulder. "I'm sorry about your friend, Ramirez."

"Thank you," he replied. "It is a tragedy. There is trouble out there, Runa, more than you know. I will explain things later, about before; I just need some time to think. Also, one more thing—if anything should happen to me or Caliste, Darcus will protect you. He's a good man."

She hugged Cathal, burrowing her head in his chest. "Please don't say that," she begged. "Nothing can happen to you. I won't let it. After all, you're the greatest sorcerer ever."

"I wish I were, you stubborn, silly girl," he muttered, holding her tight.

~ * ~

Caliste and Runa prepared the impromptu feast for their guests using magic, their hands emitting bright streams of sorcery, sparking knives to chop up large batches of potatoes, carrots, onions, and greens; scoops of barley floated from the grain bin to the large iron cauldron that hung over the cooking hearth. Bread dough kneaded itself and rose in seconds to large golden loaves, with large pats of butter melted on top. Runa stirred the iron cooking pot with a wooden spoon as the stew simmered with delicious aromas, adding spices of dill weed, pepper, and hot mylsap powder with a deft hand. Mellypip's tummy growled with anticipation. The aroma of baking bread was one of his favorite things in the world.

"The stores of honey and jam will be gone tonight with this group of men, Runa," Mellypip said. "I think they can eat a lot more than me!"

Sanura helped by staying out of the way and sleeping in the windowsill.

"Why don't you go play outside," Runa suggested, mixing a batch of batter for oatmeal cookies. "It's still sunny out, and it's our last night at home."

Mellypip had not thought about that. The enforced seclusion seemed to be lifted for the moment. Also, if he stayed in the kitchen, the wonderful smells of food would soon drive him mad, so he bounced out the door, sniffing flowers and climbing the tree.

The strange visitors smiled at him when he ran past them. He decided to explore—just a little. It was their last night here, after all. He scurried along the woods, enjoying the freedom, until he found a patch of clover. He snuggled in the clover, feeling a sense of calm, and nibbled at the buds. Male voices startled him, and he saw Cathal and Darcus walking toward him. Afraid he would be scolded for straying too far from the tower, he searched the area with a frantic eye, and discovered a hole in an old oak. He climbed into the hole. The voices became heated as they came closer, and Mellypip huddled in his hiding place. His nose twitched from the moldy leaves, and the twigs scratched his bottom.

"You can't keep her in the dark, Cathal! I can't believe she knows nothing," Darcus said.

"How do you tell a child her father was evil? That he murdered her mother and grandmother! Explain to me how you share such wretched facts with an innocent girl? Or that I, and the people she loves, killed him."

Mellypip gasped and stuck his tail in his mouth to keep from crying out.

"Ashur had to die. You know that. I know you want to protect her. Runa's a wonderful girl. I know how much she means to you."

"No, you could never know. Family means everything to me. I thought I had lost everything when I lost them in the war. They found Runa alive, and I have thanked the gods each and every day for her. The last thing I want to do is destroy her innocence or faith."

"What have you told her?"

"Just that her parents and grandmother were killed in an accident at sea when she was a baby," he said.

Belwyn alighted on a branch in Mellypip's tree. "Darcus is only trying to help. We are going out into the world. Do you think no one is going to mention her father or her mother?"

"If they had any manners, they wouldn't," Cathal said in a tight voice.

"They're people," Belwyn cried. "People have no manners. They are loud, smelly and untrustworthy—present company excluded, of course."

"Thanks," Darcus replied.

"You can't keep Runa in a glass cage like some fairy tale. She needs to know the truth now," Belwyn said. "I hate this too, but if she hears it from anyone else, it will be worse. The past is going to hurt her, Cathal, and you can't comfort her if she doesn't trust you anymore."

"Damn it," Cathal said. "I never wanted her to know."

"I know, Cathal," Darcus sympathized.

They walked away, their voices fading with the sun. Mellypip stayed in the tree hole for a long time. It was all a whirlpool in his mind. Poor Runa. He didn't know what to do about it. He crawled out of the hollow, and ran down the tree, thinking about all the terrible things, when Belwyn landed in front of him, flying down on silent wings. A puffed-up figure of gray and white feathers, golden eyes staring down at him with sharp intellect, Mellypip stumbled. "Taken up spying, Furball?"

"Oh no, Belwyn. I wasn't spying. It was…serendippy. I was just hiding because I didn't want Cathal to be mad about me being too far from home, and then all this stuff was said. Poor Runa. I'm sorry, Belwyn!"

"Serendipity," he corrected.

"What?" Mellypip whimpered.

"Never mind," Belwyn said. "Cathal is with Runa now. She is going to need you."

"What will I say?"

"Just love her. Before you go, let me explain the whole sordid story. Then I never want to talk about it again."

After Belwyn's words were spoken, Mellypip and the owl returned to the tower. Dusk shadowed the forest, and the two men standing watch outside nodded at them as they went inside. Caliste and Darcus were standing together, their faces etched in sympathy. Mellypip ran up the stairs to Runa's room.

Cathal was with her, sitting on the edge of the bed, holding her hand, his face a mask of pain. Runa was curled up on the bed, harsh sobs soaking her pillow. Mellypip went to her, snuggling next to her while she cried out her grief. Belwyn turned his head and pushed the door closed against the world.

CHAPTER 5

"Are we there yet?" Mellypip asked, yanking Runa's braid. "Soldier Darcus said we would be there today. I'm tired of riding stinky horse. I want to be there now!"

Weary, Runa shifted Mellypip in front of her. "Have a little patience, Melly. Here have a drink," she offered, uncorking the water bag and holding it to his mouth.

Mellypip gulped, water dribbling down his chin. He wiped his muzzle. "Adventure is boring," he muttered. "In fact, it's quite overrated." He scratched his ear uncomfortably; sure the mammoth animals had infested him with vermin.

"I know," she sighed. "Not exactly as thrilling as it is in books."

"You didn't sleep much again last night," Mellypip said. "It's hard to sleep when sharp-toothed wolves and lions roam the wilderness—and you have bad dreams!"

"I'm sorry, Melly. I kept you up again last night, didn't I?"

"Your scary dream has returned almost every night, Runa. The nightmare is changing too. It's not just red crystal and scary man in black fire. There's that angry woman with blue eyes and black hair; and then there are those—"

"Demons? I know," she whispered, her brilliant green eyes shadowed with dark circles. "Our bond entwines our dreams for some reason. I'm sorry, Melly. I guess learning the truth about, well, you know, made them return."

"Maybe you should tell Grandpa Cathal about it?"

"They're only nightmares. He's got enough to worry about," she insisted. "I don't want to worry him—not now."

She fell silent again. Mellypip grasped the saddle horn with chubby paws; swaying with a sick rhythm no matter how hard he held on, counting how many times the horses ahead swished their long tails at buzzing flies. He sighed, wishing he knew what to do.

It was during those sleepless bouts he got to know Darcus and his soldiers better—Timoth, Lichor, Korun, and Pol; they were very nice and gave him snacks, promising no wild lions or bears would eat them. Mellypip practiced his snarl, much to their amusement, and was glad of the warriors and their heavy swords. The hardest thing was the rift between Cathal and Runa. A difficult silence had wedged between them since Cathal told her about her father, Ashur.

Pungent, salty winds prodded him out of his reverie. "Are we there yet?"

Belwyn swayed on his saddle perch on Cathal's saddle and moaned. "Doesn't he ever say anything else?"

"Belwyn, it's his first time away from home. The trip has been hard on all of us, especially my bottom." She winced. "Riding horses is such agony! I've been chafed and stiff for days."

Darcus rode to Runa's side. "It takes some getting used to. I've had years of practice to toughen my body on long campaigns." He called ahead, "How are you doing, Cathal?"

"When I'm able to walk again without tumbling over, I'll let you know," the sorcerer replied. He looked at Runa for a moment, and then turned away.

Caliste was in discomfort too, though Sanura the cat didn't seem to suffer at all. She spent most of the journey curled up in her traveling pouch, sleeping.

"My charm is only kept intact by the promise of a long, hot soak when we reach Sea Haven," Caliste said.

Darcus signaled the caravan to stop near the cliffs. "Well, that should be soon now, Caliste. Below is the town of Sea Haven. It's a wild place, so take care and stay close. We will rest there tonight. The ship should be docked there now, awaiting us."

Runa and Mellypip were speechless at the sight of the ocean for the first time. "Look Melly," she said, hugging him, "isn't it beautiful?" The view of the wide ocean took Mellypip's senses by storm. Blue water lathered the dun-colored cliffs, and gulls cried in the air. The water seemed to expand, threatening the rocky shore and the defenseless town below; going further with each wave, while the earth remained still. Ships dotted the horizon, slowly moving through white fog that rolled across the ocean.

Mellypip shaded his eyes with his paws. "The sea looks angry."

Darcus led them down the rocky path that led to town. "Let me guide your horse, Runa," he offered. "The path is steep." He took the reins of Runa's mount, leading her down the rough trail.

"Thank you, Darcus," Runa said.

"Can you steer this horse with more care, Cathal? I'm getting dizzy," Belwyn complained, weaving to and fro on his saddle perch down the stony road.

"A bit cranky today, aren't you?" Cathal inquired.

"Rustic travel does little for my disposition," the owl retorted.

"What was your excuse before, featherhead," Mellypip asked, scratching his fuzzy toes.

Belwyn hooted. "Oh, the furry one is developing an ironic vocabulary!" He noticed Mellypip kneading his little body; round ears flattened in frustration. "Do you have parasites, Furball?"

"No, I've got itchies," Mellypip replied painfully.

"Looks like you get a bath too," Runa said.

"Wonderful," Mellypip sighed. "But if it gets rid of the itchies, I'll endure it. Wash off stinky horse smell too." The horse stumbled on the stray rocks along the path and pitched Mellypip forward. Runa's firm hand gripped him tightly. "He did that deliberately." Mellypip grimaced.

"Nonsense, little one," Darcus assured him. "It's a tough trail, that's all. You're quite safe with me."

Mellypip scowled at the horse that had been his bane since the journey began, knowing the falter was a dirty trick by this oversized hack; same as he *knew* the horse tried to bite his ear and ate up his apples. Another rocky lurch and he clung to Runa with desperation.

~ * ~

He still clung to Runa, wild-eyed and nervous, when they reached the bustling port town. They dismounted their horses at the local stables, and Mellypip was not sorry. He was positive the horse gave him a wicked look when they parted.

The stone streets of Sea Haven were crowded with every type of human imaginable—merchants, paupers, unsavory pirate-types, rough-looking mercenaries, and women dressed in garish finery with painted faces. But the Dancing Troll tavern was worse. A three-story white stone building with red trim; the paint was weathered and chipped.

The interior was even more dilapidated. The squalid building reeked of nasty odors. The lobby's worn and threadbare carpet was moldy. On the right, a large dining room crowded with long, rough wooden tables; on the left, the ale room with its long wooden bar and barrels of ale perched on logs with several round tables and chairs clustered together. Mellypip was glad he could not see the kitchen. It might spoil his appetite.

The inn was packed with seedy people milling about the large hostelry, marking their territory with the stench of unwashed human bodies, harsh perfume, bad food, strong liquor, and stale air.

"The atmosphere is a bit…ripe," Runa commented.

"It's a cesspool," Belwyn said.

"Hush, Belwyn," Runa whispered. "The innkeeper may not appreciate your views."

"I don't appreciate his hygiene," Belwyn said.

Meryc, the innkeeper, did reek of sweat and other nasty things. He was a corpulent man with greasy black hair and wrinkled, coarse skin. He wiped his hands on a soiled white apron.

"Are the rooms ready?" Darcus asked.

Meryc nodded. "Aye, Captain, the rooms are prepared. The entire top floor, as requested. Private chambers for the two ladies and their critters, the gentleman, and two rooms for you and your men. They're housebroken, aren't they," he asked, beady eyes looking over the trio of animals like they were a plague.

Sanura, curled in Caliste's arms, lifted her head and blinked. "We're cleaner than most of your guests, so mind your tongue."

Meryc cleared his throat and glanced away. "I didn't know they'd be familiars. Need to inform folks of such details. Must be important folk, to have an Imperial escort and all. Mighty fancy folk too," he added, his foul eyes drifting to Runa and Caliste's bodies with lust.

"Keep those eyes in your head, else you might lose them," Belwyn warned Meryc.

Darcus scowled. "I would listen to the owl. Also, I won't stop him if he decides to make good on his promise."

"My apologies, Captain. Didn't mean no disrespect."

"See baths are sent to our chambers. Make sure the water is hot …and clean," Darcus ordered, dropping circles of silver into Meryc's oily palm. "No one is allowed near their rooms without my permission. Do you understand?"

Meryc grinned, revealing uneven yellow teeth. "Yes, Captain. Special guests. Enjoy our fine accommodations."

Meryc led them to the top floor and opened the door to a small room with peeling paint and broken shutters.

Caliste inspected the room. "At least the bedding is clean," she remarked. "If not well-used." She noted the faded rose pattern quilts on the two narrow beds.

Meryc dropped their overstuffed satchels on the floor and scratched his armpits. Darcus examined the rooms. "Thank you. You may go Meryc."

Meryc grunted and left the room. Darcus turned to them. "Your baths should be here soon. Cathal and I have rooms right across the hall. The men have the other rooms, so there should be no strangers except for the staff on this floor. One of my men will be on watch, so if you need anything, tell one of them. Do not leave by yourself."

Caliste sat on the bed, taking off her boots with a relieved sigh. "Darcus, I don't know what we would do without your gentle care. Thank you."

"We'll call you down for supper when it's ready," Darcus said.

Servants entered with large round metal tubs lined with linen, towels, soaps, and many buckets of hot water. Pol, one of Darcus' men, stood by until the baths were ready and then left with the servants.

Runa flopped down on the lumpy mattress. "I'm exhausted."

"Of course you are," Caliste replied. "You've hardly slept in days." She removed her tunic and trousers, then stepped into the steaming water.

"I'm fine," Runa said. "It's just that, well, I have had too much to think about."

"I know dear."

"Finding out your father was evil incarnate does not exactly bring sweet dreams," Runa said, stripping down for her bath. "I know Grandpa didn't want to tell me the truth about…him."

"Your father," Caliste said, soaping up.

"I can't think of him as my father. It's too horrible."

"I know, dear," Caliste said gently. "Cathal's very worried."

"I know," Runa said. "I'm sorry. I know Grandpa is concerned. I just don't know what to say."

"You needn't say anything. Just take care of each other," Caliste said.

"I'm sorry if I've been distant. I don't want to hurt anyone."

"Just remember we love you, Runa. The truth will take time to bear. I know that. Your mother was my best friend. We grew up together. You are so much like her."

"Thank you, Caliste," Runa said. After a moment of silence, she asked, "Was my father ever good?"

"Yes, else your mother Rualla would never have looked at him. He was such a brilliant scholar, and handsome too, with black hair and deep blue eyes. He was a relic hunter of great skill."

"That's what Grandfather said."

"Ashur loved your mother. I witnessed their wedding. But something happened to him, something we cannot explain. We sorcerers live a long time, so it's best to keep the past in perspective. Just give it time."

"I wish I could stop thinking about it," Runa said, scratching her head. "I think your itchy buddies are spreading, Melly."

"Sorry," Mellypip said.

"Well, let me bathe first, and then it's your turn for a thorough scrubbing." She sank into the water and lathered with lilac-scented soap, washing her hair as well. "Ugh, I hate being so dirty. I literally had to peel off my clothes."

"I hate having itchies," Mellypip cried, scratching.

Sanura also began scratching her bronze coat with vigorous intensity and glared at Mellypip. "This is your fault!"

"Don't blame me," he said. "Blame stupid horse."

"Well Sanura, I guess Mellypip isn't the only familiar about to get a bath," Caliste said.

"Oh, no…I hate baths," Sanura replied.

"You're infested," Caliste said, washing a long, slim leg. "Deal with it, my beauty."

Runa stopped rinsing with the pitcher, raking thick strands of wet hair from her face. She wrapped a thick towel around her head and dried off. "Your turn, Melly," she said.

His skin crawling, he bounced over to the tub and leapt in, splashing water all over. Caliste finished her bath, wrapped herself in a towel, and carried a reluctant Sanura to her bath.

"My, you are dirty," Runa said, scrubbing away.

"Horses fault. Do you have a spell for killing bugs?"

She smelled the potent, unused soap the staff brought. "I have a feeling this stuff will eliminate a lot of things."

Mellypip's eyes chafed from the soap's strong odor but he got a second wash with the nice lilac soap. Sanura was not so cooperative and howled during the entire bathing, causing Pol and Timoth to knock on their door to check on them.

"It's all right," Runa called out. "Just killing the bugs on our familiars. Sorry."

After they were finished, they dried off their petulant familiars. They finished dressing in clean clothes. Runa waved her hand, and her wet hair dried to soft waves that flowed to her ankles.

"Come on, I need yummies," Mellypip said.

"You have a one-track mind when it comes to food," Sanura commented.

"It's a gift," Mellypip replied.

~ * ~

Belwyn ignored the rowdy crowd of the inn. It was best to disregard most humans anyway. Darcus was one of the few people he didn't want to peck. Captain Darcus had arranged for a private room to dine in, if you could call a shabby drape circling a table private. It was still noisy and rank, but it gave the illusion of solitude. Low-lit candles in yellow glass sconces lined the walls of the dining hall, and this area had several such draped niches.

"Shady dealings going on, no doubt, behind those curtains," Belwyn remarked.

Darcus poured strong amber ale into tankards. "This is a rough town. I'll be glad to be gone from here, especially for Runa and Caliste's sake."

Cathal passed a cup of ale to Belwyn. "I feel the same way. I never liked this place. Food's good—at least it was years ago. Did you talk to the Captain of the ship yet?"

"Yes, this afternoon," Darcus answered. "He will be ready to sail at dawn. More ale, Belwyn?"

"Yes, please," Belwyn said. Darcus understood familiars were not pets or quaint, docile creatures. The last person who had cooed at him suffered a bit finger. Darcus still looked scruffy despite a bath and shave, his face deeply tanned and lined by the sun. Darcus' ring-mail leather armor and steel-ringed leather bracers did not conceal the scarred and lean muscled arms. Darcus was no longer the youthful warrior they knew fifteen years ago, but had now been seasoned by battle and time.

Belwyn glanced at Cathal, who had *that* look again. "She'll be fine. You worry too much," he said, dipping his beak in the foamy nectar.

"She's been so quiet lately, and I know she's not sleeping either," Cathal said, his voice edged with worry.

"Runa just learned some gruesome and tragic facts about her father," Belwyn said. "She needs time. Have a few drinks and relax, Cathal. I'll buy, thanks to Darcus."

Darcus grinned strangely, shaking his head. "What's so funny?" Belwyn asked.

"I don't know if I'll live down losing to an owl in a game of dice," Darcus said.

Belwyn chuckled. "It can be something you tell your grandkids someday. You ever marry, Darcus? And where did you get that magnificent scar?"

"Belwyn!" Cathal gasped. "That's very rude."

"Nonsense," Belwyn replied. "Scars are the mark of a good warrior. It means they aren't dead."

Darcus leaned back and shrugged. "I haven't married. Been too busy in the legions to find a wife. This is my last assignment though."

"Really?" Cathal said surprised. "I thought you would be a lifer in the army."

"I want a plot of land and a plump wife. I'm thirty-eight now, and my bones feel the strain of fighting more than they use to. This scar across my eye was the result of a war in Urgonclaw about five years ago. The camp doctor said I was lucky. I could have lost my eye or been blinded. Now it's just an ugly scar."

"It's very intimidating," Belwyn complimented him.

"Thanks. Now, I just want to grow crops. My pension should help. Plus, I have saved a bit over the years."

"I hope you get your dream, Darcus," Cathal said. "I'm glad of your sword arm, should something confront us between here and Tiamet. This journey has been too easy and that makes me uneasy."

Darcus' craggy face glowed in the candlelight. "It would be a short confrontation," he replied, his hand on the hilt of his sword. "I'm not that old yet. Speaking of which," he said, leaning closer. "Why is your hair silver as the moons, Cathal? I know sorcerers live a long time and age differently than mortal men, but your hair was dark the last time we met."

"Well, he wanted to look like a grandfather," Belwyn said. "I told him it was silly. But if he was going to do that, maybe he should have added more wrinkles and used a cane."

"Belwyn!" Cathal warned.

"Maybe go for that toothless look," Belwyn teased.

Darcus laughed. "You will do anything for that girl, won't you?"

"Yes," Cathal answered firmly.

Pol escorted Runa and Caliste to the table. They looked more relaxed. The barmaid brought a platter of food for them just as they arrived.

"Good timing, ladies," Darcus said.

The men stood until Runa and Caliste were seated. Mellypip's large round ears perked up when he sniffed the food. Fresh herb bread, butter, crab cakes, greens, and roasted potatoes covered the rough-hewn table.

"At least it looks good," Runa commented. "I'm famished."

Cathal filled her plate with generous portions. She took the heavy dish. "Thanks, Grandpa." She smiled for the first time in days, which softened Belwyn's mood—and concern.

Mellypip's nose twitched and his little paws reached for a crab cake.

"Mind your manners, Furball," Belwyn warned.

"Mind yourself," Mellypip chirped, taking a big bite. "Surprisingly good. Spicy too. What is it?"

"Crab cakes," Cathal replied. "They do smell good. I haven't had any in eons."

"Do you mean that literally?" Belwyn asked.

"Don't start," Cathal replied, scooping some cakes onto his plate.

Sanura, sitting next to Caliste on the table, devoured her crab cake with ladylike bites. "Quite passable," she said, licking her whiskers afterward.

"I agree," Mellypip said. "I think we should have another to make sure. Do we get dessert?"

Suddenly, the curtain ripped from its metal rings, and a masked man swathed in black, wearing a red turban raised a long, curved dagger over Darcus. Darcus flung his tin plate at the attacker, striking him in the face and throwing him off balance. Darcus leapt to his feet and unsheathed his sword. He thrust it into the man's stomach.

Cathal and Caliste didn't have a chance to react. Heavy nets were thrown over them and several men wrestled them both to the floor. Belwyn, who circled above them, shouted, "Eat claw, you bloody buggers!" and dove to attack the men holding Cathal and Caliste.

Jolted by the abrupt shock, Mellypip fell backward into Runa's lap. The patrons screamed and fled, knocking over tables and chairs as the enemy advanced. Poor Pol was down, his head bleeding. Darcus pulled a stunned Runa to her feet, shielding her with body and blade. About two dozen men in black robes and red turbans circled the room. Their feral eyes glimmered in the dusky light, and their scimitars gleamed.

"Rashurkeen!" Darcus hissed, kicking the table over.

"What?" Mellypip squeaked.

"Assassins and mercenaries," Belwyn cried.

"Darcus, get Runa out of here!" Cathal ordered.

"Had to mention how easy the trip was didn't you Cathal!" Belwyn said, avoiding the sweep of a sword.

"This isn't the time!" Cathal struggled with the Rashurkeen who tried to carry him off.

Darcus' soldiers came running with swords drawn. Several Rashurkeen swarmed into the crowded dining hall fighting them. Runa and Mellypip had the good sense to stay behind Darcus, but their exit was blocked.

"Oh hell," Darcus groaned, flanked on all sides by the enemy.

"Why can't Grandpa use his sorcery?" Runa asked, holding a terrified Mellypip.

"Those nets are laced with sarod metal—sorcerer's bane. Magic won't work," he answered quickly.

A hulking assassin raised Cathal up by the shoulders and laughed. "Helpless now, aren't you sorcerer."

Cathal replied with a head butt, knocking the man down.

"Grandpa!" Runa cried, clutching Mellypip to her chest.

Sanura detangled herself from the curtain and grew to the size of a panther, stunning the enemy into sensible fear. She roared and leapt at the assassins with razor-sharp claws extended; the grim sound of shredding flesh and screaming followed her pounce.

"Sanura just exploded!" Mellypip cried.

"Yeah, she does that," Belwyn said, sweeping down on another enemy with sharp claws.

Caliste kicked the man trying to bind her, and Runa smashed a pitcher over the man's head.

Darcus dragged Runa back from the fray. "Don't do that again!" he said hotly. "Stay down!" he said, pushing her to the floor as an assassin jumped at him. Darcus rammed his sword into the man's throat, gushing blood over him. The man fell to the floor, dead. "Don't you dare move!" he ordered Runa and Mellypip, shoving them under a table.

"But I can use magic!" she protested.

"Not now!" Belwyn cried. "Too risky!"

Belwyn turned to the shadowy men blocking their escape. Focusing on the fallen knives and chairs scattered everywhere, and levitating them. He aimed them at the swarms of Rashurkeen and shot them through the air at the Rashurkeen as they charged, striking several.

Good. That should hurt, Belwyn thought.

Next, Belwyn sent chairs flying through the air, blocking the enemy so Cathal and Caliste could throw off the nets. Once free, Cathal and Caliste sent the Rashurkeen flying with beams of magic.

An assassin tried to throw a rope around Cathal from behind. Annoyed, Cathal spun around, casting green sparks of sorcery, burning the rope that bound him. He then grabbed the man and slapped him, magic still streaming from his fingers. The enemy's mask caught fire and he screamed. Falling to the ground, he beat at the mystical flames, writhing in agony. Cathal delivered a rush of fiery sorcery at the cluster of men attacking. The men trapped in its path howled, falling to the blood-soaked floor as their clothes sizzled and smoked, slapping at the mystical flames. They scattered and fled the building.

"I don't think this establishment is appropriate for the children," Belwyn said. "Let's go."

Bloody and tired, Timoth, Lichor, Korun, and an injured Pol surveyed the carnage.

"What now sir?" Timoth asked. "Should we pursue them?"

"No. We're going to the ship—*now*. The town watch will be here soon, and we don't have time to explain this mess," Darcus said.

Caliste picked up Sanura, normal size again, though her paws and whiskers were stained red. She cleaned them with delicate licks of her tongue.

Cathal grimaced. "Where's Runa?"

Frantic, Belwyn searched the wrecked room with his impeccable vision. "Oh no…she's gone."

CHAPTER 6

Waking up in the dark, Mellypip was confused and sick to his stomach. Cramped and uncomfortable, he soon realized he was in a smelly, old burlap sack. The last thing he remembered was Runa being hit on the head and hands smothering him. *Runa*, he cried out with his mind. *Where are you?*

She didn't answer. That was bad. Hushed voices penetrated his ragged prison, and he held his breath, listening, recognizing Meryc's voice, but not the other.

"My part's done," Meryc argued. "I want my money now."

"When we have all the goods, Meryc," A strange voice whispered back. "Runa is not all the goods."

That slimy Meryc! May he eat gruzzy worms, Mellypip fumed with anger. Frantic with the need to escape and find Runa, he chewed at the decayed cloth. It tasted terrible—like rotten turnips.

"You promised me a hundred gold dracons if I helped you!" Meryc shouted.

"When we have Cathal and Caliste, you will get the rest of your money, Meryc," the strange man replied harshly. "Runa will serve as bait to bring them to us."

"What about this rodent?" Meryc asked.

Rodent? Me! A rodent! Mellypip thought angrily, gnawing at the sack. That stinky, stupid human!

"I don't care. I understand wampu meat makes a juicy roast, however."

Mellypip…no value? A roast! Fear shifted to wild panic as Mellypip chewed and scratched through the material. It split open, and he dropped to the stone floor at Meryc's feet. All Mellypip saw of the retreating stranger was the sweep of a black velvet cloak as he exited the backdoor. Meryc's beady eyes were glaring down at him. Mellypip bolted for the door.

"Come here, varmint!" he shouted, grabbing him by the tail. He dangled him in the air and laughed. "You're gonna be stew, you mangy runt." They were in the inn's kitchen, hot with blazing hearths and iron stoves covered with large cooking pots.

Mellypip heaved his body up, and bit Meryc's thumb hard. A

sour metallic taste flooded his mouth as Meryc wailed. Meryc yanked Mellypip from his bloody, torn appendage and threw him across the room into a large pot of cooling drobba pudding on a long wooden table. Soaked and sputtering pudding, Mellypip crawled out of the pot. Meryc seized a cleaver and gripped the slippery wampu by the tail. He held him down, cleaver raised high, the metal gleaming in the firelight. Mellypip screamed as he squirmed and twisted in Meryc's grip.

Talons flashed before Mellypip's terrified eyes. Belwyn ravaged Meryc's face, who dropped the cleaver and let go of Mellypip while trying to protect himself.

Blood streamed between Meryc's fingers as he whimpered. "Stop! Stop! Mercy!"

Mellypip coughed and wiped drobba from his muzzle.

Belwyn clacked his beak. "Hurt him and I'll rip out your eyes, scum!"

Darcus and Cathal were there, shoving Meryc to the floor.

"Are you hurt, Furball?" Belwyn asked.

"No hurt...but they took Runa somewhere," Mellypip said. "They said she was bait."

Cathal cradled Mellypip in his arms, despite being smothered in brown pudding, and soothed him. "It's all right, little one. We will find her." He turned to Darcus. "Make him talk. I don't care how."

Caliste and Sanura ran in, guarded by the soldiers. Pol had regained consciousness and looked dizzy; his blond hair soaked with blood from his wound.

"She's not here," Meryc whimpered.

"Meryc gave her to those Rashurkeen for a hundred gold dracons," Mellypip said quickly. "And this strange man in a fancy cloak said to make me a roast and left."

"Where is the Lady Runa?" Darcus asked coldly, pressing his sword into Meryc's fat neck. "I've had a really bad night and my sword arm gets twitchy when that happens. I just can't help myself." Darcus hauled him up and threw him against the wall. "So speak, because two very put-out sorcerers are angry with you. They can do things to you I can't even imagine. I can only break bones or cut off your fingers and toes for starters—but that hurts too."

Sanura transformed into her large panther form. Darcus grinned and stepped aside. Sanura pinned Meryc with her massive paws and growled. "Hmmm...chew toy." She licked her chops and roared for emphasis.

"They took the girl to trade for the old sorcerer and the sorceress," Meryc blubbered, tears mingling with blood on his ravaged face. "A man and woman came to me, backed by Rashurkeen assassins. They gave me gold. No names exchanged. I didn't even see their faces. I don't know where they took her! I swear!"

Darcus winked. "Thanks, Sanura."

"My pleasure, Captain," Sanura replied.

"We can't leave him to run off and tattle," Darcus said. "Cathal, do you mind?"

"My pleasure," Cathal said. Within seconds Meryc was bound from head to toe with mystical white ropes, unable to move or speak. "That will hold him."

"For how long?" Darcus asked.

"Until they find a sorcerer who can undo my spell—which is doubtful," Cathal said.

Sorcery charged the air around them, and a transparent shadowy figure appeared. Darcus' blade passed through the shape.

"It's an illusion," Cathal said.

It spoke with a feminine voice. "Surrender to me Cathal and Caliste, and Runa lives. Go to the beach beyond the docks east of town. Come alone or Runa will die." The image vanished.

"I really hate ultimatums," Cathal said.

"You two aren't going alone," Darcus insisted.

"I have an idea," Cathal said. "Don't worry, you're included."

Pol stumbled. Darcus steadied the young soldier and held up three fingers. "Boy, how many fingers am I holding up?"

"Six," Pol replied weakly.

"You can't fight," Darcus said.

"But sir—"

"No arguments," Darcus ordered. He turned to Cathal. "What's your plan?"

"I'll explain along the way," Cathal said. "Belwyn, you fly reconnaissance. The rest of you follow me."

"Already in the sky," Belwyn hooted, and flew out the door.

"What about Meryc?" Darcus asked.

"Let him rot," Caliste said.

"Perhaps young Pol can perform an errand that won't endanger him," Cathal suggested.

"Come on then," Darcus ordered. "Let's show some folks there's no rest for the wicked."

~ * ~

Cathal floated in shadows along the stony path ahead of Darcus and his men. The night fog rolled in, making it difficult to see. On the right, there was only a wall of jagged rocks, on the left stood row upon row of buildings made of wood or stone. No lamps burned in the alley, only the dim illumination that shone from inside the structures and the twin moons above.

As they trekked to the beach, Mellypip kept calling out to Runa with his mind, but no answer came. Sanura in panther form ran alongside, her blue eyes glowing in the night.

When they reached the scrubby beach, they saw a cluster of torches below and a band of soldiers. They crouched in the dunes.

Belwyn landed next to Cathal. "Runa is there. I think she's all right, but she's still unconscious. Bound and gagged too. I count about a dozen men, and there's a woman with a crill lizard in her lap giving orders, so she must be their leader. No sign of Koll, however."

Cathal frowned. "Are you sure Runa isn't hurt?"

"See if Furball can speak to her."

Cathal looked at Mellypip. "If she's not confined by sorcerer bane, she can speak to you. I need her to wake up."

Mellypip sent out more cries, determined to reach Runa. Finally, her frightened, groggy voice replied. *Melly?*

"I'm able to speak to her," he whispered to Cathal.

"Good. Talk to her. Keep her calm!" Cathal whispered. "And, nothing foolish either!"

Runa! Are you hurt? Cathal says to stay calm and don't be a fool. We're coming to rescue you.

I'm fine, sort of. My head's puffy. I repent the remark about adventure being boring, however. Oh, they're taking me to someone.

Who is it?

She's looking at me now. And Melly, she is the one from my bad dreams.

"Let's move in, quietly," Darcus commanded. "Let's hope your cloaking spell works, Cathal. What about your—"

"The illusions of Caliste and me should convince them long enough to give us the advantage." Hidden in the shadows of mystical camouflage, they closed in.

The mysterious young woman sat on a black horse, petting a winged crill lizard in her lap. Her long black hair floated in the wind, her fingers flashing with jewels. "Azmadu, now the wintry sorcerer will have no choice. Soon he will come."

"We go home then, my Panthara," Azmadu begged, wagging his long tail.

"What now?" Darcus whispered when they were about thirty feet from the enemy.

"You get to fight, but only after Runa is safe. Wait for my signal," Cathal said.

Runa managed to sit up. With bound hands she pulled the gag from her mouth. "Who are you? Why are you doing this?"

"Talkative, isn't she? Perhaps cut out tongue and she be quiet," Azmadu suggested, wiggling his wings.

"It would be an improvement," the dusky sorceress replied.

"Try it and I'll make a belt out of you," Runa threatened.

The crill lizard hissed, but the woman cooed to him. "Behave, Azmadu."

Runa! Cathal said no foolish, Mellypip called.

Sorry. They ticked me off, she replied. She looked at her captors. "You don't scare me. And this…is unnecessary," she said, indicating the ropes, which slipped off her hands and feet.

Panthara sighed. "Unimpressive, but bold for such an insignificant girl."

"Look they come, my Panthara!" Azmadu cried, bouncing in her lap.

Cathal and Caliste step out of the mist, solemn and silent. At Panthara's gesture, an assassin pulled Runa to her feet and pressed a dagger to her throat. Hidden in shadows, Mellypip bared his teeth. How dare they treat Runa like that! Cathal and Caliste continued their march.

Panthara spoke imperiously. "Surrender Cathal and Caliste. Come with me and I will spare your precious Runa. If you resist, I will kill her."

The figures of Cathal and Caliste knelt before her. The woman smiled. "Bind them with sorcerer locks."

The man holding Runa dug the blade deeper into her throat, releasing a thin ribbon of blood. Mellypip sensed her panic. Runa flared, her whole body glowing like sunlight, stunning the brute who held her. A flare of orange magic burst from the dark, striking the man unconscious. Runa turned to find Cathal standing there in his place, his staff glowing. She threw her arms around him. "Oh, Grandpa!" she cried.

The false images of Cathal and Caliste vanished.

"What is this trickery?" Panthara cried.

A flash of gray and white feathers smacked Azmadu in the face, knocking him off Panthara's lap. His startled sorceress shielded her face with her hands. Darcus, backed by his men, charged the Rashurkeen warriors. Two immense bronze panthers now fought at their side, for Caliste had shapeshifted too, attacking the enemy with powerful blows from their massive paws. The sailors from the Imperial ship charged from the beach, bursting from the night fog like angry ghosts to battle the mercenaries. Darcus had sent Pol and Caliste with a message to the ship to ask for aid.

Panthara screamed her fury. "I am deceived!"

"You sound surprised—or is your sorcery that inept, my dear?" Cathal said. "Get back, Runa and Mellypip."

Sanura pushed Runa out of harm's way, baring her dagger-like fangs at any who dared to come near. Mellypip followed them, glancing back at the battle.

Panthara's hand sizzled with scarlet magic. She shot a fiery bolt at Cathal.

Cathal blocked her blow with his staff. Her sorcery glanced off his shield and he sent it flying back at Panthara.

The bolt struck her, and she fell back but clung to her mount, disoriented by her own magery.

Azmadu, furious at their defeat, pounced on the nearest victim —Mellypip. Mellypip kicked and bit, but Azmadu was bigger and stronger, his sharp teeth anxious to taste Mellypip's blood.

"No Azmadu! Wait!" Panthara cried after him.

Belwyn's talons raked across the spine of Azmadu, forcing him off Mellypip. Azmadu twisted around and faced the enraged owl.

"Get off him, you vile lizard," Belwyn spat. "Fight me, not an infant—if you dare, you stinking coward!"

Azmadu hissed through spiny teeth and shot into the sky with Belwyn. Shaking, Mellypip crawled away. The crill lizard and Belwyn spiraled into the misty sky in combat, their raging howls echoing in the air. "Go get' em Belwyn! Make the scaly head sorry!" he managed to whimper, then collapsed on the damp sand, exhausted and panting. Sanura scooped him up in her huge, powerful jaws, carrying him to Runa's waiting arms.

"Poor Melly," she cried, cradling him. "You are safe now."

"Azmadu...come back," Panthara cried out.

Several of the Rashurkeen lay dead on the beach. Darcus and the others surrounded the sorceress, swords and staves raised. She backed her horse away, panic on her face. She raised a shield around her to prevent anyone from attacking her, and it glowed with pale yellow magic.

The heated sky-born conflict between the crill lizard and Belwyn ceased abruptly. Azmadu plummeted to earth, yowling, one eye socket hollow and bloody. The dark sorceress wept. "Azmadu!" With a flash her steed transformed into a horse of black smoke, with a tail and mane of blue fire. She swept the injured Azmadu into her arms with a sorcerous call and flew away into the ether of night across the sea.

Cathal rushed to Runa. "Are you hurt?"

She wrapped her arm around his neck and mumbled, "I'm fine. Just dizzy, that's all."

"You shouldn't have tried fighting with magic. You could have been hurt," Cathal said, patting her back, relieved at last.

"I didn't," she sniffled. "It just happened."

Crushed between them, Mellypip felt safer for it. Caliste and Sanura shimmered back to their normal shapes.

"Damn, I nearly had her!" Darcus complained, bloodstained and filthy.

"I'm sorry too. She knows the fate of my friends," Cathal said grimly.

The Captain of the Imperial Ship, summoned by Pol as part of the plan, bowed before Cathal and Captain Darcus.

"Thank you, Captain Tigara, for your assistance," Cathal said. "Your help turned things around."

Captain Tigara, wild red hair vivid even in the night, sheathed his sword. "We are honored to be of service, especially against the Rashurkeen, Sorcerer Cathal. We should return to the ship now and leave this place."

Belwyn landed at Cathal's feet and spit out a crimson eyeball. "This is what happens when you cross me or mine!"

In an odd way, Mellypip was comforted by that.

~ * ~

"Runa look out!" Mellypip warned, bouncing up and down on the deck.

"Keep eye contact!" Belwyn hooted, swaying to the rhythm of

the ship, claws latched to a barrel.

Nimble and quick, Runa blocked Darcus' blow with her staff. His soldiers whooped and hollered, applauding every successful block by Runa, and scoffing at Darcus when he made the rare error. Runa stumbled, but recovered quickly, deflecting his next blow, perspiration streaming down her face.

"Come on Runa," he taunted her, "you can maneuver better than an old foot soldier like me! I've got more than twenty years on you."

Clenching her teeth, she charged, swinging with fierce effort against Darcus' rapid fighting style.

"Good. Reflexes should be quick for the young—right Cathal?" he shouted.

"Cathal's not so young," Belwyn corrected him. "He's older... much older."

"Just don't break anything," Cathal shouted.

The sailors, garbed in loose trousers, flowing shirts, and high boots, milled about the ship, performing their duties. They were very nice, and told great stories too, except for the ship's pilot, who was a sullen fellow. Yesterday he made a very scathing remark about the stupidity of owls, familiars or not.

Belwyn's golden eyes burned with revenge. He relieved himself on the man's head for the insult. The pilot grimaced at the irate owl, but kept silent after that, knowing sorcerers were on board and retribution might result from his opinions. It made Mellypip laugh so hard he fell into a pile of ropes until tears matted his fuzzy face. Belwyn remained unrepentant, despite the half-hearted scolding he received from Cathal about his manners.

Sanura slept a great deal, drained from too much excitement and shapeshifting into a panther, which turned out was her special ability. Mellypip sighed with envy, wondering if his special magic would ever surface.

During the last three days of their journey, Runa spent much of her time sparring with Darcus. Cathal thought Runa should learn some self-defense after her scary abduction, and Darcus was more than happy to teach her.

The staves were wound with heavy cloth to prevent serious injury. Her youthful stamina could not outfight the seasoned warrior, but each bout took longer and required more effort.

"Land Ho!" one of the sailors cried.

Runa spun around to look, and Darcus swept his staff across

the back of her knees, knocking her flat on her back. She landed hard on the deck. "Darcus, that's not fair!" she challenged, pushing herself up on her elbows.

"Battle never is," he replied. "That is also a lesson."

He turned his back. Grinning, Runa unfooted him with a wicked swing. "Like that, Master Darcus?"

The men burst out laughing. "I guess that means you were paying attention," he replied good-naturedly, picking himself up.

Mellypip romped over to Runa, licking her face. "You're salty. Just like the sea."

"I'm sweaty," she sad with a laugh. "Come here, silly wampu." She tickled him until his paws spun like furry wheels.

"Help! Warrior Sorceress has trapped me!" he cried.

"Come on," Caliste called. "Breakfast is ready."

They all followed Caliste downstairs to the small dining room. Tea, bread, and cereal were ready. Darcus and the men sat down as Caliste served them their meal. Runa washed and sat down to eat. Mellypip was famished from watching the battle.

"I'll be glad to be on land again," Runa said, pouring a heavy amount of honey on her cereal. "The ocean is beautiful, but being confined on a ship is a bit dull."

Belwyn ate bits of toast. "Yes, dry land and none too soon, young Runa. Bloody nuisance this water travel. It attracts the wrong elements—clumsy sea gulls and other scavenger types. Not real predators."

"Not like you," Mellypip said, and slurped his knurly cereal. "It must be a burden to be Belwyn."

"You have no idea," Belwyn sighed. "Any ginger for my tea?"

"I think you're full of enough ginger," Cathal commented. He turned to Runa. "How are your dreams? Anything…unusual?"

She shook her head and spoke between mouthfuls. "Nothing since the confrontation in Sea Haven. Panthara is the only one I have met from my dreams though."

"Perhaps she's a dream seer?" Caliste suggested.

"Perhaps," Cathal nodded, "but that's an Ilyrran ability."

"I am partly Ilyrran Grandpa, even if I don't have the elegant ears. Were…mother or grandmother gifted in such a way?"

"Your Grandmother was a Drusai, but prophetic dreams weren't one of her gifts. Your mother was a sorceress. I confess Yllia was a bit disappointed her daughter didn't inherit more of the Drusai magic."

"Well, I promise I will tell you any strange dreams from now on."

"Good. When we find our friends again, we will take you to Ilyrra. It's your homeland too, and they better understand such gifts."

"We should get dressed now," Caliste said. "I want to look my best when we arrive. You need to change too Cathal."

"I am dressed," Cathal said.

"Don't you have any clothes that aren't tattered and patched?" she asked sadly.

"I like to be comfortable," Cathal replied.

"But we are seeing the Emperor," she said.

"He can deal with me as I am."

"Stubborn as ever," Caliste said, resigned.

"A family trait," Cathal added with a grin.

Runa and Caliste went to change. The tiny cabins were cramped but nice. Runa shed her dirty clothes, redid her braids and donned her best dress of light blue cotton, her teal birthday cloak, and her least worn shoes. It was fortunate that before they left Sea Haven, Darcus and his men snuck back to the inn to get their bags and supplies.

Mellypip was glad, because his little pillow and blanket would have been lost otherwise—and Runa's new crystals, which he liked to play with, enjoying the sparkles of color even if they didn't have any magic in them.

"I've never been to a real city before," Runa said excitedly. "I've dreamed about it all my life. I just wish—" She sat on the slim cot and sighed. "I just wish it was for a happier reason. Our friends missing; the Archon murdered. I forget sometimes there are more serious elements to our journey. People will also know I'm Ashur's daughter. They may judge me for that."

"Then they're stupid humans," Mellypip said,

"Now you are sounding like Belwyn. How do I look?" she asked, turning around.

"Pretty as a princess."

"Come on, let's see if we can get a good view of the city," Runa said, picking him up.

On deck, the panorama of Tiamet amazed them. The day was clear, so the visionary feast of white stone buildings in bright sunlight did not end within eyesight. Flags resplendent with a white dragon design danced on the winds. "It's very beautiful," Runa gasped.

A great palace loomed above the wild sea on the cliffs. Darcus pointed to it. "That is the palace of Emperor Tarsicius."

"It's so big for one man," Mellypip commented.

Cathal and Belwyn joined them. "Is it everything you hoped for my dear?" he asked Runa.

"It's wondrous. But my real hope is we find our missing family."

"That's my dream too," he said quietly. "And we will."

The ship docked at last. Soon, a small assembly of soldiers arrived, dressed in rich crimson silk cloaks, with matching deep crimson leather vestments with the imperial emblem of a white dragon on their chests. Even the trappings of the horses were encrusted with gold and jewels.

"Who are they?" Runa whispered.

"Imperial Dragon Knights. They are very elite. Part of the Emperor's personal guard," Cathal said.

"They are too soft to be real warriors," Mellypip said, nodding at Darcus.

"You are quite right there, Furball. These puffy boys would crumble in a real battle," Belwyn agreed.

The leader of the band dismounted and removed his white plumed helmet. A young man with short-cropped blond hair marched on board. "I am Commander Priem of the Imperial Dragon Knights. Are you Captain Darcus?"

"Pompous twit, isn't he?" Belwyn commented.

Mellypip nodded in vigorous agreement.

"I am. I have delivered safely Cathal and Caliste to Tiamet as ordered by Emperor Tarsicius."

Priem pointed to Runa. "Who is that young woman and the furry thing?"

"Runa, granddaughter of Cathal, and her familiar Mellypip. So speak with respect," Darcus warned.

"What is it...some sort of squirrel?"

"I'm not a squirrel," Mellypip chirped. "I'm a wampu."

"Well, there is nothing in my orders about her. She cannot attend the palace without proper clearance."

"Deal with it, Commander," Darcus said. "She is coming, or we aren't leaving the ship."

"Very well, but hurry, His Majesty is waiting," Priem commanded.

"A bit arrogant, isn't he?" Runa commented.

"He's a poopy head," Mellypip agreed.

On the ride to the palace, Cathal said, "I hope you can still instruct Runa daily. I'm not sure how long we are going to be here, and I want her time spent in the company of proper folk." He looked at Priem.

Darcus nodded his head. "I would be honored, Cathal."

"Thank you," he smiled.

After a long trek up the hill, they arrived at the white palace. They left their mounts at the rich, white-washed stone stables, which looked as fancy as any house.

But the palace! Mellypip never imagined such opulence. Though Priem was a sullen and silent guide, not even he could spoil the myriad of colors and textures. They walked upon rivers of blue carpets on polished marble floors. Ornate tapestries lined the walls, broken by lofty windows with real glass. Mellypip was afraid to shed a hair in this pristine place.

At last, they came to two grand golden doors, embossed with a frightening design of a dragon in full wingspread, which guards opened to the throne room. Runa held her breath as she entered the grand chamber, Cathal and Caliste by her side.

The vast chamber was lined with jade pillars and Imperial guards.

On a dais, a man reclined on a throne. His rich blue velvet robes covered a thin, frail frame.

Priem walked ahead and bowed deeply. "My Emperor, as you have commanded I have brought—"

"Leave us," Tarsicius commanded.

Priem bowed his head and departed.

Tarsicius coughed weakly. "You took time coming here, Cathal."

Cathal bowed. "We came quickly as circumstances allowed, Your Majesty."

Tarsicius gestured to Caliste. "Welcome home. My daughter, Opaline, will be glad of your return. I question her attachment to mages, but she does not listen to me. Still I am glad you are safe, Caliste."

"Thank you, Your Grace," Caliste replied. "I look forward to seeing Princess Opaline again."

Cathal put his hand on Runa's elbow and gently led her forward. "With Your Majesty's permission, I would like to present my grand-daughter, Runa."

A flash of anger lit Tarsicius' eyes. He leaned forward; blue-gray eyes leveled at Runa. "Ashur's daughter!" he said harshly.

CHAPTER 7

Tarsicius gestured to Runa. "Come forward, girl."

She approached the dais and curtsied. Tarsicius studied Runa for a tense moment. "You have your mother's coloring, including those Ilyrran eyes—like green crystals. Good. There's no mark of your father upon you…at least that I can see."

"Leave her alone," Cathal said, coming to Runa's side. "She's just a child and innocent. She is not answerable for her father's sins."

"I'm sorry if my heritage offends, Your Majesty. But you only warred with Ashur," Runa said softly. "Ashur killed my family, so I think I hate him more than you, Sire."

"Impudent little wench, aren't you?" Tarsicius replied, and then laughed; but his humor was overcome by a coughing spasm.

Runa dispensed with protocol and rushed to his side, taking a cup of water from the low table next to the throne, and holding it to his lips. "Drink this. It will help." He took small sips and began to breathe easier.

"Thank you, child," the Emperor said.

The old king's pasty complexion and labored breath concerned Runa. The rich clothes hung on his wasted frame, and the ruby ring, almost as big as a robin's egg, seemed to weigh down his hand. Despite the heavy perfume, he reeked of medicines and sickness.

Maybe we should get off the dais, Mellypip suggested. *It's safer.*

Runa took advantage of their conversation to descend the dais and stand by Cathal again.

"Runa is my granddaughter. I will tolerate no prejudice against her, Your Majesty. The past is not her fault."

"You haven't changed much either, Cathal. I see where Runa inherited her cheeky nature. I also notice your hair has become gray. How did that happen?"

"I'm going to develop a complex if people keep pointing that out," Cathal muttered.

"How old are you now, girl?" Tarsicius asked.

"Fifteen, Your Majesty."

"Has Cathal at least given you an education in the backwoods he exiled himself to? What have you studied, besides magic?"

"Yes, sir, I mean, Your Majesty. Mathematics, history, philosophy, poetry, eight languages, including Dwarven and Ilyrran—"

"Enough," the Emperor relented, and smiled faintly. "I see Cathal has kept you studious. Best thing for girls. Keeps them virtuous."

"My plan exactly," Cathal said with a grin.

"But now we must speak of more serious matters. The assassination of the Archon, Ramirez, has done more than send a shock wave through the community of mages; my subjects are afraid Koll has returned," Tarsicius said harshly. "The Sorcerer War is still fresh in the memories of my people. Ramirez was murdered here—in my kingdom!" he emphasized, rapping his cane on the marble floor. "Cathal, I charge you with hunting Koll down. Before I die, I want his head on a pike."

"*That* I agree with wholeheartedly, Emperor," Cathal replied firmly.

"Then we have much to discuss," Tarsicius said. He rapped his cane and four guards lifted his chair. "We will adjourn to the council room. Send for my physician, Hemio. I need my medicine to brace me for the coming hours."

The council chamber had a long table of polished teak Mellypip wanted to slide across, but knew both the Emperor and Belwyn would chastise him. Hemio, a fussy, rather fat, short man with short-cropped brown hair, attended Tarsicius with strong-smelling tonics, and remained in the background while everyone related the dreadful incident in Sea Haven and the birthday fiasco with the giant ravens.

Runa began to squirm and whispered in Mellypip's head. *I need to use the privy. Oh, Melly, I don't know how to interrupt the Emperor. What should I do?*

I dunno. You're a sorceress. Sorcel!

Don't make me laugh, she whimpered in his head.

Sorcel, Sorcel, Sorcel—

Cathal noticed Runa's discomfort. "If it please Your Majesty, perhaps my Granddaughter should retire to her room. She is too young for such a serious assembly."

The Emperor gestured, and a servant in plain brown robes stepped forward and bowed. He was a very old man, with thin grey hair and a face crinkled with age, but he stood straight and strong despite his great years.

"Take Lady Runa to her chambers," Tarsicius ordered.

"As Your Majesty Commands," the servant replied.

The servant guided them through the endless halls of the palace.

"It's a very big palace," Runa commented as they walked.

"All palaces are large, Lady Runa," he replied. "That is why they are palaces." The old man's pale blue eyes twinkled with humor. Runa and Mellypip began to relax.

"What is your name?" she asked.

"My name is Malcolm," he answered. "Thank you for asking. You would be surprised how many do not."

Mellypip, who wanted to be included in the conversation, said, "I'm Mellypip."

"A fine name," Malcolm replied.

The walls were covered with large golden shields and masks, or tapestries of vivid colors that were violent with scenes of battle.

Runa pointed to the rich silk tapestries that covered the walls in the corridor. "They are beautiful, but very violent."

"Symbols of the Ivory Kingdom's conquests," Malcolm said.

"They all seem to relate tales of war. Did the same artist weave them?" Runa asked.

"The ones in this hallway, yes," Malcolm replied, as they walked up broad milky marble stairs, draped in rich midnight blue carpet. "War is a common theme in the design here. War is what made Tarsicius the Emperor he is today."

"You have served him long?" Runa asked.

"I have served the royal house all my days. I am a slave. I serve Tarsicius, and his father before him."

"Do you mind being a slave?" Runa asked.

"What is a slave? A form of status? Rank? I have never gone hungry or been beaten. A freed man can suffer that fate. I have no complaints, Lady."

Runa paused before a large tapestry of a dark, masked figure on a throne of skulls, carrying a bloody sword.

"Ugly," Mellypip said, "and scary."

"That is Rygon, the God of War," Malcolm said. "He is a favorite image here at the palace. There has not been a lady to supervise the décor for many years. The Emperor has not remarried nor taken a chief consort in years. Such violent pictures are not suitable for the eyes of a young girl, so I apologize."

"No need," Runa said.

"Ah, we are here," Malcolm said as he opened the door to an

enormous chamber.

Mellypip and Runa gasped at its beauty, decorated with fine glossy black furniture edged in gold. Unlike the rich but stark décor of the palace, the room was soft and feminine. Carpets with brilliant patterns on polished floors; the walls were painted with frescoes of pale leafy trees and pastel blue lakes, snowy lace-edged sheets and pristine sapphire blue bedspread on a huge four poster bed.

"Are you sure this is for me?" Runa asked in a surprised voice.

Malcolm nodded. "Yes, as arranged by the Princess Opaline. Is there anything else you desire, Lady Runa?"

Mellypip tapped her on the head. "Food, Runa! It's eons past tea time and my tummy rumbles."

"Excuse me, Malcolm. We are a bit hungry. Could you also show me where the kitchen is?" Runa asked.

"Oh no, Lady, you need not go there. I will have your meals delivered here."

"I'm famished too. My nerves are to blame. What should we ask for, Melly?"

"Lotsa food! Scones, butter, jam, especially blackberry jam, honey, fruit, tea, nuts, and drobba! The Emperor is rich! He must have drobba!"

She laughed. "All right! All right!" She gave the gentleman her long request. He smiled, bowed and departed.

"Ok…where's that privy?" she asked, searching with frantic need.

Mellypip leapt to the high bed and bounced on it. "This is the best bed ever."

"A person could die falling off that thing," she said, until finally finding the privy in the far corner of the room, behind an elegant screen painted with white swans and long, green leaves. She returned with a relieved expression and washed her hands in the basin.

Someone knocked on the door.

"Maybe that's our feast?" Mellypip said, rolling around on the big bed.

"Do you know how silly I felt ordering so much food?" Runa asked.

"Not silly. Save for late night snacks—not wake cook."

She opened the door, and saw instead a beautiful, tall blond girl who smiled graciously. "Hello. You must be Runa. I'm Princess Opaline."

Runa curtsied. "Oh, I'm sorry Your Highness. I was not

expecting—"

"May I enter?" she asked.

"Of course, I mean, it's your palace."

Melly…I'm sounding like an idiot.

No, just nervous. Ask her where her crown is?

"It's my father's palace actually," the Princess said, sweeping into the room, her gown of lavender silk clinging to her voluptuous curves. Her blue-gray eyes were youthful replicas of the Emperor's, but other than that there was no similarity. "I've looked forward to meeting you, Runa. Caliste always talks a great deal about her favorite, 'niece,' so I'm glad you're finally here, even if the reason is grim." Opaline sat upon a cushioned stool, and looked at Mellypip. "Is the wampu your familiar?"

"Yes, his name is Mellypip."

"Hello, Princess," he said. "You're very pretty."

"My, he is adorable—and such a honey-tongue. The wampu here in the south come in different shades, white, gray, and even some black ones; but the golden-brown shade of his fur is the most attractive, I think."

"I like the Princess, Runa."

"Well, of course you do," Runa said. "Princess Opaline said you're adorable."

"No formalities. I want us to be friends," Opaline said. "Only refer to my title when my father is present; he can be such a sour quince about court etiquette." She fingered Runa's long tresses. "Your hair is magnificent! I envy the length!"

"Thank you," Runa said, blushing. "It's a bit hard to take care of though."

"That's a lovely silver locket. It's Ilyrran, isn't it?" Opaline commented.

"My Grandfather gave it to me for my birthday. It has pictures inside of my mother and grandmother." She opened the locket to show her.

Opaline looked at the tiny portraits and nodded. "They were beautiful. You look like them."

"I'm not that pretty," Runa shrugged. "I wish I could remember them, but I was just a baby when they died."

"I lost my mother and brother years ago, so I understand that loneliness," Opaline said.

"I'm sorry," Runa said.

Someone knocked again, and Runa excused herself. Mellypip jumped to Opaline's lap. "Do crowns make your head hurt?" he asked.

"Yes," she laughed. "But the sparkle is worth it."

Servants carried in several trays of food. They arranged the silver trays on the central table and left.

"Having a party?" Opaline asked.

"Mellypip got hungry," she explained, blushing. "Would you like to join us? I *think* we have enough."

"Yes, I would," Opaline replied. "Thank you."

They chose little delicacies of scones and cream, cucumber sandwiches, and fruit. Mellypip tried to be well-mannered, until he found a dish of drobba cookies. He gobbled three very quickly.

"Melly! Watch your manners!" Runa scolded.

Opaline laughed indulgently. "It's the nature of wampu to eat a lot, especially when they are still growing. I'm glad they excused you from the council early. It became rather dull."

"I didn't see you," Runa said, pouring cups of tea.

Opaline added a lump of sugar to her tea and shrugged. "Well, the secret corridors of this citadel would grow dusty if not for my footsteps."

"The palace has secret passageways?" Runa asked. "Does everyone know?"

"No, not really. This place was built over three hundred years ago. The whole stronghold is laced with them, though. I discovered the old plans crumbling on a shelf in the royal library when I was researching Tiamet's history. I transcribed a copy for myself, of course. I'm not sure my father knows…or cares. I'm just Princess Opaline, left to my own devices before I am sold on the marriage block to some foreign prince. So, I amuse myself by listening in on council meetings to which I am not invited."

"You spy!" Runa exclaimed, dunking a cookie in her tea.

"True, but only out of boredom. Tell me, do you really speak all of those languages or were you showing off for the Emperor?"

"Grandfather was very insistent I study many tongues. We never went anywhere, so I wondered why I needed to learn them. Grandfather would always say, 'I must be learned to understand the responsibilities of magic.'"

Opaline began to discourse in Ilyrran, Dwarven, Ithuli, and several other tongues. Runa replied in each language with flawless precision.

"Excellent," Opaline commented. "As an Imperial Princess, I am hostess for many functions. So language skills have been an asset." She set her cup aside. "Caliste is my good friend, but it will be wonderful having a friend my own age too. I think we're going to be quite close, Runa."

"I would like that. I adore Caliste, but I never had a friend of my own age to share things with either, living in the forest. How old are you, if I may ask?"

"I'm sixteen now. So we are almost the same age. There are few people I can trust. As an Imperial Princess, I accept this. I am surrounded by many people, but in a sense, I am always alone. My father's harem is a swarm of frightened butterflies; the girls of noble birth only chatter about cosmetics and clothes or ask me favors for their families. Life would have been very tedious without Caliste's friendship."

Knocking interrupted them. "Excuse me," Runa said. "I'm so sorry." She opened it and Cathal, Belwyn, Caliste and Sanura entered.

"I see Furball got the munchies," Belwyn commented.

Cathal kissed Runa on the cheek. "Do you like your room?"

"Yes, it's very grand."

Opaline rose and Runa introduced her.

"I'm honored, Princess," Cathal bowed.

"Come join us, and no titles, Cathal. Caliste, I'm so glad you're back!" she said, embracing her. "I'm so sorry to hear about your friends and Ramirez. You've had an exhausting journey getting here!"

"Thank you," Caliste replied. "You're using the secret passageways again, aren't you, Opaline?"

"Yes, I must confess I did."

Cathal looked confused and Opaline explained.

"Very clever," Cathal commented.

"I wonder if Tarsicius knows what a crafty daughter he has," Belwyn commented.

"Males never appreciate the female mind," Sanura said.

"It's nice to meet you, Belwyn," Opaline said. "You are a magnificent owl, of the gray mountain clan, I believe."

"Why, yes I am. You're a smart girl."

"Thank you," Opaline replied with a charming smile. "Sanura, you look plump and sassy as ever."

"I'm not plump, I'm *fluffy*," Sanura replied.

"I noticed in the meeting Belwyn and Sanura did not speak,

Grandpa," Runa remarked. "I've never seen Belwyn so silent!"

"The Emperor thinks familiars should be seen and not heard," Belwyn explained. "His bloody loss." He glanced over at the table. "Are those cucumber sandwiches?"

They gathered around the table for the impromptu feast. Sanura lapped a dish of cream and Belwyn nibbled on a cucumber sandwich.

"Cathal, I'm going to the market dome tomorrow. May Runa accompany me?" Opaline asked, pouring more tea for everyone. "She will need proper clothes for court, and there is the state dinner in two days welcoming the new Dwarven Ambassador, Hinkleburr Crowyn. I know Father expects you to attend."

"I know Hinkleburr. He's an interesting fellow. I last saw him about twenty years ago when he was the aide to the Ambassador of Thill," Cathal commented.

"Then it shall be a reunion. A warning though, the High Priest of Rygon is here too, from Urgonclaw."

"Rygon is the God of War," Runa commented. "I read they are a very strange sect."

"Very strange and violent. My father honors Rygon above all the other gods, I'm sorry to say, as does my brother, Levandius."

"Thank you for the warning," Cathal replied. "What's he doing here? Captain Darcus mentioned something about a war with Urgonclaw five years ago?"

"Yes, they attempted an invasion of one of father's kingdoms. They ended up being defeated, and their king deposed. Their current High Priest is Zhelon Thor. He looks like a beautiful boy, but don't let that deceive you. There are rumors he led the sacrifice of the previous High Priest when there was a revolution in the temple after they lost the war."

"They killed him?" Runa said, aghast.

"Rygon's worshippers are brutal and don't forgive mistakes. I think Zhelon Thor is officially here to pay the annual tribute, though I am sure he has another agenda. But the banquet should be splendid otherwise."

"I'm still concerned about Runa going into the city, Opaline," Cathal said.

"Runa and I will be protected by armed escorts, so she will be quite safe. The Imperial Dragon Knights need to earn their keep, after all."

"That would ease my mind, Princess," Cathal said, buttering a scone. "I'm also sorry the Emperor is so ill."

"Thank you, Cathal. It grieves me that he worsens each day," she said sadly. "He has seen many doctors but is very attached to Hemio for his daily care. I find the mousy little man a fool, but my opinion is not welcome."

"What exactly is his ailment?" Cathal asked.

"They cannot say, specifically. The doctors say his lungs and heart are weak and fading. He's been declining for months. I don't know how much longer he will last."

"I'm so sorry, Opaline," Runa said genuinely.

"Thank you, Runa," Opaline said softly.

"Well, take care tomorrow. If Runa could be escorted to the Sorcerer House by Darcus afterward, I would appreciate it," Cathal said.

"Excellent," Opaline said.

"I hear Tiamet's market dome is one of the largest merchant exchanges in the west," Runa said. "Is it true the ceiling is made of amber?"

"No. Just a thick, amber-colored glass, though it's quite pretty. Father hates it when I leave the palace grounds, but I like to see the people and get away from court. The sun in Tiamet is brutal though, Runa. You should wear a veil."

"My face is already freckled and sunburned from the journey here," she said, touching her peeling nose.

"Well, I have some buttermilk lotion that will do wonders for that. I can loan you a veil for tomorrow." Opaline dabbed her mouth with a linen napkin and rose. "We will leave after breakfast, Runa. Caliste, I wish you could come too."

"Alas, duty calls me," Caliste said. They kissed on each cheek.

"Well, I will see if the silk dealers have anything worthy of you." Opaline added seriously, "I do hope you find Ramirez's killer—and your missing friends. Ramirez was a good man. I only know of Koll through my history lessons, but I hope you do deliver his head on a spike."

Cathal stood and bowed. "Thank you, Opaline."

She left the room. Belwyn belched and received a dirty look from Sanura.

"A little indigestion, Belwyn?" Sanura asked.

"All that talk of shopping," he explained.

"Well, my dear," Cathal said to Runa, "Opaline is not like the rest of the family."

"Opaline is genuinely nice too. I like her," Runa said.

"She has grown into a woman with a face to do battle for," Belwyn commented. "The last time I saw her, she was about a year old. Shame about her mother and brother dying so young."

"I think she's lonely," Runa said.

"I've no doubt she is," Cathal agreed. "Levandius is only her half-brother and much older. Tarsicius is a hard man with an empire to rule, and I'm sure most of his attention was focused on his son. Now tomorrow, there are enemies out there we know nothing of yet," Cathal warned. "Promise me you will be watchful. It's your first time in a real city."

"I promise I will be very careful," Runa assured him.

"Just control yourself when you scour the silk bins," Cathal said.

"Thanks, Grandpa," she said hugging him.

"Well, every girl deserves pretty dresses," Cathal said.

Caliste fingered the sleeve of Cathal's worn and faded blue shirt. "You might want to consider a wardrobe change yourself."

"Don't push it," Cathal warned.

"The Imperial Banquet will not let in beggars," Caliste said.

"I will be attired appropriately," Cathal insisted. "Stop fussing, woman, I'm quite capable of dressing myself."

"Of course you are," Caliste agreed solemnly.

Cathal lifted a covered silver tray, and instead of exotic pastries, found a rolled piece of paper. "What's that?" Caliste asked. He unrolled it and read, "Cathal, tomorrow go to the Scarlet Mermaid Tavern at noon in the north of town. Urgent news regarding Ramirez."

"That's suspicious,' Belwyn commented.

"Yes, but intriguing," Cathal said. "Runa, who delivered the trays?"

"Just three servants. I didn't notice anything about them."

"They may not have put the letter there," Sanura remarked. "It could have been slipped there by anyone."

"It could be a trap," Belwyn grumbled.

"We will be prepared if it is. Perhaps someone knows something but is afraid to come forward. I'll also request from Tarsicius an armed escort, just in case. I would prefer Darcus' men. I trust them."

"Keep your staff charged," Belwyn warned. "There's always trouble in taverns."

~ * ~

Azmadu whimpered with pain and Panthara took him in her lap. "There, there, let me see," she whispered.

Azmadu covered his ravaged face with his wings and whined. "No. Ugly. Hurts. Hate owl. Took my eye!"

"I need to make sure there is no infection, Azmadu. Let me look," she begged patiently.

He lowered his wings ib submission. One bitter amber eye watched Panthara as she unwound his bandages and examined his empty eye socket. "Ouch!" he cried.

"But I didn't touch anything!" she exclaimed. "Stay still, baby." She finished her examination. "Good. There's no sign of infection. It's healing quite nicely." She picked up the vial of the precious remedy for his agony. He turned up his blue and green scaled face for it, anxious. She measured drops of the soothing balm into his injured…well not his eye anymore.

"Hate owl! Stole my pretty eye. Now I'm a cripple!" he bawled.

"Nonsense, you are not a cripple. You are my wonderful, fierce familiar," Panthara insisted. "My tiny dragon of the desert."

He sniffled, but the cooling sensation was calming, and the pain decreased.

"Better now, my sweet?" she asked, stroking his head.

"Yes, my Panthara. Better."

"We will have it, Azmadu. Vengeance shall be ours. You may eat Belwyn the owl for dinner, and his little wampu friend for dessert if you like."

"Yes! Yes, I like!" Azmadu cried.

She set him on the table and retrieved a wad of black satin from her bodice. "I have a surprise for you. Do you want it?"

"A present! Love presents. Give me now," he begged, fluttering his little wings, his blue-black tongue rushing in and out of his jaws. She held up an eye-patch of black satin, with a red lightning bolt embroidered on it for added flair. It shimmered in the glow of the light crystals.

"I sewed the design myself. It helped me to think. I may take up sewing while I plan revenge and spells. You could pretend to be a pirate of the wild seas."

Greedy, he plucked the item from her hand and tried it on, posing in front of the long mirror framed in ornate copper on the cabin wall. He studied his reflection, and decided it was quite becoming. He began to make ferocious growls and faces for effect. Panthara enjoyed his antics and clapped her hands.

A knock on the door interrupted his imagination…and the attention she was giving him.

"Enter," she commanded, sitting on her throne of gold.

The Captain of their ship walked in, and knelt before Panthara, head bowed. "My Queen, we have arrived at the coast of Tiamet. What are your orders?"

"Keep your distance from the land, Captain. My enchantment will conceal the ship in mist."

"As you command, Your Majesty," he said.

"You may go, Captain."

"Thank you, Great Queen."

He departed quickly. Panthara went to the large oval crystal that rested upon an elaborate gold stand. Its dull glow pulsated with sorcery, and she swept her hand across it, bringing it to vivid light. A woman's form appeared in the crystal, veiled in dark silks but for angry bronze-colored eyes. Panthara bowed to the hostile visage.

The woman's voice echoed from the crystal. "Where are you? It's about time you contacted me!"

"I am near Tiamet. Where is Koll?"

"He is in the desert. He has much to do before the time comes. Do you have them?"

"Not yet, but I have a new plan—"

"You are useless! A heartless child who forgets her debts!"

"I will capture Cathal and Caliste. They will be delivered in time," Panthara cried.

"See to it," the woman demanded, and her image faded from the crystal's light.

"I will…Mother," Panthara whispered.

Panthara poured a cup of wine in a golden goblet, and began to pace the rich room, sipping with slow methodical grace, until her beautiful face twisted with frustration and she screamed, hurling the cup against the wall. Burning with dark emotions, she sat on her throne and wept.

Azmadu hated the withered shrew who made Panthara unhappy. He crawled into her lap, nuzzling her hair. He comforted her until her weeping subsided. "What now, my Panthara?"

"Chaos," she whispered.

CHAPTER 8

*Runa and Mellypip faced the giant red crystal radiating fiery light in the
dark cave. From the crystal's core flames erupted. A specter rose from this dark
fire—a man with black hair and blue eyes. Runa reached for him, but Panthara
barred her way.*

*A strange sorcerer with a scorpion snake coiled around him stepped from
the shadows and then the cavern shook with Otherworldly power. He laughed at
Runa.*

*Panthara read from a scroll, ancient and powerful, sealed with a bloodstone
that pulsated with dark light.*

The earth shook again.

*Runa cried out, "No!" and tried to touch the scroll. But it was hot and
burned her.*

*The spirit of the man spoke, "Daughter…the wraiths come." Suddenly, a
flash of light brought flying demons, their ethereal power burning the air. A
weeping black eagle lay at their feet. A wraith shot toward Runa and Mellypip,
hungry for their souls. Runa screamed.*

Runa woke up covered with sweat. Mellypip rolled off the pillow, shaken by their dream bonding. She kicked off the damp sheets
and cried. "Oh, Melly, that man in my nightmare is my father. He
called me daughter. Oh gods, he must be Ashur. I'm dreaming about
my father!"

"Don't let it upset you, Runa. Just bad dreams," Mellypip said,
crawling back on the pillow.

"What if this dream is a fragment from the future?"

"Tell Grandpa Cathal," he said. "You made promise."

"I will. I'm sorry I woke you." She took a few deep breaths and
lay back down. "How's your tummy?" she asked after a moment,
stroking his head.

"Still aches and gurgles," he moaned.

"Well, I warned you about eating all that cake. Let's get some
sleep."

"Like that's going to happen." Mellypip sighed, pulling his little
blanket up over his head. Runa didn't fall asleep again either, and
finally got out of bed to open the damask drapes. Sunshine flooded
in, but Mellypip lay a motionless furry ball. She washed her face in

the basin, lathering up with rose-scented soap. "Eat something proper for breakfast," she insisted. "You'll feel better."

"I'm not hungry," he groaned.

"Now I *am* worried," she said. She dressed in blue trousers and chose a blue and red tunic. She brushed her lush hair and finished twining it into a thick plait just as Cathal and Caliste stopped by.

Cathal kissed Runa on the cheek. "I would say good morning, but the circles under your eyes tell me you had another bad night."

Belwyn and Sanura hovered around Mellypip, looking down on the lethargic wampu. Sanura batted him with her paw, but Mellypip didn't respond.

"Is it still alive?" Sanura inquired.

"What's wrong, Furball?" Belwyn asked.

"Drobba…poisoning," Mellypip whimpered.

"Last night they sent up a whole cake for dessert—drobba cake," Runa emphasized.

"I considered its defeat a challenge," Mellypip explained.

Belwyn shook his beak. "Furball, you don't conquer pastries."

Cathal laughed. "I'm not even going to indulge in this conversation." He stroked Runa's hair. "Are you all right, dear?" he asked. "What's wrong? Tell me."

Runa sat down. "My nightmares are back. This time the man in my dreams, the dark one with blue eyes, called me daughter. I think I'm dreaming about Ashur."

"You dreamed of your father? Are you sure?" Cathal asked.

"I don't know what else it would be. I was in a cave. He came to me as a spirit and said the wraiths were coming. Panthara was in the dream too, and so was this terrible man with black eyes and a scorpion snake. Could that be Koll?"

"Unfortunately, yes," Cathal nodded.

"Then the wraiths came. It was terrible. And there was a black eagle there too. He was crying."

"Cathal, she couldn't have known," Caliste said, sitting by Runa.

"Known what?" Runa asked.

"About the black eagle," Caliste said. "It must be Urvuz, Ashur's familiar, that you see in your dreams."

"Dear, we won't be staying in Tiamet long," Cathal said softly. "I need to look for our friends—and hunt Koll down. I already spoke with the Emperor. I am leaving to go east; to Mowad. All the clues point there. The attack by the Rashurkeen, which are an eastern cult, your dreams, the disappearance of our friends. Your dreams are not just about the past. The people in them are enemies we face now, like Panthara and Koll. But the wraith demons are from the past. I never wanted to see those wraiths again."

"Grandpa, how exactly did you kill Ashur?"

"It involved forbidden magic," Cathal said.

"Runa, it was hard enough telling you the truth about your father and what he did to Rualla and Yllia. I never wanted to tell you how I killed your father using sorcery Urvuz brought us."

"Urvuz. That's the familiar who was bonded with Ashur."

"Yes, but I didn't tell you Urvuz was a black eagle at the time. Just the bare truths were hard enough to confess," Cathal said.

"Is Urvuz still alive?" Runa asked. "Could I see him?"

"Yes, Runa, he still lives. But what happened to Ashur crushed his spirit. He won't see us. His sorrow and shame are too great. But he loved you, Runa, and your mother. He gave up everything to help us. Someone I trust is caring for Urvuz. The bond Urvuz had with Ashur was severed when he became evil. Urvuz helped us, though it broke his heart. He stole a scroll from Ashur, a relic from the last age—a bloodstone scroll from over a thousand years ago."

"You used that sorcery to kill Ashur?" Runa asked.

Caliste nodded. "There was no other way. People had tried everything and failed. I witnessed a sword pierce his body. He pulled out the blade like it was an annoying splinter."

"The seven of us—me, Caliste, Riva, Myrsalian, Ulan, Liat, and Jiana, we used the scroll to call the guardian wraiths to take his soul." Cathal stood and began to pace. "It was a last resort. The conjuration opened a doorway, a dangerous doorway, to the Otherworld. There are ancient beings, demon wraiths that guard the gates to that realm. The sorcery trapped Ashur in red crystal and black fire. We witnessed the wraiths rip the soul from his body. The essence they took was twisted, black. I know the only way to resolve this is to go to Mowad. That is where all this happened fifteen years ago. If I can find Koll, I will also find our friends."

"When do we leave?" Runa asked.

"The morning after Ambassador Crowyn's reception," Cathal whispered. "But you're not coming with us."

"No! You can't go without me!" Runa protested.

"I will not risk your life. Koll is hunting down the circle that killed his old master. He will stop at nothing to achieve whatever vengeance he is planning. You were very lucky the last time, young lady! You will go to Ironia and stay with Cousin Raghnall," Cathal insisted.

"Oh no, not that!" Runa blurted out. She lowered her head. "I'm sorry. I adore Cousin Raghnall, but his wife, Greta, is so annoying," Runa said.

"I know Greta can be difficult, but you will be safe there. I will ask Darcus if he can escort you to Ironia."

"But I want to stay with you," Runa begged.

"I know. I want that too. But it's for your own good." Cathal kissed her on the forehead. "I know it's hard. But I promise you I will be fine. I'm a thousand years old, give or take a birthday or two."

"Or a hundred," Belwyn added.

"Thanks, Belwyn," Cathal said dryly. "In my early days, I faced dark gods and demons. I will defeat whatever is out there now, but only if I know you are safe and protected."

"Very well, but I fail to see how something that makes you feel so wretched can be good for you," Runa said, wiping tears away.

"I'll walk you to the stables. Do you have enough coin?" Cathal asked.

"You gave me plenty last night," Runa said sullenly, pulling on her boots.

"Runa, I hate this too," Belwyn said. "I also raised you! And I hate desert climates. They make me cranky. Do you think I would let you go unless there was another way?"

"I know Belwyn," she said, picking Mellypip up.

They walked in solemn procession down gleaming hallways and stairs then exited to the well-manicured grounds of the palace. Unable to speak aloud for fear of breaking down, she spoke to Mellypip through the bonding, while he walked slowly at her side.

I hate this Melly.

I know, Runa. Our family is being broken. Hate evil people. They ruin everything, Mellypip replied in a grumpy tone.

The long rows of white stone stables reeked of horse, which made Mellypip cover his nose. His tummy was still delicate. They passed by a building, and a different smell intrigued Mellypip. He followed his nose and found a separate stable apart from the horses that caged a strange creature he recognized from Belwyn's lessons. A gryphon!

"Runa, there's a gryphon here! Come see." Mellypip called.

Maybe this will cheer her up, he thought.

Gryphons were funny looking, part eagle and part lion. This one was black and must be full-grown, since it was the size of a horse. Curious, its feathery crested head poked out and sniffed. The eagle-like head had high tufted ears and a long neck. The front legs resembled an eagle's too, though the body and hind legs were more like a big lion. It had a long tail and the wings looked huge, even folded against his body.

Large, luminous brown eyes lit up when it saw Mellypip and Runa.

"Hello, I'm Mellypip," he said cautiously.

"You're very fuzzy and tiny. I'm Rono. I fly," the gryphon replied excitedly. "Want to go fly?"

"Grandfather, look! It's a real gryphon! He's quite friendly," Runa said.

They gathered around the gryphon. It trilled with pleasure as they stroked his head.

"Poor thing, he seems so lonely in there," Runa remarked. "He's so lovable."

"He belongs to Hemio, the court physician," Caliste said, petting him. "Rono is very gentle. It's rare for a gryphon to be pure black."

"He's so sweet," Runa said. "He needs space to run and fly, though. Has Hemio always been your owner, Rono?"

Rono hung his head. "No. Was baby with tiny, feathered wings when gryphon wranglers took me away. Hatched not long from egg when they capture me." Large tears welled in his eyes. "No see mother and father again."

"I'm sorry, Rono," Runa said, rubbing his forehead.

"But lady bought me. She nice. Then give me to Hemio. Hemio nice too and brings me apples. Not get to fly enough. Love to fly."

"Gryphons are not known for their intellectual conversation," Belwyn said, perched on Cathal's arm.

"Hush, Belwyn," Runa said. "You'll hurt his feelings!"

"I do feel sorry for the creature," Cathal agreed. "They should be free. They may not be the brightest of the magical animals, they but should be protected from wranglers. They are the only magical animals a mortal can possess. Come along. Opaline and the others are waiting."

"Bye, Rono," Mellypip said.

"Bye-bye," Rono said wistfully.

There have been too many goodbyes lately, Runa thought.

Opaline waved to them, attired in a simple, but exquisite gown of dusky pink velvet, the bodice a rich brocade over a white blouse of sheer linen with long sleeves gathered with becoming ribbons. White leather gloves protected her soft hands, and her head was covered with a sheer veil of pink. Priem, the Imperial Dragon Knight they met at the docks, held her mount, which had an odd-looking saddle.

"Welcome Runa," she said, sitting on a magnificent white gelding. "Good morning, Caliste, Cathal."

"Opaline is sitting funny on her horse," Mellypip remarked.

"It's called a side saddle," Runa replied. "A proper saddle for a princess I guess, especially wearing all those petticoats."

"Darcus can take you to the Sorcerer House after your shopping," Cathal said, hugging her again. "I'm sorry, sweetheart."

"I know," Runa whispered. "I'm going to badger you to take me along, you know."

Cathal laughed. "I wouldn't expect anything less." Cathal took Darcus aside for a few moments. Runa fought back tears when she realized what they were discussing.

"Oh Melly, I don't want to go to Ironia. Grandpa needs me."

"I'm sad too. Will miss Belwyn, even though he's strict."

Darcus returned with a horse for Runa. "Morning Runa, morning Mellypip," he said.

"Hi, Darcus," Runa said, giving him a hug. "Did Grandpa tell you?" she asked, mounting the horse and placing Mellypip in front of her on the saddle.

"He did, Runa. It's a wise decision. You will be safer there. I'm done with my service officially tomorrow, so I will be happy to take you to Ironia."

"Still sad though," Mellypip said.

"I know little one. But it will be a new adventure," Darcus said.

Runa and Mellypip noticed the Imperial Knights resentful stares toward Darcus. "What's wrong with fancy knights?" Mellypip asked.

"They don't approve of me tagging along."

"Well, I am glad you're with us," Opaline proclaimed as she rode up to meet them. "An experienced battle officer of my father's legions makes me feel doubly safe. You can shock my maiden's heart with tales of combat. Didn't you receive the medal of valor twice for your service to the crown?"

"Yes, Your Highness, but I was only doing my duty," Darcus replied.

"Which makes you doubly worthy," Opaline nodded.

Imperial Knights surrounded Opaline like an armed cocoon, but they picked up a good pace down the long, private, tree-lined path to the palace gates. Once free of the palatial grounds, the streets became narrow and they were surrounded by buildings and homes of white stone of various sizes, and conditions. Some were pristine, and others crumbling and decayed.

They reached the heart of the city a short time after they left the palace grounds. Runa saw a collage of people mingling in the hot sun.

Indeed, there were people of every color and caste that walked the streets of Tiamet.

The poor and beggared mixed with the working class. People in simple clothes, hawking goods, or shopping for the night's dinner. Others stood in filthy rags, holding hollow cups for alms.

Runa noticed too that Opaline's guards generously tossed coins to the beggars.

"The poor never leave us," Opaline commented. "But we should never ignore them because of that."

"I notice most buildings are white, but I see some painted with color; pale shades of turquoise, coral," Runa noted.

Opaline smiled. "The stark bone color of the city is symbolic, I fear. Perhaps my ancestors should have thought of something other than Ivory."

Runa noted upon closer inspection, the starkness of the bleached city had a dirty edge to it. There was an undercurrent to the smell of the city, a combination of salt air, refuse, people, spices, food, and animals. The white buildings, so purely white from a distance, had a dingy film of soot from hearth fires. The foundations on many buildings looked crumbly and cracked. Even the more pristine well-cared for buildings showed signs of age.

"You observe our city with a critical eye," Opaline remarked, observing Runa's expression. "Good. Tiamet is powerful. It is a great city. But like all great cities, it is old and worn with use. For my city, this jewel of the empire, it is the people who should be its heart, not the glory of new pillars and villas that grace the shores and hills."

"Tiamet is filled with so much life," Runa commented.

"We are a city of over ten thousand now," Opaline said. "We are the heart of the Empire, and many come here to seek their fortune.

People of all colors and races walk the streets of the White Dragon City. Commerce is a great equalizer of peace, I believe."

The busy streets teemed with activity. Beggars in rags and rich folks wrapped in colorful silks rushed about their business. Slaves carried litters of rich, veiled women, and poor women in ivory homespun bargained with street vendors for fish and vegetables. Exotic visitors, like the gaunt, brown-skinned nomads from the southeastern tribes of Sojanu, drove teams of great, shaggy kundra beasts through the streets.

Mellypip covered his nose when they crossed their path. "Oh, kundra beasts stinky!"

"They are a bit ripe in this heat," Runa agreed. "They are so sweet though."

Opaline spoke excitedly. "The caravans must have arrived. That means new shipments of goods from the east."

"They don't use horses in the caravans?" Runa asked.

"Rarely," Darcus said. "Kundras are sturdy desert animals. They fare better on the long travel routes from the east. They are gentle, but also quite stubborn. They can go without water for weeks and can carry large loads. They are priceless to the caravan routes."

Talk of travel made Runa think of her coming banishment.

Opaline leaned over. "You look quite sad, Runa," she whispered. "Tell me what is troubling you."

"Oh, I am sorry Opaline. Grandfather is sending me to Ironia for my protection. I'm leaving the morning after the Ambassador's reception. I wish I didn't have to go."

"I wish you could stay here too," Opaline sighed. "I will miss you, Runa. Perhaps you can come back and visit me when all this dreadful mess is done."

"I would like that," Runa said. "Still, I wish he wasn't sending me away."

"It's for your protection, Runa," Darcus said. "I know Cathal wouldn't part with you unless it was a last resort. I was in the camp when they brought you to him, after we thought you had been killed. He was a broken man. When Ryen put you in his arms, he came to life again. But with Koll's return, and the disappearance of your friends, he only wants you out of harm's way."

"I know," Runa sighed.

"Darcus is right," Opaline said. "Sometimes a person must make great sacrifices to help those they love."

Opaline's sunny smile vanished for a moment. She seemed to have retreated into a private world, and then regained her bright disposition.

Mellypip looked at Opaline. A Princess must keep many secrets, he thought.

The people often waved or cried out Opaline's name with joy as she rode through the city. "Speaking of love, the people adore you," Runa commented.

"I'm a young Princess and free of the constraints of rule, and the blame it can bring. I give them hope."

"I haven't met your brother, Prince Levandius, yet. What is he like?" Runa inquired.

"Levandius is the heir," Opaline said stiffly. "The Ivory Kingdoms has many other demands on his time."

They rode past a splendid blue building several stories high, with sweeping windows of colored-glass. "That temple is breathtaking! Which god does it honor?" Runa asked.

"That is the cathedral of Rhone and Araema," Opaline said.

"It's beautiful," Runa commented. "The Mother and Father creators should have a special temple. But what is that dreadful thing," she pointed to a twisting tower of black stone that covered a whole block.

"That…is Rygon's temple," Opaline whispered.

"It's scary," Mellypip said.

"Rygon hates life," Darcus added.

"That is a strange remark, coming from a soldier. You must have killed many men in battle," Priem said. "As a warrior you should pay homage to the God of War."

"I fight to defend the people and the crown, not because I enjoy killing," Darcus replied. "I don't regret what I've done, but I don't enjoy taking life, nor do I glorify it. Only a fool does that. I have never stepped foot in one of Rygon's holds and never will."

Priem turned away to sulk.

Opaline rewarded Darcus with a dazzling smile. "Well said, Captain Darcus."

They reached the merchant district, the air heavy with spices, food, animals, waste, salty air, and human odors. Mellypip's tummy had not yet recovered from last night's debauchery or nightmare and was not even tempted when they passed a stall with honey pastries.

The merchant dome was an enormous structure of ivory stone,

wide as a whole city block, and two stories high. The ceiling was domed with amber glass that glittered in the sunlight. Several open archways at least twenty feet high were filled with people coming and going.

"It looks more like a temple than a marketplace," Runa said.

"It is a temple—to greed," Darcus remarked.

"It's still beautiful," Runa remarked.

Stable boys took their horses under Priem's supervision. The Princess slipped her arm through Runa's and led her through one of the looming arches. "Now, the guards can carry all of our packages," Opaline encouraged. "Keep your purse tucked, Runa. This is my treat."

The presence of the Imperial Knights and the pure force of Opaline's personality made people step back from the royal princess and her party with quiet respect, which at least allowed more room to breathe.

Inside, Runa was stunned by the impact, not only of the immense interior of the merchant dome, but the hundreds of merchants who plied their goods. The noise was also deafening, voices shouting over each other, begging the people to come and buy their marvelous items.

"Too loud," Mellypip whimpered, holding on to Runa's shoulder.

"It is intense," Runa agreed.

"It's like a battle," Mellypip said.

"Except there is no bloodshed," Runa replied.

"You have not done a lot of shopping, have you?" Opaline quipped.

The combined smells of bodies, animals, food, and perfumes were heavy on the senses. Mellypip was still queasy, and hoped this shopping was not a long affair. He wanted to curl up on a silk pillow and sleep.

"You could buy anything here!" Runa exclaimed.

"That is why I love it," Opaline grinned.

They browsed a perfume booth with vials of colorful glass or smooth clay pots glazed with artful designs that stoppered perfumes from exotic lands.

Greedy faces visited them from every stall. A leather tanner displayed fine-tooled goods, a smithy showed off beautiful, crafted swords and daggers, some set with glittering gems.

"There are so many booths, smithy, leather tanners, cosmetics, rugs, weapons, pottery...do they sell everything here?" Runa asked.

"Almost everything," Opaline said brightly.

Runa was pulled along by an exuberant Opaline. They passed a red-faced money changer arguing with a large woman in a lemon-colored gown, her hair the same shade of yellow, frizzy beneath its brimless cap. An apothecary displayed remedies in bottles and jars, while he sat aloof, reading a scroll.

Opaline guided Runa to a stall of perfume makers. "Come see if any are to your liking. A lady can never have enough scent on her dressing table."

Runa obeyed and sniffed the sweet and spicy fragrances poured from vials of dark colored glass or smooth clay pots. Silver jars decorated with jade or pearl inlay were opened and tested by Opaline's sensitive nose. The musky scents of exotic lands floated around them.

"Oh, there are the silks."

Mellypip was soon bored despite the hubbub around him. Then a man cloaked in black velvet at the apothecary stall made him hold his breath. The mysterious man he heard in Sea Haven had a black velvet cloak too, but when he turned around, he saw it was only Hemio, the court physician. Hemio looked across the crowded floor and waved to them.

"I think Hemio's coming over," Mellypip said.

"He's such a frumpy little man," Opaline said.

He was gasping for breath and holding his fat stomach as he ran to them, he bowed, face perspiring from his efforts. "Princess Opaline, I did not know you would be at the great dome today."

"Just a simple outing to show my friend Runa the city," Opaline replied graciously.

"I was getting fresh herbs from the apothecary for the Emperor."

"So many doctors, and yet my father's health declines," Opaline commented.

Hemio cleared his throat. "Any healer's skill can be challenged by a severe illness. I am doing all that is within my power, Your Highness. I promise you!"

"I like your gryphon," Runa said, hoping to change the subject.

"Excuse me?" Hemio said, flustered. "Oh, you mean Rono."

"Is that blood poppy?" Runa asked, seeing the vial of red liquid in Hemio's hand.

"Yes," Hemio replied. "It's used as a sleeping drought only."

Runa furrowed her brow. "Blood poppy is very dangerous. There are safer sleep drafts you could brew."

"I agree, Physician. Why are you using such a strong narcotic on my father?" Opaline demanded. "His heart is weak."

"Ah, but beloved and royal Princess, I am making this for another patient at court. Only the tiniest drop goes into a large batch of a sleeping remedy that will last many days. I would never give this to our blessed Emperor!"

"Well, you would know best," Runa said. "My grandfather taught me about medicinal plants. That is why I asked."

He bowed several times. "Of course, to the common person, it would not be suspect. You have a good eye, Lady Runa. Alas, I must return to the palace. Good day." He bowed and walked away on small, quick feet.

"Well, I guess I was wrong," Mellypip said.

"About what?" Runa asked.

"In Sea Haven, the man in the black velvet cloak who was talking to nasty innkeeper. His voice was different. And I think he was taller too."

"Hemio is too ridiculous to be dangerous," Runa said.

"I'm still concerned," Opaline whispered, draping a sample of teal silk on her arm. "I have studied a great deal about medical herbs. It is true blood poppy is used in sleeping droughts but would not be recommended for a man with a weak heart. I know he said it was for another, but his eyes kept looking away. I may be wrong, but I don't trust him. Thank you, Runa, for your sharp eye." She held up the material to Runa's face. "This will enhance your coloring." She turned to the gaudy merchant. "I'll need enough for a gown and also enough to make matching slippers."

"As you command, Princess." The merchant bowed.

"If only my commands could save my father's life," Opaline whispered.

Runa squeezed her hand, sensing her sorrow.

~ * ~

"Well, that was certainly grim enough," Belwyn hooted. "I think I need that ale now."

"I know. After telling Runa I'm sending her away and visiting the Sorcerer House where Ramirez died, and seeing Koll's name written in blood, I need a drink too," Cathal said dismally.

"Maybe I should wait at the Sorcerer House. The note was for you Cathal," Caliste said.

"No. Splitting up is the worst thing we can do," Cathal said firmly. "We're not taking any chances."

"Then explain why we're going to the tavern? The note screams TRAP," Sanura said with a growl.

"Because I'm a curious fool." Cathal shrugged. "And we do have extra protection, thanks to Darcus' men," he added, pointing to the young soldiers—Timoth, Korun, Pol, and Lichor—who rode ahead of them.

"Curiosity is my job," the cat said, "not yours."

The noon crowd at the Scarlet Mermaid Inn was full of every sort; merchants, nobles slumming, workers lunching on stew and beer, and travelers. The atmosphere was common, though almost respectable, Belwyn thought. Dark wood floors and tables, the barmaids dressed in dark skirts and white blouses, and the lack of dead bodies on the floor.

"How do we know who to look for?" Belwyn complained.

A drunken man grabbed Caliste. "Hey, wench, wanna dance?"

Pol and Timoth pounced on the hapless man, and had him on the ground in a heartbeat, the tips of their swords aimed at his vitals.

"Sorry, Sorry," the man cried. "Just looking for a bit of fun that's all. Don't kill me!"

"Thank you, gentlemen," Caliste said, "for keeping the riffraff at bay. I think he's harmless now."

"Darcus trained you well," Belwyn approved.

The soldiers backed away and sheathed their swords. The man crawled away, cursing and shaking, but not looking back.

"Any orders, Cathal?" Pol asked.

"Watch for anything strange or suspicious," Cathal said.

A shimmering orange orb with beating wings buzzed toward them.

"Like that Cathal?" Pol asked with a grin, pointing.

"Follow me," the orb said.

"I don't like this," Cathal grimaced. "But I guess we follow the damned thing."

The floating orb guided them upstairs and down the hall. The people either pointed at the orb with curiosity or ignored it in a drunken stupor. The soldiers drew their swords. The orb floated before a door, and then vaporized.

"Well, that narrows it down," Caliste said.

The men took point on either side of the door. Cathal knocked. "It's Cathal. I'm here as your note requested."

The door opened. The room was in shadow; the curtains were closed.

"Don't even think about going in," Belwyn warned.

"Cathal? Belwyn? Is that you?" whispered frightened, familiar voices.

Belwyn and Cathal exchanged glances and stepped inside. Cathal cast a light to brighten the gloom. Huddled together on a large stuffed chair, were three familiars—Buzzy the sloth, Rosepetal the hedgehog, and Dabiro the badger.

"Oh Gods," Cathal exclaimed. "Everyone inside. Pol, close the door."

"Who brought you here?" Belwyn asked.

"I did," a deep, feminine voice answered.

Cathal and Caliste turned toward the voice. The men raised their swords. From the shadows a woman stepped forward, shrouded in black robes from head to toe, her veils decorated with silver beads and chains. Only her light blue eyes offered color. A white raven sat upon her shoulder.

The soldiers blanched. "That's a Necromancer," Pol said.

"Yes, I know," Cathal said, lowering his staff. "Iona, how are you?"

CHAPTER 9

The late afternoon brought little relief from the heat. Opaline returned to the palace with her silks and sundries, and Darcus and Runa rode to the Sorcerer House, which was built between the Temple and Residential Districts.

"Is it always so hot here?" Runa asked, wiping sweat off her face.

"Most of the year it's hot. It rains a great deal in winter, but we don't get any snow."

"What's snow?" Mellypip asked, bouncing on the saddle.

"It's white frozen rain that makes pretty shapes," Runa said. "And you can build a fort with it too. I use to make a fort and an arsenal of snowballs. Belwyn was often my unfortunate victim. He would get even by hurling my own snowballs back at me."

"Frozen rain sounds bad," Mellypip decided. "I like it warm and green. City is so big; how do you find anything?"

"The town is divided into districts," Darcus explained. "There's the temple section, warehouse and residential, merchant…and other areas not so respectable. I won't tell you about those. I'm tired of city life. I want to retire and grow a few crops now."

"I find it hard to imagine you planting corn, Darcus. I can't picture that somehow," Runa said. "Have you ever been inside the Sorcerer House?"

"A couple of times," Darcus replied. "I think you will like it. And here it is." He pointed as they turned a corner on the narrow road.

Before them rose a tower of white stone, five stories high, with a small garden in front and circled by slender trees, their long, light green leaves shading the yard. Six horses were tethered to the iron gate.

"Good. It looks like they're here," Darcus said.

"It's really big, but I don't see anything magical about it," Mellypip remarked.

A twisting tree, tinted with patches of moss, bent towards them. The slender branches reached down to take the reins of Runa's and Darcus' horses.

"Why is the tree moving, Runa?" Mellypip gulped.

"Grandfather did say things were a bit eccentric here," she

replied.

Mellypip clung to her shoulder, watching the animated tree with dubious eyes. He reached his paw to touch a slim bough. The delicate branch dipped low and tickled him under the chin. Mellypip's resistance broke into chuckles.

"See! It's only magic," Runa said, dismounting the horse.

When Darcus opened the iron gate shaped like a crescent moon, Mellypip's curiosity was brimming. He jumped down to inspect the silly flowers. Their strange flowers shook with giggles when Mellypip touched one.

"Very strange when flowers laugh," Mellypip commented. His furry face screwed up with confusion. "But why are the flowers laughing at me?"

"I don't know, Melly." Runa bent down and stroked a large yellow blossom until it curled around her hand, buds opening, releasing a sweet scent. "I believe they are wards of some sort."

"What do they do…spray petals at intruders?" Mellypip asked. He sniffed one. It smelled yummy. When he opened his mouth to take a bite, it sprayed him with blue pollen. "Argh! Flowers nasty!" He broke into a sneezing fit and wiped his watering eyes with his paws.

"Here little one," Darcus said, picking him up and wiping his face with a handkerchief. "I don't think they are meant for snacks."

The front double doors were wooden and carved with many runic symbols. The aura of magic here made everything shimmer. Runa knocked.

"Runa! Darcus!" Caliste called as she flung open the door and pulled Runa inside.

"What's going on?" Runa cried.

"Not now dear. Just come with me," she said. "Darcus, you too. We need your help." Caliste waved her hand, and mystical beams of orange magic roped the doorway for added security.

"What's wrong?" Runa asked. "You just activated enough wards to keep out an army!"

"I need to show you," Caliste said breathlessly.

They followed her up the stairs. Mellypip loved the vivid wall murals and starry ceiling. It reminded him of their sorcery chamber at home. The entire house had the toasty whiff of magic underlying everything that they had in their tree house. Darcus' four soldiers were guarding the doors. They nodded in greeting and opened the two wide doors where Cathal was waiting inside.

"Dear, something's happened," Cathal said. "We have a few guests."

Runa and Mellypip saw in the middle of the room a hedgehog, hiccupping and weeping at the same time, a morose-looking badger, and a strange looking creature Belwyn explained was Buzzy the sloth. Runa ran to the familiars. Mellypip remained behind, thinking they needed a private moment with Runa during the tearful reunion. Darcus scooped him up in his strong hands and held him.

"They lost their sorcerers. That must be awful," Mellypip said.

"It is tragic, Mellypip," Darcus said. "But they were stolen, not lost. We won't give up hope either. If anyone can find them, it's Cathal."

Rosepetal the hedgehog was so small Runa cupped her in the palm of her hand. Her little quills shook as she sobbed, hiccupping in spurts. The sloth was the slowest of animals. He wrapped his long, shaggy arms around Runa's shoulders and moaned. The badger was very bold. He grunted and flopped by Runa's feet and laid his head in her lap.

"Where did you find them?" Runa asked excitedly, cuddling the spiky hedgehog with a glove Caliste handed her.

"They were at the tavern. Iona brought them here," Cathal said.

"Who is she?" Runa asked.

"Iona's an old friend," Caliste said. "A very trusted old friend. She has a contact at the palace. That's how she sent us the message."

"Who?" Runa asked.

"She cannot say. Iona is to be trusted absolutely though."

"Why do you trust this Iona so much?" Runa asked.

"I told you someone cared for Urvuz," Cathal said. "Well, Iona is that person. She is a Necromancer from Thill. Like Urvuz, she is very private."

"I remember the story," Runa said. "Urvuz lives in seclusion now. I never met a Necromancer before. Is it true they speak to the dead and their familiars are only white ravens?"

"Yes, to the white raven part, but their magic is more unique than that. Rosepetal and Dabiro went to her because they knew her too, and she was closer to where they were at the time. Iona brought Dabiro and Rosepetal to meet with Ramirez," Cathal said.

"At the time we didn't realize all of us were marked. We contacted Eberr of Ithuli at the local Sorcerer House," Dabiro grunted. "We saw Koll and a strange sorceress called Panthara kidnap our sorcerers. They used lots of muscle too. Rashurkeen from the east, other mercenaries, and even other sorcerers. We were on our way to your birthday celebration, Runa. Sorry."

"That doesn't matter," Runa said, hugging the gruff badger. He pretended to scowl but laid his head on her shoulder and whined.

Dabiro sighed and continued. "Well, Eberr took us to Iona. Iona is Myrsalian's friend, and when she couldn't contact him, she feared him missing too, as well as Felisia, his familiar. We went to Myrsalian's daughter—"

"Wait," Cathal said. "Myrsalian has a daughter? How did this happen?"

"How do you think?" Dabiro said with a grunt. When no one laughed, he continued. "It's a long-lost tragic story. You do remember he was married about forty years ago to a mortal? Well, the family was supposedly butchered by an invasion of the Urgonclaw army. He was away at the time and never forgave himself. Turns out his daughter didn't die though. She was taken as a slave, but her sorcerous ability never manifested until she was an adult. When Myrsalian finally found out she was alive, he stayed away because she had a happy life. But when something bad happened to her, he brought her to Thill to live with him. He didn't tell her who he was until last summer though. That's why he never said anything to anyone else for so long. Don't know much else about her. She's a fabulous cook though. Myrsalian was wracked with guilt about the past."

"Looks like we're not the only family with traumas," Runa said.

"We sent a message to Ramirez," Dabiro said. "He contacted Riva and Buzzy in Tiamet and we were all supposed to meet here. Iona made it here the night Koll killed Ramirez and his familiar, Derena. Poor old cat, I'll miss her. All hell broke loose after that. They took Riva. Ramirez managed to hide poor old Buzzy away in a cupboard. When we got here, it was too late."

"Buzzy, I'm so sorry," Runa said.

Buzzy blinked back tears and spoke slowly. "Koll laughed as he stood over Ramirez. He said the circle of seven will pay for the death of Ashur. He stabbed him with a sword. Ramirez was bound up in a sorcerer net and couldn't use magic, but he fought hard. So did his familiar, Derena. When Iona found me, Ramirez was already dead, but he had managed to write Koll's name in his own blood before he died. I guess he thought, in case I was killed too, he should leave a clue. We've been in hiding since that night. Iona sent a message to her contact at the palace. If we had realized what was happening, that all of us were marked, we would have contacted you sooner, Cathal. I'm glad you were spared."

Rosepetal broke down into fresh sobs and Runa cradled her gently. "Do you know where Jasper is?" Runa asked. "Or Felisia?"

"We haven't seen them, but know their sorcerers have also been stolen," the badger growled. "We have another clue, though it may mean nothing. Koll didn't care to abduct us with our sorcerers but was very careful to make sure he had our sorcerer's staves." The badger turned baleful eyes on Mellypip. "Who's the runt?"

"Oh, you don't know yet! I have a familiar. Come here, Melly," Runa said.

Darcus put him down and Mellypip shook his head. "Nope. Badger looks mean."

Belwyn gave Mellypip a little push with his wing. "Go on now. Dabiro won't hurt you—much."

"Belwyn!" Cathal warned.

Mellypip went to them.

"Everyone," Runa said. "We have a new addition to our magical family. This is Mellypip, my familiar. Be gentle. He's still a baby."

Dabiro grunted and rubbed his nose all over Mellypip. "Smells fancy!" Dabiro said suspiciously. "Fat little fellow too."

"Well, we did visit a perfume merchant today," Runa laughed as Mellypip wiped badger drool off his fur.

"Hello, Mellypip," the sloth said slowly, enunciating each syllable.

"I'm happy to meet you," hiccupped Rosepetal.

"I'm sending the familiars with you Runa," Cathal said. "It will be your duty to protect them until we get our friends back. Also, Caliste is going with you."

"No you don't!" Caliste said. "Do you think you can go in and save them by yourself? Don't go lone mage on me, Cathal. You need help."

"Caliste, I know that. I can hire a few mercenaries too. I do have friends out there who owe me a few favors, sorcerers, wizards, and a few kings too." His face softened and he lifted her stubborn chin. "I regard you as a daughter, Caliste. I raised you. Do not defy me in this. Protecting Runa and the familiars will be a great help to me. Plus, whatever Koll is planning, he seems to require all of us. If we can prevent that, it may give us valuable time. Koll has a talent for dark magic. I don't need to be a genius to realize he's planning something grisly, but we don't know anything right now except he has the backing of people with a lot of gold. Rashurkeen assassins are not cheap."

"Let's not forget Panthara," Runa added.

"You don't think I am going to run with my tail between my legs, do you!" Dabiro challenged.

"Dabiro, we know you have a thick skull, but we need more than that to rescue our friends," Belwyn said.

"You will do as I say, Dabiro," Cathal commanded.

The badger lowered his head and grumbled, "I still don't like it."

"Welcome to my world," Runa said.

"The familiars can't be left alone while we are still in Tiamet," Caliste said. "We aren't leaving until after the reception. They need to be protected."

"I know. The Emperor is expecting us tomorrow night. He is very strict about these things," Cathal said. "I feel unsure about leaving them here alone too."

"Where is Iona?" Runa asked.

"She is investigating something for me," Cathal said. "Iona will be helping us, but I need to keep her time free for the next day at least."

"I can protect myself," the badger grumbled. "I am a fierce fighter."

Rosepetal sniffled. "I want my Ulan back. I think we should obey Cathal. He was the Archon, Dabiro. Stop being so difficult!"

Buzzy lifted his head. "Fighting is not what we need at this time. We need to find our stolen mages first, then Dabiro, you can tear out hunks of flesh to your contentment."

"My men and I will guard the familiars," Darcus said.

"Thank you, Darcus," Cathal said. "It's a relief that you are here to help us."

"We'll cast more protection spells around the house," Caliste said.

"What do we do now?" Runa asked.

"Return to the palace. Pretend like nothing new has happened. Go to the party," Cathal said.

"Act casual," Belwyn added.

~ * ~

Gorvanus entered Panthara's cabin, and lust overcame his senses when he looked at her.

Panthara was dressed for battle.

Panthara lounged on the silk cushioned divan, the scent of musky spices coiled about her. The dusky red light of oil lamps glowed, highlighting her smoky blue eyes lined with thick kohl and scarlet lips. Only a thick rope of black pearls covered her breasts, and a skirt of red gauze tied around her waist. A luscious leg bent with seductive promise as she reached out her hand. "Welcome to my ship, Gorvanus. I have been waiting for you."

Disgusted, Azmadu waddled to the corner to sulk.

Gorvanus threw off his black velvet cloak and joined her on the couch, stroking her legs. "It was dangerous to send word, Panthara."

"Yet you come to me, as I desire," Panthara whispered.

"Cathal and Caliste are at the palace now," Gorvanus said. "My spy tells me he plans to leave Tiamet after the grand dinner for that ridiculous dwarf. So we must act quickly."

"Excellent? We will help him leave the Ivory Kingdoms in chains. Is that mousy Runa still with him?"

"Yes. But she is no threat to us."

Panthara rose from the cushions, her pearls shifting dangerously. "What of our other plans?"

"Levandius is with us," Gorvanus said. "He's poisoning his father very slowly and carefully—with my help of course. It must look like natural causes; otherwise, he cannot join our new order. Prince Levandius thinks he's going to marry you."

"Well, I have no plans to marry him, Gorvanus—but I do have an agenda." She kissed him passionately and lay back against the pillows. "Of course, I cannot give myself to you yet, not until you have given me a proper dowry."

"The seven sorcerers," he said. "You shall have them."

"Well, we only have five, and we need all seven of them. Koll is very impatient, and time is closing in on us, so you must make sure things go well tonight. It's a long journey back to Mowad. I do not want to return empty handed."

"I have everything prepared," he said. "The plan must work." Gorvanus began to nuzzle Panthara's neck.

I am very embarrassed by your behavior when he is here, Azmadu whined through the bonding.

I know, dearest. Think of how I am suffering.

"You're talking to your familiar," Gorvanus accused.

"No, no," she promised.

"You had the look in your eye again. It's cruel, Panthara. I never had a familiar bond to me. Do you know what shame that is for our caste? No magical animal wanted to bond with me and share the magic."

"But Azmadu adores you," she said, stroking his cheek.

Liar, Azmadu said.

Panthara handed Gorvanus a goblet of wine to change the subject. "I brought something special for tonight." From a velvet bag she drew a smoky vermillion crystal. "The spell is ready, stored in this crystal for when it is time. It took Koll an entire day to prepare it."

"What sorcery is inside?" Gorvanus asked.

"A powerful one. It will ensure Cathal and Caliste will be conquered, with your help of course. Is our spy prepared?"

"Yes." He nodded. "We may need more funds to ensure silence."

"I have gold for a thousand such spies. I hope that Runa does not cause trouble. Her innocence is so banal."

"But she's—"

"Don't even say it, Gorvanus. Make sure she is dealt with. Go back to the palace. Prepare, for the ball tonight is about to get very tempestuous." She caressed the crystal in her palm, ignoring the sorcerer as his hands lingered on her naked shoulder, and then drifted down to hazardous territory. She stopped smiling, her features feral in the ruby light. "Stop it, Gorvanus."

"Why wait, my love," he begged. "You said—"

"No!" Panthara commanded. "Not until my quest is complete. When the seven pay for their crimes, then I will be free." A smile curved her crimson lips. Her expression calmed like an ocean after a brief storm. "Beloved, the ritual requires I be a virgin. Old magic has its rules. Be patient. You will be rewarded," she whispered, stroking his cheek.

"You're a dangerous woman, Panthara," Gorvanus mumbled, caressing her mass of black hair.

"Of course I am."

~ * ~

Belwyn perched atop a chair looking out the window. Mellypip directed his boredom at a silver dish of ripe fruits and nuts. The weather was unusual for this time of year. Since dawn an oppressive mist clung to the ground and the sky was shadowed by storm clouds threatening to unleash rain and thunder.

"I'm going to miss you, Belwyn," Mellypip said.

He looked into Mellypip's big sad eyes. "I will miss you too. Do you promise to behave?"

"I'm always good," Mellypip said, his enormous round ears drooping.

"Well, you'll be better off in Ironia for now. Raghnall has a familiar named Baldur. He's better with children than I am. Damn. I hate this humidity. Makes my feathers feel sticky."

"What is Baldur? Is he an owl too?" Mellypip asked.

"No. He's a grizzly bear."

Mellypip's eyes became very wide. Belwyn shook his beak. "Don't worry. You will like him. He's very jolly. Don't let him spoil you though. And don't eat so many sweets. It's bad for you," he said sternly.

"Yes, Belwyn. Are you crabby today?"

"What? No, I'm not crabby. Just concerned. I wish it would just rain. I won't feel right until we are out of the city either. I got a prickly feeling down my back. It makes me itch."

"Want me to scratch it?" Mellypip asked.

"No, I don't...sorry. Come here, Furball."

Mellypip bounced over to the chair and perched alongside Belwyn. He snuggled close to the owl.

"Now, I want you to take good care of Runa. Make sure she studies and doesn't blow anything up."

Mellypip crunched another walnut in his mouth and nodded, his cheeks puffy with nuts.

"When I get back, I will begin to teach you some magic."

"Promise!" Mellypip cried, swishing his thick tail.

"Promise. Now I wonder what's keeping Cathal."

"Didn't he go to the baths? Opaline and Caliste took Runa there too. The princess was talking about oils and milk baths and perfume. Why would you want to take a bath in milk? Better to drink, I would think."

"Well, it's best you stayed with me. No self-respecting member of the male clan needs to be exposed to all that female ritual. We need time to relax and meditate."

"Are they giving Cathal a milk bath too?"

"Oh no...the male rituals involve steam."

Cathal entered the room. His short silver beard was trimmed and he wore a new dark gray tunic that reached his knees, trimmed in silver embroidery, and tied with a black velvet sash. His black trousers and boots looked new too.

"What happened to your scruffy clothes?" Belwyn laughed.

"The women sabotaged me," Cathal said. "But at least they picked out something appropriate. Runa and Caliste promised to return my clothes after the reception." Cathal scooped Mellypip in his arms. "Let's see what they've done to Runa. Opaline sent word they would be in her apartments."

Belwyn perched on Cathal's shoulder. The halls were very busy with servants running everywhere. He knocked on Opaline's door.

A servant opened the door, then stood aside, bowing. Opaline was standing in the middle of her beautiful chamber, surrounded by her maids. "Welcome, Cathal," she said, resplendent in a gown of golden brocade silk, sleeveless, with a low neckline. "You look splendid."

"Thank you," he replied, bowing elegantly. "You are every inch an enchanting princess."

"Thank you. Belwyn you look noble as ever. How is our Mellypip?"

"I'm fine. You look very pretty," Mellypip said.

"You are sweet," she replied. "They will be here in a moment. Please sit," she said graciously. Opaline stood while her ladies jeweled her with gold and pearls, and a maid put the finishing touches on her soft blonde curls. A crown of slim, delicate gold was placed on her head.

Caliste entered, Sanura walking at her side. She looked stunning in a gown of white silk, and tiny pearls woven into her mass of black braids. Her black face glowed with pampering, and a dusting of gold flecked powder.

"You look magnificent, Caliste," Cathal said.

"Thank you, but you have not seen everything yet," Caliste grinned. "Runa, Cathal is here!"

Runa ran in from the dressing chamber, maids still chasing her with combs and brushes. Cathal's mouth dropped and Belwyn's eyes popped. Runa's mass of hair flowed to her ankles in soft waves, swept off her face by emerald hair combs. A simple gown of blue-green silk with short sleeves clung to her youthful curves. The colors made her light green eyes even more vibrant. An emerald bracelet and ring accentuated the ensemble, and as always, she wore the silver Ilyrran locket on a long silver chain.

"How do I look?" Runa asked breathlessly.

Cathal got misty-eyed, and Belwyn pretended not to notice.

"You look beautiful," he said, kissing her on the cheek. "You grew up, and I didn't even notice."

Mellypip danced around Runa's feet. "You look like a fairy tale princess!" he chirped.

Opaline clapped her hands. "Shoo now, ladies. Any more primping and all the mortal men will faint." The maids retreated with giggles into the background. "We should repose to the banquet hall now. Will you be so kind as to escort three maidens to the ball, Cathal?"

"I would be honored," he bowed.

"You are such a handsome man," Opaline said boldly. "I'm sure you will break many hearts tonight. And you can tell me all about the new Ambassador. Perhaps you can also tell me secrets about the Dwarven race."

"You know, Princess," Cathal said. "There are things I know that are not in any book or scroll."

"How delicious! I made sure you were seated next to Ambassador Crowyn. I arranged for Zhelon Thor of Urgonclaw to be seated next to my brother. I dislike the man. I think he is a worm."

"The Princess has good taste," Belwyn commented.

"Of course I do, Belwyn," Opaline replied. "I picked out Cathal's new tunic. But I promise you I did not steal his old robes."

"No, I'm guilty of that," Runa confessed with a grin.

"Bad sorceress," Cathal teased.

CHAPTER 10

Mellypip had never seen so much food in his life! The long tables were laden with platters, heaped with many varieties of food; steaming fish and roasted meats, golden bowls of fruits and vegetables overflowed with bounty, and mountains of fresh-baked bread piled high, gleaming with butter that made Mellypip salivate.

"Is he rabid?" Sanura gasped.

"No...it's just all this food," Belwyn replied. "It affects the wampu senses. Down Furball, your turn will come."

Light crystals hung in golden baskets from the ceiling in the immense banquet hall. The light was warm and bright. On the tables, candles glowed, but for decoration rather than need. Many fancy dressed folks gathered at several long tables, laughing and drinking. Several of the Emperor's Imperial Knights were in attendance in an official capacity, including Priem, while others made merry.

Opaline led them to the Emperor's chair at the head of the main table. Tarsicius was dressed in rich red satin robes and wore a heavy golden crown. The vibrant colors only enhanced his pallor and his pewter hair looked dull. Tarsicius nodded. "Welcome, all of you."

They all bowed. "Thank you, Your Majesty," Cathal said. "I am honored to be here."

"I wish you good hunting, Cathal. Are the arrangements complete for your journey?"

"Yes, Your Majesty. I leave at dawn."

"Good. I pray you find your friends unharmed. Koll's capture will be a great victory, and his death will bring me greater gratification, not to mention a handsome reward for your troubles," Tarsicius said.

"No reward is necessary for bringing him to justice," Cathal said seriously.

"My brother, Prince Levandius," Opaline gestured to an aloof young man with short-cropped flaxen hair. His maroon and black satin doublet already stained with wine, Prince Levandius did not acknowledge them except with a bored nod. His blue-gray eyes were much like Opaline's, but that was where any resemblance ended. He had a sour look about him that Mellypip did not like.

Opaline turned to Ambassador Hinkleburr Crowyn of Ironia,

who sat next to the Emperor. A jolly fellow with wild carrot-red hair and a bushy beard, Hinkleburr smoothed his green velvet coat. "Cathal, you old mage, where have you been all these years?" he shouted. "And how are you Belwyn!" He hugged Cathal with enthusiasm, though he only came up to his waist.

"I'm quite well, Hinkleburr. You've come up in the world. Congratulations," Cathal said joyfully.

"I think my parents are finally proud, but now they want me to find a wife! Who is this ravishing goddess with ebony skin and eyes so luminous, my heart is fluttering?" he asked, kissing Caliste's hand.

"I am Caliste, Ambassador. This is my familiar, Sanura." Hinkleburr's buoyant charm was hard to resist, and she rewarded him with a magnificent smile.

"Sanura, you are the most elegant of felines," Hinkleburr complimented her.

Sanura lifted her head and allowed Hinkleburr to scratch her ears, and then went back to sleep.

Hinkleburr bowed deeply. "I must commend our gracious Princess Opaline for her wise seating arrangements and the exquisite planning for this lovely party."

"Thank you, Ambassador," Princess Opaline said softly. "Enjoy the festivities."

"I will, Your Highness," he said. Hinkleburr's attention turned to Runa. "And this girl must be your granddaughter. You are lovely my dear Runa, and those green eyes will melt the heart of every man here," he said, kissing her hand.

"He likes kissing hands…so strange," Sanura commented.

"Is that cuddly little wampu your familiar?" Hinkleburr asked.

"Yes," she said with a nod. "His name is Mellypip."

"Ah, I can see he will be a fine fuzzy warrior someday," he said, tickling him under the chin.

"Hello," Mellypip chirped. "Are you one of the Dwarven folk?"

"I am indeed," Hinkleburr laughed.

Opaline took her chair between the Emperor and her dour-faced brother.

"Tell me Runa, did you enjoy my city?" Tarsicius asked imperiously.

"It is a wonder of beauty, Your Majesty," Runa replied.

"Good. I'm pleased. Living in the woods can often limit a person's perception. Culture is vital to the growth of the mind and soul,"

Tarsicius said.

"My goodness, the plates and cups are all solid gold," Runa commented softly, sitting down and placing Mellypip on the table by her. "And look, they have jewels around the rims!"

"Look Runa, I have my own little dish and cup, with tiny utensils!" Mellypip said.

"Thank you, Princess Opaline. It was very considerate of you to consider our familiars," Caliste said.

"My pleasure, Lady Caliste," Opaline nodded formally.

"I think the Emperor is more interested in impressing the new Ambassador," Sanura said softly. "Otherwise he would send us to the corner with his hounds."

"That must explain why we are seated near the Emperor at the main table," Cathal whispered. "We are getting some jealous stares from the other nobles."

Mellypip noticed the massive dogs hovering near the Emperor's throne. They made Mellypip a bit nervous, but the colossal canines ignored the familiars in favor of the chunks of beef Emperor Tarsicius tossed them.

Musicians were clustered in the far corner and played soft music on pipes, tabors, and harps. The walls of the dining hall leapt to life with painted scenes of battles, showing soldiers wielding bloody swords and war horses with vicious red eyes and wild manes. The White Dragon Imperial Flag hung on the wall. Even in this huge hall, so many people crowding about made it hot and uncomfortable. The long windows, which ran floor to ceiling, were open to let in the night breeze, which had yet to arrive. Behind Tarsicius was a gigantic shield in ebonite, a rare black precious metal. But the face engraved on it was ugly and cruel.

"That's a scary mask," Mellypip said. "Who is it supposed to be?"

"Rygon, the God of War," Cathal answered.

"We saw Rygon's temple in the city. I've also seen Rygon on some of the tapestries and sculptures in the halls here in the palace," Runa said. "Bloody swords and skulls. It was quite ominous."

"Of course, my girl. Rygon is the god of men—not maidens. I rank Rygon first among the gods," Tarsicius said. "War has made me supreme in the Ivory Kingdoms. Isn't that right, Zhelon?"

The High Priest of Rygon had just arrived and bowed before Tarsicius. "Rygon is the greatest of gods, Your Majesty. He has shown great favor for your house. War is the maker of kingdoms...and kings." Zhelon Thor's porcelain skin had the soft look of a youth who did not need to shave, cold pale blue eyes, and golden hair that flowed down his back. His rich black robes trailed the polished marble floors as he took a seat next to Levandius.

"The God of War has always protected my realm. As a young man, I first achieved manhood in the temple. So did my son, Levandius. I was very proud of my son that night!" Tarsicius said.

"The ceremony was too long, but the girl was pleasant." Levandius laughed, downed his wine and poured more.

"What does the Emperor mean?" Runa whispered to Cathal.

"Nothing I want you to hear," Cathal replied.

Opaline looked uncomfortable.

"Come sister," Levandius said, "you should not be embarrassed. Isn't that how our beloved father met your mother, Sirahnami?"

"Yes," Opaline whispered. "But this is not the place to discuss it."

Levandius smirked. "Opaline's mother was my father's chief concubine, but once she was a temple slave in Rygon's Temple. At the holy mass honoring the birth of Rygon, my father saw her dance in the ceremony of Lilitu in Urgonclaw. My father lusted for her and bought her that night. So you see, my sister, you too should honor Rygon, for without him, you would not have been born."

"My ancestry doesn't shame me, Brother," Opaline said calmly, though anger lit her eyes.

"That's enough, Levandius," Tarsicius said firmly.

That wretched man! He's tormenting Opaline deliberately, Runa fumed.

Why is he so mean to his sister? Opaline's so nice, Mellypip thought back, chewing a piece of juicy purple gutchuli fruit. He considered spitting the fruit's seeds at the mean prince but chose to ignore his impulse. He didn't want to end up in a dungeon.

Tarsicius turned his attention to Hinkleburr. "Your people understand war, Ambassador. Dwarves make the best weapons on the continent. The strength of your steel is sought after by many."

"My people have occasionally taken up the sword to defend their borders or aid an ally, but we prefer peace. Many nations find it preferable. I was in Thema last year and their history—"

"Thema!" Tarsicius spat. "A land ruled by women."

"And yet no man has ever successfully challenged their rule for a thousand years," Opaline added.

"Perhaps they should be our next conquest?" Levandius said. "Of course, my father has resisted expanding our empire that far east."

"Enough! Levandius, this party is to honor Ambassador Hinkleburr, not to hear your political diatribes. Let the feast begin," the Emperor commanded. "Perhaps full bellies will soften everyone's mood."

Chilled fruit was served first, and Mellypip nibbled the sweet orange slices.

"Levandius is already drunk," Caliste whispered to Runa. "Best to not make conversation with him."

"Not a problem," Runa replied, digging into her fruit with restrained anger.

When they were done, the fruit dishes were removed. Servants ladled thick soup into his tiny bowl. Its sour aroma made him pucker.

"What's the matter, little one?" Hinkleburr asked.

"Soup stinks like rotten moss!"

"I never cared for this dish myself," Cathal said. "It is an acquired taste, though it's a favorite of the Emperor. No idea why, but it is." Cathal casually covered his bowl with a napkin.

"Eat your soup," Belwyn said to Mellypip.

"No. It's icky." He stuck his little spoon in the soup, and it remained erect like a pole in the mud.

"The soup is a bit…pungent," Runa commented, stirring the concoction, but not tasting. Caliste simply pushed the bowl aside and drank her wine, sharing it with Sanura.

"What do you know? There is something that Furball won't eat!" Belwyn tittered.

"Go dunk your beak. And you're not eating it either!" Mellypip said, sticking another utensil in the mess.

"Birds of prey don't eat soup."

Sanura ignored the whole episode by washing her face.

"Grandpa, may I have some wine?" Runa asked.

Cathal raised an eyebrow, and Mellypip was sure he was going to refuse her, but he relented. "Very well, but only a little."

She sipped the wine and winced. "It's very strong."

Cathal laughed and took back his cup. "It's much like the soup. An acquired taste, for adults."

The Ambassador snapped his fingers. The offensive soup was removed and a plate of egg pie, stuffed with cheese, mushrooms, and spinach was placed before them.

"Thank you, Mr. Ambassador," Mellypip said happily.

"Call me Hinkleburr, little one."

Mellypip enjoyed the egg pie. It was very good. "I wish dessert would come," he commented between bites.

"We have much in common, my wampu friend. I love to eat and drink too, especially dessert," Hinkleburr said.

"Drobba is my favorite dessert," Mellypip said enthusiastically. "Though I have learned too much can be hard on the tummy."

"Drobba is my favorite too!" hc laughed, slapping his knee. Crinkles lined his ruddy face when he smiled, and he smiled often. "So Cathal, the last time I saw you, your hair was dark as a walnut. Why is it all silver now? I thought sorcerers aged slower than molasses."

"Running after Runa for fifteen years took its toll," Cathal grinned.

"Grandpa!" she laughed.

"Cathal, let us talk of good times and bright futures. And beautiful women." Hinkleburr laughed and raised his cup. They toasted each other and drank. "And to the defeat of Koll. Give him a good lashing for the Ironians," Hinkleburr added.

"To that I will drink!" Belwyn agreed, dipping his beak in a gold cup.

Thunder crackled and lightning lit the room with sudden brightness. Mellypip felt his dinner curdle in his stomach. He hated storms.

"Finally, it's raining," Belwyn sighed.

Let's hope Darcus' men are not delayed, Runa said to Mellypip through the bonding. *They are meeting us tonight after the reception. Darcus wanted to make sure Grandfather made it to the Sorcerer House safely.*

I'm scared, Runa. Storms are a bad sign.

Don't get superstitious on me, Melly.

The Emperor dropped his goblet, clutching his chest painfully. Opaline leapt to her father's side. "Oh, Father! Guards! Summon the doctor! Help me get him to his chambers."

Levandius knelt by the Emperor. "Just try to breathe, Father. It will be all right soon."

Cathal jumped up to assist, but Levandius barred his approach. "We don't need help from your kind, Sorcerer."

"He can't breathe, Your Highness. Just let me—"

"Stay back, Sorcerer," Priem commanded, lifting the Emperor's frail body. The guests knelt in mute respect as the Emperor was carried out of the hall, with Opaline and Levandius following. A hum of whispers filled the hall with their exit.

Cathal's slammed his fist on the table. "Damn it!"

"Poor Opaline," Runa said. "She looked so frightened. I wish I could be with her."

"Me too, dear, but we dare not interfere," Caliste cautioned.

"Come on. Let's get out of here," Cathal said. He grasped Hinkleburr's arm. "Sorry your party was ruined my friend. Let's hope the Emperor recovers."

"That is my wish too. Tarsicius is not the kindest person in the world, or anyone I would ever trifle with, but if his son takes the throne, I would have to resign my post. He's a wretched boy."

They left the great hall and went to Caliste's chamber. "I think Tarsicius is being poisoned," Cathal said once they were inside.

"Opaline had such fears too," Runa said. "She suspected the royal physician, Hemio, may be involved. We saw him buy blood poppy at the market dome. He claimed it was for another patient."

Cathal leaned against a satin chair, rubbing his forehead. "Blood poppy is only one of many ingredients if this is the type of poison I'm thinking of. If Tarsicius is being poisoned, we may have run out of time. I suspect it may be mystical based, which is why the other doctors have not been able to pin down his condition. The only way to reverse it may be through mystical means too."

"Magic poison?" Runa asked. "But how would you know how to cure it, even if it is?"

"There is a very complex antidote for this type of poison. I know Tarsicius doesn't like any mage folk around him, but that doesn't mean a mortal didn't commission someone. Tarsicius was always a robust man. His sudden illness is suspicious. I'm not fond of the man, but I don't want to see him die like that. People do get diseases, but if it's not a natural ailment, the potion will reverse its effects," Cathal said.

"Who is making the potion then?" Runa asked.

"Iona is making the potion as we speak," Cathal said. "It is very volatile and sensitive. It can't be rushed! With Caliste and I occupied here, we needed someone experienced to make it. We are lucky to have her here."

"I hope for Opaline's sake Iona can help," Runa said.

"And if they don't allow us into the Emperor's presence," Caliste added. "What do you intend to do? Charge into the sick room?"

"My dear, Tarsicius knows what I am doing," Cathal said. "If they refuse it, then someone is guilty of treason and attempted murder."

"Did you share all your fears with the Emperor?" Runa asked.

"I did. He insists everything is tasted and extreme precautions have been taken since his illness began. Now we may be too late," Cathal said with regret.

"Iona should have it prepared soon," Caliste whispered. "Perhaps all is not lost?"

"In the meantime, I need to finish packing. Runa, come along; let's have a few moments before Lichor and Timoth arrive. Oh… where are my clothes?"

"Under the mattress in your room, Cathal," Caliste replied.

They went to Runa's chambers. The light crystals in the hall cast colorful lights, though long shadows clung to the halls too, which scared Mellypip. Once within the chamber, Cathal and Runa became very sad.

Mellypip realized they knew they had to part soon.

"Remember to thank Raghnall and Greta for me," Cathal said at last. "Try not to worry…and say nice things about Greta's cooking—even when it's burnt. Study hard, and try to not blow up their house."

"I will," Runa nodded, wiping away an unwanted tear.

"There, there," he said, taking her in his arms. "No more of that." Cathal rubbed his forehead again. "This whole mess has given me a miserable headache."

Belwyn blinked. "Me too. I think the wine was too heavy. I should have asked for ale instead. I should remember wine gives me a headache."

After they left, Runa sat in her finery with Mellypip in her lap, desolate. "I feel so terrible," she said.

"Headache too?" Mellypip asked.

"No…well, a little. I only had a little wine. I meant about us being apart. Grandpa hunting evil sorcerers in hostile lands doesn't give me peaceful thoughts."

Another crash of thunder unnerved Mellypip. "I wish the storm would stop."

"It will soon, Melly," Runa said, soothing him with gentle strokes on his bristled fur. She looked at the sparkling emeralds on her wrist. "Oh my, I must return her jewels. I know Opaline's with her father, but maybe one of her maids can take them. I don't want to leave these lying around." She removed the emeralds and wrapped them in a silk towel. "Let's go. It should only take a moment."

With Mellypip in one arm and the royal jewels in the other, she left her room. The hallway was well lit with oil lamps, but seemed oddly quiet. "Where are all the guards and servants?" she asked. They went up the stairs and knocked on Opaline's door. Mira, Opaline's personal attendant, opened it. "Hello, Runa. It's so terrible about the Emperor. Any news?"

"No. I hope he recovers. I wanted to return the emeralds Opaline loaned me," Runa said.

"Thank you, Lady Runa," she said, taking the jewelry. "Princess Opaline and Prince Levandius are with the Emperor."

"Tell Opaline that I'm so sorry about her father. I will pray for him. I will write her from Ironia when I arrive. Could you tell her that?"

"Yes, Lady."

"Thank you," Runa said.

They went down the wide marble steps. When Runa passed Caliste's room, the door was wide open and when she called to her, no one answered.

"Maybe she's with Grandpa?" Mellypip said.

When she passed Cathal's room, the door was also open, but it was silent. Runa froze in her steps. "Grandfather?" she said.

"Okay, I don't like this," Mellypip murmured fearfully.

Runa pushed the door open, and saw Cathal and Belwyn lying unconscious on the floor in the dim-lit room. Lightning illuminated the chamber with terrible radiance.

"Grandpa! Belwyn!" she cried.

She ran to him and turned him over. Runa shook him. "Wake up!" She tried slapping him, but he didn't respond.

"Guards!" she cried. "Someone help us."

Mellypip tried to rouse Belwyn, shaking him. "Please Belwyn, it's scary now." He looked up and saw the bodies of Caliste and Sanura by the bed. "Runa; Caliste and Sanura are over there." He ran to them, trying to wake them. "They're asleep too!"

"Where are the guards!" she cried, going toward the door. Runa collapsed and gasped. "I'm so dizzy. I can't get my legs to move. I think we've all been drugged."

Panthara stepped from the shadows. "How astute," she said.

"Runa!" he cried, running to her. He could sense her fading consciousness and bounced on her to keep her awake. "No sleep! Stay awake," he begged.

"Oh no, Melly. Get help...I can't keep my eyes open."

He ran for the door, which slammed shut magically.

"Don't go away, wampu."

He ran to Belwyn and burrowed his head in his warm feathers, weeping. "Please wake up, Belwyn. I need you!"

Melly, you need to run. Get help. Now!

Reluctant to abandon her, Mellypip also knew he had to obey. As the door opened again, Mellypip tried to rush through but smacked into a man wearing a black velvet cloak.

"Going somewhere?" the man said.

It was the same voice he remembered from Sea Haven.

Mellypip tried to run around him, but a wave of gray sorcery tossed Mellypip across the grand room. He rolled, banging his head against the four-poster bed. Mellypip looked up to gaze upon the stranger.

"Where have you been, Gorvanus?" Panthara demanded. "Stop playing and help me!"

"Taking care of loose ends," he said casually. "The Emperor is near death, but Hemio had to be taken care of. Levandius wanted to make sure he didn't suspect anything and ask embarrassing questions. We can blame the emperor's death on Hemio if anything comes up." He threw back his hood; it was Priem! "I will be glad to be out of this damned armor," he said. He looked down at the wampu. "Don't look so shocked. You don't have to be a sorcerer to pretend to be someone else." He turned to Panthara. "Where's Azmadu?"

"He was not well, so I had him wait on the ship," Panthara said impatiently. "Hurry up."

Gorvanus shrugged. "Their bodies will not function for hours. Look, even the little sorceress cannot speak or move, and she only had a tiny amount of wine. Most of the dinner guests will be unconscious, except for some stray servants. I drugged the guards too. I made sure their food was spiked quite liberally with my special recipe. It was timed very carefully so we would not be rushed." He laughed at Mellypip, who hovered near the bodies of his family, tears matting his furry face. "He's afraid. Isn't that cute?" Gorvanus dragged Caliste's body and laid it next to Cathal on the floor.

Panthara took a smoky red crystal from her cloak and beams of crimson burst from its core, covering the prone bodies of Caliste and Cathal. They began to shrink smaller and smaller, until they were the size of mice. Panthara put their miniature bodies inside a small cage and locked it with a key.

"Close the door! Let's not take any chances," Panthara said harshly.

Gorvanus, once called Priem, turned to shut the door, and confronted Timoth and Lichor, two of Darcus' soldiers. Timoth rammed his fist into Gorvanus' face.

"He's a sorcerer!" cried Mellypip. "Be careful!"

Panthara exhaled black vapors that drifted across the room, enveloping Timoth. He fell to his knees, dropping his blade as he fought the enchantment. Lichor swung at Gorvanus. The sorcerer laughed. He disarmed the blade from Lichor with a flash of his sorcery.

Mellypip surged with anger and jumped at Gorvanus, biting him on the knee. Panthara's dark mist stunned him too and his knees buckled.

"Guards!" Lichor called out. "Help! Guards!"

"Rotten little rodent," Gorvanus howled, reaching down and ripping Mellypip from his leg and throwing him across the room. Panthara grabbed for him, but he bolted under the bed. He weaved to and fro, avoiding the sorceress' angry bursts of magic. He scampered out from the haven of the bed. Timoth recovered and reached for his fallen blade.

"Oh no, there'll be none of that," Gorvanus scolded, unsheathing his sword and ramming it into Timoth's body. He cried out once, then died. Gorvanus pulled the blade back, and Timoth fell to the carpet, his blood staining the floor around him. Gorvanus walked to Lichor, who still struggled against the enchantment, but was helpless as Gorvanus ran him through. The sorcerer was covered with blood. He wiped his dripping sword on the white silk sheets, and then strode toward Runa and Mellypip.

Runa's faint voice entered Mellypip's mind, her face wet with tears, *Oh…Melly…run…RUN.*

They'll kill you Runa! he cried in her head.

You must save yourself. Get help, she cried. He felt her magic rise, shaky and weak, and the window blew open with her sorcery, letting in the violent tempest. *Go,* she cried. He wept as he ran toward the storm and darkness.

"Stop him you imbecile!" Panthara cried.

Mellypip jumped out the window and fell several feet to a rough bed of rose bushes. The thorns scratched his body. He untangled himself from the thorns and continued to run.

Breathless and alone, Mellypip took shelter beneath a willow tree as the rain lashed the night. Soaked and terrified, he covered his face with his paws and sobbed.

CHAPTER II

Opaline woke with a raging headache and a sour taste in her mouth. She blinked and cursed the candlelight. She looked around the room, recognizing the large teak desk and her father's collection of swords mounted on the wall.

I'm still in father's apartments, except now I'm in his study, she thought hazily. *The last thing I remember was holding Father's hand while he struggled for breath.*

She sat up and a wave of dizziness overwhelmed her. She frowned with suspicion. She had never been prone to fainting spells or vapors, and drank very little wine last night.

Muffled voices and the audible click of the door handle startled her. She lay back down and closed her eyes. She prayed her thumping heartbeat would not be heard.

"Is she still out?" Priem whispered.

"Yes, for now," Levandius answered.

The door closed and after waiting a painful thirty seconds to make sure it wasn't a trick, she stood up, praying her stomach would not revolt. She tiptoed to the door, thankful for the thick carpets. Holding her breath, she pressed her ear against the door.

"Clever ruse with the drugs. I commend you," Levandius said in a low voice.

"I merely coated certain goblets, instead of tampering with the wine. The precise seating charts your sister arranged made it quite simple. The others will simply think they overindulged."

"What about Runa?" Levandius asked.

"I put her in the abandoned part of the dungeon for now. She's chained and bound with a sorcerer lock, so she won't be tattling to anyone. It'll be simple to convict her of killing Hemio and the soldiers. Murder is always easier when it's judicial. We can blame Ashur for her corruption. Tainted bloodlines. A bad seed. People love to blame something," Priem said.

Levandius laughed. "That should make Panthara happy. She was very insistent Runa not leave Tiamet."

"I put Hemio with the other dead bodies in Cathal's room where the guards found her," Priem said. "I covered her with their blood too, for good measure. Her fate is sealed."

"Panthara demanded this girl be punished. But I don't mind. I like to punish women—in many ways."

Opaline was disgusted.

"Panthara also sends her gratitude to the new *Emperor*," Priem said.

"What about Runa's damned familiar?" Levandius said.

"The creature hasn't been found yet. I have my men out looking for it now. It's a useless thing."

"I don't want any complications, Priem. My ascension to the throne must be unquestioned. I wish we had just poisoned my father outright."

"Tarsicius was a robust man. A sudden death would have provoked too many questions. Oh, speaking of that, I also summoned the Imperial Warden."

"Why?" Levandius hissed.

"Because when an Emperor is dying it would suspect for us not to follow protocol. Don't worry. Tarsicius will be dead by morning."

"Zhelon Thor will be quite pleased…and grateful," Levandius said. "I must reward him for sending you to me. What about the others?"

Others, Opaline wondered.

"I'll personally handle their disposal," Priem laughed. "I'll burn the bodies. The less evidence the better."

She gasped and put her hand to her mouth. "I'm an idiot," she cursed silently.

"Did you hear something?" Levandius said.

Opaline rushed to the sofa. She lay down and threw her arm over her face just as the door opened. "Father…father?" She moaned.

Opaline feigned relief when she looked at Levandius and held out her hand. "Oh dear…Levandius…what happened?" He rushed to her side, his face a cocoon of false sympathy. He helped her to stand. She broke into tears. "Is Father dead? Oh, I feel so ill and weak."

Not a complete lie.

"Hush now, Opaline. He's still alive, praise Rygon. I fear he won't last long though. Father sent the physicians away. He insisted. He said he would rather die like an Emperor."

Even if it means being murdered by his son, Opaline thought bitterly.

"Your fragile nature overcame you. You fainted, and I carried you in here," Levandius said gently.

"Thank you. Our poor father languishes, and I behave like a silly woman!" She broke down, harsh sobs wracking her body. Opaline's violent weeping was not a complete façade, since her own fear and rage threatened to explode. She had no idea how deep or far-spread this conspiracy went or who could be trusted now. She wanted to scream treason! But to do so now would mean her immediate death. She needed to get out of here. Quickly. She pretended to swoon. The touch of her brother's hand as he caught her made her feel dirty, but she endured his spurious concern with an equal sham of meek compliance.

"Go to your chambers, Opaline. I will stay with father and watch over him."

"Father does hate tears," she said in a choked voice. "I must compose myself for his sake. Would you please send word to me immediately if anything changes?" she begged sorrowfully.

"I promise. I've thought a great deal these past hours. We have never been close, Opaline, but must put aside our differences for the good of the kingdom. Make a fresh start."

"Yes, for the sake of the empire," she agreed. "We must make a new beginning."

In a perfect world that would be the blow of a sword to your traitorous neck.

"Let me send for your women to assist you," he offered.

"No—I can manage." He helped her to the door. Priem had already departed—or was hiding. "Thank you, Levandius," she whispered. Her brother's hand remained on her elbow as he guided her out the door.

How anxious he is to get rid of me.

They passed her father's large bed. His breathing was labored and hollow. So helpless now. Genuine weeping overcame her as she left the room. Only two Imperial Knights were outside the royal door. Levandius closed the door behind her. Opaline walked for a few moments, watchful of the guard's eyes, wiping tears off her face.

"Stop this!" she chastised herself. "No time for this foolishness!" When she was certain she was out of their vision, she lifted her skirt and fled. She ran down the steps and raced to her private apartments. Once inside the safety of her rooms, she locked the door and nearly collapsed with panic.

One of her ladies came out of her bedchamber and jumped in surprise. "Oh, Your Highness, you startled me. I've been so worried.

Runa returned your jewels last night."

"Give me your dress, Ada."

"What? Is this a game, my lady?"

"I wish it were. Send all my ladies and servants away. Tell everyone I'm in seclusion while my father is ill. We don't have much time." Opaline tore off her exquisite yellow gown and tossed it aside like a rag. She ripped the pearls and gold from her arms and fingers, except for her gold luck ring. "I have important errands for you too, but you'll need help. We can trust Mira, but only her, so fetch her after I leave. I will leave written instructions." She splashed water on her face and tried to rinse the foul taste from her mouth. "Listen carefully while I explain. This is life or death." The stunned maiden had not moved but stood frozen with her mouth open. Opaline sighed and spoke impatiently. "Quickly dear, unlace your gown."

~ * ~

Wet and shivering, Mellypip was watchful of Priem's guards who had hunted him all night. Weary and beaten by grief and hard rain, he still searched for someone to help. He ran along the ledge on the second level of the palace, peeking through windows, desperate to find help. It was almost light and the rain had waned. The last sight of his magical family haunted him. When he fled at Runa's command, he knew it was the only choice. If only he were big and strong! Had powerful magic! Mellypip could have saved them! Panthara succeeded in taking Cathal and Caliste, their bodies reduced by sorcery to the size of mice and caged. She flew away on a horse of smoke and shadow, just like she did in Sea Haven.

"Runa, Runa, I failed you!" he cried silently. He could not even seek her out through the bonding and the loss was traumatic. He prayed if they lived, he would be the best wampu ever! He would study hard and never smart off again!

I wish Belwyn were here. He would know what to do, he thought. "Can't be weak. Must be strong," he mumbled as he walked along the ledge. He didn't know who to trust in this strange place, except Hinkleburr and Opaline. He scoped several windows, but had not seen either of them yet. He did not see any of his family either. He tried to sneak into the palace, but all the entrances were guarded. The windows were also locked against the rain as people slept. He hoped the Ambassador was a true friend to Cathal. If he wasn't, all would be lost. Mellypip also craved the strong, comforting presence of Darcus. He could not go to the Sorcerer House. He didn't even know how to find it. He would get lost in the big city too, and the violent storm was also a problem.

Two guards with sodden cloaks trailing the grass beat against the bushes with long sticks and clubs. Mellypip huddled against the windowsill, hoping the shadows would conceal him. He had been evading them all night. The dreadful storm had protected him at first, but now that it had waned, he was vulnerable.

"Hey, what's up there?" one of the men said.

They looked up in his direction and grinned maliciously.

"Kill it," one of them said. "That's what Priem ordered."

The other raised a bow and arrow in his direction.

Mellypip bolted to a nearby tree limb, avoiding the arrow. The rush of another arrow whizzing by his rump propelled him to leap to another tree limb. He ran along the bough of the tree and jumped to another window on the ledge. Another arrow struck the stone wall right by his head and bounced off. Desperate, Mellypip ran along the narrow ledge to another window that glowed with soft light. Someone must be awake! He had to risk it. Frantic, Mellypip looked through the moist glass, and saw two small children. No wait…their faces looked older. They were Dwarves! He scratched against the window. "Help me!" A young man looked up from setting the table for morning tea. He saw Mellypip's little face pressed against the glass. The young man rushed to open the casement window just as the archer loosed another bolt. He grabbed Mellypip by the scruff of the neck and dropped him on the carpet. The arrow whizzed through the portal, deflected from the stone ceiling of the room, striking a pitcher of water on the table, shattering it. The other young dwarf ducked in confusion, then ran to shut the window and pulled the drapes closed. Mellypip clung to the leg of the one who saved him, his heart thumping.

The dwarf pulled him up and Mellypip grabbed the spotless white collar of his rescuer, smearing it with his muddy paws. "Please help me! I'm a familiar being hunted by bad humans. They're gonna hurt Runa! Belwyn and Sanura in danger too—"

"Ambassador!" one of the young Dwarves called. "We have a situation, sir!"

"Good heavens, what's all the racket! Broda? Talwyn? Where are you boys?" Hinkleburr grumbled. He staggered into the room holding a cloth to his forehead. "Blast, but my head hates me today!"

"Hinkleburr!" Mellypip cried, and he jumped from the arms of his savior and climbed up Hinkleburr's blue-brocade robe and babbled his story between crying fits. The young aides brought a thick towel to dry off his soaked fur and hot milk to warm him. Mellypip could not think about eating though, not until he rescued Runa and the others.

Hinkleburr's already flushed face burned with anger. "There are a lot of dangerous folks involved in this. We can't risk trusting anyone, except Captain Darcus."

"But Opaline's good," Mellypip said.

"She may be, but we have no idea if she's involved with her brother's plot. Are you sure, Mellypip? This is very serious."

"I heard him say it. Levandius wanted no loose ends, and they killed Hemio. What are we going to do! They'll hurt Runa!"

"Calm down," Hinkleburr said gently. "All is not lost. I have a few folks who work for me here, along with my trusted aides."

"Spies?" Mellypip whispered with wide eyes.

"It's part of the diplomacy. We'll find Runa, Sanura and Belwyn, don't worry. That old owl has weathered tougher situations. But we need to be extremely careful. There are deadly plots about. Damn, I feel for poor Cathal and Caliste, but there is still hope my boy. However, our first priority is rescuing Runa and the familiars."

Someone banged on the door. Hinkleburr gestured to his aides and took Mellypip to wait in his bedroom. He closed the door, but left it open a crack to listen.

"Who is calling?" asked Broda.

"The Emperor's Imperial Guard!"

Broda opened the door. "How may I be of service?"

"There was a creature that ran into your room through the window a short time ago. A wampu. I have been commanded—"

"One of your arrows flew into our chamber," Broda interrupted.

"Well, he's a dangerous creature. Magical and—"

"It nearly struck the Ambassador. It also destroyed a glass pitcher and left a dreadful mess to clean up."

"I'm sorry, but I am here to apprehend the animal."

"It's not here," Broda said. "The animal ran out the door into the hallway. I was too occupied cleaning up glass fragments and caring for the Ambassador to chase after it."

"Just let me search the room, in case the animal is hiding."

"No," Broda said softly.

"You cannot refuse me! I am an Imperial Guard!" he shouted.

"I can. A step across that threshold and you are in the sovereign land of Ironia, according to the treaty we have signed with your Emperor. That could be misconstrued as a declaration of hostility between our nations," Broda replied calmly. "Do they *teach* archery at all in Tiamet? Or manners?"

"Is there trouble, Brother?" Talwyn asked.

"No, Brother, but thank you. This rude soldier was just leaving."

"I will speak with the Ambassador now!" the guard demanded, pounding his fist against the door jam.

"He is taking a nap now and cannot be disturbed," Talwyn said.

"So good day to you," Broda said and closed the door. They waited a moment and then opened the door to check the halls to make sure the annoying knight had gone.

"Fine work, my boys!" Hinkleburr complimented them.

Hinkleburr went to his desk and placed Mellypip there among a messy pile of papers. He summoned his aides with a wave of his hand and sat down at the desk. The two young brothers, Broda and Talwyn, waited with stoic patience for their master as he scribbled several notes. They looked like twins, but there were subtle differences up close. Broda's face was more slender and Talwyn had a broader nose. The youthful Dwarves had shiny brown hair and round chestnut-colored eyes. Their matching moss green jackets, walnut-brown trousers, and white shirts were ironed and spotless, except for Mellypip's paw prints. Hinkleburr handed them the papers. In three breaths they were cloaked and gone.

"What now?" Mellypip asked.

"You must wait here. They're hunting you." Hinkleburr said. "Gods, I need a drink," he said, pouring a glass of brandy. "My aides are very well trained. They can find anything. A pretty sorceress like Runa is hard to miss. They'll fetch Captain Darcus too!"

Mellypip covered his face in his paws. "I was a coward. I shouldn't have run."

"That was the bravest thing you could do. Runa was right. You're the only one able to save them. If you stayed, Priem would have killed you. That arrogant knight, or sorcerer, whatever he is, has a lot to pay for. So does the Emperor's son. What you discovered Mellypip, not only involves this horrible conspiracy with Koll and the missing sorcerers, but the fate of an entire kingdom. That's a lot for your little wampu shoulders, my furry friend."

"I just want my family back," Mellypip said sadly.

"We all want that," Hinkleburr agreed gently, taking Mellypip in his arms.

Mellypip prayed with every ounce of faith he had they were not too late.

~ * ~

After Opaline donned the plain gray dress and bound up her mass of flaxen hair in a maid's white turban, she slipped a dagger in her bodice and a light crystal in her pocket. She left the room, her head bowed and carrying a stack of sheets. Two palace guards passed her, and she longed to ask them for help, but she had no idea if they were loyal. They whistled as she walked by them.

"Feather my bed anytime," one of them snickered.

In your dreams, toad. she thought angrily.

She ran down the stairs. The large oval windows on the staircase showed the storm had calmed, but it still rained heavily. She went to a wall sconce in the shape of a dragon head and twisted the dragon's iron ear. A crack opened in the wall. She pushed against it and entered the passageway. Closing the door, the sudden blackness disturbed her. She dropped the sheets and retrieved the crystal from her pocket. In the shadows of the secret halls, she ran.

The twists and turns of the old passageway were familiar, thanks to months of bored exploration. She had no idea that someday the knowledge would mean life or death. She sneezed, cursing the mold and dust that infested the ancient halls. Even hidden passages should be swept from time to time. She reached the narrow stone steps that led to the bowels of the palace. They had grown crumbly with age and she almost twisted her ankle when a piece broke off and caught on her heel.

The lower levels of the fortress were dank and dirty. She opened the secret door and stepped inside. Torches burned along the walls, so someone must have been here in the last couple hours. She longed to cry out Runa's name, but fear someone was lurking about kept her mute. She gripped the dagger and put her crystal away. The only sound was the occasional squeak of a rodent. She hated rats.

The old iron-banded, wooden doors of the cells were wide open and unoccupied. She checked each one, and the wretched holes reeked of stale human filth and blood. Even though they were long unoccupied, the odors never washed clean. A rat squeaked and darted across the hall. "I will not scream at the sight of a silly rat!" she promised with quiet panic. "Even a scruffy, smelly, rat!" At the end of the hall, the room opened to a larger chamber, with bright torches in wall sconces that cast amber shadows everywhere. Horrible implements of torture hung on cracked walls. She gasped when she saw on a wooden table splintered and marred by decay, were the bodies of Belwyn and Sanura!

She rushed to them and from her peripheral vision she saw a figure. She turned and saw Runa chained to the wall.

Runa was unconscious. A narrow band of sorcerer bane was around her neck. Opaline checked the familiars' bodies. They were still breathing. She ran to Runa and slapped her. "Wake up," she whispered. "Oh please, wake up!"

Runa moaned and her eyes fluttered. She pulled against the cuffs binding her wrists. "Opaline? Is that you? Where…Oh…they took Grandpa and Caliste! Priem-"

"Shhh! I'll get you out of here. We are all in danger." Runa's fine silk gown worn in happiness just a few hours ago was torn and smeared with blood. She reached up to unlock the iron cuffs.

Runa's eyes widened. "Priem!"

"I know. He is conspiring with my wretched brother."

"No—behind you!" Runa warned.

Opaline spun around. The annoying rat shimmered with sorcery and shapeshifted into Priem.

"You're a sorcerer!" she cried, shocked.

"Old news, Princess," he said darkly.

She stabbed at him with her dagger. He avoided her thrust, and caught her by the wrist and twisted it until she dropped it. He held her close, breathing into Opaline's ear. "I was wondering when you would get here Princess," he laughed. "I've been waiting." He spun her around and punched her hard in the stomach. Opaline crumbled to the floor, groaning. The pain choked her. Runa cried out curses. He grabbed her throat.

Opaline scratched at his face.

I can't fight him, she thought weakly. Her luck ring! She had to risk it. She pulled the golden ring off her finger, and it dropped to the floor. She must fight with—

Priem punched Opaline hard in the face with his fist. She fell backward on the stone floor. She moaned. Her head exploded with pain.

"Feisty little thing," Priem laughed. "I could have subdued you with magic, but this was more fun." He hauled her up as Runa cursed at him like a veteran seaman, struggling against her chains. He shoved Opaline's body against the wall next to Runa. He locked her hands in the hanging cuffs on the wall. She hung limply. "The new Emperor will be pleased. He wanted to get rid of you, Opaline. This just makes it easier."

"You dirty bastard!" Runa shouted.

"Actually, I'm Gorvanus. The bastard and Priem part are just facets of my personality." He fingered Runa's silver Ilyrran locket and ripped it from her neck. "A token...for my beloved Panthara. She will want proof you are no longer a hindrance to our plans. It will also upset Cathal to no end." Runa spat in his face. He wiped away the spittle. "Such bad manners," he said. She kicked him hard in the groin. He doubled over with pain and sucked in his breath.

"How's that for manners?" she shouted.

Eyes on the ground, he saw the delicate golden ring gleaming on the filthy floor. He reached to pick it up. "Another token for my troubles," he said. "Must be my lucky day. A bit snug, even on my pinky finger-but lovely."

He took a moment to recover, then straightened. He drew his sword and stood over the vulnerable bodies of Belwyn and Sanura. "Excuse me, but I have to kill them now. You might want to close your eyes, Runa. It's going to get messy. But then...your pretty gown is already ruined, so no matter." He raised his sword.

Runa screamed.

CHAPTER 12

Gorvanus' sword, poised to strike Belwyn and Sanura, descended. Even in her grief and anger, Runa sensed an abrupt rise in mystical energy. Just as he brought down his blade, a rush of gray-hued magic burst around them. It hit the table, not Gorvanus, and the gloomy room exploded with blinding light. Runa shut her eyes against the glare. The magical energy left a tingle in her mouth and on her skin. When she opened them, the force had thrown Gorvanus back several feet. He lay dazed against the back wall on the filthy floor. The heavy wooden table had been tossed several feet across the room and flipped over on its side, causing Belwyn and Sanura to roll across the floor. Stunned, Runa looked at Opaline. The vapors of raw sorcery sizzled around her.

Runa blinked and gasped. "You're a sorceress!"

Opaline nodded. "I know. Long story."

"Can't wait to hear it,' Runa replied.

Gorvanus groaned and pushed himself off the ground. He glared at Opaline. "You did that!" he accused. "Looks like I'm not the only one with secrets, but yours will die with you, Princess." He extended his hand, but no magic emitted from it. He stared dumbly at his hands.

"Tough to cast a spell wearing *sorcerer bane*, isn't it?" Opaline said.

Gorvanus glowered at the golden ring he had stolen a moment ago. He tried to pull it off, but it remained stuck on his pinky finger. "The ring! No! No! Damn it!" he howled. Gorvanus frowned and looked around for his lost sword.

"Better free yourself before you taunt him any further," Runa suggested in a frightened voice. "I'm a bit trapped now."

Opaline concentrated on her locks. Her manacles sparked with magic and broke open. She tried to unlock Runa's. Runa was bound by the sorcerer bane metal, so she had to do it manually.

Gorvanus snatched up his sword and advanced on Opaline.

"Look out!" Runa cried.

Opaline spun around, retrieved a light crystal from her pocket and hurled it at his head, striking his forehead. He moaned and staggered, blood streaming down his face. She grabbed a broken wooden leg from the table and struck him across the back of his head. He fell unconscious at last. Opaline, breathless and flushed, returned to Runa, trying to unpin the other manacle.

Runa's heart raced. They could not use magic on Gorvanus while he wore the sorcerer bane. "Why do you wear a ring of sorcerer bane ...obviously coated in gold?"

"To hide my secret," she said quickly.

Gorvanus straightened and wiped blood from his eyes. "Oh... you're dead, Princess," he threatened.

"You need to hit him harder!" Runa shouted. She pulled against the iron manacle as he grabbed Opaline by the throat and threw her to the grimy floor. Opaline kicked him hard in the groin. His face contorted with pain, but his grip remained firm. Runa wondered if he was getting use to being kicked in his privates, since she had also done so earlier.

Suddenly, Sanura leapt toward Gorvanus. In midair she shape-shifted into her impressive panther size. She pounced on Gorvanus violently, exposed claws ripping armor and flesh. He screamed and rolled off Opaline. Opaline crawled away, coughing and gasping for breath. Belwyn flew around and raked him with his talons. In desperation, Gorvanus shielded his face with his hands.

"No way to treat a lady!" Belwyn said sternly. "You need to learn some manners, boy!"

Gorvanus curled into a fetal position as Sanura sat on him in her panther-size form. She roared; sharp claws poised to do more damage.

"Don't kill him yet," Belwyn warned. "We need him to give us information." He shook out his feathers. "Damn, I have a vile head-ache." His head rotated around. "Runa, are you hurt?"

"No, I'm fine, except for a bit of nausea," Runa said.

He hopped over to Opaline, lying pale and shaky. "Opaline... breathe girl!"

"I'm trying," she replied hoarsely.

"Oh, Belwyn, Grandfather and Caliste have been taken," Runa said.

"And Levandius is poisoning my father," Opaline wheezed. "Priem is helping him."

"Priem's real name is Gorvanus," Runa spat. "He's working with Panthara too." Runa sucked in her breath. "Oh dear! Poor Mellypip! Last night I made him flee into the storm rather than be captured by Gorvanus and Panthara. Oh, my poor baby! He must be so alone."

"Oh, Runa, I'm so sorry. I haven't seen Mellypip," Opaline said.

She glared down at Gorvanus. "But I do know Gorvanus sent his men out to hunt him. I spied on him and Levandius when they thought I was still drugged."

"Deceitful bitch!" Gorvanus spat.

Sanura dug her claws deeper into his back. He shrieked with pain. "No way to speak to a lady either! Perhaps you need etiquette lessons?" Sanura suggested ominously.

Belwyn sighed. "Gorvanus, you are so stupid."

"If they hurt Melly, I'm going to feed you to Sanura in pieces!" Runa promised bitterly.

Sanura dug her claws even deeper into his back. Red rivulets of blood ran down to the cold stone floor. "Where is he?" Belwyn asked hotly. "And where are *our* sorcerers?"

"I don't know," whimpered Gorvanus.

Sanura growled. "I don't believe you!"

"I don't know where that wampu is!" he cried.

"Excuse me, but I'm still chained to the wall," Runa said, shaking the chain that still bound her.

"Oh, sorry," Opaline said, and she got up and freed Runa.

Runa massaged her wrists. "Thank you. I must get this off though," she said, pointing to the band of sorcerer bane collar. "It's chafing me too—not to mention preventing me from doing magic."

Opaline examined it. "We need a key to remove it." She turned toward Sanura. "Check his body for any keys—thoroughly. Don't be shy."

"Gladly," Sanura said, pawing at the ragged and bleeding Gorvanus, who whined even louder.

Belwyn hopped over to Runa. "Don't worry. We'll find Furball," Belwyn comforted her. "He's a wampu. Furball can move pretty fast when motivated."

"I need to get Iona to my father before it's too late," Opaline said. "Priem…Gorvanus, or whatever his name is, is working with Levandius to poison him."

"You're the contact Iona had at the palace?" Runa asked. "Grand-father told me Iona had one. He also suspected your father was being poisoned, but couldn't be sure. She has been making the antidote."

Opaline nodded. "Yes. I hope Iona was able to finish it, and one of my women reaches her. It is a very complicated potion. Iona and I are old friends. I'll explain about everything—I swear, Runa. I just couldn't tell you yet. Only a few people know about my secret. If my father ever found out, I would be exiled—or worse. He hates magic. Right now, I just want to save my father."

Sanura sniffed around a weeping Gorvanus and extracted a small ring of keys with her teeth. Opaline took them and after a few tries, found the right key and unlocked the band around Runa's neck.

"Thanks," Runa said, rubbing her throat with relief. "Now we need to make Gorvanus talk. We don't dare remove that ring he's wearing though. He's a sorcerer."

"Then the old-fashioned way will just have to do," Belwyn said.

Sanura bent down and gripped the back of his head with her massive jaws.

"I suggest you talk," Belwyn said sharply. "She looks hungry."

"I only know Panthara has Cathal and Caliste. She is taking them to Mowad by ship," he wept pathetically. "She has a head start so perhaps you should follow them and leave me alone."

"Not a chance," Belwyn barked. "Where is Koll?"

"He's in Mowad—waiting for them."

"What are they planning?"

"I don't know! I was sent here to work for Levandius months ago. I displeased Panthara when I failed to deliver Cathal and Caliste. After that I was told very little."

"He sings quite well when motivated," Sanura commented. "But he is still holding back."

"Chain him to the wall," Opaline suggested. "There are numerous instruments of persuasion here that may assist our investigation."

"I knew I liked you girl," Belwyn hooted with approval.

The sound of running feet alerted them.

"Oh no, someone is coming," Runa said.

"Now what!" Sanura growled.

Belwyn took the front position. "Behind me, girls."

Runa grabbed a large rod of wood from the ruined table and held it ready to swing. Opaline grabbed Gorvanus' sword.

Three Imperial Knights ran into the room, swords drawn. Opaline held the sword out in warning. "Stand back you traitors!" she commanded.

Gorvanus wiggled beneath Sanura's weight and cried out. "Where have you been? Kill them you fools! What am I paying you for?"

The leader of the trio removed his helmet. It was Darcus! "Thank the gods you are all safe," he said. The two men behind Darcus took off their helmets. Beneath them were the youthful faces of Pol and

Korun.

Runa threw her arms around him. "Oh, Darcus! So much has happened!"

Darcus hugged her and spoke softly. "It's all right, Runa. I know. I've been informed of everything. We'll get them back. Don't worry. Worry later, when there's time."

"How did you find us?" Runa asked.

"I promised Cathal I would look after you, and I keep my promises. I also had some help."

Hinkleburr Crowyn and his aides rushed in. A girl Runa recognized as one of Opaline's servants was with them.

"Dear me," Hinkleburr said, panting. "I'm getting too old for this. Is everyone quite all right?"

From Hinkleburr's coat pocket, Mellypip poked his head out. "Runa!" he cried and jumped out.

"Melly!" Runa cried. Mellypip jumped into her arms, licking her with happy kisses. Runa hugged him and felt the worry knot loosen in her belly. "I was so worried. How did you find us here?"

"Ada knew I was coming here to save you, Runa." Opaline said.

The young servant curtsied and smiled. "Opaline sent me to fetch Darcus, but he was already on the palace grounds, with Pol and Korun."

Darcus nodded. "Even with the storm last night, I knew Cathal and Caliste were in trouble when they didn't arrive by midnight. We came here last night, but no one was being allowed into the palace. I managed to pound a couple heads and got in anyway."

"Where are the other familiars?" Runa asked.

"Pouting in Ambassador Crowyn's apartments. They wanted to come along for the fight, but I decided they should remain out of sight for the moment," Darcus said. "When I finally got into the palace, I checked Cathal's room. I found the bodies of Timoth and Lichor, and that of Hemio, the court physician. I tried to see the Emperor, but I was informed rather rudely by an imperial guard he was on his deathbed. After that I skulked around for hours trying to find out where you were when Mistress Ada found me."

"I'm so sorry about Timoth and Lichor," Runa whispered. "They were very brave and tried to save me." She pointed to Gorvanus. "And he killed them. Priem was just a cover. His real name is Gorvanus. I saw him cruelly stab them to death." Angrily, Darcus stalked toward Gorvanus, but Runa held him back. "We still need more information from him. Believe me; I want him to be punished —severely."

"I want him dead too," Opaline said hotly. "He's poisoning my father."

"Take a rune and stand in line," Belwyn said. "But in the meantime, would someone explain how you all arrived together?"

"I am Broda," One of the young dwarves said. "The Ambassador sent me to bring Darcus here when we rescued Mellypip from knights who were shooting at him."

The other bowed. "I am Talwyn, Broda's brother. We considered contacting you, Princess."

"But we were not sure if you were involved. I apologize," Broda added.

"Quite all right," Opaline replied graciously.

"Thank you," Broda said before continuing. "I found Mistress Ada in conversation with Captain Darcus. We soon discovered we had similar secret missions involving palace intrigue, so we banded together as an act of faith."

"We all got together rather quickly after that," Hinkleburr added. "We immediately came here when Ada said Levandius and Priem had you here, Runa. I managed to procure imperial knight uniforms to enable them to move more freely around the palace."

"What of Iona?" Opaline asked.

"She is waiting for you in your room, Your Highness," Ada replied. "But Prince Levandius has barred all from entry to the Emperor's chamber. Iona fears it may be too late."

"Oh, I'll get us in," Darcus said grimly.

"How?" Opaline asked.

"Just leave that to me," Darcus said, putting the imperial helmet back on.

"What about him?" Runa asked, looking at Gorvanus.

"Oh, I know just what to do with him for now," Darcus said with a wicked grin. "If he's a sorcerer, we should put that collar on him for safekeeping, just in case. If he gets that ring off, chains won't hold him." He turned to Sanura. "Would you mind moving back a bit so I can snap this on him?"

"No problem," she said. She remained sitting on his rump, licking her chops for further intimidation.

Gorvanus pulled at his finger with frenzied desperation. Darcus knelt and pulled back his head. At last, his fingers slick with sweat and blood, the ring slipped off just as Darcus bent to put the collar on. The ring chimed as it hit the stone, and Gorvanus shapeshifted into a rat.

"No! Stop him!" Sanura cried, rolling over onto her back when Gorvanus' body disappeared.

The grungy rat squeaked hysterically, and escaped Darcus' blade as he swung hard, chipping the stone floor.

Gorvanus scuttled to a hole in the wall and vanished.

Frustrated, Darcus cursed in colorful and imaginative verse for several seconds.

Runa's hand flew up to her neck. "Oh no! He still has my locket! He took it from me while I was chained down here!"

"We'll get it back," Belwyn promised grimly. "Rats never stay hidden for long. They like to cause trouble."

"I hate rats!" Opaline shivered.

"In more ways than one," Runa agreed.

~ * ~

Opaline and Darcus guided them through the beautiful halls of the palace. They took the secret passageways until they reached the floor with the Emperor's chambers. Everything was strange and silent—and devoid of people. The jade and ivory pillars and gleaming white walls looked abandoned. The elaborate doors of carved wood and gold inlay were closed.

"This is creepy," Mellypip commented.

"I know, Melly," Runa said. "This feels like an elegant decorated tomb."

"What's happened to everyone?" Opaline asked.

"Prince Levandius has commanded everyone remain in their chambers while the Emperor is on his deathbed." Ada explained. "He said it was to pray for the Emperor's deliverance from death."

"I'll give my half-brother Levandius in trade," Opaline said frostily. "Except he's not worth much."

They stopped around the corner from the Emperor's private chambers. Mellypip chewed his tail. Not because of what they were doing, but the presence of Iona the necromancer. Her face concealed by dark veils, only her pale blue eyes were visible. Her white raven familiar, Amun, perched on her shoulder with stoic patience.

"You are afraid of me," Iona said softly.

"Oh no," Mellypip lied. "I just never met—"

"A necromancer before?" she said. "Few do. We like to keep to ourselves. But I'm quite harmless, my little friend."

Opaline, flanked by Darcus and his men still disguised in imperial armor and helmets, marched up to the guards stationed before her father's door. "Please stand aside," she commanded.

One of the two guards shook his head. "I beg your forgiveness, Your Highness. The Imperial Prince Levandius has commanded that no one is allowed to disturb him or Emperor Tarsicius."

"I'm so sorry then," Opaline said softly and stepped aside.

The confused expression on the guard was replaced by shock as Darcus struck one across the jaw with the iron hilt of his sword. The second guard drew his sword too late. Pol smashed the other knight's face with his sword. They both fell unconscious. Darcus and Pol dragged them out of the way.

Darcus signaled it was safe. Everyone had a weapon, even the Ambassador and his aides were armed with small swords. Opaline had a dagger and Runa carried a staff.

Opaline tried the door. "It's locked. Stand back." A wave of sorcery exploded the doors. Opaline covered her face and fell backward from the force. Darcus caught her in his arms. The smoking remains of charred wood were in pieces.

Runa ran up to her. "That was a bit much."

Opaline shrugged. "Sorry. My powers are untrained."

"No kidding," Belwyn said.

Levandius fanned away the mystical smoke. "Guards!" he shouted. "Help me! Assassins!"

"You're no one to cry assassin!" Opaline accused. She walked up to Levandius and punched him hard in the eye with her fist. He dropped to the floor, dazed. She withdrew her hand and winced with pain. "How do men do that?"

Darcus took over and knocked Levandius out with only one blow. In a moment he had him bound and gagged. "Now what?" Darcus asked.

"Lock him up in the closet for now. We don't dare kill him—yet," Opaline warned.

Pol and Korun dragged the unconscious prince into one of the closets. Hinkleburr took out a vial of dark green liquid.

"What's that?" Darcus asked.

"Moonshade. It's made from a night blooming flower that grows only in Ironia. Place one or two drops in his mouth and the prince will sleep for hours. Do the same for the guards outside. Be careful, too much can cause a quick death."

"Lead me to the Emperor," Iona said, stepping into the room.

"This way," Opaline said, guiding her to the royal bed.

Tarsicius looked dead. His complexion was ashen, and he was very still. Opaline tried to shake him.

"He's in a coma," Iona said.

Opaline felt his heart. "But he's still alive. His heartbeat is so weak though. And his skin is so cold."

Iona took out a potion bottle. The contents shimmered with many colors. "Then let us hope this will revive him. But even if it heals him, it may take hours, or even days, before he wakes."

"How is he going to swallow?" Runa asked.

"He won't have to," Iona said. "The potion is designed to work its magic as long as it can enter the body." She opened his nightshirt and uncorked the mystical potion. She poured it on his chest and the liquid sparkled and then absorbed into his skin.

"We can't leave my father here while he is so helpless. Where can we hide him that's safe? I have no idea who to trust except for you folks."

"Order the stables to get a cart ready and some horses," Darcus replied. "If he can survive the journey, the Abbey of Araema will be the safest place. I will also send a message to my legion. They are loyal, Princess. I was their Captain. They are quartered outside the city too, so it could take a little time to get them to our aid."

Opaline rewarded Darcus with a brilliant smile. "That's genius! The abbey is about thirty miles outside the city. We will also have the added protection of sanctuary there."

"I don't think Levandius will honor that ancient law," Darcus commented. "But it is too dangerous to stay here—for all of us. And he won't know where we are for a while at least. The Abbess is also my sister," Darcus added. "She won't mind doing a favor for her baby brother."

Belwyn nudged Darcus with his beak. "Priem is on the loose. Also, stablemen can talk."

"That shouldn't be an issue," Hinkleburr said, "at least regarding the stable." He tossed the vial of Moonshade to Broda. "Go to the stables now. Take a bottle of wine and add that to their drink. They will be spared from being witness to all this, as well as tattling on us. Can you boys handle the horses?"

"Yes, Ambassador," the two young dwarves answered in unison then departed.

Belwyn nodded. "Let's go then. I don't like it here anymore."

"Not to mention being chased by nasty humans with arrows," Mellypip agreed.

"I've had a bounty on my tail feathers from more interesting people," Belwyn said. "No one has ever collected on it either. And they won't start now."

CHAPTER 13

The wooden stairs creaked with each delicate step Panthara took as she descended to the lower decks of the ship. The velvet wrapped staff she carried with reverence still had the faint odor of sorcery, though it had not been used in many years. Azmadu was confused too. He thought now that Cathal and Caliste were prisoners, she would be happier—but she wasn't. She had not smiled since they had overcome their enemies last night.

"Don't like it down here," Azmadu mumbled.

"You are quite safe," Panthara said. "I just need to inform them why they are here. They may be dissatisfied with their accommodations, but that is part of the fun."

A special place had been constructed in the bowels of the ship. It had been scrubbed with soap and water, but it still stank. Azmadu scratched his eye patch. That moldy, salty rank odor never washed away. Barrels and crates of supplies crowded the small space. Light crystals hung from the ceiling, offering dim illumination. Panthara had considered keeping them in total darkness, but she was also practical enough to know two such clever sorcerers needed to be watched. In the back of the hold, two separate iron cages, eight feet tall and six feet wide, stood. Within each cage, bound with sorcerer locks around their necks and in chains, were Cathal and Caliste. Azmadu hesitated, hearing both of them curse quietly with unrestrained gusto.

"Come, Azmadu, we must see that our *guests* are comfortable… and *secure*," Panthara insisted. Her smoky blue eyes glowed in the hazy light. She stroked his head tenderly. "Come along, they won't hurt you. I have neutered their powers."

Azmadu grunted and obeyed. "After we taunt them, I want my ointment and treats. My eye socket itches!" Azmadu whined. "Burns too. I need cuddling. The angry sorcerers are mean. And Gorvanus didn't deliver mean owl like he promised."

"Hush, my sweet," Panthara said quietly. "He will deliver the wretched owl and his wampu friend for you to eat. Gorvanus has other things to take care of right now. Now come along like a good crill familiar." She walked to the cages, and he padded after her reluctantly. Cathal and Caliste stopped cursing and focused their hostility on Panthara with hateful stares.

Panthara greeted them. "I am glad you are both awake at last. Did you enjoy your nap?"

Cathal kicked at the cage. "Where is my granddaughter? Where are our familiars?"

"They aren't here on this ship if that's what you're wondering. Gorvanus, whom I believe you also know as Priem the Imperial Knight, will deliver your familiars later. He had other pressing duties to perform first. Poor Azmadu needs fresh meat and they should provide an ample meal. Runa's fate, however, might be more…grim."

Cathal turned bright red with rage and reached his arm through the narrow bars of the cage. "If you hurt Runa or Belwyn I will—"

"What?" Panthara asked, tilting her head and smiling. "Hurt me? How? You are in a cage, old man. Your sorcery is contained. You are at my mercy."

"I thought that arrogant snit Priem was up to no good. I just never realized it was treason and murder," Caliste said. "Or that he was an imposter."

"It is of no matter. Gorvanus' role as Priem was simple enough. A young man from a noble family, the parents conveniently dead. It is nothing to kill and hide a body. Gorvanus needed help of course. That is where Prince Levandius was useful. The Prince adores me, you know. But Gorvanus' sojourn here is nearly completed. Then we will sail to Mowad. There you will pay for your crimes."

"Your threats are juvenile, Panthara," Cathal replied. "But then, Koll wouldn't employ anyone with backbone and intelligence. You're working for evil. Koll is a ruthless butcher. Only Ashur himself was more despised and feared. Why do you work for him?"

"I work for no one," Panthara said.

"Why are you helping Koll hunt us down?" Cathal demanded.

"I am the one who has hunted you, Cathal. You and your revered circle of seven—Cathal, Caliste, Myrsalian, Jiana, Riva, Liat, Ulan. The plan to capture all of you was not Koll's idea. It was mine," Panthara said smugly.

"Don't you have anything better to do?" Cathal asked.

"Justice has been my vocation," Panthara said with pride.

Caliste rolled her eyes. "Oh yes, I see now! Murder, abductions, attacks, threats—all very noble causes."

"I will show you my cause!" Panthara cried. She unfurled the velvet wrappings and laid a staff on the floor with care. It was a sorcerer's staff. The dark wood gleamed, and the head was carved into the shape of an eagle's head. "Do you recognize it? It belonged to someone who was once quite close to you, Cathal."

Cathal's face clouded. "That resembles Ashur's staff. But there have been many mages with eagles as familiars over the centuries. It could belong to anyone."

"It *is* Ashur's staff. You should know! You laid it on his ashes after you cremated his body in that cave!" Panthara said with a chill calm. "You murdered him. Now you will pay for your crime."

"Pay for what? Ashur became evil. In a rather short time Ashur had managed to kill thousands of people and take over several countries." Caliste said.

"A Sorcerer King who reigned supreme! Ashur was a warlord! A god! A titan among pathetic fools. And you took his life! You and all of your friends turned against him and plotted his assassination with forbidden magic! You opened the nine gates to the Otherworld and summoned the Alzghoul to take his soul," Panthara said with a shaky voice.

"Ashur became a monster, Panthara," Cathal said darkly. "He killed my wife…my daughter…friends…and many innocent people. I don't regret what I did, Panthara. I only regret that it came to such extreme measures, and I was too late to stop him before he wrecked so many lives. How could you care for such a man? Were you his lover?"

"Lover? No. It is not simple, old man. Ashur was my father!" Panthara said with grave solemnity. "I do this for family honor. My honor…and love."

Cathal and Caliste were stunned into silence.

Panthara's smile was triumphant as she continued. "He never told you, did he, that he had a daughter from a previous relationship when he married your precious Rualla? Your daughter stole Ashur's heart, just when my mother learned she was pregnant with me. She never told Ashur, because she could never marry him, of course. As a princess of Mowad, their affair was forbidden. Only royal blood could ask for my mother's hand in wedlock. My mother quickly married a prince her father chose when Ashur returned to the west. I thought the man my mother married was my father. I never knew about Ashur until I was three when he came back to us after Rualla abandoned him. My mother welcomed him back with joy. He picked me up and called me daughter, his precious jewel. He said he would make me queen of the world.

"He nearly kept his promise. Until his death turned our dreams to ashes. I was there that night in the great caverns of the mountain in the Salomm desert. My father hid me and my mother high in one of the many small hidden caves and cast a shield for our protection. He wanted me to watch as he defeated his greatest enemy—you! That cave was his private sanctuary. He discovered many relics from other ages there. He knew you would seek him out, and he was ready. I was only four years old. Then you opened the gates to the Otherworld. I witnessed black fire erupt, the rise of the Alzghoul wraith guardians, my father trapped in a red crystal—using magic you stole from his personal tome of ancient knowledge he found in these caves. Imagine, Cathal, being a small girl and watching your father's soul ripped from his body by demons! My mother never stopped screaming. She is still mad with grief. The roar of the demons shrouded her cries." Panthara lifted her chin. "But I did not scream. I did not weep."

"You should have wept, Panthara. Your grief might not have twisted you," Cathal said. "What you plan is evil, no matter how much warped sentimentality you frost it with. You are mad."

"You have not seen true madness. I have watched my mother descend into the pits of insanity. You are to blame. I vowed I would have revenge on the murderous circle of seven who destroyed my father. You are the last members, and the most difficult to catch. But I have you now."

"Revenge can be bitter, Panthara. Our deaths will not bring Ashur back. If death is what you desire, why take us alive?" Cathal asked. "You have gone to a great deal of effort, planning and work just to see me dead. What are you really planning? Come now, surely you want to gloat about it."

Panthara smiled and replied. "You must die together, all seven of you. How—that will be a surprise. You will soon learn the hand of justice is hard and cruel." She picked up Azmadu, stroking his scales lovingly. "I must retire now and take care of my familiar. Your vile owl hurt him deeply. Now my poor Azmadu must wear this eye patch. Another sin against my royal person, Cathal. But you will never hurt me or mine again." She turned away from them as four guards entered the hold. They knelt at her feet.

"Guard them well. They must be alive when we reach Mowad,"

Panthara commanded them.

"Yes, Your Majesty," the lead guard replied.

Regal and satisfied, Panthara ascended the stairs, leaving her prisoners in the depths. Once on deck, Azmadu was relieved. He didn't like the way the two sorcerers looked at him. When they entered Panthara's luxurious private cabin, she was still distant and quiet.

Better now, my Panthara, Azmadu asked through the bonding.

No…not yet, my little dragon. Soon. When justice is done. She put him on the couch and went to the great crystal of calling.

Azmadu scratched at his patch, and whimpered. "Can I have my medicine now? Hurts."

"In a moment, my love. I must do this first." She swept her hand across the gigantic crystal and it radiated with life. "I must contact Koll," she explained.

Azmadu hung his head. *Him.* He didn't like Koll. He scared him. Koll's familiar, the scorpion snake Xabral, was even more terrifying. He had tormented Azmadu since he was a hatchling when Koll brought him to Panthara. He adored his Panthara, but Koll and Xabral were a bane to his existence.

The crystal's intense brightness lit up the cabin. A sharp face appeared in the crystal, dark hair flowing from a widow's peak, and deep black eyes. Koll. Xabral was there too! He coiled around Koll's shoulders; his black and red scales glistened. His stinger tail twitched back and forth. Azmadu scurried under the bed to hide. The scorpion snake was always cruel to him. He hated learning the arts of familiar magic from Xabral.

The face in the glowing stone spoke. "Well, my Sorceress Queen, have you taken them at last?"

"It is done, Koll. I told you I would be victorious! You were right to keep Gorvanus out of it. He has failed us too often. We will sail for home soon. I should arrive home in about fourteen days with clear weather."

"Your blessed father Ashur would be proud of your devotion. Your mother, Naloia, will be relieved. What of Ashur's other daughter?"

"I am Ashur's *only* daughter," Panthara pouted.

"You are his firstborn, true. You are sisters," Koll corrected her. "Runa could be swayed. You are born of the same blood. Perhaps she could be an ally in our new holy war."

"She is simple and pure. Runa is not very bright either," Panthara added. "Besides, Cathal has had too much influence on her morality. She is not worthy of us. Also, there were some unanticipated deaths in the palace. Gorvanus got carried away—"

"How carried away was he?" Koll asked sternly.

"Nothing extreme. Some unimportant soldiers who had the misfortune of being witnesses, that's all. Gorvanus thought it would be best to blame Runa for their murders. She makes a convenient scapegoat. As soon as the Emperor dies and Levandius takes the throne, she will be executed immediately. What of my father's remains?"

"His bones and ashes were gathered. The ancient sorcery has done its work. Now we need the seven to make it complete."

"Where is Azmadu, my apprentice familiar?" Xabral's chilling whisper came through the crystal.

Azmadu cowered, covering his face with his wings. "Azmadu is helping to guard our captives" Panthara replied. "But I will be sure to tell him you inquired after him."

"Good," Xabral said. "I miss the lizard."

Azmadu shivered. *Lying serpent,* he cried to Panthara. *Mean snake. Snake hates me! Threatens all the time to sting me with its barbed poison stinger. Makes me scared. Hate Xabral!*

"Excuse me, Koll. But the Captain has a question for me." Panthara looked under the couch. *Calm down! I would never let him harm you, Azmadu,* Panthara comforted him. *Xabral and Koll would never risk my wrath by harming you. Not even my mother would be foolish enough for that, and she's crazy!*

Maybe Xabral could eat your mother, Naloia. Give nasty snake indigestion. Naloia tough meat.

My mother would be deadly to digest, even for Xabral, Panthara retorted through the bonding. She returned to the crystal. "Forgive me, Koll. But the weather here has been volatile. The storms I invoked to cover my activity have yet to calm."

"Do you require assistance?" Koll offered.

"No, Koll. That won't be necessary. You have trained me well. Did you not say I was your most talented apprentice?"

"You are, my Sorceress Queen," he said passionately.

Too passionately, Azmadu thought. He did not like the way Koll looked at *his* Panthara.

"How did my mother react when you told her my father's remains were required? She has never parted from that urn since his death."

"Naloia is here in the cave. The scroll specified the essence of his body was a requirement. She finally surrendered the urn after many tearful protestations."

"Is she…calm?" Panthara asked.

"Sometimes Naloia became difficult," Koll replied. "Once the ritual was completed, she was more cooperative. I will see you in Mowad."

"Can the magic truly bring my father back?" Panthara whispered.

"Do not fear, Panthara. I have taken care of you since you were four. I have never failed you. I made you a promise, and I will keep it. We are in a way, family, after all. Soon, you will keep the promise you made to me."

"I understand Koll," Panthara said gravely. "I will honor that promise."

~ * ~

Koll passed his hand across the crystal and the image of Panthara's somber beauty faded to oblivion. His protégé was raw and excitable; but he had trained her well in the arts of sorcery and leadership.

"Gorvanus is becoming a liability," Xabral said. "He thinks he can rise above his station. We have too much riding on this, Koll, to allow an imbecile free reign, especially one so ill-regarded. No animal familiar has ever bonded with him."

"I agree," Koll nodded. "But Gorvanus is creative with deadly mystical poisons. His purpose there is nearly served. He was the liaison between Zhelon Thor of Urgonclaw and Prince Levandius. Now that the alliance is agreed upon, and the Emperor is dying, we will soon rectify his position in our circle. I do dislike his cloying affection for Panthara. I will eliminate him on those grounds alone. Come along, Xabral. We cannot leave Naloia alone too long with the remains of Ashur. She is also a hindrance. But we can do little about that for now."

Xabral slid down Koll's black robes and crawled along the cool ground. The gigantic cavern was lit with braziers but did little to brighten the deep shadows. "Once, this had been a sacred temple to *Her*—Obsydia the Bloodstone Queen. Light was never welcome in her hallowed altars. It's a shame this is not her tomb."

Koll looked around the ancient carvings of demons on the walls of the cave. Even a thousand years later, faint traces of blood from sacrifices long dead clung to the rocks. "Obsydia had many temples, many followers before her defeat. Ashur learned where her ancient palace was before he died. Unfortunately, he did not reveal its location to me before his death. When he is raised, we will learn of her secret tomb and resurrect her," Koll added with confidence.

Xabral raised his head, tongue flicking in and out. "But Panthara thinks we are raising Ashur for her. Once we have the secret, how will we get rid of Ashur so you may keep Panthara too? Ashur had become very powerful in the end. Plus, you are the one who wants to marry Panthara. Not me. My snake clan is more practical. Scorpion snakes do not mingle except for breeding. Humans are too stupid to realize that is a much more logical relationship. You also don't like sharing glory, Koll. I know you far too well to think you would bow before another again." Xabral coiled around a rock and laid his head on it to pout. "It's still too chilly down here, Koll. I am having difficulty staying awake. One would think a place associated with hell would be better heated."

"We are deep within the cave. Perhaps we could—"

"Hush!" Xabral hissed, lifting its large head off the stone, tongue flicking in and out. "I smell blood. *Fresh* blood." Xabral glided over the dust along the wall. His barbed tail stung a plump sand rat. It squealed once in pain, and then lay paralyzed from the venom. It would die soon, so Xabral swallowed the furry creature. It was still warm. Unlike most snakes, scorpion snakes swallow their food and digest it at a much faster rate. Xabral raised his red and black scaled body, feeling his prey move downward to his belly.

"Feel better?" Koll asked.

"A mere snack, Koll. I hate to see good food go on living."

"Go rest by one of the braziers. It will be warmer," Koll suggested.

"Where are you going?"

"To inform Naloia Panthara has been successful."

"I'll just stay here and digest," Xabral said.

"I thought you would say that," Koll replied.

Koll left his familiar to find Naloia, Panthara's mother. He knew where to find her of course and went to the main chamber where a circular altar of bloodstone was elevated about three feet off the ground. Some lost ancient magic kept it afloat. The patterns in these ancient tiles were elusive and mysterious. Koll had spent hours sitting on the altar, trying to copy the images that would appear and then vanish. Along the back of the wall, a semi-circle was tiered with carvings of cruel looking creatures—inhuman and mysterious. These images in the amber-colored rock were harsh and feral—ancient demons or gods? He did not know. But he desired that knowledge. Perhaps they were guardians of the temple that would leap to life with the correct words or were they just artistic replicas of Otherworld chaos that if seen in true form, would burn a mortal to ashes?

Floating upon the altar was a red crystal, the length of a man and throbbing with power. It was a mystical sarcophagus that held within it a body—Ashur's body. The scroll Koll had discovered a year ago finally bore fruit. The ashes and bones of his dead master had been resurrected. It had taken only days to remake the physical shell, but it had no life—not yet. It had no soul. The crystal's magic gave it form, but the ritual required to bring Ashur back would come later when the seven who killed him were gathered around it and offered in exchange. Kneeling before the crystal was Naloia, her bronze-colored eyes wet with joy.

Naloia turned to Koll, her face veiled. "He looks like an enchanted prince awaiting a kiss to wake him," she whispered. "If only I could do this rare magic, I would bring him to life now."

"He will wake, Princess Naloia. Panthara has contacted me. She has captured Cathal and Caliste. They sail now for Mowad."

"She took long enough to perform such a simple task. I have suffered so long without my beloved. My pain has been a knife in my heart, while my daughter has offered little balm to my grief." She touched the crystal tenderly. "Soon he will rise and take his crown as king of the world. I will sit at his feet once more."

"We all will," Koll assured her. "But we must still take care. We must proceed with caution. We have many enemies."

"I care nothing for that! I have slain many enemies to come to this moment. The blood of my family I willingly sacrificed to ensure my daughter Panthara became Queen of Mowad. Even my own father! I poisoned him with a smile on my lips. The Rashurkeen's coffers are bloated with my gold that paid for the extermination of any who would precede my daughter's rightful place as Queen. I did all this so we would have the resources and power to achieve the return of Ashur. If bringing Ashur back meant cutting out Panthara's beating heart, I would do it gladly!"

"Your daughter is devoted to our cause. Panthara has obeyed our wholesome instruction and guidance. She is Ashur's true daughter."

"But Ashur had another child by that bitch sorceress he abandoned me for. You said she was raised by Ashur's greatest enemy, Cathal. She could be a threat to our holy cause."

"Runa will not be a concern. She is a mere child. A fifteen-year-old girl whose talents are nowhere near as polished—or powerful—as Panthara's. Gorvanus has further ensured she will not be a hindrance. She will be executed for murder in Tiamet. Now that Panthara has captured the last of the circle, it is only a matter of time now."

Naloia turned away from Koll. "Time is cruel. It has teeth that rake my flesh. You remain the same for centuries, you and your whole sorcerous lot, while I suffer the bitter aging of mortal women. It has marked me cruelly. It is bad enough that I had to wait years for his return, a martyr to love! But now I fear I am no longer beautiful enough for his eyes."

"I will leave you to your…reflections," Koll said and bowed before leaving her to worship Ashur's shell. *You are insane,* Koll thought as he went to his private alcove. It was a bare and simple room. Upon a table of newly unearthed scrolls he discovered hidden in this ancient hold tantalized him. He unrolled them, touching them with the tenderness of a lover. They were from an age of dark dreams and dark magic. Upon each scroll of ancient parchment, free of decay, was a glowing bloodstone.

CHAPTER 14

Opaline guided them through the secret tunnels holding the small light crystal. The dim light did not provide ample illumination in the gloomy passages, so Runa used a light spell on Korun and Darcus' swords which helped them navigate. Darcus and Korun marched behind Opaline, swords drawn. Pol carried the unconscious Tarsicius, who still lived.

Mellypip rode on Runa's shoulder, proud of his assignment as lookout. Runa took care of the familiars, except for the sluggish sloth Buzzy. Hinkleburr Crowyn carried Buzzy, his head draped over his shoulder like a rag doll. Dabiro the badger carried Rosepetal the hedgehog on his back. Sanura padded along, unencumbered by the dark. Belwyn perched on Darcus' shoulder.

"Are you sure this passage opens up near the stables?" Darcus asked.

"Near enough," Opaline said. "I just hope the Ambassador's aides are successful."

Hinkleburr shifted Buzzy in his arms. "Young Broda and Talwyn are very persuasive. They are also very clever; else they wouldn't be working for me."

"I'm sure they are very bright boys," Darcus said. "But right now our lives depend on them." Darcus sneezed. "This damned dust is thick as fog in here. How much further, Princess?"

"Not long now," she said. "I just hope I didn't take a wrong turn."

"Wrong turn?" Belwyn exclaimed. "*Wrong turn!* Listen, Missy, our lives and those of our sorcerers are in peril, not to mention old royal butt here."

"Runa, would you smack the owl for me? I'm busy," Opaline said.

"I would, but he would smack back," Runa replied lightly. "I just hope Iona is all right."

"Iona's a resolute woman and also very clever," Opaline said. "Iona will put any guards and servants to sleep who might be roaming about. I'm concerned about Gorvanus, or whoever he is. He's still a threat. I just hope my maid Mira was able to reach the Imperial Warden."

Hinkleburr moaned. "Next time I will decline any offers of

noble rank my King decides to bestow upon me. Go south, he said. Make a new trade treaty with the Emperor of the Ivory Kingdoms. It's warm there! It never snows in the south; it is balmy warm in Tiamet. Make a profit for us and live in a palace! Ha!"

"Keep quiet!" Belwyn warned. "Else I'll peck you!"

"Be nice, boys," Darcus chastised them.

"We are here!" Opaline announced. Runa removed the light spell from the swords, and Opaline doused the glowing crystal inside her cloak.

Opaline pressed against the door. At last it opened, and the rush of fresh air was a welcomed change for everyone.

Mellypip breathed deeply. "Better. I don't like the stuffy tunnels."

Outside it was still raining but had calmed to a light drizzle. "I would bet my feathers this isn't a natural rain," Belwyn said, perching on Darcus' shoulder. "I smell sorcery afoot. All these storms during the dry season? I think not! That wench Panthara and Gorvanus are behind this. I'd love to give them a taste of my claws. Wouldn't be so pretty then, would they?"

"Is *he* always like this?" Opaline asked.

"Oh, this is a good day," Mellypip quipped, but bowed his head when Belwyn gave him a dirty look.

"Come on…move quickly," Darcus ordered.

They ran through an orchard of cherry trees and well-trimmed elegant bushes.

"The stables are close now," Opaline assured them.

After a few moments, they finally reached the long white stone buildings with red tile roofs. The shelter brought welcome relief from the rain.

The horses were restless and wild-eyed because of the turbulent weather. This unsettled Mellypip, but he decided to be brave. Even worse, the rain had not washed away the strong odor of offal and horses, Mellypip thought, holding his nose.

"I don't see anyone" Runa said. "Where are they?"

"We are here," the two young Dwarven aides said.

Hinkleburr jumped and turned around. He almost dropped Buzzy, who whined and opened his sleepy eyes. He put the disgruntled sloth on the ground. "Damn, don't scare me like that!" Hinkleburr puffed.

Broda grinned. "All the stablemen and guards are sleeping." He held up the little vial of Moonshade. "Thanks to this little seasoning that we added to their wine."

"Yes, they found it quite good," Talwyn added. "They love to drink good wine." He held up a bag of coins. "We also took their dice winnings."

Hinkleburr chuckled and slapped the two young men on the back. "Excellent work. We can use the money."

"Are you sure you want to come with us?" Darcus asked Hinkleburr. "You've already put yourself at risk for us."

Hinkleburr nodded. "Oh yes. This place is way too dangerous right now with renegade sorcerers and a traitorous prince prancing about. I think I'll take a holiday until the carnage and body counts are done. I also owe Cathal a few favors. He's an old friend, and I dislike people messing with my friends."

"I just hope my women are safe," Opaline said. "Ada is on her way to one of my friends in the city. Mira should reach Lord Rhudon soon. He has been the Imperial Warden since my father's coronation."

"But can he be trusted?" Darcus asked.

Opaline nodded. "Lord Rhudon is from one of the oldest and most noble families in the empire. I've known him since I was born. His honor is above reproach."

Darcus checked the four horses hitched to the long wagon. Pol and Korun laid Tarsicius in the back of the wagon and covered him with horse blankets. The familiars boarded the wagon quietly.

Opaline mounted the rickety wagon and sat in the front seat. "Let's get out of here," Opaline said, looking around nervously.

"I'm all for that," Runa agreed.

Runa gasped when an crossbow bolt struck her right side. The bolt knocked her backward to the straw covered ground.

Mellypip wailed. "Runa, oh Runa!" He ran to her as she moaned with pain.

"Runa!" Belwyn cried. He flew to her side. "No! No, no, no!" The owl rotated his head to see her assailant, Gorvanus, standing several feet away, backed by at least twenty Imperial Knights. Gorvanus lowered his crossbow and laughed. In the opposite entry of the stables, another group of knights also barred their way. "You're a dead man, Gorvanus!" Belwyn said coldly.

"Thought you could escape so easily?" Gorvanus asked smugly.

Darcus' scarred eye twitched. "Think you can live through the next five seconds?" Darcus marched towards him, oblivious to the blockade of guards that protected the sorcerer with swords and spears. Darcus howled a chilling battle cry and charged.

Gorvanus retreated behind the knights.

Crossbow bolts fired, but Darcus deflected them with his sword. The bolts bounced off the flat of his sword as Darcus swiftly moved forward. Enraged, he smashed the guard's faces with the thrust of his booted foot and fist. Blood splattered as he struck down one after another as he battled toward Gorvanus.

But Darcus was not alone.

Pol and Korun joined the fray swinging. Sanura shapeshifted into her panther form. Her roars were met with blood-curdling screams. Dabiro growled and leapt from the wagon. He rammed and bit anything in his path. Rosepetal rolled into a ball and shot quills at the advancing men.

The clashing of metal made Mellypip's head ache. He wept as he hovered next to Runa. Opaline knelt by Runa's side, holding her hand and trying to shield her from the fracas. The crossbow bolt pierced all the way through her side, the barbed tip exposed through her back. She was so pale and her blood so red.

Darcus cut a bloody path to Gorvanus, who cowered behind the knights. The sorcerer yelped and transformed into a falcon. He flew upwards out of Darcus' reach and laughed until he ran into Belwyn.

Belwyn confronted the falcon with sharp talons. "Now you are in my domain, Gorvanus."

Gorvanus screamed and tried to fly away. But his falcon form was no match for Belwyn. The owl pursued Gorvanus with vengeful determination. Blood-stained feathers mingled with the falling rain as they battled in the air.

Three guards dragged Opaline off Runa. She struggled and her chaotic sorcery erupted. Two of the men were tossed through the air like leaves. The third man punched Opaline in the face. She dropped unconscious next to Runa. Broda cracked a rake over the culprit's head. The soldier fell, and Hinkleburr added a few more blows to his skull for good measure. Hinkleburr and his aides then formed a protective circle around Runa and Opaline.

The bleeding Gorvanus, still in falcon form, escaped Belwyn's talons and spiraled down to the ground and shapeshifted into a rodent. Belwyn dove for him, but Gorvanus scurried into one of the mouse holes in the building. Belwyn cursed at his ruse with wild fury.

Then the sloth joined the fight. Buzzy lumbered out of the wagon. He took a deep breath, and then sped across the ground so fast a mere blur was all Mellypip saw. The lightning quick sloth attacked the knights with deep precise bites to their ankles. It drew their attention away from their opponents to leave them vulnerable.

Darcus was a force of unleashed wrath. He left a trail of blood and gore. His leather armor was smeared with crimson. Three more advancing knights tried to challenge him, but his intense rage and fearlessness frightened the warriors, and they fled.

Mellypip watched over Runa during the mayhem. He clung to her hand and bawled harshly, the tears hot and salty in his mouth. "Don't die, Runa," he begged. "Please, please don't die!"

Four knights charged the Dwarves. They were caught up in the scuffle except for one who loomed over Mellypip and Runa. The hard-faced warrior raised his sword to kill Runa. "No!" Mellypip wept. "Don't hurt her!" Mellypip began frothing at the mouth and his body pulsated with strange energy. He was so hot! The combined feelings of love, protection, and fear exploded. Just as the sword descended, Mellypip metamorphosed into an enormous creature with huge dripping fangs and long razor-sharp claws. As large as a grizzly bear, Mellypip felt his fuzzy head bump the ceiling as he roared. He ripped the sword from the killer's stunned grip. The knight blanched with terror and ran away! Overcome by a wave of nausea and dizziness, Mellypip could not even enjoy his heroic triumph.

"Uh-oh, I think Mellypip found his special ability," Belwyn said with dismay. "Oh, dear…this is not good. It's too early!"

The moment of dire need passed and Mellypip shapeshifted to his own small size. The strain of the internal magic exhausted Mellypip, and he tumbled over, his little heart beating rapidly.

Two white ravens landed in the midst of the turmoil. Iona transformed into her human form. Without fear she approached the well-armed men with nothing but her staff and familiar.

"You're a bold wench!" remarked one, swinging his sword.

"I see a bold fool," Iona replied.

"She's a necromancer! See her white raven! Get away from her, lest death touch you," one cried fearfully.

"Yes, I am a Necromancer."

The warriors backed away from her, but her staff sprayed a wave of dark blue sorcery and the remaining soldiers passed out.

Hinkleburr and Talwyn helped a dazed Opaline to stand. Her eye was already swelling and bruised.

"Where the hell have you been?" Darcus asked Iona as he

rushed to Runa.

"Busier than I anticipated," she said, lowering her staff. "The entire Imperial Guard and several mercenaries have been hunting for you. I have left a trail of sleeping bodies everywhere. I'm so sorry I did not come in time to save Runa. How badly is she hurt?"

"I'm not dead yet," Runa groaned weakly.

Belwyn winged to Runa's side. "Runa, it's going to be all right," he said tenderly. "Just hold on!"

Darcus examined Runa and shook his head. "It's too dangerous to pull that bolt out. She could bleed to death. We need to get her somewhere safe." He stroked her hair, concern knotting his features. "Runa, can you hear me?" he asked.

"I...can hear. Hurts though," Runa whispered weakly.

"I know," Darcus said softly. "Try to stay awake. I know it's bad, but I swear I'll make it better."

"Poor Melly..." Runa said faintly, "...is he—"

"I'm here!" Mellypip said quickly.

"My brave little wampu," she whispered.

"We won't be able to get her to the Abbey in time," Opaline said in a worried voice. "We can't trust anyone here."

"Not if I have anything to say about it," Darcus said, lifting Runa in his arms. He marched to another stable in the next row.

"Darcus, what are you doing?" Belwyn asked. They all followed him, except for Broda and Buzzy who stayed with the sleeping Emperor.

"We need a speedy solution. I know where to get it," Darcus said as he carried Runa to the enclosure where the gryphon was kept.

The gryphon huddled in the rear of its stable, its black feathers shaking with terror. "I hear swords and smell blood," the gryphon cried, tears welling in its large eyes. "I'm scared."

"We won't hurt you, Rono," Opaline assured him. "Please calm down. We need you to help us." Opaline opened the gate and led him out, patting his head with affection.

"Rono, yes please help us Rono!" Mellypip cried.

"Furry little familiar. I remember you. Nice to me. Been so lonely here. Hemio not visit me," Rono sighed.

"Hemio has gone away for a long, long time," Opaline explained. "But we will take care of you now. Isn't that nice?"

The gryphon sniffled and looked at Darcus with Runa in his arms. "Pretty sorceress girl hurt?" Rono asked sadly.

"Yes. We need you to fly us to Araema Abbey so Runa can get help," Darcus said gently.

"I can fly! Will it save nice girl?" Rono asked.

"I hope so," Darcus said.

"I will fly fast," Rono nodded, stretching out his wings. "I'll help pretty magic girl."

"Get a rope and tie Runa to me," Darcus ordered as he mounted the gryphon. "I'll need one hand to steer. Korun, you get word to my men at the camp. Pol, guard the others on their way to the Abbey."

"Yes, sir," Pol and Korun answered in unison, bringing some rope.

Pol hesitated. "Have you ever ridden a gryphon before, sir?" he asked Darcus.

"There's a first time for everything," Darcus said.

Pol and Korun bound Runa's body to Darcus with a thick length of rope. Opaline brought a blanket and wrapped Runa with it. Darcus cradled her in one arm and made sure she was secure.

"Can I come too?" Mellypip begged.

"I'm sorry, but I can't watch over you, little one," Darcus said gently. "We must think of Runa first. I'll take good care of her, Mellypip. I promise. I'll see you at the Abbey."

"Fly now?" Rono asked.

Darcus took the reins. "Fly like hell!" he shouted.

The gryphon unfolded his wide wings and took a few bounding strides; then Rono took swift flight across the sky. Within a few breaths, they were out of sight.

Mellypip wiped his face with his paws. His head ached and his tummy was in knots, from both the tragedy of Runa's injury and what he had brought forth during that time of terror when Runa's life was threatened.

Belwyn wrapped his wing around him. "Are you all right, Furball?"

Mellypip leaned against Belwyn and sobbed. Then he turned away, sick from too much adventure.

~ * ~

Panthara strolled the decks, her deep blue cloak protecting her from the light rainfall. She carried Azmadu in her arms. "Soon we will be home, Azmadu. The desert sun will warm us, and all this tragedy will be behind us," she said soothingly.

"Miss home," Azmadu agreed. "I don't like sailing. I miss my heated rock...I miss my eye."

"My poor sweet," she cooed. "I will let you choose from my collection of jewels. Perhaps a ruby might be becoming?"

Azmadu was busy imagining himself with bright gems in place of his missing eye until a clumsy seagull interrupted his reverie by landing on the deck before them. Azmadu sniffed magic in the air. The bird shimmered into Gorvanus. He was bloody and bruised. Good. He didn't like the oafish sorcerer. Azmadu sensed Panthara's aggravation when he appeared. She got *that* angry look in her eyes.

"Beloved Panthara, are you not happy to see me?" Gorvanus asked.

"You are a mess," she replied. "What are you doing here?"

Gorvanus shrugged. "Well, I just thought I would advise you of what's happening."

Panthara turned away. "There are other ways to contact me, Gorvanus! You're a sorcerer! Instead of chasing me you should be making sure the Emperor is dead and that mousy sorceress Runa is dead!"

"Oh, but I have news that will make your heart sing!" Gorvanus said. He removed something from his pocket. It was silver and bright. "This should make you happy," he said.

"I possess chests of jewelry, Gorvanus," Panthara retorted impatiently. "Please, get to the point!"

"This is Runa's locket. You said you wanted to know when she was dead." He dangled the locket.

"Runa was executed?" Panthara asked excitedly.

"Uh...no, not exactly. But she was shot with my own crossbow bolt when she tried to escape. I assure you she is not only dead, but she suffered greatly in the process."

Panthara nodded. "That does please me. What about the Emperor Tarsicius?"

"He is breathing his last breath."

"Good. Now go back and make sure he actually dies!"

"Where is Cathal?" Gorvanus asked.

"He is caged in the lower decks. Why?"

"I just thought a little salt on the wound might add the right seasoning." Gorvanus said with a shrug.

"Very well," she said. "Follow me."

"He is caged and bound with a sorcerer lock?" Gorvanus

inquired nervously.

"Of course," Panthara replied impatiently.

"I don't like it down there!" Azmadu said with a grunt.

"It's all right, my precious," she said, patting him affectionately. *Let's just give him what he wants for the moment. Then I can send him away.*

Gorvanus followed them down to the prisons that held Cathal and Caliste. The guards kneeled when Panthara appeared.

"Cathal, I have a visitor for you," Panthara said.

"Well, what do you want?" Cathal said gruffly.

Gorvanus showed Cathal the silver locket. For a terrible moment Cathal was silent. Gorvanus broke the tension. "You should recognize it. It has a picture of your wife and daughter. Your granddaughter Runa wore it. The writing on it is Ilyrran, I believe."

"I can't believe you know how to read," Cathal said.

Azmadu snickered, but then stopped when Gorvanus gave him a dirty look.

Gorvanus frowned. "I'm sure Panthara informed you of Runa's plight. Well, the foolish girl tried to escape. I was compelled to punish her. A crossbow bolt can be quite painful I understand. She's dead, sorcerer. I was very—"

A scream of rage split Azmadu's ears. Cathal's fury shattered his manacles.

Caliste gripped the bars. "Cathal! No!" she cried.

Gorvanus tripped and fell as he backed away. "You can't hurt me," he stammered. "You can't do magic!"

Panthara fled, crying for help. Azmadu took refuge in the ceiling.

Cathal ripped the cage door from its hinges. The guards tried to block his way, but the sorcerer's strength tossed them aside easily. Frantic, Gorvanus began throwing beams of sorcery at Cathal, but they vaporized. It was a useless gesture since the sorcerer lock around his neck evaporated all magic that touched him. Cathal pursued Gorvanus with the rage of a god. Gorvanus squirmed like a worm trying to climb the stairs. Cathal knocked the guards out with his fists and snatched up one of their swords. He seized the squealing Gorvanus by the ankle and dragged him down the steps. Cathal grabbed him by the hair and rammed his face into the wooden steps. Splinters and blood splattered as Gorvanus cried for help. Cathal swung the sword down. Gorvanus managed to turn away, the blade grazing his cheek. He kicked Cathal hard in the face.

Cathal was stunned only briefly, but it allowed Gorvanus to

scurry up the stairs. Cathal bounded after him just as Gorvanus reached the open decks. Azmadu followed, flying a safe distance above. Cathal grabbed Gorvanus by the throat and pitched him to the deck. He beat Gorvanus' face into oatmeal. The feeble smoking beams of sorcery Gorvanus attempted dribbled off Cathal. Gorvanus' screams dissolved into pathetic, gurgled whimpers. Several soldiers pounced on the maddened sorcerer. One brought down the heavy hilt of his sword on Cathal's head. The sorcerer crumbled, unconscious and bleeding at last.

Gorvanus lay there, his face a messy pulp, gasping for breath and shaking. He pushed Cathal's limp body off of him, groaning with the effort.

Panthara stood over him, tapping her foot. "You are a fool!" Panthara said harshly. She turned to the guards and pointed at Cathal. "Take him back down. Make sure he's restrained. I don't care if it requires every inch of chain and rope we have!"

"Yes, Your majesty," they replied, and dragged Cathal away.

"That could have gone better," Gorvanus said weakly. He leaned over and spat out two teeth.

"Speaking of gone…your presence is a liability now. Leave the ship, Gorvanus. Find another ride to Mowad for the ritual. Make sure we have the allegiance of Levandius and the Emperor dies!"

"But beloved!" Gorvanus cried.

Panthara turned and added with disdain. "And one more thing, Gorvanus…you scream like a girl."

As she walked away, Azmadu stuck his little tongue out at him before they disappeared into Panthara's private cabin.

~ * ~

Zhelon Thor surveyed the damage to the Emperor's private suite when he stepped into the chamber. The Emperor was gone and the doors blasted into pieces. A muffled sound came from one of the closet doors and Zhelon opened it to discover Prince Levandius tied up and gagged. Zhelon knelt and sighed impatiently. "I was wondering where you were?" He untied him and removed the gag so he could speak.

"Damn, I thought I would die in here," Levandius said hoarsely. "Bring me wine." Zhelon Thor brought him the decanter and Levandius gulped and wiped his mouth. "My sister did this—and her damned sorcerous friends. They took my father away."

"Pity. If your father lives, you will be in a rather difficult position, Prince Levandius. I do, however, have a small gift for you." Zhelon motioned to a waiting guard and a young woman was dragged in. "Do you recognize her?"

Levandius looked at her for a moment. "That's Mira, one of Opaline's maids!"

Zhelon forced her to her knees. "She carried a letter for the Warden. My spies stopped her before she reached him."

"I'm too tired for this! Where is Priem?"

"He is pursuing your enemies, I believe. There are several dead soldiers by the stables and several sleeping ones in the palace. Your enemies have been quite efficient. Too efficient."

"Do you know where they took my father?" Levandius asked groggily.

"No. But we need to find out soon." Zhelon said.

"Interrogate the girl, but be quick about it. Kill her when you're done with her. I need to change my clothes. Meet me in my chambers in an hour," Levandius said as he left the room.

"As you wish," Zhelon said. He ran his finger along Mira's dark hair and down her smooth cheek. "She is a pretty morsel. Shame it's not time for the sacrificial rites. She would be an excellent offering to *Her*. Still, death can be enjoyable even without the sacred mass."

"Be careful about what god you mention here. Until we are in power, our devotion to Obsydia must be a secret."

Mira cried out as Zhelon pulled back her head, exposing her throat. He teasingly ran his dagger along her exposed skin. "Now my dear, tell me what you know."

CHAPTER 15

Darcus flew eastward until he recognized the well-known Abbey entrance below, marked by a simple arch of twisted green boughs. The large two-level stone building in dusty gray rose amid lush gardens and old trees. A few other smaller buildings and Araema's temple surrounded it. Darcus held Runa close. "We're here, Runa."

She moaned and looked up at him with glassy eyes. "Where did I go?"

"It's all right," he whispered. He tugged on the reins. "Rono, we need to land here. Set down carefully though. She's very fragile."

"Yes, Darcus," Rono responded and dipped low in the sky. "I'll be gentle for Runa. How is she?"

"Still with us," he replied cautiously, hiding his concern. Her blanket was soaked with blood, and she shivered from shock.

The gryphon swept across the lawns gently, until he hovered a few inches above earth, and then touched ground and slowed to a gentle trot. Several nuns ran out to greet them.

"Darcus! How nice of you to visit us!"

"Is that a gryphon?"

"How wonderful!" they chattered as they approached. They reminded Darcus of fluttering bluebirds in their light blue robes and veils. Their excited voices dimmed to solemn murmurs and gasps when they saw Runa in his arms.

"Fetch Mother Eshra, quickly," Darcus said.

A few ran inside the Abbey to do his bidding. Darcus held Runa as he swung his legs over and dismounted Rono. His sister Eshra appeared in the doorway; a dignified, older woman in a white turban holding a staff of carved oak in her hand. Her blue robes were a darker shade than the other sisters. When she saw Runa in his arms, she hiked up her skirts and ran towards him.

"Sister, I need your help," he said simply.

Eshra's hand touched Runa's pale cheek. "Dear heavens. Inside —quickly!" She spoke in quick, decisive tones to the circle of sisters. "Bring my medicine bag, bandages, and hot water."

"Yes, Mother," one of the sisters bowed and ran to obey her commands.

She pointed to two wide-eyed nuns. "Take care of the poor gryphon," she ordered. "Take him to the stables and make sure he is fed and tended to."

"What do gryphons eat?" a nun asked apprehensively.

"They eat anything," Darcus said.

Rono sniffed the shy nun's hand and gazed at her with sorrowful eyes. She relaxed and stroked his head. The gryphon followed them to the stables, but looked back forlornly. "Runa be healed?" he asked, his inky wings drooping.

"She will be soon, Rono," Darcus said in a choked voice, marching away. "The sisters are kind. They'll take care of you," he called over his shoulder.

Eshra guided Darcus into the soft-lit halls of the Abbey. She opened the dark wooden door to a tiny cell with plain, white-washed walls, a small table and a bed. "Put her on the bed, Darcus. What happened to this poor child?" She laid her staff against the wall and examined her. "Who did this vile thing?"

"It's a long story, Eshra. Vile doesn't even begin to cover it."

"I look forward to hearing it—later. We must work quickly to save her."

Darcus stroked Runa's forehead. "There are others coming too. We all need sanctuary. And the Emperor is with them."

"You never did do anything small, Darcus," she remarked. "Even as a boy your exploits were mythic."

Three nuns entered the room with Eshra's medicine satchel, a bucket of water, and a stack of towels. More lamps were brought in to provide brighter light by which to work. Eshra opened her medicine bag and took out several vials and little bags of powder. She uncorked a vial of yellow liquid and added a few drops of it to a cup of water. The nuns organized the sick room with silent efficiency.

"Lift her up so she can drink this," Eshra said. "This will ease her pain and help her to sleep. What is her name?"

"Runa," Darcus replied. He held Runa up while Eshra put the cup to her lips.

"Drink this Runa," she said. "It will help, my child."

Runa regained consciousness. She gazed at Eshra and Darcus. "Where am I?" she said. "Where's Grandpa?"

"You're safe now," Darcus said fervently.

She sipped the drink and coughed. "Bitter," she said. When Eshra was satisfied Runa had drunk enough, she nodded, and he laid her down. She peeled back the bloodstained blanket and removed it.

"Extracting the crossbow bolt from her body, even with the help of my drugs, is going to be excruciating."

"How can I help?" Darcus asked.

"Scrub your hands and hold her down firmly," Eshra said, rolling up her sleeves.

~ * ~

Mellypip did not feel the warmth of the fading sun. Hinkleburr held him in his lap, petting him and consoling him with kind words. The strenuous journey over the rough back roads jarred every bone in his body. The wagon got stuck in the mud three times and took the combined efforts of everyone, even Opaline, to get them moving again. They were all muddy, exhausted—and worried about Runa.

"Is every inch of this road jagged with stray rocks and holes?" Belwyn complained.

"We are taking the back trails. It's safer," Opaline said. "How's my father?"

"Still breathing, and he looks less a corpse," Hinkleburr said. "He actually has some color."

The badger Dabiro hung his head over the side of the wagon, cursing a great deal. "Can't these hacks move any quicker?" he rumbled. "Buzzy can move faster."

"Stop jabbering," Rosepetal said. "Runa is hurt, and all you do is whine." The hedgehog had finally calmed down after a ong bout of hiccups.

"That son of a demon is going to pay for what he did to our girl," Dabiro groused.

Only the sloth seemed unperturbed by the chaos. He sat against the side of the wagon in a meditative posture.

On the surface, Belwyn looked calm, but Mellypip knew better. Anger lit Belwyn's round golden eyes. Mellypip understood that since he was angry too.

"How much further?" Sanura asked sharply, her tail swishing.

"Ten more miles," Opaline answered.

"Don't worry, Mellypip," Hinkleburr comforted him. "Captain Darcus will save Runa. And gryphons are very speedy creatures in the air."

"Too bad they're slow as molasses on the ground," Dabiro said with a grunt.

Mellypip fumed a moment, then turned to the badger. "That's not nice. Rono is gentle and sweet. He can't help it if he isn't smart. Being smart sure hasn't helped your disposition cranky butt!"

"The fuzzy runt is developing a pair of—"

"That's enough!" Belwyn commanded and gave Dabiro a sharp peck on his rump.

"Ouch!" Dabiro shouted.

"Shut up and leave Furball alone," Belwyn said impatiently.

Dabiro growled a moment, then lowered his head and mumbled gruffly, "I'm sorry."

"How did you shoot quills like that?" Mellypip asked Rosepetal. "Hedgehogs can't do that, though you are pointy and dangerous to touch."

The hedgehog turned her delicate little nose toward him and sniffed. "Well, it's my special magical ability—well, one of them. I have another. My sorcerer Ulan is better at fighting than I am. He is very rugged, tall, and his skin is a beautiful black—just like Caliste. I prefer magic and reading."

The badger snorted and curled up in the wagon next to the sleeping Emperor. Mellypip wondered how a man who so despised magic would feel about sorcerers and familiars saving him? Opaline was a concern too, now that she had so revealed herself as a sorceress. What would happen to her?

"I hope they don't track us somehow," Sanura said in a worried voice.

"Iona said she would watch the palace and fly to warn us of any danger." Opaline said. "If Korun can reach the legions safely, we'll have more protection. Until then it's just us."

"*Us* is just fine, Missy," Belwyn said. "I trust us. I'm having issues with trusting anyone else of late."

Mellypip leaned against Hinkleburr, wishing they could just magically be at the Abbey now. He did not even realize he had dozed off, until Belwyn shook him awake.

"We're here!" Belwyn said in a hushed voice.

Mellypip rubbed his eyes. "It's dark out," he said.

"It's after midnight," Belwyn said. "Come on, Furball."

Darcus rushed out to meet them. He looked worn out, but the first thing out of his mouth was, "Runa's going to be fine. She has a fever right now, but Eshra says that's normal. Follow me. Rooms have been prepared for all of you. Pol, please carry the Emperor to his room. One of the sisters will show you where to take him."

"Yes, sir," Pol said. He lifted Tarsicius out of the wagon.

"Everyone else, follow me," Darcus said.

There was a collective sigh of relief from everyone. Mellypip felt like a horrible black cloud had been lifted off his heart.

"Oh Darcus, I'm so relieved!" Opaline said with tears in her eyes.

"Great news indeed, people," Hinkleburr said jovially, the spring restored to his step. "A fit occasion to tip a glass of wine in celebration. They do have wine here, don't they?" he whispered to Mellypip. He cradled Mellypip in the crook of his arm and jumped down from the buckboard.

Anxious, they followed Darcus. Even the lethargic Buzzy moved at a fast clip. Inside the Abbey, the austere plainness nevertheless had a warm feeling of home which Mellypip found very comforting. Women in matching blue robes and veils gathered around them when they entered.

"How come all the ladies dress alike?" Mellypip asked quietly.

"They are nuns. They devote their lives to charity and the religious ideal of monastic life. Their patron goddess is Araema." Darcus replied.

Pol carried Tarsicius upstairs, guided by one of the nuns holding a lamp. Darcus led them down the hall with deep-toned wood trim and spotless plain walls.

A young nun sat outside a room on a simple wooden stool. She smiled when Darcus appeared. "I'll tell the Abbess you're here," she said. She opened the door and after a few hushed whispers, she waved them inside. "You can only stay a moment," she advised.

Within the small simple room Runa lay pale and fevered in the narrow bed. Belwyn flew to the bedpost. "How is she?" he asked.

An imposing woman with wise hazel eyes looked up at them. "Fevered, but I have given her willow bark for it. I'm glad you arrived safely," she said. She turned to the owl. "You must be Belwyn."

"Yes, Abbess, I am." Belwyn nodded. "Thank you for helping Runa," he said with respect.

She looked at Opaline and inclined her head. "Welcome, Princess Opaline. It's good to see you again, though the reasons are not. Darcus has told me everything." She wrung out a cloth and placed it on Runa's head.

"Thank you, Mother Eshra," Opaline said softly.

"You must be Runa's familiar," Eshra said to Mellypip.

Mellypip nodded nervously, chewing his tail. Eshra picked him up and carried him to Runa's side. "The owl and wampu may stay. Their presence will be a comfort to the child since they are family. She needs her rest, so go."

"We're all family here," Opaline remarked sincerely.

"You can take turns sitting with her tomorrow, when her fever breaks. Now go get some food in your bellies and sleep. You all look exhausted. Sister Dian will lead you to the bath house first. You all need a good wash."

"But Eshra!" Darcus protested.

"Runa is safe in my care, Darcus. The rest of you go—now. That's an order." Eshra's tone brooked no argument.

The others were directed out the door by Eshra's firm hand.

Belwyn remained on the bedpost, watching Runa. Mellypip curled into a ball above her head, just like he did at their old tree house, a home he missed now more than ever. After untold hours of vigilant watching, Mellypip succumbed to sleep. Runa's fevered dreams entwined with Mellypip's. They entered a strange new land…

Runa and Mellypip fled as dark forces pursued them. Breathless and frightened, they looked back. A large shaggy troll chased them, grunting and slobbering with rage. They stepped across a shimmering border into a wild, exotic forest. The troll howled in the distance, unable to cross from the bleak lands to this haven. Runa and Mellypip wandered the ethereal woodland dusted by falling blossoms and the leaves. Strange folk appeared above them on flying deer. Ilyrrans with pointed ears and eyes bright as crystal. Runa and Mellypip chased them through the mystical woods.

"Wait," she cried as they flew overhead. The forest was full of shadows now. They came to an ancient willow oak ringed with red and white toadstools that glimmered. A red panther crouched high in the old tree. He looked down upon them, but Runa and Mellypip felt no fear. Runa reached up to the great cat. His roar shattered the shadows.

Runa and Mellypip snapped out of their uneasy sleep together. He rubbed his eyes, and cried happily, "Runa, you're awake! I had funny dreams, but no scary crystals and black fire. I dreamed we were in a forest. Oh, there was a troll though."

"Me too. There was a red panther also. But I wasn't afraid."

Belwyn was perched on the bedpost at the end of the bed and sighed with relief. "Welcome back, Runa. Striker was a red panther," Belwyn said. "Perhaps you dreamed of him?"

"I don't know. I remember you telling me about Striker and how he saved me from Ashur." Runa stirred and tried to move. "Ouch," she winced painfully.

"Don't move," Darcus said gently, sitting next to the bed. He leaned over and brushed her cheek with his callused hand. He had bathed and shaved, and smelled of soap. "We got the crossbow bolt out and my sister says no internal organs were injured, but you need to heal."

"Thank you, Darcus. Where are we?" she asked hazily.

"We are in a *holy place,*" Mellypip whispered with reverence. "Darcus' sister is a *holy woman.* She took care of you. So you have lots of holy blessings."

"We're at Araema Abbey," Darcus said with a laugh. "You gave us quite a scare, Runa, but fought like a good soldier."

"Thanks," she whispered.

Dabiro and Buzzy popped up at the foot of the bed. Sanura was curled up at the end of the bed, and Rosepetal chirped from the low table.

"Hi everyone," Runa said weakly.

"We're glad you're better," Dabiro said.

"You gave us quite a fright," Buzzy agreed.

Darcus patted her hand. "I'll fetch my sister. Don't even try to get out of bed."

She smiled faintly. "Yes, Darcus."

Darcus turned to the familiars. "Let's give Runa a moment. Keep an eye on her, boys," he directed to Belwyn and Mellypip. The other familiars followed him out of the room with some firm coaxing.

After they left, Runa looked around the room. "How long have I been out, Melly?"

"Oh, forever…since yesterday. You had a fever and Abbey Eshra gave you stitches and everything."

Runa laughed and then winced again. "Oh, blast," she whimpered. "I think she's called Abbess, Melly. My poor baby, are you okay? No one else was hurt?"

Belwyn nodded. "Just some scrapes and bruises. That moron Gorvanus is the culprit who shot you. I tore him up a bit, but the scum for magic got away."

"You missed lots of battle," Mellypip said. "Darcus slew many bad knights. Belwyn was hooting mad when Gorvanus escaped. And I turned into a big wampu and scared someone who tried to hurt you. It was very scary. Then I threw up. Now Belwyn is upset about that too cause he says I did it too young."

"I'm doomed," Belwyn groaned.

"I missed all that?" Runa said, amazed.

Mellypip nodded excitedly. "Oh, and Rono is here too! He flew you and Darcus to the Abbey. We rescued the Emperor too, and he's finally awake. He's mad too. Opaline is with him now. She was sitting with you earlier. Everyone took turns sitting with you, after they all had a bath and something to eat. Eshra insisted on the bath. Do you want some breakfast? You need to build up your strength," he said. He fluffed her pillow and covered her up with the blanket.

Abbess Eshra entered the room carrying a tray laden with broth and tea for Runa, and a dish of sliced apples, nuts and bread for Mellypip and Belwyn.

"No meat?" Belwyn inquired in a disappointed voice.

"I'm sorry. But we are vegetarians here, Belwyn. Our barn, however, has rats."

"Big ones?" Belwyn asked hopefully.

"Yes," she nodded and set the tray on the table. "Our barn cats are sorely outnumbered, I'm afraid. Would you be so kind?"

"Well, I am a bit peckish," Belwyn agreed.

"Go on, Belwyn," Runa encouraged. "You need to keep your strength up. You can check on Rono. You could pretend the rats are Gorvanus. It will give you an edge."

"If you'll excuse me ladies, I'll be back shortly," he said, and winged out of the room.

Eshra sighed and looked at Runa with amused eyes. "The familiars are a very devoted group and love you. They are also stubborn and refused to stay out of your room all night. That owl opens doors with his magic!"

"Belwyn is a bit…stubborn," Runa agreed.

"I finally gave up," Eshra sighed. "Opaline and Hinkleburr also checked on you. You are lucky to have such good friends."

"I am lucky, but my Grandfather and Caliste are in danger. We must—"

"Hush. I forbid any talk of adventures," Eshra commanded. "When you can stand on your own two feet without wobbling or bending over in pain, you may resume your dangerous hobbies. Until then, you are under my care," Eshra said firmly. "How's the pain, dear?"

"My side hurts, but that's to be expected." Runa said. "I don't think I'll be taking up archery anytime soon."

"A sensible plan," Eshra said. She placed a napkin around Runa's neck and sat next to her. She began to spoon broth to her.

"Aren't you hungry, Melly?" Runa asked between mouthfuls.

"Nope. Gotta take care of you first," Mellypip insisted.

"It must be wonderful to be magical?" Eshra commented.

"It is, but sometimes there is a price," Runa replied.

"There is always a price, Runa. Nothing in life is free. But I believe good must overcome evil. Sometimes fighting is necessary, because there is evil in the world. The Book of Eternals shows us that. But our way is the way of peace. Not all of us need to fight."

"Darcus is a good fighter," Runa said.

"Yes, my younger brother has always been a warrior. Even when we were small, though he was the youngest, he took care of us. It's in his blood. Though he claims he wants to retire from the legions, he will not put his sword down for long. It's in his blood."

"How is Opaline? Is she with her father?"

Eshra nodded and set the bowl down. "She is paying a price of her own. The Emperor despises magic as you know. Though she has risked her life to save him, I fear what he will do now that she is revealed as a sorceress."

"Poor Opaline, what she must be going through now," Runa said.

Mellypip sighed. "It's sad. Somehow I don't think a good breakfast is going to help Opaline. What do you think the Emperor's going to do?"

"I don't know, Melly," Runa answered. "I'm too afraid to think about it."

~ * ~

Opaline sat with her head bowed. "I'm sorry, Father."

Tarsicius paced the small room, his color and energy had been magically restored thanks to the potion that Iona gave him. But he was too furious to be grateful.

"My son is a traitor! My only son!" Tarsicius raged.

"Not your only son!" Opaline corrected him.

"Taran is dead to me, as you must be now," Tarsicius said bleakly. "Now my only heir has betrayed me! Me! When I was fading from the poisons he has fed me for months, I heard him taunt me as I lay at death's door! He gloated about it. My mind heard him, but I was unable to cry out my pain. Priem was at his side, my most trusted knight. It is no surprise the villain turns out to be a sorcerer."

Opaline burst into tears. "But Father, I only kept my sorcery a secret to help you. Levandius, your precious Levandius, has become a drug addict and traitor! How long could your great empire survive with such a ruler? He was so greedy for power, Levandius tried to assassinate you for the crown. He is no mage, but his treachery is no surprise to me! But sorcery also saved you too! Cathal and Iona risked their lives to get you that potion; though staying in Tiamet put them at deadly risk. Cathal and Caliste are prisoners now, doomed to who knows what fate!"

"Opaline, I regret what I must do. You have been a good daughter. But from this day forward you are dead to me...and all here. You will have a royal funeral, like I did for your mother and brother. The empty coffin covered with flowers will be placed in the royal necropolis. I will not attempt to keep you in a secret prison like I tried with your mother and brother. They escaped with the help of their sorcerous friends. I have done nothing because they keep silent about their true fates and live in quiet exile. Accept that voluntary exile. Leave the Ivory Kingdoms forever. Your mother and brother must miss you. That is the only clemency I can offer. It's my gift for saving my life, Opaline."

"How is exile a gift, Father? Those that have truly loved you have all been rejected on the prejudice of magic."

"No one can be of sorcerous blood and be in line for the throne, Opaline. That is the law of my kingdom."

"We never wanted your crown," Opaline cried passionately. "Just your love, but there can be no room for love when a crown is at stake." She wiped her eyes, composed herself and walked to the door. She turned and curtsied deeply. "Farewell, Emperor Tarsicius," she said formally. "I will leave with Runa and the others to help search for her family. After all, they are my own kind, are they not?"

Before he could reply, she fled quietly, leaving him alone as he commanded.

CHAPTER 16

The temple of Rygon burned with crimson light from hundreds of candles ensconced in red glass. Feeble and bleeding, Gorvanus leaned against the stone wall. His body and face throbbed with pain, and he was sure his ribs were broken. His energies were further depleted by the effort it took to shapeshift into a bird again to fly back to Tiamet after Panthara banished him.

Sullen and humiliated, he regretted losing the silver locket during the fight on the ship with Cathal. Gorvanus hated Cathal. His stature in the mage world was legendary. Mage and mortal alike still revered him. No one ever spoke of Gorvanus with such admiration. Gorvanus was the sorcerer without a familiar because they would not bond with him. He envied Cathal's status for years. He wanted him to suffer. Gorvanus rejoiced when he killed Runa because it would bring him great pain. Well, he hoped she was dead. Surely, the stupid girl could not have survived!

Zhelon Thor interrupted his thoughts. He walked with solemn grace; black robes sweeping the floor and long blonde hair framing his boyish face. His golden beauty contrasted with his savage reputation. Gorvanus bowed as he approached.

Zhelon looked him up and down for a moment. "What happened to you?" he asked.

"Cathal escaped his chains on Panthara's ship. It took a dozen guards to restrain him. I delivered the news of his granddaughter's death. It...upset him."

"Cathal is still contained, isn't he?" Zhelon asked sharply.

Gorvanus wiped his face with a bloody rag. "He is, fear not. How bad do I look?"

"Close your eyes before you bleed to death," Zhelon remarked and turned away. "Follow me."

Gorvanus spat blood into a kerchief and limped after him, every step an agony. It was an eternity down the long, narrow nave toward the altar that reeked of incense and blood. The large circular shield stamped with Rygon's warlike countenance was on a wall behind it. The metal shield was ebonite, that rare black precious stone that rivaled gold for wealth. Thirty feet high and as wide, it seemed to glare down at its congregation with hungry demands for battle and sacrifice. He followed Zhelon through an oculus to the private chamber of Tiamet's High Priest of Rygon, Azrul. The dark stone walls were decorated with more masks of Rygon, and another face worshipped here—Obsydia the Immortal, daughter of Ahridum and great Queen of the Bloodstone Age.

Zhelon bowed to Azrul and stood at his side. Decades of remorseless sacrifice to Rygon marked Azrul. The dark eyes were like black stones, seasoned by the bloody rites Azrul led with devoted vigilance.

Levandius lounged on a couch smoking dream herbs through a water pipe. His right eye was swollen and bruised. He exhaled the strong-smelling smoke then glanced up with lazy eyes. "You've been truant, Gorvanus…or do you still require the facade of Priem?"

"I am as Your Majesty wishes," Gorvanus said.

"I like the sound of that," Levandius said languidly. "*Your Majesty*. I am the new Emperor; at least I will be once I find my father and kill him if your magical poison has not done its work. This debacle with my sister has caused me trouble, Gorvanus. Now Opaline has spirited my father away." Levandius breathed in more smoke and the pungent smell made Gorvanus lightheaded. Levandius exhaled. "Why is that? How could she possibly escape when you had scores of knights under your command?"

"I tried, Your Majesty," Gorvanus stammered. "But I was overcome by forces—"

"Not good enough!" Levandius screamed and kicked over the water pipe. The angry prince grabbed Gorvanus by the ears and pinned him to the wall. The Prince's bloodshot eyes were enraged. "You had over fifty knights! They had what? A trivial renegade group hampered by a comatose Emperor, two teenage girls, and some dwarfs! How were they able to escape you, Sorcerer? Now we have to eliminate them. I planned on murdering my deceitful, sorcerous sister eventually. But now my timing is ruined!"

Gorvanus raised his hands to fend off Levandius' assault. "Opaline will suffer. I assure you now that—"

"I waited a long time to have my revenge on Opaline," Levandius said hotly. "I managed to expose her mother and brother as sorcerers, but she kept eluding me. She always tested negative when the mages examined her."

"Well, she wore a ring of sorcerer bane," Gorvanus said. "I

found that out the hard way. I made the mistake of putting it on after I first apprehended her in the dungeon."

"And why did you do such an idiot thing? "Did it shine pretty and bright?" Levandius sneered.

Embarrassed, Gorvanus looked away. "It was golden. I had no idea it—"

"Idiot!" Levandius screamed. His hands squeezed Gorvanus' already bruised throat.

"She deceived us for years," Gorvanus whimpered. "You had spies watching her all the time! I discovered her secret!"

"If my father had died even a week ago from the mystical poisons you administered, this would not be happening!" Levandius screamed. "Now it's complicated and messy! I hate complications. Clean it up or you will find yourself on Rygon's altar!" Levandius released Gorvanus and stepped back. Gorvanus crumbled and coughed, spitting up more blood. Levandius poured wine into a silver cup. "What news of Panthara, my beloved?" he asked.

"She sends you her eternal love," Gorvanus said hoarsely. "She sails for Mowad now with Cathal and Caliste."

"Good," Levandius said. "She must bring back Ashur. Everything depends on that!"

"I know she is obsessed with bringing back her father Ashur. Why are you so anxious for his return?" Gorvanus asked nervously.

"Ashur will lead us to the hidden tomb of the Bloodstone Queen," Zhelon said with reverence. "That is why we are assisting her. With Ashur's return, Obsydia shall be returned to us, and with that the yoke of Tarsicius will be broken from Urgonclaw."

Azrul stood, his bent body moving slowly. "Gorvanus, now that Ashur's resurrection is near, you must know why it is so urgent. Ashur learned of Obsydia's hidden tomb before Cathal killed him. That is why he must be raised! Our chief goal is to resurrect our dark goddess, Obsydia," Azrul said in a voice brittle with age.

Zhelon Thor nodded. "The location of Obsydia's temple in the wasteland of Skarros has been a mystery for a thousand years. Many have hunted for it and failed. When Koll found the scroll that would raise Ashur from the dead, we had hope. Koll would not bother with Panthara's desire for vengeance to restore her father unless it would lead to Her return. Koll is your master, but he has kept you ignorant to protect our secret. He instructed us to tell you when all seven sorcerers were safely in our hands."

"Instructed you?" Gorvanus asked shakily.

Azrul and Zhelon revealed the bloodstone amulets they wore under their robes. Zhelon spoke roughly. "Koll is Her High Priest. We sheltered Koll in Urgonclaw after the Sorcerer War ended. Koll told us of what Ashur told him before he died."

"Tarsicius cared only for his own kingdoms," Azrul said harshly. The rites of blood served the Emperor's selfish desire for power. Levandius is a true believer. Koll is Obsydia's High Priest. He lives only to restore Her."

Gorvanus hesitated a moment. "Queen Panthara never mentioned this ambition to find Obsydia. Many believe Obsydia to be myth. I only ask so as not to make an error of judgment when I speak to her."

Zhelon smiled. "Koll's instruction on the Gospels of Obsydia is merely educational for Panthara at present. Koll felt that until he could bring Ashur back into the world, it was best to keep her placated and ignorant of our true goals before we bring her into the fold. We are telling you now so you understand the grave importance of raising Ashur. You do understand that; don't you, Gorvanus?"

Gorvanus nodded vigorously. "Of course."

"Failure in any way will not be met with compassion," Zhelon added in a smooth voice. "Koll is your master, but he serves a higher purpose."

Levandius sipped his wine a moment. "That is enough for now," he finally said. "Go clean yourself up. Then use your sorcery to find out where my sister is hiding. Zhelon's enthusiastic torture of Opaline's maid caused her to expire before she confessed anything useful."

"As my Emperor commands," Gorvanus replied humbly.

He fled the shadowy chamber.

~ * ~

In the dark corridors of Rygon's temple, two white ravens hid in the shadows. The sorcery used to hear through the walls of the High Priest's chamber was easy enough; it was the words they heard that were difficult to bear. Iona shook her feathers and turned to Amun, her familiar.

She spoke through the bonding. *It won't be long before even a moron like Gorvanus finds out where Runa and the others are. They need to leave the Abbey.*

Amun blinked and replied, *the evil here makes my feathers itch. Their plans are more dangerous than we realized. They want to find the Bloodstone Queen! This goes beyond common palace intrigue.*

That must be prevented. But for now, we can only help our friends.

They fled the dark temple through an opening in the high vaulted dome. Iona noticed not even bats nested in the high pinnacles of this wicked temple.

~ * ~

Runa donned the simple, long sleeved, white robe of soft woven cotton. "Eshra says the new postulants wear this when they enter the Abbey." She looked down, smoothing the folds of the snowy material. "I'm afraid I'll dirty it up though. How do the nuns manage to look so scrupulously clean all the time?"

Mellypip nibbled on sweet, crunchy apple slices. "They're pure, I guess. Maybe that deflects dirt?"

Runa bent down to pick up the borrowed sandals and winced. "Oops. I guess I'm still broken." She sat down on the bed again, holding her side.

"Be careful, Runa. If you pull your stitches, you'll really dirty it up. Abbess Eshra says you have to rest. Did you use the salve?"

"Yes, right after I washed up this morning. It smells awful, but is soothing. "I'll be glad when these stitches come out. They itch! I also need to get out of this room. Then we will find Grandpa and all of our friends. Panthara has a few days lead on us. I don't like those odds." She braided her magnificent hair into a single plait.

"But you're still wounded!" Mellypip argued.

"I feel much better. Really!" She slipped on the plain sandals. "Come on. Let's join the others for breakfast."

"I'm gonna tell Abbess Eshra you're not obeying her commands," Mellypip said.

"Please, Melly, I'm hungry for some real food this morning. I've had enough vegetable broth to last me a lifetime. It's your fault. You're the one who mentioned pancakes."

He leapt off the bed and followed. "If you were really recovered you could pick me up. But you can't...*can you?*" Mellypip pointed out.

"Don't be difficult." She grinned. "Give me a day or two and I'll be good as new."

Darcus met her in the hall. He frowned. "What are you doing out of bed, young lady?"

"Hunting for pancakes," she replied. "Look. I'm walking."

"I think the correct term is shuffling," Darcus said and took her arm.

"Am I too late for breakfast?" Runa asked.

"No, we are just gathering now." He helped her walk down the hall while she took baby steps. "You could have breakfast in bed, you know."

"I know, but I need to feel normal again," Runa said softly. "I don't know if I've thanked you properly—"

"There's no need," Darcus replied quickly.

"Darcus, you saved my life. I'll never forget that. You are the great friend that Cathal said you were when we first met. I hope we will always be good friends."

"Now, Runa," Darcus said, flustered. "I only did what anyone would do."

"No, Darcus. Not anyone. You are special," Runa insisted. They walked a moment in silence. "How is Opaline?" she finally asked.

"Her black eye is much better," Darcus said.

"I don't mean that. I mean about the Emperor exiling her. That must be wretched. To be rejected by your own father. How could he? After all she did for him!"

"She's being stoic," Darcus replied carefully. "But that won't heal so easily, I imagine."

"Then we must help her," Runa said decisively.

Mellypip agreed as he bounced along. "Yes, I like Princess Opaline. We must make her happy again." His little nose wiggled. "I smell breakfast, Runa," he chirped. They entered the large common room where the nuns gathered for meals, but it was empty except for their own group of friends and familiars. "Where are the nuns?" Mellypip asked.

"They eat breakfast at five in the morning," Darcus answered. "We're a bit tardy."

Runa was greeted with gentle hugs and joy. Opaline fixed her a plate with a large stack of hot cakes and topped them with generous helpings of butter. "You should still be in bed, Runa," she chastised her.

"I'm much stronger today. Mellypip mentioned pancakes and my craving overcame my wound," Runa said. "And this breakfast will make me even better." She smothered the cakes with syrup and passed the pitcher. She looked at Opaline across the table. "Are you okay?"

Opaline smiled and nodded.

Runa ate with gusto. She cut small pieces for Melly and shared her meal with him. "I do want to tell all of you, though it risks being quite mushy, that I am grateful to you for all that you have done for me."

Hinkleburr blushed bright as his red hair. "Nonsense. You helped me reconsider my life goals. Ambassadors rarely get to be heroic. I rather enjoyed it. I may take it up as a hobby." Hinkleburr passed the maple syrup to Broda and Talwyn.

Eshra entered. "I have a fresh pitcher of chilled milk. I thought it would be good with your breakfast." She poured tall cups of frothy milk for everyone. She even had tiny cups for Mellypip and Rosepetal.

Hinkleburr added a few more pancakes to his plate. "Abbess Eshra, the breakfast is delectable. My compliments to your cook."

Eshra smiled. "I made them. It's my own recipe."

Darcus laughed. "My sister is the best cook in the Ivory Kingdoms."

Pol and Korun rushed in. The two young soldiers who served with Darcus were flushed with excitement.

"Captain," Pol said. "You won't believe it! The Emperor has made us Imperial Knights. Us!"

Darcus stood up and shook their hands. "I'm glad for both of you."

"He is coming now. He wants to talk to you too!" Korun said.

The Emperor entered, flanked by several guards and the Imperial Warden, Lord Rhudon. Lord Rhudon was a distinguished gentleman of mature years. His silver hair and wise brown eyes looked over the group. Everyone bowed before the Emperor.

"Rise," Tarsicius said. "All of you have played a part in saving my life. I thank you. I am leaving now that the legion has arrived with reinforcements. I am returning to Tiamet to reclaim my throne."

"We wish you victory, Emperor," Abbess Eshra said.

"And I shall have it," Tarsicius replied. He turned to Hinkleburr. "I will award you with a special medal of valor, Ambassador, and send a letter of praise to your King."

"I thank you, Emperor Tarsicius. I wish you good fighting," Hinkleburr said simply.

Eshra glanced at Opaline. Her sorrowful face was not lost on the Abbess. "Do you not have a word for your daughter, Emperor?"

she asked Tarsicius. "She was chief in your liberation. In fact, she risked more than anyone to save your life."

Tarsicius did not look at Opaline. "My daughter is dead, Abbess. I will mourn her in my own time—after I have defeated my traitorous son. But if I can help your abbey in some small way, please do not hesitate to petition me. You did shelter me in my time of need. You will find my gratitude quite bountiful."

Tarsicius then summoned Darcus to his side. Darcus went to the Emperor and saluted him. Tarsicius looked the stalwart warrior in the eye as he spoke. "And you, Captain Darcus, I offer the position of Captain of my Imperial Knights. I need loyal blood in the ranks. You have proven yourself noble despite your common lineage. Will you follow me to victory?"

Darcus bowed. "I am honored, Emperor. I know the position of Imperial Knight is normally reserved for those of noble blood. But I must decline this generous offer."

Tarsicius' face shadowed with anger. "What! You? Refuse me? I offer you a commission most men in my kingdoms would die for."

"I am not ungrateful, Your Majesty. But I made a promise. I promised Cathal I would look after his granddaughter. I also intend to rescue Cathal and his friends from those same forces that threatened your throne. I cannot accept this honor. Forgive me." Darcus bowed again. The heavy silence that filled the room was palpable.

Tarsicius glared at Darcus with contempt. "Then help your sorcerer friends," Tarsicius spat. "I will not hinder your quest. Perhaps your loyalty is not as shining as I believed."

"A man must keep his promises, Your Majesty," Darcus replied bravely.

"Then so be it," Tarsicius said. He swept out of the room.

Lord Rhudon paused. He went to Opaline, took her hand and kissed it. "I wish you well, Princess Opaline," he said with sorrow.

"Thank you," Opaline whispered.

Lord Rhudon nodded to them all and left the room.

"Please come with us," Pol pleaded.

"Yes," Korun insisted. "We need you."

"I can't. Be well, boys. I'm proud of you. My path is different now." Darcus put a hand on each of their shoulders and smiled. "Go fight bravely and with honor."

"We will always remember you, Captain," Korun said.

"And I you," Darcus said.

The two young knights embraced Darcus and then hurried after their Emperor.

Opaline's pale face was calm, but her eyes were glassy with unshed tears. Runa went to her side and comforted her. "Damn him!" Runa said. She lowered her head. "Sorry," she said to Eshra.

"Don't be," Abbess Eshra replied.

"He's your father," Runa said. "How can he treat you so! I'm so sorry."

"It's all right. I was not expecting anything else." Opaline sat down and sighed. "Secrets never keep anyway. I knew someday mine would be revealed."

Darcus turned to them. "As long as we are all gathered, it's as good a time as any to tell you that I will be leaving tomorrow morning. Runa, Hinkleburr said he would take you to Ironia. I am going east to find Cathal and the others. I just hope I'm not too late to save them."

"I'm not going to Ironia. I'm coming with you," Runa said. "You can't stop me, so don't even start lecturing."

Darcus shook his head. "I forbid it, Runa."

Sanura's head poked up. "Oh dear…he picks the one thing that should never be said to the female clan." She shook her furry head. "*Males* never learn."

"You can't forbid me, Darcus," Runa said calmly. "I may not be a fully trained sorceress, but my magic can do a lot of damage."

"Yes, well that damage should be directed at the enemy, not a backlash on your comrades," Belwyn said. "Need I remind you of your exploding potions?"

"Exploding potions?" Opaline asked.

"I'll explain later," Runa whispered.

"Cathal left Darcus and *me* in charge, young Runa," Belwyn said. "He wanted you to go to your Uncle Raghnall's—*remember?*"

"Things have changed since then," Runa replied. "All of the sorcerers Panthara and Koll hunted are prisoners now. We know they are headed for Mowad. We just need to make up for lost time. If we could get more gryphons, we could fly and even beat Panthara there."

Darcus shook his head. "There are few enough gryphons in captivity in the west. Rono was a very expensive item. Many are not as well-trained or gentle as he is either."

"Then we can take a riverboat, avoiding the coastline delays, and cut straight through the continent," Runa said confidently. "We can reach Ilyrra in a few days. They have perytons and warriors. I'm part

Ilyrran and Grandpa is a good friend of a ranger named Ryen. They will help us."

"And I can help too," Opaline said. "I can take care of Runa and the familiars."

Darcus threw up his hands. "Oh no, Princess, you—"

"I'm no longer a Princess, Darcus. I'm just Opaline now. The Emperor has exiled me. I'm dead to him now. I always will be."

"I'm sorry; I know you've just lost a great deal. But you shouldn't put yourself at risk over a conflict that has nothing to do with you."

"But it has everything to do with me," Opaline insisted. "Myrsalian, one of the sorcerers abducted, is my Grandfather."

"How is that possible?" Belwyn asked in a stunned voice.

Opaline sighed. "It's a long story."

"Humor us," Belwyn said.

Opaline folded her hands demurely. "My mother, Sirahnami, is Myrsalian's daughter. Myrsalian thought she was dead for years. When she was a baby, their village was attacked by an Urgonclaw army. Myrsalian's wife was killed, but she was sold as a slave when she was just a baby. The village and most of the people were burned beyond recognition, so he never knew. My mother eventually served as a slave in Rygon's temple in Urgonclaw as a dancer. My father saw her dance during one of his visits. He fell in love with her and brought her to Tiamet. My mother was only fifteen then. She bore him two children, twins, Taran and myself. My mother's magic manifested when we were five years old. Father told us she died. I still remember how much I cried at her funeral.

"We never learned the truth until Taran and I turned twelve, and his sorcery revealed itself. My mother was exiled—not dead. Well, at first my father tried to keep her a prisoner on his Island of Nirous. But she was rescued—by Myrsalian. He never knew his daughter lived until years later when he asked Iona to speak to his dead wife's spirit in the Otherworld. Her spirit told him my mother was still alive. He never forgave himself for being away when their village was attacked, you see. Myrsalian spirited Taran away after he was discovered. My stake in this is as strong as Runa's."

"Why did you stay here Opaline? You had family that would welcome you," Darcus asked.

"When I was little, I realized Levandius was the worst sort of man. My father needed me. I thought that someday, perhaps, he would soften his views on sorcery, and we could be a family again."

"You are Sirah's daughter!" Dabiro exclaimed.

Sanura rolled her eyes. "Gods, you are slow!"

Dabiro shook his head. "Myrsalian only recently revealed your mother to us! We have known her for years! Myrsalian didn't tell her —or us—he was her father until recently."

Opaline nodded. "Yes, well…now you have it. So you see, my family is in danger too. My family is important to me. I stayed in Tiamet out of love and duty. My Mother and Taran were right. I should have gone home a long time ago."

"Then you must come with us," Runa exclaimed.

"I will come too," Hinkleburr announced. "Facing a pack of renegade sorcerers is light weight compared to what is happening here. I smell civil war brewing and the ramifications of that are never pretty."

"You've all gone mad," Darcus said.

"It seems to be an epidemic," Belwyn hooted.

"Darcus, I am afraid you must comply," Opaline said sweetly. "We are all quite determined."

"Then it's settled," Runa said. "More pancakes anyone?"

CHAPTER 17

Runa lay on the bed in her plain room. Mellypip cuddled next to her, snuggled in her long braid. He yawned and stretched. "You should take a nap Runa. Breakfast was very tiring. Too many pancakes."

"I'm not tired, Melly."

She got out of bed and went to the table to pack her satchel with clothes the Abbess gave her. Eshra had managed to gather some good practical clothes for her journey; a pair of trousers, a couple tunics, a belt, and a pair of sturdy boots that fit.

"It's nice of the Abbess to give you clothes," Mellypip said.

Runa picked up the dagger. "And nice of Darcus to give me this too." She balanced the blade in the small her hand. "I guess *this* is in case my sorcery goes wrong. When this is all over, we must come back and repay the Abbess for her kindness." She folded and packed the garments away. "I wish we had Grandpa's crystals. But he left those at our tree house."

"Magic too powerful for little sorceress," Mellypip said. He hung his head forlornly. "I miss Grandpa Cathal. I know Belwyn does too. And poor Sanura, she cries a lot in the barn. Belwyn's very quiet about it. But I know he's miserable too."

Runa nodded. "I miss him too. And Caliste…and all the friends you never got to meet, Melly. I *will* find them. And I will make Panthara pay for hurting Grandfather and our friends. I can't be a little girl anymore. I must grow up. Darcus told me this wasn't a game. And he's right. It's serious. Very serious."

"Abbess Eshra says we should forgive," Mellypip said. "But Panthara is nasty. Maybe you can forgive her after you turn her into a toad." Mellypip rested his chin on the bedpost. "I guess you need to be really holy to forgive."

"I suppose. I never really had to think about forgiving until I learned about Ashur. How can I ever forgive him? He was my father, yet I can never ever think of him in that way. He was an evil sorcerer who murdered everyone around him. He killed my mother and grandmother," she said bitterly. "Yet, Abbess says we must have faith. She says the Goddess Araema will hear my prayers. I've always honored the gods, but I never picked a special one to pray to. Grandpa told me when I was old enough, after I studied all the Holy Scriptures, I could choose a patron god. Araema's Abbey is the one that helped me in my time of need. Maybe that's a sign. Araema is the mother of all things. I always wanted a mother. Perhaps a spiritual mother will be good to have."

"Belwyn says that signs can be misleading. He thinks that many signs are…rationalizations. Did I say that right?"

Runa laughed. "Yes. You did. Belwyn is a very skeptical owl. I'm going to the Temple to think. Want to come?"

"Darcus said you need to rest."

"I promise I will take a good long nap before supper. Hop on my shoulder. I can carry you there as long as I don't have to bend over." She slid the dagger into her belt.

Mellypip sighed. "Okay…but I'm gonna make sure you nap later." He jumped onto her shoulder.

They walked through the Abbey. Nuns went about their duties and smiled at them as they passed. Outside, the late morning was still cool. The rain had stopped. The raw earth smelled rich and green, and the sun shined above.

The sun-ripened air was fresh. "It's so peaceful here," Runa commented. "The sky is very blue and cloudless today. I think I understand why the sisters love it here so much."

They took a short walk to the Abbey's Temple, a round building of pale bluish stone. The structures of the Abbey all had the same similarity of circular design. Even the barn in the distance was round. The morning sun was bright, and the raw earth smelled rich and green with the radiance of a new day. They entered the Temple of Araema. Inside, the smell of spicy incense tweaked Mellypip's nose.

"Look at the colored windows, Runa!"

The stained-glass windows' bright scenes shimmered in the sun's glow. One exquisite glass design had ethereal winged beings with celestial faces that hovered above the earth.

Mellypip pulled her braid. "Are those the Winged Feys of the Ilyrrans?"

"No. I think they are the Seraphim, the winged messengers of the Eternals."

"They look like the Winged Feys in our magical history book back home. I remember the pictures. They were pretty."

"The Seraphim are connected with the legend of the Winged Feys. The Seraphim loved the Elfsharans, which is what the Ilyrrans use to call themselves until the wicked Bloodstone Queen conquered their lands. They changed their name out of grief for what was lost to them. They founded a new country which they call Ilyrra now. But long ago according to myth, the Elfsharans were the first race the Eternals made. They made us all of course, but Belwyn said they liked to take their time with some things. No war or strife tainted the Elfsharan people. Some of the Seraphim did the forbidden and fell in love with the Elfsharan's purity. In time, the women the Seraphim loved bore immortal children that have the bodies of the Elfsharans and the wings of the Seraphim."

"That sounds nice," Mellypip said. "Their wings are colorful. They look like butterfly wings."

"They are beautiful, but their love had a tragic price. The earthly Elfsharans were mortal, made of earth and water. The Seraphim were immortals made of fire and air. All the women who gave birth to the Winged Fey died. The Seraphim grieved for their loss. Their poor children were also cursed with grief. The Winged Fey folk are caught between the two worlds and cannot live in either. The Seraphim gathered their sad children and hid them away. Many say they are only myth now."

Mellypip's ears drooped. "That is a sad tale. Are there any happy gods or legends?"

Runa shrugged. "Very few, I'm afraid. The Eternals of Light fight a great deal against the Eternals of Darkness."

They walked down the aisle toward the altar dominated by an exquisite statue of a veiled woman. The stone eyes seemed to look upon them with kindness. Piles of fragrant flowers rested at her feet.

"She looks so kind and mysterious," Runa said softly.

"It is Araema," Eshra said, walking down the aisle, candle in one hand casting a dusky light and a bouquet of wild flowers in the other hand.

"Abbess, I didn't hear you come in," Runa said.

Eshra smiled and laid the flowers at the feet of the image. "It is an image of Araema, The Mother Creatress of all things.

"Is that what Araema truly looks like?" Runa asked.

Eshra smiled. "No one can ever know the true visage of an Eternal. This is how people imagine their gods to be in their hearts."

"Why is her face veiled?" Mellypip asked. "Isn't she pretty?"

Eshra laughed. "She is beautiful, but she has many faces. Some are pleasant, some terrifying. She is the First Eternal, and Her light shines throughout the heavens."

The Abbess walked to the shrine. She motioned for Runa and Mellypip to follow. She opened a great book, massive and bound in a design of many colors. Runa was tantalized by the great volume. She touched the pages with respect. "Is this a Book of Ages, Abbess? It's so lovely."

Eshra nodded and turned to the beginning of the holy book. "This book was written hundreds of years ago by the founders of the first Araema Abbey. In the beginning, there was the Diamond Age." She pointed to the first page of the soft, ivory-shaded paper. A tiny diamond was at the top of the first page.

Runa looked at the writings, which were in a language Mellypip had never seen. "Is this Chaotul script?"

Abbess Eshra nodded. "Excellent. You have studied it?"

"It's one of the oldest languages. Grandfather was teaching me before we left home. He has some scrolls written in this ancient language. The flow of the script is amazing. So intricate and beautiful. The Diamond Age was the first era, when the Eternals created life and light."

Mellypip was fascinated by the book too. Many illustrations depicted disturbing scenes. "The gods battle a lot, don't they?" he asked.

Eshra rubbed his ears and smiled. "Yes, Mellypip, the Eternals rose from the deep Abyss, infinite power that took on mystical life. But from the beginning, Light and Dark have battled." She turned to another chapter, and this one had a tiny emerald marking the beginning. "The Emerald age is when life was made, all life, with Her Touch. The Goddess Araema, the First Eternal, is the timeless heart, the soul, the dream of the world."

Runa turned to the next chapter, The Sapphire Age, when peace and magic ruled a peaceful world. Mellypip liked that chapter. The next age was much grimmer. A bloodstone marked that era.

"That is the darkest age," Eshra said solemnly. "The Bloodstone Age, when the world was in chaos. A dark star struck the world when the Eternal of Darkness, Ahridum, sought to eclipse the light. He chose a bride, a mortal seer named Lilith during this time of evil. His essence filled her and he planted his seed. That seed was Obsydia, the Bloodstone Queen. She was born only moments after her conception. Her birth consumed Lilith like fire, turning her to ashes. Obsydia slept for thirteen nights and awoke fully grown. Half-god and half mortal, she conquered nations during her reign. Blood sacrifices flowed from her wicked altars. She was defeated a thousand years ago, and Light was restored," Eshra said. "We live in the Topaz age now. Darkness may win battles, but it can never defeat the Light as long as there is a resistance of soul. Our age is still new. The fate of this time is known only to the Eternals." She kissed Runa on the cheek. "You have a great task ahead of you. I will leave you to meditate, my child. Araema will listen to you."

"Thank you, Abbess Eshra," Runa whispered.

After she left them, Runa knelt before the statue of Araema. "I want to ask Araema for protection. I should make an offering to show her I am sincere. I have never done this before. But I would like to ask Araema for luck."

Mellypip sat next to her, resisting the temptation to nibble the blossoms that tantalized him. "Araema is good. Maybe we can pick some more flowers for her. She likes flowers. The nuns give them to her all the time."

Runa shook her head. "No. It must be special." Runa touched her long braid and sighed. "If I am to ask for luck in my quest, I think I need to do more than pick flowers. I have little else to offer." She raised the dagger before the statue. "I ask for the protection of Araema, not for myself, but for my Grandfather and friends. I am not very religious, Goddess. I mean, I know you are out there. One would be a fool to think otherwise. You're a goddess, so you know what my task is. So I won't bore you with the details. But I need all the help I can get. In return for your blessings, I make this humble offering." She sheared the braid off at the nape of the neck and laid the long golden-brown braid at the base of the statue. Runa's warm scent mingled with the blossoms there.

Mellypip's fur puffed with shock. "Runa! Belwyn's gonna swat me good for letting you do that! He'll hoot and bark like a mad owl!"

Runa smoothed his ruffled fur. "No. He won't."

Opaline burst into the Temple, flushed and breathless. "Runa, we have trouble. Iona is here. She says we need to leave right away." She ran to Runa and helped her up. Opaline froze and her delicate mouth fell open when she saw Runa's shorn locks. "Oh my gods, what did you do to your hair?" she cried.

"I cut it off." Runa touched her short wavy hair. "Do you like it? I must admit I feel naked without it."

"Don't blame me. It's not my fault," Mellypip said to Opaline.

"But why?" Opaline gasped.

"Let's just call it an act of faith," Runa said.

~ * ~

After Iona's warning, Belwyn scouted the roads from the air, watching for enemy forces. He hoped they could leave before anyone showed up to cause trouble. A train of twenty horses at heavy gallop below burst Belwyn's hopes of a peaceful exodus.

"Damn," Belwyn muttered, when his keen vision spotted Gorvanus leading them.

Belwyn's silent wings turned and flew back to the Abbey. In front, Darcus and Talwyn had already saddled the horses and Rono the gryphon. Fortunately, yesterday they had sold the wagon in the nearby village. The generosity of Hinkleburr (and the dice winnings his aides acquired) helped to purchase three Dwarven mountain ponies and horses for the journey.

Belwyn swooped down and perched on Darcus' shoulder. "Twenty horses coming this way—fast. Gorvanus is leading them."

Hinkleburr joined them in the yard, carrying a sack of food. "I do worry about rushing off so, Captain Darcus," Hinkleburr said. "Runa is not fully healed."

"I'm not an officer anymore," Darcus said. "And Belwyn just spotted Gorvanus leading several soldiers down the road, so we leave now."

"My feet are suddenly swift," Hinkleburr said.

"Everyone is losing rank around here," Belwyn grumbled. "What's that all about? Good guys getting shafted by evil overlords, that's what!" Belwyn looked around. "Where's Runa and Mellypip?" Belwyn asked in a concerned voice. "I haven't seen them since breakfast. When Iona got here, I took scouting duty."

"Opaline and Runa are bringing the familiars," Hinkleburr said. "Runa looks quite charming with her new look too."

Belwyn turned his head. "What?"

Runa and Opaline led the familiars to the courtyard. "Where have you been? I—" Belwyn said in a relieved voice. He looked at Runa's short hair. "What did you do to your hair, Runa?" he snapped.

"I'm traveling light for the trip. I'll explain later, Belwyn," she said. "Which one of you can take Dabiro and Buzzy? Opaline can carry Sanura easily, and little Rosepetal is quite happy in a satchel.

"Oh yes, she is indeed," Opaline agreed and lifted the flap of her bag, and the tiny hedgehog poked her nose out.

"I'm quite secure in here. Let me know when we're out of danger. Thank you." The hedgehog then retreated to the comfortable dark.

"Where's Mellypip?" Darcus asked, helping Opaline mount her horse.

"I'm here!" Mellypip said, poking his head out of Runa's satchel. "Rosepetal is right. It is comforting."

"Much like mother's womb," Belwyn retorted.

"I'll take Dabiro," Talwyn offered, lifting the stout badger with comparative ease. The badger grunted but allowed the young boy to carry him to the shaggy, stout pony.

"I'll ride with Buzzy," Hinkleburr said, carrying the sloth to his pony. "We're old companions now."

The sound of iron-shod hooves drew closer. "Darcus…is your sword ready?" Belwyn asked.

Darcus drew his blade. "Always."

A compact ball of fire dropped in the middle of the yard and exploded. It stunned everyone, throwing them several feet and spooking the horses. Poor Rono cried out and flew up to the Abbey roof. Runa rolled across the ground. The hem of Opaline's cloak caught fire. Runa crawled over to her and helped her stamp it out. Mellypip pushed himself out of the bag, wild-eyed but brave. Darcus was knocked unconscious. Hinkleburr and the others were dazed and useless.

Belwyn was not affected by the blast, though his head buzzed painfully. He flew to Runa and Opaline and placed himself between Gorvanus and his charges, ready to draw blood. "The bloody cheater!" Belwyn mumbled. "Dropping flame bombs on our heads!"

Furious, Abbess Eshra ran out to help them. Staff in hand, she met the riders led by Gorvanus as they entered the sanctuary of the Abbey.

The arrogant sorcerer reeked of the magic he had just cast. He pulled the reins of his horse stopping the animal and laughed. He held up a smoking crystal in the palm of his hand. "Flame star spells are very useful," Gorvanus said.

Eshra marched toward Gorvanus and his heavily armed soldiers. "You will anger the Goddess with this blasphemy. Go now, Sorcerer. You are in violation of ancient laws. This is holy ground."

Gorvanus dismounted his horse. "I do not fear *your* goddess."

"I am giving you the chance to leave with your bones unbroken.

I suggest you take it," Eshra threatened.

"Or what?" Gorvanus laughed, walking toward her.

All the nuns of the Abbey marched into the yard from all sides. The hundred blue-robed maidens, young and old, formed a protective circle around their friends. The sisters of peace did not look so peaceful now. Each carried a staff, a rake, a club, and even cast-iron frying pans, as weapons.

The Abbess smiled. "We have faith. We also have had the fortune of my brother, Darcus, who has taught us self-defense over the years." She spun the staff in her nimble hands. "He is an excellent teacher. Attack these infidels, sisters."

The nuns attacked the soldiers with the fury of angry wasps. Belwyn would have found it amusing if he had the time for it.

Gorvanus removed his helmet and threw it aside. His face was swollen and covered with bruises.

"Having a bad day, Gorvanus?" Belwyn said.

"Bad?" Gorvanus shouted. "Your sorcerer did this to me!"

"Grandfather! Where is he?" Runa demanded.

"Sailing to his fate, brat," Gorvanus replied. "I lost your pretty locket when I told him you were dead. It's not true it seems…yet."

"You're scum!" Runa cried.

"Take down the sisters," Gorvanus ordered. "Now!"

"I do not think so," Iona said.

Gorvanus turned just in time to get a dose of fiery anger from Iona. Her beam of white sorcery threw him several feet across the yard. She stepped into view, her dark veils concealing all but her pale blue eyes, and her white raven Amun upon her shoulder.

"A necromancer!" the soldiers cried, backing their horses away.

Gorvanus pulled himself up from the mud. "I said attack! It's just a necromancer! She can't bring you death, but I can!"

Talwyn and Broda revived and threw a bucket of water from the well on Darcus, which woke him up. Darcus did not stagger or wonder when he opened his eyes, but jumped up and raised his sword. He stalked toward Gorvanus with a murderous look.

Gorvanus grabbed his sword and rushed toward Runa. Opaline pushed Runa out of the way. Gorvanus grabbed Opaline by the hair and crushed her to him, pressing the sharp steel to her bare throat. "You will do, Opaline. Come a step closer and she dies!" he threatened.

They all stopped in their tracks. Gorvanus smiled and held her tighter. "That's better."

"Hurt her," Darcus said darkly. "And I'll make you pray for death."

"Are you quick enough, Darcus? Can you save the maiden before I slice her throat open? Can you risk attacking me with magic before I act? I think not." He looked down at Opaline. "Your brother Levandius is angry at you," he whispered. "Your maid, that pretty little thing named Mira, kept your secrets. She's dead because of it, Opaline. It's your fault."

"You bastard!" Opaline cried.

"Tsk, tsk...language!" Gorvanus warned, pressing the blade against her skin. "Levandius wants you dead. I intend to deliver your head to him."

"Let her go! She's leaving Tiamet, Gorvanus. Tarsicius has exiled her." Runa pleaded.

Belwyn focused on the sword, and his magic ripped the blade out of Gorvanus' grip. Gorvanus gasped with surprise when his weapon flew out of his reach. Darcus did not have time to pull Opaline to safety. A new wave of magic burned the air. It was not from Runa or the familiars, or even Iona. Opaline glowed with it.

Oh no, Belwyn thought. *This isn't good.*

A furious burst of sorcery bubbled from Opaline as her anger unleashed. Incensed, Opaline turned on Gorvanus, pummeling him with her small fists. "You wretched beast! Let me go! Mira's dead, and you laugh! You stupid troll! Evil, heartless troll!" she cried. Just as the words *troll* escaped her lips, a flow of purple sorcery poured from her whole body. Streams of purple magic coiled around Gorvanus like mystical ropes. The sorcerer howled and struggled, falling to his knees as the cloud cloaked his body. Opaline stepped back and crumbled to the ground in shock.

Holding her side, Runa stumbled to help Opaline up. The whole congregation of friend and foe witnessed Gorvanus transform before their shocked eyes.

"Oh dear," Runa whispered, holding Opaline close. "This is going to be very bad."

"What...what did I do?" Opaline asked in a frail voice. "What is happening?"

Rapt by the scene of Gorvanus' transformation, they witnessed the wicked man hunch over and scream with pain. Coarse gray and black fur sprouted all over his body. His face twisted into a demonic shape. Two long yellow tusks shot from his mouth. The eyes altered to a dark red. He howled as long claws shot from his fingertips. He grew to an enormous size. His clothing ripped apart to make way for the massive bulk and height of a troll. Horns grew from his skull. The voice was no longer human, but changed to the guttural, slobbering howls of a troll. The apparition was terrifying. Gorvanus was no more. Instead, an eight-foot troll stood, smelly, with shaggy fur and dripping tusks. The mist of sorcery faded at last, but the troll remained. The light hurt its eyes, and it yowled pitifully. Covering its gruesome face with long, ape-like arms, it ran away.

Mellypip crawled back into his satchel. "I think Opaline made a big oops."

Opaline looked at her hands in horror. "Oh, I didn't...mean... to do that!" She buried her face in her hands and cried.

Darcus took Opaline by the shoulders and shook her. "It's going to be all right, Opaline. Come on."

"We need to leave now while the enemy is dumbfounded." Sanura suggested.

Indeed, the forces of Gorvanus were not only stunned, but turned their horses around and rode away.

Iona bowed to them. "Go now. I will be in contact with you if I can."

Eshra hugged her brother. "Iona is right. Go now before they come back."

"Thank you, Iona," Darcus said. He turned to his sister. "Take care, Eshra...and thank you for everything."

Hinkleburr bowed with elegance despite his disheveled appearance. "Thank you, Abbess. I promise to send bountiful donations for your good order. Please send me your recipe for gooseberry pie. I found myself in bliss after such a delicacy."

Eshra embraced the shocked Opaline. "You did not do evil my girl. But I think a little self-control might be prudent the next time you cast a spell."

"I'm so sorry," Opaline sobbed. Talwyn and Broda helped her to her horse.

The Abbess hugged Runa last. "Remember the dark cannot eclipse the light for long. Have faith."

"I will," Runa whispered. "Thank you."

"Belwyn, scout ahead!" Darcus commanded.

"Aye, Darcus," Belwyn replied as he soared into the sky.

They mounted the horses, except for Darcus, who leapt upon a nervous Rono who had returned to earth. He patted the gryphon's head. "Let's go! We'll run for a space, boy. Then we'll fly to give Belwyn a rest." The gryphon nodded happily.

Eshra waved. "And Darcus, do not wait a whole year to visit me next time!"

"I won't!" Darcus shouted as they sped away.

CHAPTER 18

Darcus and Talwyn returned from the river town of Kupa down the hill with their passage tokens.

"Did you have enough money for all of us?" Runa asked.

Darcus nodded. "Yes. Barely, but we had it. The riverboat should be here in about two hours. We'll rest here until then. Kupa is small, but crowded with bad elements. We'll just stay camped outside of town on the bank until the riverboat comes. We have no idea if Gorvanus had other spies hunting for us," Darcus said.

"The river looks wild," Runa commented. "And it's so wide!"

Mellypip climbed a tree to get a better view of the rushing currents. Darcus said the river was a mile across. The rapid currents looked hostile to Mellypip.

"Did you use the salve, Runa?" Darcus asked.

"Yes, a few minutes ago," she replied.

"You're lucky you didn't pull your stitches at the Abbey," Darcus said seriously. "At least you can get some decent rest on the ship for a couple of days."

"I hate water travel," Sanura said. "But we have no choice if we want to reach Ilyrra in time." The cat curled up in Broda's lap and nibbled a wedge of cheese he shared with her.

In the distance, the town of Kupa reminded Mellypip of Sea Haven, just less stinky. "I'm glad Darcus decided not to venture into the town, especially after what happened in Sea Haven." He scurried down the tree to join the others.

Darcus searched through his pack. "It was extra to bring the horses and Rono, but we will need them later."

"Unless we get to ride perytons after we reach Ilyrra," Opaline said. "I've dreamed of seeing a peryton someday. I've only seen drawings of them. I hear they are quite beautiful." When Rono lowered his head, Opaline noticed his forlorn face and gave him a good hug. "There now, Rono. We love you too! You are the most handsome gryphon ever," she said.

"Really?" Rono asked. The gryphon raised his head, large dark eyes shaded by long black lashes.

"Yes. And very brave too!" Runa added. "You helped to save my life with your swift flight." Runa wrapped her arms around his feathery neck and hugged him.

"What a ham," grunted Dabiro.

"Stop being a poopy head," Mellypip said. Dabiro gave him a dirty look, and Mellypip bounded over Rono. The gryphon lowered an inky wing and lifted him on to his back. Better to be safe than sorry where that cranky old badger was concerned.

"How's Rosepetal?" Runa asked.

Opaline patted the satchel at her side. "She's inside my bag. She finally calmed down and stopped hiccupping. I think she's napping now. She asked for some grubs, but I have no idea how to even look for such things."

"Look under a rock or fallen log," Sanura suggested. "That's where slimy things live."

Opaline made a sour face. "That's a bit too revolting for my taste. Maybe I'll just give her some bread and cheese," Opaline said.

Dabiro laughed. "Speaking of slimy, that last fight took a dramatic turn—especially for Gorvanus. Rotten turd got what he deserved."

Opaline's expression crumbled. "I still can't believe I did that. I don't even know how I did that!" She sat on a log and put her face in her hands.

Buzzy the sloth glared at Dabiro. "Now you've done it. Can't you keep that mouth of yours muzzled for five minutes?"

"But it's true," Dabiro protested. "That evil slime deserved to die. I never considered a fate worse than death, but Gorvanus living out his sleazy life as a troll works for me. I was paying her a compliment! Does everyone here enjoy twisting my words on purpose?"

"Are they always like this?" Opaline asked.

Runa nodded and laughed. "Always. Since I can remember. Welcome to the world of sorcerers and familiars, Opaline. Magic laced with adventure, rigorous study, and throwing mashed potatoes across the dinner table."

"I'm never going to live that down, am I?" Dabiro grumbled.

"Never," Buzzy said with a wry look. "Cathal had to scrape food off the ceiling after you and Jasper got into a philosophical debate about…what was it? Oh, I remember now. It was about the ethics of using beer as a potion base. Cathal banned you from drinking ale in his tree house for a whole year."

"Gorvanus got what he deserved, Princess," Darcus comforted

her. "My only regret is that I didn't get to run him through at least once."

"Thank you, Darcus," Opaline said. "And you don't have to refer to me as 'Princess' anymore. That part of my life is over."

Darcus grinned. "To me, you will always be Princess Opaline, the Jewel of the Ivory Kingdoms."

Belwyn got that irritated look again. "Will everyone pipe down," he said. "I'm trying to think! This spell must be done very carefully."

"Are you sure you remember everything?" Runa asked.

"I'm just cautious—and not so old that I would forget an incantation. I wish we had Cathal's tomes, or his old scrolls just to verify, however. This enchantment transports our thoughts and image, while our bodies still remain here. And it's not just words that make the spell. Oh no, there are other factors involved. The words are the icing on the cake, but not the cake itself. People who think that saying some silly words will make spells happen have no clue to the mystical intricacies of sorcery. It takes concentration and control. I'm also including a tether as a safety net, Runa. That's your job, Sanura."

The cat stretched out on Broda's lap. "I'm quite capable of that," Sanura replied lazily.

"Are you sure you want to do this, Runa?" Darcus asked. "It sounds potentially dangerous."

"My whole life is dangerous right now," Runa replied. "Somehow, I must communicate to Grandfather that I'm not dead. I hate to think what he must be going through. Belwyn told me what grandfather was like in Mowad before the rangers brought me to him. When I think of how Gorvanus gloated about killing me! Ugh!" She calmed down and put her arm around Opaline. "Gorvanus deserved to be turned into a troll, Opaline. So stop beating yourself up over it. Don't forget how he killed Timoth and Lichor too! Who knows what that wicked man had done over the years? And if he's working for Koll and Panthara, that makes him extra evil."

"Extra evil?" Buzzy asked. "Things are good or evil, Runa. If you are evil, you're limited only by your own power. Evil is evil... plain and simple. It is the same for good. There are no degrees—"

"The philosopher is awake," Dabiro said. "Prepare for boredom."

"Your attitude is getting on my nerves," Buzzy warned.

"I didn't think a sloth had nerves," Dabiro grunted. "All you do is sleep!"

"I meditate!" Buzzy protested.

"Stop it now! Both of you!" Runa chastised them.

They lowered their heads. "We're sorry, Runa."

Mellypip bounced over to Runa's lap and munched on a piece of bread she gave him, glad to be out of the tussle.

Opaline sighed. "I'm not heartbroken over Gorvanus' fate. But I know my untrained magic is responsible for what I did. I never hurt anyone before. Well, I sort of did once, but it wasn't that bad and it was an accident too. But I haven't had any instruction since my sorcery manifested."

"When did your magic appear?" Darcus asked, sharpening his sword with a whetstone.

"My sorcery came to me only a year ago," Opaline said. "I was fifteen. I was afraid. Levandius was always on the lookout to expose us after my mother became a sorceress."

"Why did Levandius hate you so much?" Runa asked.

Opaline shrugged. "Who knows? He hated any type of competition. Levandius was always vice-ridden and cruel. He was born from my father's first marriage to a Princess of Talreja. She died when she gave birth to him. For years Levandius was the center of attention, until he was ten years old, and father brought my mother home. Then she gave birth to twins, me and Taran. Levandius didn't like sharing our father and he was a poor scholar, too. My brother Taran and I excelled at study. That irritated my half-brother. He liked to be the center of attention at all costs. He rejoiced when my brother Taran was exiled."

"How did you realize you were a sorceress?" Runa asked.

"And what did you do that was an *accident*?" Darcus added curiously.

Opaline shrugged. "It was only last year, when my father had a new favorite from the harem who annoyed me. She was very vain, especially about her long, curly red hair. It wasn't even natural. She used henna to color it. She fawned over me in front of father. I found her to be offensive and false, but I remained silent. After he sent my mother away, he rarely attached his affections to another woman. Then, at a banquet one night, she got very drunk and told me she would be queen one day and I would be sent away to marry some petty prince. I remember sitting there, wishing, wishing very hard, that her precious hair would fall out. Suddenly, it did! Right there, long locks of flaming red hair began to fall out at the banquet table. She was bald as an egg before the second course arrived."

The group began to laugh. "Stop laughing," Runa scolded.

Opaline shook her head. "It's all right. I know how it sounds. Her hair grew back—eventually. But I was still mortified. Father never realized because he was so drunk that night. Fortunately, Levandius wasn't there. He was in the country hunting. The physicians said it was an allergic reaction to the dream herbs she smoked. I was lucky. After that, I began wearing the *luck* ring my brother Taran sent to me, a ring of sorcerer bane coated in gold. He wrote me and said if I insisted on staying with father, I needed protection."

"You're a dangerous woman, Opaline," Hinkleburr chuckled. "Do you still have that ring handy? You may want to wear it just in case. I don't fancy being transformed into anything unseemly if you get miffed."

Opaline dropped her head into her lap and sobbed.

Hinkleburr was very contrite. "Please don't cry my dear. I was only teasing. Quick, Talwyn, get some cookies from the food pack," he begged.

"Is a little silence too much to ask?" Belwyn grumbled.

"Sorry, Belwyn," Runa said sheepishly.

"Furball, we need you," Belwyn said.

Mellypip's large round ears perked up. "Really?" he asked.

Belwyn nodded. "She needs her familiar for this. Runa, stand over there in the clearing. There is a good bit of sun there. We need a clear range without any hindrance. We'll cast the circle of protection first. Sanura, since you're the binding force to bring us back if anything happens, sit by Runa's feet. I want everyone to be absolutely silent during this spell. Talwyn and Broda, get the jar of salt Eshra gave us and a cup of water. Pour a circle of salt around Runa, then pour the water and stand back."

Broda poured the salt in a wide circle around Runa. Darcus laid out the map and secured it with stones at her feet.

"What's the salt for?" Opaline whispered.

"It's a symbolic circle of protection," Sanura said quickly. "It represents the earth."

Runa stood in the sunspot with Mellypip in her arms within the ring of salt. "Now what?" Runa asked.

"Use your magic to call up a bit of wind. Cast a small flame in your hand."

Runa held out her hand and a small, bright flame appeared. The wind stirred around Runa and Mellypip.

"Let the wind circle you, but control it. Now repeat these words," Belwyn said.

"How come Grandpa never goes through all of this ceremony?" Runa asked.

Belwyn glowered. "He's an experienced sorcerer with centuries of practice, young Runa. The added ritual is necessary when you're a novice to high magic. Now, *without interruption*, repeat these words: I summon the sacred elements to circle me from harm. Earth, air, fire, and water, above and below, make the circle whole."

Runa repeated the words. The salt and water encircling her glowed brightly. The air charged with energy and the white flame in the palm of her hand flared.

"Good," Belwyn approved. "Now think of the ocean. It doesn't matter if we don't know Panthara's ship; we are looking for what's inside—Cathal and Caliste. Imagine it. Think about Cathal and Caliste. Clear your mind of everything else. Furball, use the bonding to stay in her thoughts. Help guide her through the journey. Your thoughts must be as one. Focus, children. Call up your sorcery, and let it carry you through the sky, across the seas, to Cathal. Command the elements of air, water, fire, and earth to meld. Feel your magic grow within. Summon the magic, but hold it in. Now repeat these words:

"Air, Fire, Water, Earth
Elements of Eternal birth
With pure heart and spirit I do now speak
Carry me to those I seek
Sacred elements, we summon thee
Carry me across the sea."

Runa and Mellypip closed their eyes and said the charm. The tingling sensation of magic flowed inside both of them.

I feel warm in my tummy, Runa, Melly said to her mind.

So do I, Runa whispered.

Belwyn's voice echoed around them. "Think about Cathal and Caliste. Let the winds carry you. Now—let go."

The hum of magic whirled around Runa and Mellypip. Belwyn hovered above them now, his silent wings sheltering the two young ones. The ring of salt and water began to sparkle, and a circle of glowing beams appeared. Belwyn floated down into the shimmering lights.

"Focus, Runa!" Belwyn encouraged. "I sense the enchantment taking hold. Brace yourselves!" the owl warned.

Clinging to Runa, Mellypip breathed in the sorcerous sparkles. Suddenly, Runa glowed in a burst of light like the sun. Another burst of light carried them through a colorful maze of blues and yellows. Inside the radiance that enclosed them, Mellypip soared through the sky with his Runa. Harsh winds beat his face. "It feels so real!" Mellypip gasped, dazed from the whirl of sorcery. "Is this what it's like to fly, Belwyn?"

"For an amateur," Belwyn replied.

A mere heartbeat ago they were on solid ground far from the sea. Now Mellypip and Runa gazed down at frothy waves. Winds tangy with salt and hot sunshine spiced Mellypip's senses. Runa and Mellypip's thoughts were entwined with thoughts of Cathal and Caliste clear in their minds.

Mellypip concentrated real hard, just like Belwyn told him to. He guided Runa through the journey, aware of her magical strength and watching for any weakness that might cause her to falter.

Then a grand ship appeared below, sailing with great speed over white-crested waves. Could that be it? Mellypip wondered.

"Fly down," Belwyn said. "If your focus was true, it brought us to her ship. Follow me." Wings spread wide, the spirit of Belwyn swooped down.

Spellbound, they followed Belwyn through the funnel of enchantment. The colors grew deeper. Ripples of dark green and red glided them down to the decks. And more amazing, they passed through the wood planks down into the bowels of the ship.

"This is weird," Mellypip said. "It tickled."

They traveled like ghosts through the solid ship. In a dim-lit section in the lower hold of the ship, they saw Cathal and Caliste at last. Each was in a cramped metal cage. Each wore a sorcerer lock around their necks.

Caliste sat with her knees bent, tears flowing down her cheeks. Cathal was bound in chains. His grief-stricken face was ashen.

Melly, this breaks my heart, Runa whispered when she saw his ravaged features.

Four soldiers carrying spears guarded them despite the sturdy prisons and chains. The muscular men also kept a respectful distance from the two sorcerers.

Runa and Mellypip drifted on the air toward Cathal and Caliste. Belwyn hovered above them. Her glowing form lit up the shadowy chamber and startled the guards. They shouted curses and prayers and stabbed their images with spears.

"Stop that!" Runa scolded.

They ran screaming toward the door, wailing about ghosts and curses. Caliste gasped and stood up, gripping the bars of her cage.

"Are you real?" Cathal whispered. "Runa? Is that truly you! Gorvanus said he killed you!"

Runa nodded, tears welling in her eyes. "What have they done to you?"

"I thought I sensed sorcery," Caliste exclaimed. "Oh, I'm so happy you're alive!"

"Darcus and the others rescued me," Runa said. "They got me to Araema Abbey. I desperately wanted you to know I was safe. Oh, and by the way, Gorvanus is a troll now. Long story."

"A troll?" Cathal said with a raised eyebrow.

"Credit Opaline…she did it," Belwyn said.

"Opaline did that!" Caliste said, surprised. "But that means—"

"Yes, she's a sorceress. She's with us now. Gorvanus stole my locket though. Now that he's a troll, I will probably never find it again."

Cathal looked down and unclenched his hands. "You mean this?" In his grip was her silver locket. "I took it from Gorvanus when I was pulverizing his face. I haven't let go of it since."

Belwyn hooted. "Oh, nice job by the way on the beating you gave Gorvanus. I saw the results. Well-deserved."

"Belwyn, Mellypip," Cathal said with relief. "I'm overjoyed to see you." He gazed at Runa with joy. "When Gorvanus said you were dead, I thought my life was over."

"Don't say that. I love you Grandpa, and you too Caliste. But we don't have a lot of time. The spell Belwyn taught me is only for a short time. So listen."

Cathal laughed and cried at the same time. "Yes, I have some things to tell you too."

"We are going to rescue you Grandpa," Runa said. "I'm going to Ilyrra to get help. Oh, and Sanura and the other familiars are safe and with us too."

"Thank you," Caliste wept. "But you cannot risk yourself. It's too dangerous."

"I'm afraid I'm turning into a delinquent," Runa said with a smile.

"You're not very good at obeying orders, are you?" Cathal said.

Belwyn's shining shape fluttered around the cage. "See what

happens when you let them out of the tree? They run wild, invading kingdoms." The owl blinked. "I miss you, Cathal."

"I miss you too, old friend," Cathal said. Cathal's eyes widened. "Runa…you cut your hair!"

Runa sighed. "Yes, but I feel the spell weakening. We need to share our information quickly before it fades completely."

They whispered quickly. Each received surprising and disturbing revelations.

~ * ~

Panthara arranged a large selection of glittering gems on the table for Azmadu. His wings wiggled with excitement as he touched each of the bright stones with the tip of his claw. The variety of colors mesmerized Azmadu as he pondered his decision. He still enjoyed his black satin eye patch with the red lightning bolt, but for special occasions a jewel would be fun to wear.

"Well, Azmadu, which shall be your new eye?" Panthara asked as she sat down next to him.

"So many pretty jewels to choose from, my Panthara!" Azmadu exclaimed eagerly. He picked a great ruby and examined himself in the hand mirror Panthara held up for him. "I like this one. Red for blood!"

"A bold and fearless choice," Panthara agreed. "A jewel for my precious jewel." She kissed the top of his scaly head.

A yellow citrine stone did not appeal to him, and he tossed it into the 'no' pile. The onyx was too gloomy and lacked flash and was also discarded into the 'no' pile.

Sudden, frantic knocking on Panthara's cabin door annoyed Azmadu. It distracted his Panthara from paying attention to *him*.

"Enter!" Panthara said impatiently.

Four guards ran into the room and knelt on the carpet with their heads bowed. "Your Majesty, there—" one of the men said.

"Silence. In a moment," Panthara commanded sharply. She picked up a large pink diamond. ""What about this one?"

He scratched his chin and shook his head. "Nope. Too paisley."

"At least try it," she pouted.

Azmadu relented and held it up to his eye patch. "No, Panthara. I don't want it."

"See how it reflects the light," she said. "It's from an ancient dragon hoard, stolen by a clever sorcerer."

"I thought dragons didn't actually hoard? Koll said that was a myth," Azmadu said. "Dragons prefer to eat trolls, which is why they live on Rapiveshta Island."

"You're being difficult," Panthara accused.

"Please, Your Majesty! It's urgent!" the guard pleaded.

Panthara glared at the man and he bowed his head back into the carpet.

"Pink is a girly stone!" Azmadu whined. "Everyone will make fun of me—especially nasty Xabral. He seized the giant ruby. "I want this one!"

"Very well," Panthara sighed. She turned to the shaking guards. "Well...what is it now?"

The first guard spoke quickly. "Thank you, Blessed Queen! There are ghosts in the prison hold. The sorcerers have summoned ghosts!"

"Nonsense!" Panthara snapped.

Azmadu admired the ruby and held up the mirror to see. He scratched his satin eye patch and snorted. When Panthara turned away, he grabbed the pink diamond and stuffed it in the bottom of Panthara's jewelry casket. No crill lizards in pink!

"Must I do everything myself?" Panthara complained. She grabbed her deep blue cloak and followed the frightened men. Grumpy, Azmadu followed after her. Panthara entered the prison chamber, and the guards remained in the background, their features blanched white with fear. The scent of magic was in the air too. Then Panthara saw them! The shimmering specter of Runa stood there, brightening the grim prison. With her were the two familiars, Belwyn, Azmadu's arch-enemy, and that fuzzy thing with the big ears—Mellypip.

"You! You're supposed to be dead!" Panthara wailed.

Runa glanced over her ethereal shoulder. "Not sorry to disappoint you, Panthara."

Face twisted with fury, Panthara stormed toward Runa, but her hands passed through her.

"I wish people would stop doing that!" Runa said in an irritated voice.

"You're no ghost! This is a spell! I can smell the magic!" Panthara accused. "Gorvanus said he shot you! That lying toad!"

"Troll, actually," Runa said with a laugh. Then she faced her enemy with serious resolve in brilliant green eyes that shimmered in the flickering spell. "Look well and remember me, Panthara, for I am the arrow that will strike you down. Oh, and one more thing...do not expect me to ever call you *sister!*"

The shapes of Runa and the familiars floated above Panthara, flying out of her reach.

Panthara's screams faded into a distant echo. A wave of dizziness and a flash of light sent them swirling. Mellypip held on tight, swallowing a wave of nausea. In a gust of multi-hued shades, Mellypip tumbled back into his body and fell over, his little paws dangling above him. He gulped in deep breaths, shaking his head. Runa, ethereal in vanishing waves of enchantment, fainted in Darcus' arms.

"Is she all right?" Darcus asked in a worried voice.

Belwyn nodded. "Give her a minute. It's a common side effect."

"I think the wampu is getting sick," Sanura said.

Belwyn sighed. "That is also a side effect."

CHAPTER 19

Panthara fled to the sanctuary of her luxurious cabin. The bitterness of Cathal's laughter burned her. Runa still lived! She slammed the door, almost catching Azmadu's tail as he rushed in after her.

Azmadu yelped and hovered in the air above her. "Panthara, you almost crushed my tail!" he whined.

"Curses, is that all you can think about!" she snapped. "You have no idea how terrible this is! That pansy witch is still alive!" The sight of Runa's shimmering essence unraveled Panthara's calm. "She taunted me, Azmadu! Damn her! And what did she mean about Gorvanus being a troll?" She smoldered with rage and tugged at her mass of sable hair, moaning louder and louder until her anger erupted. She screamed and pointed at a ceramic pitcher; a flow of sorcery exploded it into dust.

"Gorvanus said Runa was dead!" She flung beams of red sorcery at the tray of ornate golden goblets, pitching them to the ceiling. They plummeted, scorched and melted into the carpet. "That lying toad! He failed me! And Cathal laughed at me too! ME! The Queen of Mowad!" She unleashed more frenzied magic, hurling her exquisite silver jewelry casket upon a jet of scarlet sorcery across the room. It struck the wall, and dozens of beautiful gems spilled out. The silver casket crashed to the carpet, molten and steaming.

Azmadu took refuge under the bed, whimpering. Panthara stormed about the room, ripping pillows and blowing up glass and precious objects with unbound rage.

The Captain of the ship and a guard burst into the smoking, magically-charged room. She froze in a shower of feathers that rained around her from shredded pillows. She glared at them with dangerous blue eyes.

The Captain bowed. "Forgive us, Your Majesty, but we heard violent noises and were concerned. We—"

Panthara flicked her wrist and the Captain went mute. Stunned, he stepped back, hands to his throat as he tried to speak, but no sounds issued from his open mouth.

Trembling with fear, the soldier pleaded, "Your Majesty, we only sought to—"

Her fierce gaze sent him to his knees. He bowed his head to the carpet in fear. Panthara smiled maliciously, a black flame poised on her fingertip. "I suggest you leave…now!"

Quaking with terror, the men fled the compartment. Panthara waved her hand and the door snapped shut behind them. She unleashed another scream and flung a hot ball of sorcerous fire across the room. It struck the door, leaving a gaping hole that sizzled.

"Panthara, Panthara, stop!" Azmadu cried from under the bed. "You're scary!"

Her wrath spent, Panthara sank to her knees in the middle of the ruined cabin and wept. The odor of charred wood and molten metal stank up the room.

After a moment of weeping and no further explosions, Azmadu poked his nose out. "Are you done now?"

"I think so," she replied, exhausted.

Azmadu crawled out from his hiding place. He waddled over to her and laid his head in her lap. "Feel better now?" he asked grumpily.

She stroked him with shaking hands. "Yes…a little. Sorry, Azmadu." Panthara smoothed her black hair and took several deep breaths. Finally, she stood up and carried Azmadu to the calling crystal and passed her hand over the mystical stone. It glowed with power. In a moment, Koll's image appeared in the clear crystal.

"I hope Xabral isn't there," Azmadu whispered.

"Hush," Panthara whispered. "This is urgent."

Koll greeted her. "Panthara, you look troubled, my Sorcerous Queen."

"Troubled doesn't even begin to express it, Koll," Panthara replied. "Runa's still alive! I just saw her essence in the prison hold."

"Runa is alive," Koll said. "I hoped it wasn't true."

"What do you mean?" Panthara asked.

"There were witnesses who saw her alive at the Araema Abbey after Gorvanus said she was dead," Koll answered. "I just learned of it. I was going to contact you."

"Runa used an enchantment to visit Cathal," Panthara spat. "A powerful spell too! I couldn't even hit her, Koll, because her body was only a projection through sorcery. Runa actually threatened me! She is surely on her way to Mowad now." Panthara began to pace around the crystal, stroking Azmadu. "And that idiot Gorvanus lied to me too! He said he killed her! When I see him, I'm going to make him suffer! He needs to be hunted down and whipped like the dog he is! Where is he?" Panthara demanded.

"That will not be an issue," Koll replied in a calm voice.

"What do you mean?" Panthara said.

Koll's black eyes burned with dark humor. "He is a changed man. Literally. Gorvanus is a troll."

Panthara flashed to Runa's words in the prison hold. She called him a troll. Suddenly, she burst out laughing. "I'm sorry, Koll. But this is actually amusing. What happened?" she asked bitterly. "Did Runa do it?"

"No, not Runa," Koll said smoothly. "It was the Princess Opaline."

"Princess Opaline is a sorceress? How did Gorvanus miss that?" Panthara wondered angrily.

"According to Zhelon Thor," Koll said. "Runa and Princess Opaline managed to spirit the Emperor away to an Abbey outside Tiamet. Levandius sent Gorvanus to murder Opaline and if necessary, kill the Emperor at the Abbey. They found Runa at the Abbey too, quite alive. One of the soldiers who escaped with Levandius reported Opaline's sorcery changed Gorvanus into a troll during a battle."

"Escaped?" Panthara murmured. "Levandius? What happened? Surely he is Emperor now."

"Levandius failed to take the throne," Koll said. "Emperor Tarsicius made a miraculous recovery. Someone must have managed to brew the antidote for the poison. Obviously, Cathal was busier than we thought before you captured him. Tarsicius defeated Levandius in *one* battle. The Emperor returned to Tiamet victorious. Levandius fled with his tail between his legs to Urgonclaw for asylum."

"Why would they help him? The High Priests of Rygon are not very forgiving of failure," Panthara said.

"Levandius still serves our cause. We will make use of him in other ways."

Panthara dismissed Levandius' fate without concern. "Levandius is a drug addicted fool. We don't need him anyway." She smiled with relief. "At least I will no longer have to fend off the advances of Levandius or Gorvanus. I found their crude attentions…revolting." She stopped pacing and frowned. "Opaline must also flee the Ivory Kingdoms. Tarsicius hates magic. We must assume she is exiled now for her magical blood and traveling with Runa. I don't like that either!"

"A small group of pathetic outcasts," Koll said. "By the time they reach Mowad, it will be too late."

Panthara stamped her foot impatiently. "But what are we going to do about Runa? That mousy girl is ruining my plans."

"Leave Runa to me," Koll replied.

~ * ~

Koll summoned one of his personal warriors who knelt at his feet. "Summon the Master Assassin of the Rashurkeen," he ordered. "He should be nearby, patrolling the desert rim. Go now!"

"At once, my Lord," a soldier said and sped away.

The cavern was ripe with activity. Bronze braziers and torches filled the vast cavern to give light and warmth. The cave's entrance was fortified by Rygon's warrior priests for added security. The resurrected remains of Ashur's body in the red crystal pulsated with power on the great circular altar. The laborious hours of weaving archaic magery from the relics of death bore dark fruit ripe for a soul.

The sorcery he wove from the ancient scrolls kept the body intact; but it was only a shell until they could summon the soul it once housed. Naloia worshipped at Ashur's feet in her mourning robes. Panthara's mother was quite mad of course. When their other duties were done, Koll would arrange to dispose of Naloia. Ashur would not want her now anyway. Her beauty had faded. Not from her years, for she was only thirty-six, but her bitterness and rage had eroded her charms.

Despite the extravagant uses of fire, the cavern was still chilled and full of shadows. Koll did not mind the cold, but Xabral did. He went to his private chamber in a small alcove to find Xabral resting on a heated rock.

"Are you finally awake?" Koll asked with a grin.

"Warmth feels good, Koll," Xabral replied with a sigh.

"Rest then my sweet," Koll said gently. "I have some things to arrange."

"Interesting or dull things?" Xabral asked languidly.

"Panthara insists Runa will be trouble. Perhaps she is right."

"What can Runa do?" Xabral said, curling his lustrous red and black scales on the warm rock. "Though she's a sorceress, she is only a girl. She's alone now too."

"A girl raised by Cathal the Sorcerer. Panthara desires her death. It would make a fine betrothal gift—Runa's heart in a golden box."

Xabral blinked and flicked his tongue. "You concern yourself too much about Panthara. There are other women to amuse your lusts, Koll."

"Not like Panthara," Koll said passionately. "I have seen to it she remained a virgin. I must be her 'first.' In the early years, it was easy. She was surrounded by eunuchs and women who watched over her as a Princess. I prevented any dalliance with Gorvanus or Levandius by warning her she had to be a virgin to perform the raising ritual to bring Ashur back."

"Is that true?" Xabral asked.

"Of course not, but it worked."

Xabral laughed and shook his poison stinger merrily. "A bloodstone ritual does not require virgins, of course."

"Of course," Koll smiled. "Soon, Panthara will sit at my side as my bride. And She will be restored—Obsydia, the Bloodstone Queen," Koll added with reverence.

Xabral sighed. "In the ancient wastelands of Skarros, She sleeps. When we know where her ancient palace is hidden, we shall release Her. Then we shall be rewarded and help Her rule the world." Xabral slithered off his rock and coiled at Koll's feet. "Tell me the story again."

Koll grinned. "You just love this tale, don't you?"

"Yes," Xabral said eagerly. "It's my favorite fairy tale." The snake pouted and rubbed his head against Koll's leg. "Please!" he begged.

Koll relented. "Very well." The sorcerer sat down cross-legged on the floor, smoothing his black robes. Eager, Xabral curled in his lap, and Koll began. "Once upon a time, Ahridum, the Lord of Darkness and Chaos, decided he would make an immortal child of His essence. His child would be Queen of the world. Her empire of blood and fire would be for His Glory! Through His daughter, Ahridum would reign supreme. So, Ahridum chose a bride from all the mortal women of the world."

"Was she beautiful?" Xabral asked wistfully.

"Yes. Lilith was her name. She had a long mane of raven hair and eyes like the starless night. Her flawless alabaster skin and shapely breasts and limbs were made for a god's desire."

"Did she know of her blessed fate?" Xabral whispered.

Koll shook his head. "She knew Ahridum chose her as His handmaiden. An oracle of the dark temple, she knew one day he would call her, though she was not aware of the honor Ahridum blessed her with. The world was in chaos then. The eras of illumination shattered when a dark star struck the world. Darkness swept across the lands like a soft quilt, ice and snow purified the world, night was a constant as the sun was blotted out by a heavy veil of clouds. Many nations were wiped out during the time of cleansing. Faith in the Eternals of Light waned. The world was ripe for Her coming."

"Tell me of this wondrous age," Xabral sighed.

"Blood and fire reigned. Lilith was a priestess of Ahridum's temple. A seer. The holy priests would sacrifice to Ahridum, bringing the unworthy infidel to the blade. Blood soaked Ahridum's altars each dawn and dusk. Lilith would sacrifice too, cutting out a maiden's heart with an ebonite blade. Then Lilith would paint her body with their blood and dance naked beneath the hot torches."

"She was very devout," Xabral agreed.

"But…there was an enemy," Koll said ominously.

"Who?" Xabral cried in fear, wagging his stinger. He always asked this, though he knew the answer.

"Kronus, the Warrior King. He was a champion of the cursed Light. He sought to kill the blessed dark spark before it was conceived …and hunted Lilith. The seers of Light warned Kronus that Lilith would give birth to the dark queen who would crush the Light. The birth of Obsydia was in danger of being erased from destiny. Kronus led his armies, seeking her out. He stormed Lilith's city, setting it to flame. He crashed the temple doors of Ahridum's holiest sanctuary, seeking out helpless Lilith."

Xabral scales quivered. "What of Lilith?" he asked. "Who would save her?"

"Ahridum would save his dark bride. Kronus desecrated holy ground with the blood of fallen priests. Ahridum's altar steamed with the blood of sacrifice. Next to that altar, Kronus found Lilith alone."

"Oh no!" Xabral cried in terror. "And the priests could not protect her?"

"No. And because they failed, these priests of Ahridum died since they were unworthy. Kronus sliced open their bellies and struck off their heads. Kronus, his sword dripping gore, stalked the sacred earth of dark and blood toward Lilith."

"Oh no!" Xabral cried.

"She fled the temple and ran across the frozen earth to escape Kronus. He pursued her, hunting her beneath iron gray skies in the bloody snow. They finally surrounded her. Lilith was trapped, naked and alone in death's chill! She prayed to Ahridum for salvation. He found her worthy and Ahridum used his Eternal powers to lift her from danger and transported her far away to a mysterious desert, leaving His enemies to howl in defeat. From this barren land, she began her final journey to the shores of the violent Isini Sea."

"Then she was saved from the Light!"

"Yes," Koll said. "Dark would have her now. The desert of black sands purified her. For days she walked alone in this wasteland, wild-eyed, feet raw and blistered. The brutal sun purged her of her old life and burned her skin. At last, she saw the sea and stumbled toward it."

"Where was she?" Xabral asked. "Was it…near the sacred tower?"

"Yes," Koll exclaimed, emotions of joy lifting his soul as he told this sacred tale. "As the twin moons rose in the sky, a great tempest began to rage. The Isini Sea roiled with rage."

"And Ahridum's blessed tower rose?"

"Yes, Xabral. Lilith watched as a black tower rose in radiance from the violent currents, shimmering at the heart of a terrible gray storm. Hooded beings, servants of Ahridum, appeared in a boat of glass and came for her. They carried her to the ethereal vessel and sailed to the black tower. Within the tower, they washed her body and painted it with sacred symbols in blood. They gave her wine, which revived her spirit and body. They anointed Lilith for the ritual of marriage, for she was destined to be the bride of Ahridum! No other mortal has been blessed to be joined with an Eternal."

"Was she happy?" Xabral sighed with envy.

"Glorious with joy! Naked, with only her long black hair as her wedding raiment, Lilith knelt upon the sacred altar. The sky eclipsed, for no light of a star or moon could be seen. Then Ahridum's essence filled his bride with the divine. But to love a god is danger-ous. The touch of Ahridum's essence seared her body. A mortal is not immune to the touch of an Eternal, even in a loving caress. But to the hooded servants who witnessed this sacred union, Lilith's screams of agony were the blessed sounds of conception. Black fires filled the temple as Ahridum's holy servants sang joyous hymns of darkness. When Ahridum's Holy Presence retreated, Lilith's shrieks of pain faded to a dull whimper.

Tears of joy welled in Xabral's eyes. "To be sacrificed to Ahridum must have been her greatest joy."

Koll nodded, and stroked Xabral's scales with tenderness. "Lilith sacrificed body and soul to give her hallowed baby life. The infant fed on her soul for nourishment. In moments of this immaculate conception of darkness, Lilith birthed her child of chaos, Obsydia. Obsydia was born into the loving hands of Ahridum's Hooded Guardians. These handmaidens wrapped the new babe in crimson silk."

"And what of Lilith?"

"Her duty done, Lilith's body crumbled to ashes, her body and soul consumed by the greatest of all powers, Ahridum."

"She must have been so happy. And the little baby?"

"The handmaidens of shadow watched over Ahridum's infant for thirteen nights as Obsydia slept. In that time she grew into a beautiful woman. When she woke, Obsydia was crowned the Bloodstone Queen."

Tears welled in Xabral's eyes. "I just love happy endings."

"Excuse me," a human voice interrupted, breaking the dark spell of the tale.

Annoyed, Xabral twisted around to see a guard kneeling at the entrance. He looked terrified.

Good.

"Forgive my intrusion, Lord Koll. But the prisoners have refused to eat since yesterday. Their jailor is concerned."

"I will take care of it," Koll said. "You may go."

After the soldier departed, Koll lifted Xabral and draped him across his shoulders. "Come, Xabral. We must reprimand our guests for refusing our hospitality."

Koll left his chamber and motioned for two of his guards to follow. They left the main cavern and passed through a dark tunnel that led downward to a smaller cave crowded with tall metal cages where the sorcerers were kept. The area reeked of human waste and despair. A few torches provided dim light. There were seven cages, but only five were occupied now. The other two would hold Cathal and Caliste once Panthara delivered them.

A large, bald brute of a man was their watcher. Clad in only leather breeches, his body thick with muscles. The keeper bowed to Koll. "They refuse food and water, Lord Koll. You said to alert you—"

Koll raised his hand and the keeper fell silent. "You have done your duty. Even in this sunless pit, ragged and dirty, they refuse to surrender. Well, I shall remedy that."

The five imprisoned sorcerers looked at Koll with such malevolence he wanted to laugh. A band of sorcerer bane was bolted around their necks, preventing any magic to aid their escape.

A woman with tawny hair and flashing hazel eyes beat against the bars. "Koll, you dung eater! You won't get away with this!"

Koll inclined his head. "Jiana. Your gentle manners are always a joy. And I've already gotten away with it, my dear. You are my prisoners. Attempting suicide in this manner is foolish. You will eat."

Jiana grabbed her crotch. "Eat this, Koll."

"Charming," Koll said.

Riva stopped his nervous pacing in the small jail. "Stop it, Jiana. It won't help."

Jiana kicked at the iron bars. "Yeah! Well, maybe it makes me feel better. And Koll will never capture Cathal or Caliste!"

"Ah, but I have Cathal and Caliste," Koll said with triumph. "They will arrive soon." He allowed them a moment to absorb the news. He relished their stunned faces.

The tall black sorcerer, Ulan, leaned against his cage and shrugged. "I'll believe it when I see it. Now go away, Koll. You stink up the place."

Myrsalian and Liat were at least quiet. Myrsalian's long red hair hung in his face as he sat in his cage. Stoic and proud, Liat sat crosslegged in his prison, though his angular eyes were locked on Koll.

"Now that I have your attention, your warden says you will not eat or drink," Koll said.

"Maybe we don't like the swill you're feeding us?" Ulan said. "Rats eat better garbage than what this thug offers us."

"You must eat to keep your strength up," Koll said. "How do you expect to exact your revenge upon me when you starve yourselves?"

"Pray we don't escape," Liat said calmly, long black hair framing his slender features. "I'll hunt you down and eat on your liver. I may even take your eyeballs for dice. They would make a nice chew toy for Dabiro."

"A fine sentiment," Koll replied. "But until then, you must eat. You cannot perish of your own accord."

"So we can become sacrifices for your obscene ritual?" Riva cried. "Never! We won't help you resurrect Ashur."

Koll looked at each of them, amused at their foolish pride. "You need only be alive for the ritual. It doesn't matter if your bones are smashed or if your arms or legs are missing. As long as you have a soul and breathe, you will serve as a sacrifice. The *Gate of Souls* will be opened.

"Open Jiana's cage," he said to the guards as he lifted Xabral from his shoulders and laid him on a rock. The scorpion snake lifted its hooded head to watch the excitement.

"No!" Myrsalian cried, reaching through the narrow bars. "Leave her alone."

"Ah, Myrsalian lives after all," Koll said. "I was beginning to suspect you had already died from your morose depression."

Ulan thrust against the metal cage and swore. His curses were quite imaginative.

Liat jumped up. "Don't hurt her! Damn you, Koll! Take one of us."

"Take me," Riva begged. "You know she's got a temper! I will offer myself willingly."

"Such generous offers of sentiment," Koll said. "Your weak affections make me choose Jiana for discipline. Odd, considering she could defeat each and every one of you, with the possible exception of Ulan, in a fighting match."

The sorcerers gripped the bars of their cages and shouted as the keeper unlocked Jiana's cell. She backed away; fists raised defiantly. The guards approached the angry sorceress with caution. Jiana had already injured several guards since her capture. True to her nature, she kicked and punched at them as they tried to extract her. It took both guards and the keeper to drag her out. Jiana struggled against the men, but they managed to subdue her on the ground.

"Give me a sword," Koll commanded, "and hold out her arm."

One of the guards handed Koll a scimitar. They held out her slim arm as Jiana cursed violently. Koll raised the sword. "Now, cooperate and eat, and I will not punish her for her numerous insolent remarks."

"Let her go!" they all cried as Jiana awaited the brutal stroke. "We will eat! Don't hurt her!" they begged.

Koll looked down at Jiana's prone body. "And you my dear?" he asked. "Will you be obedient to my will?"

"I'll eat. But I won't like it!" she spat.

"Excellent," Koll said. He brought the sword down swiftly, but the blade only struck the rocky floor, a mere inch from Jiana's exposed arm. Her panic-stricken face was reward enough. The terror on the other sorcerer's faces was like sweet wine. Koll stepped back.

"Next time, I will show no mercy." He turned to the guards. "Put her back in her cage. And be careful! She's a wild thing."

With rough hands they shoved her back into the cage, shut the door, and locked it.

"Bring them bread, meat and water rations," Koll commanded. "See they all eat!" He looked at the angry sorcerers and grinned. "Or I will return with a sword to slice up fresh meat for the vultures."

"Anything else?" the keeper grunted.

"Clean their cages. The smell is revolting."

"Yes, Lord Koll," the keeper said.

Xabral pouted on the rock. Koll stroked his scales. "Disappointed?" he asked.

"Yes," Xabral complained. "I was hoping to see blood."

"Come along. I'm positive their dispositions will drive me to make at least one of them bleed before the ritual," Koll said.

When Koll and Xabral returned to the main cavern, Sefu, Master Assassin of the Rashurkeen, awaited him. His black and red robes were dusty with sand and his face masked, but Koll could recognize those cruel eyes anywhere.

"Hail, Lord Koll," Sefu said.

"Welcome," Koll replied. "Thank you for coming so quickly."

"What task will you have me do?" Sefu asked.

"A simple duty, but it will require a great deal of travel and searching to find your victim."

"No distance is too great for the Rashurkeen. The chosen victim of our blades cannot escape death."

"Good," Koll said. He drew in the air, and with each fluid stroke a glowing rune appeared and then vanished. In a moment an image formed of a young girl with vivid green eyes and golden-brown hair. He looked at Sefu. "That is your victim. Her name is Runa. She is a sorceress and a danger to our cause."

"You wish her dead?"

"Yes." Koll said. "Search the ports, forests, roads and ships. She is traveling from the western shores of the Ivory Kingdoms toward Mowad. Summon all the men you have, sparing only what is needed to protect us here. Seek her out. I will use my sorcery to help locate her. She may have a few friends with her, kill them too. Leave no one alive."

Sefu's harsh brown eyes gazed upon Runa's shining image. "So young and fresh, like a blooming rose. My blade is eager to cut down such a flower. Are there any other orders?"

Koll nodded. "When you kill her, cut out her heart and bring it to me in a silver box. I wish to give it to my Panthara as a token of my affection."

Sefu bowed. "It shall be done, Lord Koll."

CHAPTER 20

It's too hot!" Dabiro the badger grumbled, dropping under the shade of a willow tree.

Belwyn landed on the ground. "Come on! It's almost sunset. We'll rest then."

"Too hot," Dabiro repeated with morose finality. He turned his backside to them and began digging with his powerful claws.

Belwyn's feathers puffed up with annoyance. "Dabiro listen!" he said sternly. "You must go on!"

"No!" the badger snapped.

Darcus stopped their caravan and dismounted Rono. "What's wrong now?" he asked in exasperation.

Belwyn spread his wings helplessly. "He's in a mood. What can I say? He's a *badger.*"

Sanura rolled her eyes. "Just peck his rump and make him move."

"You do it," Belwyn challenged her.

"What's he doing?" Opaline asked with concern.

The owl hopped over to her. "I think he's digging a burrow," Belwyn whispered cautiously.

"I'm digging my grave!" Dabiro moaned as he dug up huge wads of dirt.

Runa and Mellypip exchanged glances. This was not the first time Dabiro had fallen into a depressed mood.

"No hope," Dabiro grunted, shoveling a wave of dirt at Belwyn, who flew back to shake off the mess. The obstinate badger continued to dig, oblivious to everyone. "We will never make it. I'll never see Liat again. Mowad is too far. It's hopeless! Can't you see that? We are doomed." Dabiro plopped down in his shallow hole. "Just go on without me."

"Dabiro, stop this right now!" Runa scolded him. She dismounted her horse and marched over to him. Mellypip jumped from her arms to the grass, not wanting to be near the cranky badger. Runa knelt next to Dabiro and spoke gently. "I know you miss Liat and feel sad."

Dabiro lowered his head into her lap and moaned. "I'm mad too!"

"What else is new?" Sanura said. The cat flopped in a warm

sunspot. "Let me know when we're ready to be on the road again. I'm going to nap."

Buzzy the sloth shifted in Broda's arms. "We are going to need you to fight, Dabiro, unless of course you aren't up to it?"

"I live to fight!" Dabiro said proudly. "I'm a badger aren't I?"

Darcus stroked Rono's head. "It will be dark soon. We might as well set up camp here. The horses are tired anyway. Maybe we can catch some fish for supper."

"I'm not tired!" Rono said excitedly.

"I know, Rono," Darcus said, scratching his head affectionately. "You're a very energetic gryphon." He watched Dabiro exhume the forest loam with ferocious claws. "But I think the others are feeling the strain of travel."

Belwyn perched on a tree limb, shaking off dirt. "Just let Dabiro pout for a while. When he gets hungry, he'll come around."

"I heard that!" Dabiro shouted.

"I'm hungry," Mellypip said, rolling in a dandelion patch. "Is there any bread left?"

Talwyn rummaged through the packs. "A little, but it's a bit stale. We'll toast it. We still have cheese, beans and plenty of apples and porridge to fix for breakfast. Fish does sound good though. I can fashion some fishing poles from a few branches."

They all worked together, laying out their sleeping blankets and supplies. Talwyn and Hinkleburr gathered wood for the fire.

Broda dug a shallow hole for the fire. "Too bad certain badgers can't use their digging talents when needed," he said.

"That would be an affront to their contrary natures, brother," Talwyn replied, ringing the fire pit with stones.

Mellypip enjoyed lying in the grass in the fading sunlight. He liked the trees here. Enormous trees loomed above the forest floor like ancient wards of nature. They reminded him of home. Rono wandered over and nudged him. They began to play a game of tag. Rono did not really try to win, though Mellypip knew the gryphon could beat him with ease. Rono just liked the company, and the large creature was gentle with him. Though the powerful creature was older, Mellypip often felt like the grownup and made it his responsibility to look after the affectionate gryphon.

Opaline cleared her throat. "May I try to light the fire tonight... with my magic?"

Runa put her hand on Opaline's shoulder. "I'm not sure that's a good idea. Maybe another time, after you have had more…supervised training."

"Oh Runa, please! I'll never be able to control my magic unless I practice," Opaline begged.

Mellypip considered taking cover in the bushes. The last time Opaline tried to start the campfire with sorcery, an oak went up in flames. It took the combined efforts of everyone to put it out.

Runa relented. "Oh, all right." She guided Opaline to the woodpile. Broda and Talwyn made a swift change of direction away from her. Hinkleburr followed his aides a safe distance away.

"I saw that!" Opaline accused.

Darcus came back from the river carrying a jug of water. "Opaline's not going to cook tonight, is she?" he asked tensely.

Opaline gave Darcus a withering stare. "No. Don't worry, I'm not cooking!"

"Just asking," Darcus shrugged. He filled the tin kettle with water for evening tea.

Opaline put her hands on her hips and pouted. "I know I'm not the most adept person for rustic travel. The skills of making fire and cooking meals were not part of my royal education." She sat down on a moss-covered rock. "Oh, blast! I've hidden my sorcery for so long, I have no idea how to control it."

Darcus scooped tea leaves into the kettle. He grinned. "You did well enough with Gorvanus. That is one sorcerous event that will become legend."

"Damn, will I ever live that down?" Opaline moaned. "I feel terrible about that."

Darcus fixed a hard stare on Opaline. "Don't," he stated. "He was going to *kill* you, lady. Never forget that. Gorvanus was also involved in the conspiracy to abduct the sorcerers. He doesn't deserve your tears."

Opaline nodded. "I know. Still, to be fated to live as a troll would be a wretched curse."

Little Rosepetal peeked out of the bag next to Opaline. "Gorvanus was evil slime. You merely made his outside match his inside."

"Thank you, Rosepetal." Opaline smiled. "I would cuddle you, but you are far too prickly."

"Get some thick gloves. That's what Ulan use to do. Then he cast a spell that made his hands impervious to my quills. It's merely common sense, you know. Is it supper time?"

"Soon Rosepetal," Opaline replied. "I'll call you when it's ready." The hedgehog retreated back into her dark sanctuary in the bag.

Runa added more kindling to the pile. "Stop fretting about Gorvanus and relax! It wasn't your fault. You were angry and afraid."

"Dangerous attributes in a woman," Belwyn added. The owl perched on Darcus' shoulder. "Don't ever be too concerned about how much you hurt the enemy. It dulls the reflexes."

Runa and Opaline stood together. "Relax," Runa whispered. "Concentrate. Think…*small* this time." Opaline closed her eyes. "Now, take a few deep breaths. Calm your mind and focus. Think about lighting the fire within the stone circle. *Only* the stone circle," Runa emphasized.

Mellypip watched from a safe distance with the others. Only Darcus was brave enough to remain close. The timber began to smoke. A spark snapped and a tiny flame appeared.

Excited, Opaline clapped her hands. "I did it!"

Suddenly, a powerful surge burst upward in a pillar of black smoke. Mellypip covered his eyes with his paws, unable to watch. He peeped when he heard the sound of coughing and laughing. Runa and Opaline were covered head to toe with soot and ash, waving away choking billows. Mellypip breathed a sigh of relief. "That was very lucky, Runa. Be careful or Opaline could make you toast."

The trio of Dwarves poked their heads out from behind a nearby tree. "Is it over?" they asked in unison.

Darcus laughed. "You can come out, boys. It's safe now. At least she didn't set the forest on fire." He went to Runa and Opaline. "You girls go wash up. I'll take care of the fire. There looks to be a good, secluded spot by the river behind those trees. Just stay close."

"I'll protect them!" Mellypip offered.

"You do that, little one," Darcus said, grinning.

Belwyn flew down from the tree he had escaped to. "I'll think I'll supervise the children.

Opaline hid her smudged face in her hands. "I'm hopeless! I'm not good for anything useful!"

Darcus raised an eyebrow and pointed to Dabiro. "I wouldn't say that, Princess. You cheered up the badger."

Dabiro was rolling in the dirt with laughter, kicking up dust and grass.

"Well see, you did some good!" Runa said brightly. She patted

Opaline on the back and sighed. "I promise you; it will get better. Remember when I told you about my exploding potions? Maybe we should practice sorcery minus the flammable part." Runa and Opaline grabbed their packs. "Call us when supper is ready." They walked to the river. Mellypip and Belwyn went with them.

Darcus called after them. "And watch out for snakes!"

"Oh dear," Opaline mumbled. "I hate snakes."

They stripped down and hung their clothes over some branches. Runa cast a clean spell on them, and with a twinkle of magic the tunics and trousers were soot free and fresh again.

"They needed to be cleaned anyway. All this traveling is so dusty and sweaty," Runa said. "Do you have the soap, Opaline?"

"Yes, I think I do." She rummaged through the bag carefully. Rosepetal crawled out and settled on a small rock into a sun patch "Sorry, Rosepetal," Opaline apologized. "I didn't mean to disturb you."

"I need some fresh air, anyway," Rosepetal said, pointing her little nose at the beam of sunshine with contentment.

Runa took out an oatmeal cookie. "Melly, I've been saving this for you."

"A cookie!" Mellypip exclaimed and bounced over to her. He took the cookie in his paws and sniffed the sweet aromas of sugar and oats.

Belwyn perched on a low tree branch. "That's just what Furball needs—a good dose of sugar to make him hyper."

"I saved one for you too, Belwyn," Runa offered, taking another cookie from her pack.

The owl's eyes lit up. "Well, I guess I need to keep my strength up." He flew down and caught it in his beak when she tossed it.

"The last of Abbess Eshra's goodies," Runa said. "Darcus was right. She is an excellent cook. I must get her recipes."

"Could we clean up with a spell as well?" Opaline asked, removing the soap from its cloth wrapping. She sat down and unbraided her flaxen hair.

"Yes, but I long for a real bath with a thorough scrubbing with soap!" Runa said.

Mellypip nibbled at his cookie. Runa dived into the bright water with eager anticipation.

Opaline stepped into the water, but froze suddenly. "What about the snakes?" Opaline asked fearfully.

"I don't see any," Runa laughed. "Come on in. The water is heavenly!" She swam around the pool. "See, no snakes!"

Opaline swam in and in a few moments managed to relax. They shared the bar of soap, lathering their hair and bodies with the sweet-smelling bar and rinsing. They splashed water at each other in the tall reeds.

"How's your side?" Opaline asked.

Runa floated in the water. "Itching, but better. Darcus said the stitches could come out tomorrow."

"Something is bothering you that has nothing to do with stitches," Opaline said. "Tell me. Is it your dreams?"

Runa looked away. "No. I haven't had a dream since we left the Abbey. It's just that, well learning Panthara is my half-sister is, oh, I don't know."

"An apocalyptic horror beyond comprehension?" Opaline finished for her.

Runa bit her lower lip. "Yes, something like that."

"Well, we have something else in common now," Opaline said. "We both have siblings that should never have been seeded. Our families tend to be in extreme levels of dysfunction. We either adore them or wish them dead!" Opaline swam alongside Runa. "I know it probably sounds silly, but it feels strange knowing Belwyn is watching us naked."

Belwyn flew down to a lower branch above Opaline's head. "You needn't be embarrassed, Opaline, especially with perfect breasts like yours."

Opaline gasped and hurled the soap at Belwyn. "You dirty old owl! Go away!"

Belwyn snickered and flew off to a higher branch.

Runa walked out of the water in a fit of giggles, with Opaline following, her arms covering her breasts.

"It's not funny, Runa!" Opaline cried.

"Yes it is," she giggled. "I can't get embarrassed around Belwyn. He used to help diaper me."

Opaline squeezed the water from her hair and studied her reflection in the pool. Her hands went up to her face. "Oh no, my face! It's peeling!" she exclaimed.

Runa toweled off quickly. "It's called sunburn. Don't feel so bad, my whole complexion molts from spring to autumn."

Mellypip bounced along the riverbed while they dressed. All that girl talk was getting boring. His scrumptious cookie in his mouth, he found a nice spot under a birch tree. He was about to take a big bite when a flash of striped fur whizzed by him and snatched his cookie!

"Hey!" Mellypip cried. Disgruntled and battle-ready he chased after the creature to reclaim his cookie. The creature ran very fast. He cornered it against a big oak tree. It was the strangest rabbit he ever saw! A large rabbit with long ears and orange and black tiger striped fur!

"Stay back!" the rabbit threatened, picking up a stick and waving it around. "This cookie is mine!"

"Think again tiger bunny!" Mellypip challenged.

"I'm a tiger hare," he snapped. "And this sweet confection is a spoil of war!"

Mellypip began to think about changing into his impressive giant form that happened in Tiamet. He strained and shut his eyes, but nothing happened. No metamorphosis to the rescue. Darn!

The tiger hare sat down and watched with amused eyes. "Are you constipated?" the hare asked.

"No!" Mellypip grunted. "I was going to scare you."

"A valiant effort, my chubby friend," the hare replied.

Before Mellypip could respond, two of the largest wolves he ever saw ran down the hill toward them. They were snowy white with huge fangs.

The tiger hare bounced on his huge hind legs. "Ah, my companions have arrived," he announced. "Prepare for battle, my fuzzy wampu!"

Mellypip climbed up the oak tree, terrified. "Belwyn! Runa! Help, help, help! Monster wolves are going to eat me!" he cried.

The two white wolves sat on their haunches. The blue-eyed wolf looked down at the hare. "Shame on you, Jasper. That wasn't nice."

The tiger hare lowered his ears. "I was just having a bit of fun."

The amber-eyed white wolf shook its head. "You scared him! Look at him shivering in the tree. And give back his cookie!"

The whole camp surrounded them. Folks and familiars, swords drawn, claws and teeth bared.

"Now look what you've done!" the blue-eyed wolf admonished Jasper.

"Well, I'm sorry!" the hare cried.

"Jasper? Is that you?" Dabiro growled.

Belwyn landed on Darcus' shoulder and laughed. "You randy

old hare! We've been worried about you!"

Runa sighed with relief. "That's Jasper. He's Jiana's familiar."

"Brothers!" Jasper cried and hopped over to his friends. There was much tussling and wrestling.

"What about us?" Rosepetal and Sanura inquired primly.

"Ah, my pointy sister Rosepetal!" Jasper added. "I would hug you, my sweet, but you are dangerous. And Sanura, you are ravishingly plump as ever!"

"I'm not plump!" the cat growled.

"Yes, she's fluffy," Rosepetal sniffed.

Darcus' sword was still raised. "Who are the wolves then?" he asked sharply.

"I know who they are," Dabiro laughed.

One of the white wolves shimmered, and transformed into a beautiful woman with long, flaming red hair and amber brown eyes. "I am Sirah," she said. "The wolf is my familiar, Arial."

"Mother!" Opaline cried and ran to her waiting arms. The two embraced in a flood of tears and laughter.

Runa smiled. With the tip of her finger, she lowered Darcus' sword. "I think we are safe now." She looked up into the tree. "Mellypip, you can come down now."

Mellypip sighed and scurried down. Jasper handed him his cookie. "Sorry, mate. Just a bit of fun. Looks quite tasty!"

Mellypip sighed and broke off a piece and handed it to Jasper. Best not to irritate the weird bunny.

"Thanks!" Jasper said.

After a few moments, Opaline and Sirah composed themselves. Opaline wiped tears from her eyes. "I'm sorry. It's been so long since I've seen my mother. Our visits have been rare since she was exiled."

Sirah looked concerned. "Where is Felisia?"

Belwyn brightened. "Felisia is with you too?"

"I'm right here!" the tiny owl announced, gliding down to Sirah's open palm.

"She's so cute!" Opaline said. "Is this Myrsalian's familiar? I have wanted to meet her and Arial for so long."

"I welcome another member of my pack," Arial replied softly, and permitted Opaline to give her a hug.

Sirah nodded, stroking the owl's head with her finger. "Felisia insisted on coming. She is an elf owl, the tiniest owl in the world."

Mellypip noted she was pretty, with fawn and cream feathers. He also noticed the change in Belwyn when the venerable old owl gazed at Felisia. He realized Belwyn must have a crush on the diminutive owl. Felisia pretended not to notice, preening her fluffy feathers.

"What are you doing here, Sirah?" Buzzy asked.

"Let's all have some supper first," Sirah said. "I could not let you go on this journey alone. Myrsalian is my father. I refuse to simply do nothing."

Opaline pulled Runa to her side. "Oh Mother, this is Runa. She's my best friend. Cathal is her grandfather."

"I have heard a great deal about Runa over the years. I've always wanted to meet her." Sirah said softly. "I'm glad Opaline has such a wonderful friend." Sirah kissed Runa on the cheek.

They prepared supper to welcome their new allies. It was a celebration too, with the reunion of Opaline and her mother, Sirah. Sirah offered her supply of cornbread to the simple feast. Broda managed to gather some wild berries. Fish cooked over the fire. Homey smells of good food shared with friends. Suddenly, everything felt safe and warm. The familiars even behaved with decorum.

Sirah and Opaline sat on a log, the wolf at Sirah's feet. "I have been hunting you since my last conversation with Iona," Sirah said. "She told me the route you were taking to Ilyrra, and I was hoping to find you. I was worried about my father, Myrsalian. I knew I couldn't remain in Thill once Iona told me what was happening, nor could their familiars." She put her arms around Opaline's shoulders. "And I was concerned about my daughter." Sirah looked at her daughter, smoothing a stray lock of hair out of Opaline's eyes. "You did a noble thing, helping your father."

"He still exiled me when he learned I was a sorceress," Opaline said. "You were right, Mother. I was a fool to stay for so long. He doesn't want us."

Sirah cradled her daughter gently. "Tarsicius cannot change," Sirah said sadly. "But that is his choice. Now you can come home to Thill with me when this journey is done. Taran will be glad to have his sister home too. We love you. Your place is with us."

"How come Taran didn't come?" Opaline asked.

"I forbade him. He wasn't happy about it. Taran also has someone to look after. He has a familiar now. A tabby kitten named MacTabbish. It was safer for both of them to stay there. Your band also needs a fully trained sorceress to help you. We are going to face some very evil folk in Mowad."

"That, Lady, is an understatement," Darcus added. "I welcome your assistance."

"Thank you, Darcus," Sirah replied with a dazzling smile.

Runa speared pieces of fish to the tin plates. "There are extra helpings of fish for Felisia and Arial."

"Thank you," Sirah replied.

The wolf and owl also thanked her. The little owl was quite dainty as she pecked at her meal. The wolf was not delicate as she devoured her share of fish.

Runa sat down across from Sirah and Opaline. "So, do you know where Iona is now?" Runa asked, sharing cornbread and berries with Mellypip.

"I don't know," Sirah answered in a worried voice. "She said there was something important she needed to attend to. Iona is a good friend, but she's also very private," Sirah said between bites. "I hope Opaline's magic will improve too, now that she can be *properly* instructed."

"A remedy we all look forward to," Hinkleburr chuckled.

Belwyn hooted. "At least she wasn't magical from birth. Runa had magic even as a baby, which caused us trouble until she was older."

"She could do spells even as a baby?" Opaline exclaimed. "I'm jealous."

"Well, not exactly spells, but magic happened!" Belwyn said, biting into his fish with relish. "Runa's particular fondness for butterflies once caused the tree tower to fill up with them. Runa sat there gurgling, covered head to toe with butterflies. Monarchs, blue fairy wings, you name it. It took hours to clear out the house. Runa loved the light too. She would curl up in any sunspot and go to sleep." Belwyn chuckled. "When she got mad, she would explode her milk bladders. Cathal finally had to brew a binding potion to keep her under control until she learned the word no."

Mortified, Runa cried, "Belwyn! You need not expose all my childish quirks to Lady Sirah and Opaline."

"Too late." Belwyn laughed. "Telling stories is the reason we adults put up with your antics as babies. It's called balance. You tell her, Buzzy." He looked at the sloth, who was curled up asleep next to Hinkleburr. "Well, he will back me up on this later. You also went through an annoying phase when you pretended I was your familiar and tried to dress me up—in dresses. I had to put a stop to it. An owl needs his dignity."

Sirah laughed. "Don't be embarrassed, Runa. I have already heard many of these stories from Myrsalian. Don't fret; I will gladly reciprocate with my own tales of Opaline and Taran when they were small to balance things out."

"I'm doomed," Opaline said, but she could not stop smiling and holding her mother's hand.

Mellypip snuggled in Runa's lap. He felt safe and secure with a full tummy. The moons were high and bright. With any luck they would be in Ilyrra tomorrow.

~ * ~

Red smoke swirled in water charged with magic. Koll stared into the black bowl. The image of Runa and her friends began to form in the mist. He heard their voices like faint whispers. Koll's black eyes glittered in the shadowy cave. "I have them!" he said with triumph.

Xabral raised his head. "The spell of seeking works at last!" he said. "Where are they?"

"A mere day's journey from Ilyrra. They are traveling east along the river."

"They have come farther than we thought they could. Panthara has not even reached the coast of Mowad yet."

Koll poured a cup of wine. "This spell should have worked days ago. Something or someone is protecting them."

"Who?" Xabral asked.

"I don't know. But it doesn't matter now." Koll took a jagged black crystal from his robes. He held it in his hand and whispered words of magic. It glowed with red light. Sefu's face appeared in the stone.

"I know where they are," Koll said. "They are near Ilyrra's borders. I will show you where."

"We are not far from their lands, Lord Koll."

"Do not fail me, Sefu," Koll warned. "I want them all dead. And remember, I want Runa's heart."

CHAPTER 21

Darcus led them through the forest. Mellypip bounced in Runa's lap astride Rono. He liked it when she rode the gryphon. He didn't have fleas. Mellypip felt extra small amid the titan trees shadowing the feral landscape. Swirling mist lingered on the ground not yet vanquished by the beams of sunlight that filtered through the black-green canopy. The two white wolves ranged ahead to scout the way.

"Belwyn?" Runa asked. "Are you sure we are going the right way?"

Belwyn flew down and alighted on Darcus' arm. "Of course, I'm sure," he replied caustically. "I may be venerable, but I am not yet infirm of memory. We are very near the borders of Ilyrra."

Darcus looked around them, his craggy features taut with worry.

"What's wrong, Darcus?" Runa asked quietly.

"I don't know," he replied. "There is something strange in the air I can't put my finger on."

They continued to ride, alert to any possibility, leaving the thick forest for more open, hilly land. The quiet green surroundings held an eerie feel. They rode in silence for an hour, until Darcus reined in his horse, signaling for them to stop. The scar over his eye twitched as he looked around. The wolves returned to the group, sniffing the air; a quiet whine escaped Arial's throat.

Belwyn spread his wings, flapping them nervously. "Darcus," he said. "Something is not right. I smell magic…the dirty kind."

"I smell it now, too." Runa nodded. "It's getting stronger."

Mellypip shivered in Runa's arms. "I thought it was because there are so many sorcerers in our party now."

"I agree, Belwyn," Darcus murmured. "It is too quiet. The land feels…altered in some way."

Rono sniffed the air. "I smell other gryphons!"

"They aren't native to these parts." Darcus unsheathed his sword.

The wolves wheeled about; their ears twitching for any sound, their eyes straining for a hint of movement.

"Rono's right," Sirah said. "And there are humans, too…many humans. The whole area reeks of sorcery. I don't like it."

"We're turning back now," Darcus ordered. "Belwyn, is there

another road to Ilyrra?"

Before the owl could answer, the landscape about them began to fade, and the false illusion of calm green grasslands melted away, revealing a detachment of at least fifty Rashurkeen, mounted on gryphons, surrounding them.

"Oh, hell," Darcus spat.

"Damn." Belwyn clacked his beak furiously. "I *knew* it was a spell!"

Sirah shimmered into human form; with a blur of motion, her wolf-headed staff appearing in her hands. A blinding charge of orange sorcery streamed from its tip, as the assassins charged.

The staff-magic flared up and out, forming a glittering dome that enveloped the group. The first wave of Rashurkeen bounced off the dome with a sickening crunch of bone; blood splattering, as rider and beast impacted against the unyielding iridescent shield.

Panicked and angered, the lead rank of gryphons fell upon the fallen Rashurkeen, tearing at their dying or lifeless bodies. The remaining assassins who had avoided charging headlong into Sirah's protective dome struggled to regain control of their own mounts, as the blood frenzy overwhelmed them, as well.

The angry shouting of men and the gryphon's howls filled the air. Inside the dome, the horses and ponies reared, dancing in wild terror. Mellypip clung to Runa's arm as she tried to calm a near-hysterical Rono.

"That was risky, Sirah, but inspired," Darcus complimented her. "Quick thinking."

Sirah nodded. "We needed protection fast."

"Now what?" Hinkleburr looked about nervously. "This is most disconcerting. I thought we were past this sort of thing, at least until we reached Mowad."

"They must have a sorcerer working for them," Sirah said. "How else could they have concealed their presence until the last moment?"

"There!" Hinkleburr pointed. A dark-robed sorcerer stepped from the turmoil, gripping a heavy staff of twisted ebony wood. He ignored the wild-eyed gryphons that tore at the earth with their razored claws, only inches from where he walked. A large black crow perched upon his shoulder, cawing at the chaos all about. Even in his distress, Mellypip could not help but choke at the stench of such unbearable evil.

The Rashurkeen sorcerer extended his staff, muttering foul,

unfamiliar words of magic that those within the dome felt, rather than heard. Smoky, dark bolts of sorcery arched from his staff, striking the shield, again and again, in a rainstorm of black sorcery. The ground beneath them shook with the force of the relentless pounding.

Sirah gripped her own staff even tighter. "He's trying to tear down my shield."

"But, I thought another sorcerer couldn't undo your magic?" Opaline did not try to hide her confusion.

"He can't undo it," Sirah acknowledged. "But, that doesn't mean he won't try to *break* it down."

Another man approached the enemy sorcerer, his garb of black robes and red turban like that of the other Rashurkeen save for a wide, red sash belted around his waist.

"A Master Assassin," Darcus muttered grimly. "Koll and Panthara have spared no expense. I'm touched."

"What will happen when the magic fades?" Opaline pressed Sirah.

Darcus raised his hand. "Quiet! They want us to panic. Frightened people make mistakes. When the shield falls, everyone stay together. We'll ride as fast as we can; retreat back into the woods. It'll be harder to catch us in there. They still haven't regained full control of their gryphons, and that may give us a few moments."

The dome was evaporating, bit by agonizing bit, as each molten black orb of Rashurkeen sorcery impacted against Sirah's own. Sanura shapeshifted into her large panther form, joining Dabiro and Arial for battle. Darcus gripped his sword tight.

"I'll stand and fight, too!" Jasper hopped to the ground.

"Get back with Broda," Darcus barked sharply. "This is a fight we can best win on the move."

The tiger hare grumbled but leapt back onto Broda's lap. Buzzy remained draped over Talwyn's shoulder.

Darcus turned to Opaline. "Where's Rosepetal?"

Opaline patted her bag. "She is secure in my pack. She's upset. I hear her hiccupping."

"I may join her when there's time." Darcus replied dryly.

"Be ready, folks," he warned in a louder voice. "Run fast, and run hard!"

The remnants of Sirah's magic bubbled and weakened; at last, the dome of protection collapsed and vanished.

"Go!" Darcus shouted, slapping the rump of his horse with the flat of his blade to spur it on.

The group bolted, frantic to stay close together to protect one another. Mellypip clung to Runa.

"Come on, Rono," he whispered into her sleeve. "Run."

The Rashurkeen rallied their mounts, setting off in pursuit. Darcus kept to the rear of the retreating horses, first striking down a Rashurkeen on his left, before delivering a mortal slash to the unprotected flank of a riderless gryphon on his right. A score of assassins flew overhead, waving scimitars and throwing the short, broadheaded lances they favored. Arial and Dabiro fought savagely, killing or crippling those assassins foolish enough to get too close to the group.

Sirah stood in her saddle's stirrups for balance, casting waves of gray magic at their pursuers. Smoky tendrils coiled around man and gryphon alike, felling them at a dead run into a deep sleep.

Four Rashurkeen dropped from the sky, only a dozen yards in front of Runa's path. Without a thought, waves of white energy sprung from her hands, repulsing her attackers a good hundred yards backwards into the heavy thickets bordering the forest.

Belwyn and Felisia set upon those foes above who flew too close, raking and slashing at unprotected eyes, flesh and wings. Sanura's bloodlust raged, rending anyone who challenged her. Dabiro rammed his way through his opponents, smiling at the sound of cracking bone and the screams of agony left in his wake.

One foolhardy Rashurkeen leapt from his gryphon in midair, tackling Darcus and knocking him off his horse. They both tumbled to a bone-jarring stop at the base of an ancient oak. The assassin, younger and more eager to kill than his opponent, gained his footing first. Speed, however, does not always grant the upper hand. Years of battlefield experience had taught Darcus to fight in any position, on any terrain. Flat on his back, Darcus parried the assassin's curved blade, once, twice, then again. On the attacker's third downward stroke, Darcus came up into a crouching position in a move so fast, so fluid, the assassin did not have time to react. Darcus slid his own blade into the folds of the Rashurkeen robes, feeling his steel nick against bone. He heard an audible gasp from his opponent, as he turned away from the wounding blade.

The assassin continued his turn; the heavy fabric of his robes catching and holding Darcus' blade before he could pull it free. It became a momentary tugging match between the two adversaries.

The harder Darcus twisted and pulled, the more the assassin turned away, attempting to keep him off-balance.

The glint of blue-tinged steel appeared in the Rashurkeen's hand. A double-edged, serrated dagger arced upward on a path toward Darcus' exposed neck. Before Darcus could react, a flash of gray-brown feathers struck the assassin between the shoulders, knocking both men aside. Belwyn's gore-covered talons found the assassin's throat, and he gripped tight.

Darcus regained his feet but did not interfere.

The Rashurkeen struggled; his breath coming in ragged gurgles as the lifeblood filled his windpipe. Soon, the struggling subsided, the gurgling ceased. Crimson spread across the grass, glistening wetly. Finally, Belwyn released his hold.

"Thanks," Darcus wrenched his sword from the dead man's robes. "Guess I owe you a tankard."

"I won't say no." He spread his wings wide and shot into the air. "But," he called back, "we're not out of this yet. Come on!"

The sound of fighting, magical explosions, and angry shouts somewhere ahead reminded Darcus of his charges. He set off at a run to catch up, fearing what he might find.

Suddenly, strange cries; neither gryphon nor horse, echoed high above the din of battle. Darcus looked up into the sun, to see another wave of flying creatures appeared overhead. Darcus could only curse himself as a fool and ran faster.

Just ahead, he saw Runa; still on Rono's back, clutching Mellypip in one arm and hurling bolts of blue-white lightning with the other.

"Look!" he heard her cry out, pointing into the sky. "Raven Wing!"

Darcus stumbled as he turned for another look.

Ilyrran rangers, astride their majestic perytons, winged deer with feathers instead of fur, filled the sky. Wings spread wide, the perytons swept down upon the Rashurkeen. The Raven Wing warriors challenged the enemy, engaging them in fierce hand-to-hand fighting high above the forest canopy. A few of the Ilyrran rangers rode the edges of the battle, glided forward when needed; lifting members of their company to safety.

The Ranger's somber black and green uniforms contrasted with the red and black of the Rashurkeen. The perytons, their feathers vibrant shades of brown, blue, gold, green, and so many others, glistened in the sun.

Fighting his way back to Runa and the others, Darcus saw the Rashurkeen sorcerer confront Sirah. A ball of dark magic crackling in his hand.

"Burn!" he shouted and hurled the ball at Sirah. She seemed to shimmer, then disappear. The black sorcery smashed into the earth, leaving a sizzling, scorched hole where she stood just a moment before. When Darcus saw her again, she was several yards away.

The sorcerer grimaced. "You spoil my plans, witch!"

Arial charged the sorcerer from behind, knocking him to the ground; her sharp teeth rending his flesh. Sirah ran forward, but before she could ready a spell, the sorcerer's crow familiar attacked Arial, digging its talons into the wolf's snowy back. Sirah seized the sorcerer's fallen scimitar and severed both claws from its legs. The crow shrieked, wings flapping in anger and surprised pain. A second stroke of the blade and Sirah separated the crow's head from its body, ending its ear-splitting cries forever.

A lone gryphon swept down from the battle above, knocking Runa off Rono before landing several yards away. The gryphon turned, screaming a challenge before charging Rono. Dazed and shaken, Runa moaned as she scrambled away, Mellypip in her arms, desperate to avoid the charging gryphon. Rono fled into the heavy thicket, his only hope of avoiding the enemy gryphon's beak and claws.

"Runa!" Mellypip shook her by the arm. "Get up, Runa!" A terrified Mellypip sucked in his breath, clinging to his young sorceress, as the red-sashed Master Assassin stalked toward them. Dagger in hand, his dark eyes burning with death. Mellypip shook her again. "Please, Runa! Get up, now!"

Runa staggered to her feet, grabbing Mellypip by the scruff of the neck, and ran. The Rashurkeen Master moved with the easy speed of a predatory beast, and soon caught her in his strong arms. He flung Mellypip aside. Runa continued to struggle, as his thick, blood-stained fingers closed about her throat. He threw her to the ground, pinning her against the hard earth.

"Koll the Sorcerer makes a special request of you, Sorceress." His laugh was deep and humorless. "A gift. He wants your heart!"

Desperate, Mellypip raced back to her, wishing with each long stride his magical ability would manifest itself. He looked to the sky, hearing himself shout above the rush of blood pounding in his ears. "Belwyn! Where are you?" he cried. "Help Runa!"

Just as the Master Assassin touched the point of his dagger against her heart, Runa screamed. A pure, white sorcery flared to life, turning her entire body into a beacon of light for one long moment. The light stunned her attacker, forcing him to let go of Runa. He stumbled back, shielding his eyes. In that instant, Runa swept Mellypip up in her arms and turned to run. The Rashurkeen Master recovered quickly and chased after her. A look of murder etched upon his cruel features—painful murder.

A flash of crimson feathers caught Runa's eye as she ran, and a great peryton, hot breath steaming in the cool forest air, landed behind her, blocking the Master assassin's path. Long-healed scars latticed the creature's powerful body. It pawed the earth, shaking its massive rack of silvery antlers in challenge. The Rashurkeen Master unsheathed his scimitar and, with a blade in each hand, attacked.

But it was no two-legged victim the Master faced this time; bent on standing his ground to fight, nor turning to run for his life. An Ilyrran Ranger on a peryton charged the assassin with speed and power the man could not have guessed. He covered no more than a few yards when the peryton's antlers impaled him through chest and stomach; the impact lifting the Rashurkeen off the ground. The peryton flung off the dying assassin. It trotted back to Runa, blood still dripping from the silvery antler points. The man astride the peryton quickly leaned over and reached out his arm to her.

"Quick. I'll carry you to safety!" the ranger said.

"Thank you," Runa said with relief and took his hand. As he pulled Runa up behind him, she felt the rider shudder, and saw a spear pierce the Ilyrran's chest. He slumped forward in his saddle, losing his grip on Runa's arm.

"Aidan!" the crimson peryton cried.

"No!" Runa shouted as she fell. Regaining her feet, Runa tried to help the wounded man as he slid from the saddle. Just then, Darcus reached them. He caught the man in his arms; blood trickled from the corner of the rider's lips. "Hold on, friend!" he said. "I've got you." Darcus pulled him free of the stirrups and laid him on the grass. He was still alive, but barely.

"Runa!" Mellypip shouted. "Look out!"

Three more Rashurkeen appeared from the nearby trees. A second spear arced toward the fallen Ilyrran, but Darcus' fast reflexes deflected it with his sword.

"Get behind me, Runa." Darcus stood, the sword in his hand

already dark with assassin blood. "Stay with him."

Runa obeyed, cradling the wounded man's head in her lap.

Darcus charged, ducking the first Rashurkeen's blade as they passed one another; decapitating him with a vicious back-handed stroke. He landed a solid boot to the second attacker's stomach, knocking the wind out of him. The assassin fell to his knees. Darcus swung about, blocking the third man's downward sword stroke. Darcus' blade flashed, slicing open the assassin's belly.

The second assassin had regained his feet, rushing Darcus; a half-moon bladed axe gripped for a slashing attack. Darcus whirled back to meet him, but the crimson peryton reached the attacker first, his powerful wings spread wide, lifting the assassin high into the air. Up and up the peryton flew, the Rashurkeen cradled on his rack. Then with a flip of his muscular neck, the peryton threw the man even higher, as a child might toss away a rag doll. The black-clad assassin fell screaming back to earth. Runa winced as his screams were cut short when he struck the ground.

"Thanks," Darcus said when the peryton landed again.

"It was my pleasure." The creature bowed its head.

Darcus hurried back to where Runa held the fallen ranger, Aidan, as the man struggled to breathe. Much of the battle was over now. Many gryphons and Rashurkeen lay dead. The green path was stained a glistening red. Mellypip looked around for their friends, fearing more death.

"You all right, Furball," Belwyn asked as he landed next to him.

"I'm not hurt," Mellypip said in weary voice. It was all he could think of to say.

The rest of the Raven Wing gathered around them. They had rescued Opaline and the Dwarves early in the battle, flying them some distance from the fighting for their safety. Sirah arrived, leading the other familiars. All were exhausted and bloody, but alive. Hinkleburr and his aides were in tears.

"Filthy Rashurkeen butchers!" Hinkleburr wept. "They killed one of the horses and two of our Dwarven ponies!"

The wounded Ilyrran, head still cradled in Runa's lap, looked up at Darcus with glassy eyes.

"You were very brave," his voice was a hoarse whisper. "Even from high above, I witnessed your courage. Many Rashurkeen lay dead because of you. When the assassins came to finish me, you risked your life to shield me. Your actions make us brothers. What's your name?"

"I am Darcus. Now be still, so we may help you."

The leader of the Raven Wing dismounted. He went to his fallen comrade and took his hand.

"Hush, Aidan," he said. "We will get you home."

"I'm dying, Ryen," he whispered. "My home is now in the Otherworld. Tell Redstorm…I shall miss him." He looked at Darcus. "Thank you…Brother," he said with his final words.

Death took Aidan in the quiet of the green forest, and Darcus closed his eyes.

The Ilyrran leader laid a comforting hand on the crimson peryton's neck. "I am sorry, Redstorm. Your rider has journeyed to the Light."

Grief filled the peryton's eyes. He lowered his head. "Then, I shall carry him one last time."

The Ilyrran then turned to Runa. "We have been searching for you."

Runa wiped tears from her eyes and looked at him. "Are you Ryen? Cathal's friend?" she asked in an unsure tone.

He stood and pushed back his hood. Pointed ears accentuated his aquiline features. His walnut brown hair was shaded with silver.

"I have not seen you since you were small, Runa. We know what is happening. We will carry you to Moonthorne." He looked at Darcus. "Aidan has bestowed a great honor on you, Darcus. Aidan proclaimed you a brother. I also remember you from the great battle in Mowad when Ashur fell. You are most welcome."

"Does that gryphon belong to the Rashurkeen?" One of the Ilyrrans pointed to Rono, who staggered toward them, bleeding and crying. "I spotted it fighting with another of its kind. So fixed on killing this one, its attacker did not see me coming until I drove my sword through its throat. I had every thought of killing this one as well, but…something stayed my hand. If you wish it…" The Ranger gripped the hilt of his sword.

Runa pulled Rono to her side to protect him. Rono was shaking and Runa stroked him. "This gryphon is with us," she said quickly. "He is…a friend. His name is Rono and he is very gentle."

"We see he is no threat," Ryen agreed.

The other Ilyrran threw back his hood. He was younger, with long black hair and storm blue eyes. "Father, we should pursue the Rashurkeen and finish them off," he said impatiently.

"Patience, Jadon," Ryen said firmly.

Runa gazed at Jadon strangely. He looked at her too for a heartbeat, and then turned away. Something passed between them, though Mellypip could not fathom what it was.

"We grieve for your fallen animal companions," Ryen said. Some of our rangers will stay and bury them with honor." Ryen looked at the field where dead Rashurkeen and gryphons lay. "The rest we will burn and scatter their ashes so as not to contaminate our lands."

The sound of a distant-sounding, angry voice caught their attention. Darcus and Ryen followed the sound to the dead body of the Master Assassin. Darcus examined the body and removed a black crystal from his robes. The voice echoed from the stone.

"Sefu, are you there?" the voice demanded. "Did you kill Runa? Answer me!"

Darcus spat angrily. "More foul magic."

"That's Koll's voice," Belwyn said hotly.

Darcus gazed into the stone. Runa and Sirah went to him and saw Koll's face form in the jagged crystal.

"I'm afraid Sefu cannot answer you, Koll," Darcus said to the stone. "If you wish to find him, I suggest you follow him into Hell?"

Darcus dropped the sorcerous stone, knelt, and crushed it with the hilt of his sword.

CHAPTER 22

The flight to Moonthorne was breathtaking and frightening as the Ilyrran rangers carried them on their perytons high above the forest canopy. Runa and Mellypip rode with the young ranger, Jadon, and his peryton, Darkleaf, who was the deepest midnight blue color, almost black. Runa held Mellypip as they soared into the sky. Jadon gripped the reins of Darkleaf with one hand and held Runa with the other. Darcus rode Rono, who looked elated to be flying in the same presence as Raven Wing.

Jadon gripped Runa about the waist as they flew. "Comfortable?" Jadon whispered in her ear.

"I'm fine, thank you," Runa replied.

Mellypip sensed Runa's rigid posture was not just from a fear of falling. *What's wrong, Runa,* he asked through the bonding.

He's holding me too tight, she answered.

Better too tight than to tumble, Mellypip said. He considered her words and then added, *He's not getting fresh, is he?*

No, I'm just upset and rattled, Melly. That poor ranger died saving my life. And I feel so bad about our horse and ponies too! Those evil men!

Mellypip burrowed his face against her neck. He was heartsick too, about the ranger Aidan, and the pain everyone had suffered because of Koll and Panthara. He didn't like horses much, but for them to be slain by the cruel Rashurkeen was sickening. Mellypip could not wrap his mind around all the wickedness in the world. There was no reason for it, and that perplexed him more than anything.

They soon reached the Ilyrran city of Moonthorne and began the descent to solid ground. They landed in a large circular clearing where other rangers waited for them. From their vantage point on the hill, Mellypip could see much of the city below.

"Oh Runa, look! It's a city of trees!" Mellypip exclaimed as he pointed.

It was indeed wondrous. The homes very much like their own tree tower, though there was a greater variety of shapes and sizes to these arboreal homes, large to small. Some soared high and slender in the air, others were squat and broad. The river that divided Moonthorne was also quite beautiful, shaded by drooping willows.

Jadon dismounted Darkleaf and lifted Runa from the saddle. Mellypip jumped to the sweet-smelling grass, grateful to have all four paws earthbound again.

Raven Wing warriors set down, and their weary friends were somber as they joined the circle of rangers awaiting Redstorm. The great crimson peryton landed, sorrow etched his rough, scarred features; the body of Aidan strapped to his back. Ryen dismounted Silverthorne, untied Aidan and lifted him from the saddle with solemn care. Two rangers bearing a litter came running. They all bowed their heads with respect as they laid the body of Aidan on the litter and covered him with his cloak.

Redstorm shook his great rack as he pawed the earth with heavy hooves. He howled with grief. The other perytons joined, their mournful keening echoing all around them. With reverence, they carried the body away.

Belwyn flew to Runa's shoulder and bowed as they passed.

"Where are they taking him?" Mellypip asked gravely. "What do they do with the dead?"

"They will take him to the temple," Belwyn answered grimly.

"There Aidan will be bathed and wrapped in a shroud," Jadon added. "Then we will take his body to the necropolis outside Moonthorne. It is a sacred grove, where our heroes are buried. The final rites will be held at sunset."

"We would all be honored to attend," Runa said softly. "If that is permitted."

"Yes, we would welcome you," Jadon said. He stroked Darkleaf's head and fed him some unusual looking treats.

Runa gazed upon the serene beauty of Moonthorne. "Your homeland is quite lovely," she said to Jadon.

"Thank you, Runa," Jadon said sincerely.

Ryen and his peryton, Silverthorne, walked toward them. "I'm going to the palace to tell the Oak and Rowan you are here, Runa."

"Thank you, Ryen," Runa said gratefully.

"What are the Oak and Rowan, Runa?" Mellypip asked.

Ryen mounted Silverthorne. "That is what we call the king and queen of Ilyrra," the peryton answered. "Our ways are different from others, little wampu." Then Silverthorne carried Ryen across the river.

Mellypip thought the rangers and perytons were quite extraordinary—just like heroes from fairy tales. He also noticed the Ilyrran

Raven Wing had both men and women in their ranks.

The rest of their group gathered together. Sirah and Arial were quite composed, but Opaline looked a bit green. The hard and fast flight seemed to have upset Opaline's stomach. Hinkleburr and his aides were still quite distraught over the loss of their ponies. Darcus, blood-splattered and ragged, calmed Rono by scratching his head. An Ilyrran approached Darcus and offered to take Rono with the others.

"Want to stay with my friends," Rono protested.

Jadon and Darcus calmed the gryphon. "They only wish to treat your wounds and give you something to eat," Jadon said in a soothing voice.

"Go on, Rono," Darcus said. "It's all right. We'll come see you later."

"I'll go then," Rono nodded. He permitted the ranger to lead him away.

Mellypip sighed. "Poor Rono. He's hurt and scared."

"We will see him later," Runa assured him, "and bring him a special treat." Runa looked at the lush green city with awe. "It's so beautiful here."

Jadon gave Darkleaf more treats. Mellypip was curious about the edibles and bounced over to see what Darkleaf was snacking on. Jadon grinned and tossed him a piece. Mellypip caught it with his paws. It was shaped like a maple leaf and had that sugary smell he so loved. He bit into it. The luscious taste of maple sugar melted in his mouth. "Thank you, Ranger Jadon," he said, remembering to be polite. He settled at Runa's feet, contemplating the handsome Ilyrran.

"They're maple crisps. Perytons love them, and so do wampu it seems," Jadon remarked.

"If it's sugar, Furball will eat it," Belwyn said.

"We should bring some to Rono when we see him," Mellypip said.

"We will," Runa said. She turned to Jadon. "How did you know how to find us? Ryen said you had been looking for us."

"Iona the Necromancer herself sent a message you would be coming our way," Jadon said. "There's been an outbreak of communication between all the castes of mages—Drusai, Sorcerer, and Wizard. News of the abduction of Cathal and the other sorcerers has spread. Koll's return has also caused a great deal of distress— and anger," he added darkly.

The other rangers departed, leading their perytons away to be cared for. Jadon remained though, and escorted them down the hill. Several local folk gathered to see the visitors.

"Everyone is so curious about us," Opaline observed in a hushed tone.

"They rarely see outsiders," Jadon replied. "They do not mean to be rude."

Eyes with the same crystalline quality as Runa's, peered out at them. There were many other colors than green, as some were blue, brown, lavender, and gold. More doors to these unusual tree homes opened, and the people stepped out. The lush, wooded land was also a city, Mellypip remembered. But the people were friendly.

Long, twisting boughs, some decorated with garlands, extended from the trunks of these unusual trees. Doors and windows of various shapes and sizes opened as curious Ilyrrans looked up at the new visitors.

A pang of homesickness stunned Mellypip. He realized it was not just the tree houses that reminded him of home, but the faint scent of magic that was everywhere in Moonthorne.

Jadon guided them along a serpentine path lined with vibrant yellow and blue flowers. Rows of slim, unusual trees the shade of honey lined the path. Mellypip inhaled the soft smell of fresh green in the air. He decided that though human cities were quite exciting, the earthy land of Ilyrra was much nicer.

A crowd had gathered by the river. Some of them attended to their needs. A tall maiden brought them chilled water in tall, beautifully carved wooden goblets. A young boy, his brown hair long and wild, carried a plate of bread to welcome the visitors. Mellypip was quite hungry after all, having survived all of the horrific excitement. He accepted a small piece of sweet nut bread. They spoke in the Ilyrran language far too fast for Mellypip to comprehend. Fortunately, Runa and Belwyn managed to say thank you for him. Poor Opaline accepted water gratefully but declined the food.

Jadon led them through the whispering crowd to a quiet meadow near the river where they waited. "Look, the Oak and Rowan come now," he said when a boat appeared on the river. Jadon noticed Runa's apprehension. "Are you nervous?" he asked.

"Only in the literal sense," Runa replied.

"Don't be afraid. They are very kind," Jadon said gently.

On the sparkling river, a dark green barge sailed, drawn by six giant swans of cloud white radiance linked by delicate silver chains. Mellypip had never seen such swans! All along the riverbed, Ilyrrans knelt at their coming. In the shade of twin dusky green willow trees, the royal couple landed and walked hand in hand upon the shore with easy grace. The Oak and Rowan wore mantles of gossamer cloth, woven into the image of a thousand leaves that trailed the earth.

The Oak was a man of noble bearing, his coloring sunlight and cream, with golden hair and fair skin. He wore a crown of iridescent oak leaves and tiny acorns. His light golden-brown eyes, like all Ilyrran eyes, were bright.

Their queen, the Rowan, was the ripe earth in beauty. Her dark brown hair crowned with rowan leaves and berries, flowed down her back in shiny waves; brilliant green eyes glowed, though they were a deeper shade than Runa's. Runa picked Mellypip up when they motioned her to come forward.

Belwyn remained perched on her shoulder and nudged her with his beak. "Go on, Runa," he encouraged. "No time to be shy now."

Runa approached, keeping her head bowed. She knelt before the royal pair.

The Rowan looked upon them with kindness. "Welcome, Runa and Belwyn, to Moonthorne." She smiled when she looked at Mellypip. "Is the wampu your familiar?"

"Yes, Your Grace, his name is Mellypip," Runa replied.

"Light's blessing upon you and your friends. I am Talaith, the Rowan of Ilyrra."

"And I am Niall, the Oak of Ilyrra. Rise Runa, for you are a sister to us. You are born of the line of Yllia and Rualla, and our spirit brother, Cathal."

Talaith smiled. "You were too young to remember, my child, but Ilyrra was your sanctuary after you were rescued from Ashur the Sorcerer. We were tempted to keep you," she added. "There are violent forces at work again. We know you're going to Mowad to save Cathal and his circle of sorcerers. You are innocent of the world. What weapons have you to fight this evil? You don't even have a staff."

"She has us," Darcus stated from the background.

"I see you have devoted friends, but the task ahead of you is hard," Niall said.

"I know it is," Runa agreed. "I have already suffered that cost, as have my friends. I know we are outnumbered, but they haven't beaten us yet, Your Majesty. I thank you for saving us. We all grieve for the loss of the ranger, Aidan, who died protecting us. But I humbly beg now for whatever assistance you would grant us. We need speed to reach Mowad. If we had perytons, we might get there in time. I won't abandon my grandfather to his enemies," Runa added fiercely.

"Perytons? That's a bold request," Talaith said. "And then what will you do, my child?"

"I will fight to save my Grandfather and our friends," Runa said firmly.

"What do you say, Belwyn?" Niall asked. "You are her guardian now in Cathal's absence."

Belwyn spread his wings. "Who can control children these days?" He then looked at them with sad eyes. "Time is running out. I have vowed to protect Runa. She is part of my clan, and I love her. But I will not let Koll and his low-life scummy minions hurt my sorcerer! We are going to Mowad. Hell itself could not stop us now."

"You're quite unwavering, Runa, as are your companions," Talaith observed. "You are also as stubborn as Yllia was. We will grant you what you need. Cathal is our ancient friend. Koll is our great enemy, and we would welcome his downfall."

Runa sighed with relief. "Thank you."

Several rangers had joined the crowd to witness the meeting. The air began buzzing with murmured voices. Niall raised his hand and all fell silent. "I will grant Runa and her friends the aid of ten rangers, and additional perytons to fly them to Mowad. Who among our Raven Wing volunteers? Remember, this is a journey into foreign lands."

Runa and Mellypip were stunned to see every ranger raise their hands high.

Niall nodded. "Your courage does you honor, Raven Wing. Ryen, you will lead them and your son, Jadon will be your second-in-command. I will choose the remainder tonight after Aidan's funeral. Then we shall share a feast to celebrate his life and to wish our new friends a victory, and a safe return. We hope you save Cathal, Runa. We will pray for you." Niall kissed Talaith's hand. "I shall see you at the ceremony, my dear."

"Thank you, Niall." Talaith turned to Runa. "Come with me," she whispered. Concerned, Runa glanced at her companions as Talaith led her toward the woods. "Your friends will be well cared for," she assured her. "Don't worry. We have much to do in a very short time. Belwyn, you come too." The Ilyrrans bowed as they passed. Soon, they were alone, away from both friend and stranger.

"Where are we going?" Runa asked.

"I will help you make a staff, Runa."

Runa followed Talaith as they walked across the grass. "You are Drusai, Rowan?" Runa asked.

"Yes, and please call me Talaith," she replied.

"How come you don't have a familiar?" Mellypip asked.

Talaith tickled Mellypip under the chin. "It is an ancient covenant with the perytons. According to legend, in the beginnings of our people, the gods asked us to make a choice, to be balanced with the mages of human and dwarf who had familiars as companions. We had to choose between familiars or the perytons. One of our seers dreamed the perytons would one day help save our people, and be part of our warrior caste. So they made that choice, perytons have served in our Raven Wing ever since."

"Is Niall a Drusai too?" Runa asked, running to keep up with her.

"No, he is not," Talaith replied wistfully. "As a sorceress, you know us mage folk live much longer. I will still be young when Niall is old. An Ilyrran or a Dwarven can live about two hundred years; a human only about half that; if they are lucky. But I love Niall," Talaith said passionately. "We agreed to rule for twenty years, and then we shall abdicate for the next in line, so we may have more time for each other." Talaith stopped. "What is your strongest power, Runa?" she asked curiously.

"Light," Runa answered in a sure voice.

"Show me," Talaith said.

Runa summoned her magic. A ball of shimmering light appeared in her hand. Talaith touched the glowing orb. "Your light has elements of both Drusai and Sorcery," she said with surprise. "That is very strange. It is not common to be both."

"Runa is not common," Belwyn said with pride. "And her heritage is unique."

She looked at Runa closely. "Have you developed any abilities recently that are not sorcerous?"

"I've had dreams lately, about the past—of things I never knew until recently. It started a short time before my fifteenth birthday. I dreamed of Ashur too, and other strange things, that have come to pass."

"When did you get your first menstruation?" Talaith asked bluntly.

Runa blushed. "Well, the week it first happened, I think. Then Grandfather talked to me about becoming a woman." She grinned. "I always thought he should have been more embarrassed," she added.

"He was," Belwyn said. "Cathal was in quite a state explaining female function to you. He braced for it with lots of ale."

"That explains the timing of these dreams," Talaith said with a nod. "Such gifts do not appear until a person begins to reach maturity. It is possible you're a dream seer."

They stopped near a waterfall that flowed into a sparkling pool. The woodlands surrounded them with quiet green.

"This is the heart of the grove, Runa. Here you will find the tree from which you will make your staff," Talaith said.

"I will guide you to shape it," Belwyn said. "Talaith and I will then help you charge it with some needed spells for battle."

"What do I do?" Runa asked.

"Open your heart," Talaith said softly. "Feel their spirits." She patted Mellypip on the head. "Help Runa discover her Drusai heart."

"How will I know?" Runa asked. "There are so many trees here!"

"You will know," Talaith assured her.

Runa and Mellypip explored, touching the bark and leaf, and breathing in the savory aroma of nature. Nothing unusual happened until they saw a tall willow oak, surrounded by a ring of red and white sparkling toadstools. It captivated Runa. Mellypip was drawn to it too. The memory of the recent dream they shared at the Abbey about the red panther loomed in Mellypip's memory.

Runa circled the willow oak. "There is something special about this tree." She took a deep breath and laid her hand upon the bark. A surge of energy overwhelmed both of them, and Runa was bound to the tree, her body glowing with light. A rapid wave of images flooded their minds. Belwyn flapped his wings and clacked his beak with concern. Visions flashed of a powerful red panther crouched in a tree, roaring in triumph. Then the bond was broken, and Runa stumbled back, breathless and shaking.

"What the hell was that?" Belwyn demanded.

Talaith rushed to Runa and helped her sit in the grass. "What did you see? What happened?"

"I couldn't move. It was like being pulled out of my body. Then I saw a red panther," Runa said. "My mother had such a familiar, named Striker. He died rescuing me when I was a baby."

"Furball, you all right?" Belwyn asked, looking down on Mellypip with concern.

Panting and lying on his back, Mellypip gasped. "That was scary."

Talaith touched the tree with respect. "Beneath this willow oak is where we buried Striker. Heroes are buried here, and Striker was a great hero. A piece of his spirit has remained, waiting…for you Runa."

The willow oak glowed briefly, and a sturdy, long bough fell to the earth. Startled, Runa reached to pick it up.

"The spirit of Striker has made this offering," Talaith said with awe. "Use your magic to weave your staff, Runa."

"Kneel and touch the wood," Belwyn said to Runa. "You must also do this, Mellypip. Concentrate on the shape of your staff. Let your love do the carving."

Runa fingered the wood gingerly, then grasped it firmly. Mellypip laid his paws upon it as she summoned her magic. Her sorcery channeled into it, and something else, woodsy and green. With a steady rhythm she moved her hands up and down the staff. The breeze became a strong wind and swirled around them. The oaken bough shimmered and became ethereal with Runa's touch. The gnarled wood began to smooth and straighten. Sparks of colorful light danced along the grain as it shifted with her magic. Sweat poured from Runa's features and her whole body blazed with white light.

Then it was done, and the wind calmed. When they looked, the wood had formed into a staff, and at the top the likeness of a wampu head was carved through mystical molding.

"Look Runa!" Mellypip said with excitement. "That looks just like me!"

Faint from her efforts, Runa smiled with pride. Mellypip saw something else, something neither of them expected. Beneath the carved wampu face on the staff, a pair of eyes was engraved into the wood. Panther eyes, much like those Runa and Mellypip remembered from both the dream and the vision.

"Those look like Striker's eyes," Belwyn said in a choked voice.

Talaith kneeled next to Runa. "You have done well, my dear. You are doubly blessed."

"You have two guardians now," Belwyn said solemnly. "Striker's spirit is now with you forever."

~ * ~

It is believed, among the Ilyrran people, that songs help guide the souls of the dead to the Otherworld.

Priestesses in pale green robes led the funeral procession of Aidan, carrying torches and singing the ancient farewell hymn of fallen heroes. The Oak and Rowan stood side by side, joining the chorus of sorrow. All the Raven Wing warriors attended, solemn in their deep green and black uniforms. Sunset cast long dusky shadows in the grove, broken only by the torch light. The perytons were there too, led by Redstorm, to say farewell to a young man who died so bravely. Runa and her friends joined the mourners. They had little time to prepare, but the people here were generous and offered all of them baths and fresh clothes to replace their torn and bloodied garments.

The body of Aidan was wrapped in a white shroud, and his funeral bier was covered with flowers as they laid him deep within the earth. The moons rose high above trees, offering a final beam of light before his tomb covered him with darkness forever. When the grave was covered, the singing stopped.

A hush fell over the gathering when a snow white peryton with luminous gold eyes walked toward the Oak and Rowan. All the perytons bowed their heads with respect.

"Who is that?" Mellypip whispered.

"Her name is Moonwave," Belwyn answered in a low voice. "She is the spirit guardian of the perytons. She is offering her blessing to guide Aidan's soul to the Otherworld."

After the blessing, Niall and Moonwave chose the remaining warriors to accompany Runa on her quest. Perytons, not yet bonded to a rider, offered to carry their friends on this journey. Three perytons, Dovetail, Starwynd, and Dawnfire were chosen.

"I commend our Raven Wing warriors for their bravery," Niall said to the people. "And the courage of Runa and her companions. You all face a hard task wrought with danger. I wish you victory."

Ryen walked to the center of the circle. He spoke in a deep, emotional voice as he faced the assembly. "True honor and bravery is rare. Aidan was young but served the Raven Wing with those very attributes. His death leaves a great void. With his dying words, he called one man brother. This is not lightly said among our people. By calling this man brother, he truly made him one of us. He made him not only a brother, but heir to all he possessed. I know this man too and understand this generous benediction." Ryen then looked at Darcus. "Darcus, please come forward."

Uneasy at being singled out from among his fellow companions,

Darcus walked toward Ryen and stood at attention.

Ryen spoke so all could hear. "Darcus, you are a great warrior. I know the strength and skill you possess as a fighter. You are fierce and resolute yet possess compassion and mercy. But more than that, you are a man of honor and self-sacrifice. What I offer you this day has not been offered to another human for a thousand years since the great Bloodstone Wars. The sacred wing of the raven has claimed you, Darcus. Her feather has touched your soul. We offer you a new home among our people. I know your service to the White Dragon throne has ended. I've been informed by your friends you gave up a position of great prestige to help Runa and Cathal. To be Raven Wing, is to defend the light, even in the deepest shadows. What do you say, Darcus? Will you join with the rangers of Raven Wing?"

Darcus paled at Ryen's words. The entire gathering was mute with anticipation. Darcus knelt before Ryen and Niall. "This honor you offer is unexpected," Darcus said. "I have always respected the Raven Wing. I thought my days as a warrior were over. I wanted to hang up my sword forever, but I realize now I need to serve a noble purpose. If you want me as a ranger, then I am yours."

"Stand, Darcus of the Raven Wing," Ryen said. He took the deep green cloak and draped it across Darcus' shoulders.

Niall handed him the sword. "Receive Aidan's sword, Darcus. May it serve you well to defend the light," Niall said. "Rise now and join your brothers."

Darcus accepted the sword and rose.

Ryen nodded. "Darcus, you also have the honor of a seasoned peryton who has accepted you," he said.

Redstorm detached from the other perytons and walked toward Darcus, his powerful body looming over him. "Welcome, Ranger."

CHAPTER 23

Cathal and Caliste sweltered in their cramped prisons as the caravan rolled across the hot sands of the Mowad desert. A team of shaggy kundra beasts pulled the wagon. Their thick, insulating sandy-colored fur and splayed hooves were well adapted to harsh arid climates. The massive beasts lumbered across the sands, grunting with mournful sounds.

The shadow of Salomm Mountain loomed with forbidding evil but offered no respite from the blazing sun. The heat baked not only the sands, but the prisoners in their metal cages. Several Rashurkeen on horseback flanked the wagon.

Cathal and Caliste winced and groaned as they were jostled over rough terrain. They languished in their searing cages, unable to even grip the bars for the burning sun heated the metal like a hot skillet.

"I hoped never to see this place again," Caliste moaned. Uncomfortable, she shifted in her cage, so she could look at Cathal. "I think I preferred it when we were at sea. At least it was cooler."

Cathal turned his head. "Less gritty too. I've forgotten how much sand irritates. Are they planning to sacrifice us or roast us! My skin is crisping." He lowered his voice. "How are you holding up, my dear?"

"I'm strong, Cathal. I learned that from you when I was growing up. When we do finally escape, I plan to soak in a cool bath for at least a week! But right now I would settle for a drink of cool water."

Cathal kicked against the bars with booted feet. "How about some water, you mangy dogs!" he shouted. "The lady needs a little refreshment!"

"Silence, Sorcerer," one of the guards replied coarsely.

"Make me," Cathal challenged.

The guard struck the cage with his spear. "I said be quiet!" he shouted gruffly. He shoved the spear between the bars and pressed the point against Cathal's throat. "You drive me mad, Mage! Maybe I should just cut your throat right now."

"You're going to have to do better than that," Cathal advised in a calm voice. "You don't intimidate me. You can't harm me. I need to be alive for the sacrifice, remember. Koll would be very unhappy if you killed me before the ritual. I hear he has a nasty temper." The guard lowered his spear. "You can't even beat me either. In order to do that, you would have to open this cage. I'm a dangerous man. The last time, I killed one of you and escaped. I've faced down worse opponents in my life. I don't fear you. You are nothing."

The guard's weathered gaze, smeared with sand and sweat, was merciless. Only his eyes were visible, for the billowing robes of black and red concealed him. "You should fear the Rashurkeen, old mage. Killing is our religion. You can't do your foul magic either, wearing that collar of sorcerer bane."

Cathal gave him a flinty stare. "I don't need magic to kick your ass."

Panthara rode up alongside their wagon, swathed in a dark blue cloak, the hood covering her face. Azmadu bounced in her lap, flicking its tongue. The Rashurkeen backed away from her. "Now what's the problem?" she asked imperiously.

"We need water," Cathal said.

"You have had your ration for the day," Panthara said.

"The water is not for me, it's for Caliste. Have a little compassion, Panthara. It's good for the soul."

Panthara's dark blue eyes glared with hatred. "Interesting you should mention souls. You will not have yours much longer, Cathal." She took her water skin and uncorked it. She drank deeply, allowing precious drops to dribble down her chin. "I have no water to spare, I'm afraid," she said when she was done. "We would not have needed to travel during the day if you and Caliste hadn't tried to escape so often," Panthara replied.

Cathal shrugged. "If I'm going to be sacrificed, you're going to work for it, Panthara."

"It doesn't matter now anyway," Panthara said. "We have arrived at last." She turned to the guard. "Summon Lord Koll and alert him of our arrival! Now!" she commanded imperiously.

"Yes, Queen Panthara," the man said and rode away.

"The entrance of the mountain is heavily guarded," Caliste said. "I hate this place. Old evil that will never be cleansed."

"The décor does little to challenge that," Cathal agreed.

Centuries ago, when this place was used for Obsydia's unholy rituals, her followers carved the cave's vast mouth into the visage of a demon. Giant fangs curved over the entrance, and an ugly monstrous image was beaten into the rock's face. Rashurkeen patrolled the area on foot and on gryphon. Panthara's Imperial Guard, their simple white kilts and brown leather uniforms contrasting with the grim black and red of the Rashurkeen, walked with guarded suspicion among the assassins.

The driver of the caravan pulled hard on the reins to slow the powerful kundra beasts. The shaggy animals stopped their rambling march.

Panthara smiled. "I'll leave you alone to contemplate your sins." She dismounted her horse and gave it to one of her personal guards. As she walked away, a veiled woman in voluminous black silk robes came out of the cave. She marched toward Panthara with quick steps.

Panthara threw off her cloak and ran to meet her. "Mother, I have returned victorious," Panthara said with joy.

The woman stopped before her and slapped her face. "Foolish girl! Do not stand there with your face exposed like a common harlot!"

"But Mother, I have captured our greatest enemy."

"Trouble in hell?" Caliste quipped as the two women argued in the distance. "Speaking of trouble, where do you think Runa is now?" she whispered.

"I wish I knew," Cathal replied. "I just hope she is being careful. I never knew how willful that girl could be," he said with a laugh.

Caliste managed a wistful smile. "You raised her, Cathal."

Koll exited the cave, swathed in dark robes. Xabral, his scorpion snake, coiled about his shoulders. The two women fell silent in his presence.

Revulsion twisted Cathal's features and his temper snapped. "Koll!"

Black eyes glittering with malice, Koll walked toward them. "Welcome to Mowad, Cathal, Caliste."

"We don't plan on staying," Cathal replied.

"Your powers must have gone soft old man," Koll observed. "Else why would you be trapped in a cage like an animal for the slaughter?"

"Animals I like. It's certain people that annoy me." Cathal laughed bitterly. "You think I'm soft, Koll? Want to duel it out?" He tugged at the sorcerer lock around his neck. "Take this collar off, and we'll see who the strongest sorcerer is—or are you too spineless to fight me," Cathal challenged.

"I will not banter with you, Cathal. I don't have time. Gorvanus told me, before Princess Opaline transformed him into a troll that is, Emperor Tarsicius charged you with hunting me down. Well, fortunes have turned, and I am the hunter now."

"Bully for you," Cathal said.

As Koll turned away, he said to him. "Your friends are anxious to see you. You will have little time though, for a reunion. At least in this world. Caliste, you are so silent. Are you well?"

"I am quite well," Caliste replied. "I just prefer not to speak to scum."

Panthara ran to Koll's side. "Did you find Runa? Is she dead at last?" Panthara asked impatiently.

Koll's annoyed expression amused Cathal. It was obvious he failed in his task to stop Runa. Koll guided Panthara out of earshot to whisper their secrets.

Cathal shielded his eyes from the glaring day. The sky was barren of clouds. A bird circled the sky high above them. Then it flew westward out of sight.

"What is it?" Caliste whispered.

"Belwyn," Cathal said in a jubilant whisper. "It was Belwyn!"

Then Cathal laughed so heartily, Koll stared at him in confusion.

"What can I say?" Caliste shrugged when Koll came closer. "He's gone mad from sunstroke. He told you we needed water."

~ * ~

Mellypip did not like this sand pit they called Mowad. The desert was a harsh place. From the rough ridge where they landed in a range of low bluffs close to the mountain, Mellypip surveyed the barren landscape. No flowers or grass broke the sea of dunes and rocks. The cruel sun in the day and the bitter cold nights would make anyone evil. Perhaps that was why Panthara was so nasty? This place would make anyone bad-tempered.

Belwyn's mood also got more irritable than usual as they traveled deeper into this desert. Belwyn had gone to scout ahead when they reached the rim of Salomm Mountain, which rose like a dark specter in the distance. The mountain looked so dark and terrible. A place of nightmares. He wished Belwyn would return.

Ryen and his rangers guarded the camp. Everyone was silent in anticipation of Belwyn's return. The familiars didn't even squabble— at least for the moment. When they landed here an hour ago, Sirah cast a shield over them that acted as a protective dome to conceal them from enemy eyes. It looked liquid from where Mellypip sat when he looked up, but Sirah assured him it was sheer as air from the outside. Even though he knew he was protected, he felt a rush of fear when a Rashurkeen flew overhead on a gryphon.

"Are you sure they can't see us?" Darcus asked.

Sirah leaned against her staff. At the tip of the staff was a carved wolf's head, just like Arial. "The shield I conjured prevents them from seeing us," she said calmly.

"Mother has a unique talent for shields," Opaline said with pride.

Sirah smiled. "Protecting oneself can never be underrated."

Runa was anxious now that they were so close to their goal. She stood at the edge of the cliff, looking at the mountain. Opaline went to her and squeezed her hand affectionately.

Sirah noticed their pensive mood and told them to feed and water the perytons for the rangers. It gave them something to do. Sirah had watched over the two girls since she joined their renegade band. She was a good cook too!

Sanura shifted from her normal small cat shape to panther size. "I think it is best I stay battle ready while we are grounded," she said.

"I must admit I do feel safer when you are big and fangy," Mellypip confessed.

"Sanura just likes to show off," Dabiro said gruffly, rolling in the dirt beneath an outcrop of rock where the ground was cooler.

Mellypip sighed. "My ability doesn't come when I want." He wished he could control his special talent, but all he ever got when he tried to manifest it was an angry tummy.

"It's all right, little one," Arial said. "Your powers will grow as you do. You are still a baby."

"I'm not a baby," Mellypip protested.

"Of course you aren't," Arial said with humor.

Mellypip laughed, feeling foolish. He liked Arial, Sirah's wolf familiar. He noticed Arial was quieter than the other familiars. Belwyn liked Arial too, and he trusted Belwyn's judgment. *Darn it, where was he!*

What are you thinking? Runa asked silently.

Belwyn, Mellypip answered. *He should have returned by now.*

Don't fret, Melly. Belwyn is a clever owl. I know he will be back soon.

Mellypip nodded, then noticed Jadon walking toward them. *Jadon is coming.* She looked around expectantly. Mellypip asked, *What is it with you two? Did you know him before, Runa!*

Runa sighed. *It was years ago. I remember Ryen visited us only once. He brought his son with him—Jadon.*

Did you like him?

Melly!

Jadon offered her a drink of water. She nodded and took a long swig and then shared some with Mellypip.

"Do you remember, Runa, when my father and I visited you some years ago?" Jadon asked. "Or have you forgotten?"

Runa dropped her head and sighed. "I haven't forgotten, Jadon. Yes, I do remember you. I hope you will take into account I was only four."

Jadon grinned. "That explains your embarrassment whenever we speak. I think I can put the past behind me."

"What did Runa do?" Mellypip asked.

"She put a frog down my tunic when I didn't want to play with her," Jadon said. "That was the first of many tricks, as I recall. Would you like the list?"

"No," Runa begged.

"I do," Mellypip said.

"Let's see, I remember there were episodes that involved spiders and the hot spices in my glass of milk—"

"Stop!" Runa cried, then sighed and hung her head in shame. "I was such a brat. I'm sorry, Jadon."

"Bad sorceress," Mellypip scolded her.

"It's all right. We were just children," Jadon laughed. "I think you were a bit lonely too. I was ten and I thought girls were a weird creation. You have grown into a lovely young woman since that time when you tormented me with frogs and spiders.

He thinks I'm lovely, Runa cried in Mellypip's head.

Ouch, Mellypip grimaced. *Too loud.*

Sorry, Melly.

"I pray your manners have improved," Jadon inquired.

"Ha-ha," Runa said. "But as I recall the spiders didn't scare you."

"That's because I had pet spiders at home. You were quite ignorant about boys."

"I still am," Runa whispered.

"Good," Jadon replied in a husky voice. "Just mind the frogs from now on." Ryen called to Jadon. "Excuse me," he said and walked away just when things were getting good.

"Look! There's Belwyn," Opaline exclaimed.

Belwyn glided to earth with mute wings and landed on Silverthorne's antlers.

Silverthorne glanced up. "Comfortable, or do you want to build a nest?"

"Quite cozy," Belwyn replied. "And I don't need your acerbity." The irate owl shook out his feathers. "I saw Cathal and Caliste arriving at the mountain."

"Then we aren't too late!" Darcus said.

"Did they look well?" Runa asked quickly. "Are they hurt?"

"A bit toasted, but they are still alive." Belwyn swiveled his head toward Runa. "You've really rattled Panthara, Runa. She's quite anxious to see you dead."

"I'm anxious to return the favor," Runa said dryly.

"We need to stop babbling and strike!" Felisia, the elf owl, cried.

"Felisia, calm down," Belwyn said, flying down to her.

Felisia sniffed. "You be calm!" She kicked sand at Belwyn, then flew to Sirah's hand to sulk.

"I think Felisia is a bit...anxious," Sirah said, stroking her feathers to calm her.

Dabiro the badger was rolling in the sand, laughing and grunting at the same time. "Women!" he guffawed.

"The badger is being weird," Mellypip whispered to Runa.

"No," Runa sighed. "That's just Dabiro."

"How many assassins did you see guarding the area?" Darcus asked, trying to focus their attention back to more important matters.

"There are well over a hundred Rashurkeen and gryphons," Belwyn said. "And that is just on the outside."

"I'm getting damned sick of those assassins," Darcus grumbled.

"Join the club," Belwyn laughed bitterly. "Plus there are Mowad warriors—imperial guards by the looks of them. Who knows how many are inside that cave!"

"We can't dally about, now that they have all of the sorcerers," Hinkleburr commented. "I don't think they'll stop to have tea and cakes."

"How many entrances did you see, Belwyn?" Ryen asked.

"There is the main opening—the one smothered with enemy assassins. There are some smaller ones along the back of the mountain, but I have no idea where they lead, or if they even lead into the main cavern. I checked out a few, but there was no easy route I could find. So we can't risk those. I know the path we need to take once we are inside the cave." Belwyn looked back at the mountain, his golden eyes brimming with violent memory of his last sojourn there. "I remember that wretched place all too well from fifteen years ago."

"We will have to fight our way in," Ryen said. "But we need to be clever about it."

"I'm good with that," Darcus said.

"A suicide mission would make all this moot," Buzzy the sloth agreed.

"I say we charge," Dabiro rumbled.

"That's your answer to everything," Felisia said. "But not all of us have skulls made of granite with little else inside."

"Hey! Was that an insult?" Dabiro asked.

"Oh no," Jasper tittered. "It was a compliment."

"We are woefully outnumbered," Belwyn reminded them.

"Belwyn is right," Jadon said. "This place is swarming with Rashurkeen and the odds are not too cheery. We have three sorceresses, two of them untrained in high magic, three enthusiastic dwarves trained in diplomacy, nine angry familiars, a confused gryphon, and our perytons of course, plus exactly twelve Raven Wing Rangers."

"Thanks for including me," Darcus grinned.

"You're welcome," Jadon said. "All this against maybe a hundred Rashurkeen guarding the cave alone."

"Not to mention Koll, Panthara, more bloody Rashurkeen lurking inside like scorpions, not to mention some wicked priests of Rygon, inside the cave," Belwyn said.

"Sounds like a fair fight. The odds don't bode well for them though," Darcus said.

"Good," Runa smiled wickedly. "I like to see a positive attitude."

"I think Darcus is delusional," Jasper the tiger hare quipped.

"Go lick your butt," Rosepetal the hedgehog said.

"The pointy one has a potty mouth," Dabiro said with respect.

"Dabiro, just stuff it," Felisia said.

"The children are fighting again," Sanura groaned.

"I suggest we meditate," Buzzy the sloth advised in soft voice drowned out by the other familiars.

"That is enough!" Runa warned.

Runa had never used such a stern voice before. The circle of familiars lowered their heads in penance. Rosepetal broke into a fit of hiccups to break the silence.

"Runa is right," Sirah said, and put her arm around her for

support. "We must not only keep our focus, but our hope, else all is lost. I know you are all frightened and miss your sorcerers very much. My father is one of them, remember."

"I may have a plan to get us in the cave," Runa said. "But I'll need your help, Sirah. And Darcus and Ryen's warrior perspective. As Jadon has pointed out, I'm not skilled in high magic yet. Opaline, though I know you must be powerful, judging by what you did to Gorvanus." Opaline winced, and Runa hugged her. "You need to get over that, but you aren't trained either in sorcery."

Sirah nodded with approval. "Koll is no fool, either. He will have laid wards close to the cave to alert him of magical attacks. Koll is expecting us. That is evident by the number of assassins he has engaged. He will also be prepared with more than warriors. We need to check out how far Koll has mined the area with mystical wards to know how to proceed. We need to get inside the cave and find out their strength and weaknesses too. You need a sorceress for such a task, and a familiar able to deceive the guards. Arial and I can do that."

"Excellent," Ryen said. "Darcus and Jadon will go as your guards."

"This should be interesting," Darcus commented.

"Oh, it will be," Sirah assured him. Sirah turned to Opaline. "Watch over little Felisia. I'll be back soon." She gently transferred the upset owl to Opaline's hands.

"Be careful, Mother!" Opaline begged.

Sirah gently stoked Opaline's cheek. "My dear, it is the Rashurkeen who will need to take care."

~ * ~

Xabral hovered over Azmadu, his nasty barbed tail swishing too close for comfort. He spoke in harsh whispers. "You must heed every nuance of the ritual. If even one thing goes awry, terrible the consequences you shall suffer," he warned. The scorpion snake paused, seeing a tiny lizard dart through the sands, and Xabral's stinger struck the creature. "I must keep my skills sharp." He laughed and proceeded to feed with delectable joy.

Azmadu quivered. In the year since he became Panthara's familiar as a young hatchling, Xabral had tormented him with many such nerve jittering tricks. The gathering of their guests here in the great cavern was unnerving too. Azrul, the High Priest of Rygon's Temple, just arrived on a red gryphon. The man was old and brittle, but his eyes were bright with bloodlust. Azrul and Koll spent a great deal of time talking together.

Panthara entered, robed in pure white gauze for the ceremony. Her black hair flowed down her back, and she had removed her silver and jewels. In the dun lit tomb, she looked just like a bride—or a sacrifice. Her mother, Naloia, stood at her side.

Panthara smiled at Azmadu. *Come to me, Azmadu. Do not be afraid. I will protect you,* she said through the bonding. He waddled over to her. She picked him up, and her gentle hands soothed his jitters. On the ominous altar of dark stone that hovered in the air with mystical power, a red crystal the size of a sarcophagus throbbed with necromancy. Within it was the body of Ashur, whole but lifeless without a soul to give it substance. Naloia knelt before it to pray.

Azrul, the aged Rygon priest of Urgonclaw, bowed to Panthara. "Your holy cause has borne fruit, Queen Panthara. Ashur would be proud of you this day."

Koll gathered Xabral in his arms and lifted the great snake. He draped him around his shoulders. "In a short time, Ashur will be able to tell her that too. Come Panthara, it is time."

She nodded, and kissed Azmadu on the head before she put him down. "Bring in the sacrifices!" Panthara commanded.

Guards dragged in the seven sorcerers. Chained and their sorcery bound, they struggled against the firm-handed men who pushed them towards the altar.

"I call the seven murderers of my father, Ashur, to justice," Panthara said triumphantly. She looked at them, and counted off each one. "Jiana, Ulan, Liat, Riva, Myrsalian, Caliste, and...Cathal! The sorcery you used to murder my father was only one of many secret scrolls discovered in this cave. We learned that I could bring my father back, by using this lost magic, but only by offering the souls of the ones who performed the magic to kill him. Now that I have all of you captive, I can call back his soul. I will summon the Guardians of the Gates. We have restored his body, as you can see."

"Bloodstone magic!" Cathal spat. "This whole cave, this mountain, was once one of Obsydia's temples. It is evil! Nothing good can come of this. Not even rebirth!" Cathal looked at Panthara. "There is a price, Panthara, for disturbing the Guardians of the Gates."

"Yes." Panthara nodded. "But that price is *your* soul, not mine."

"You are young, Panthara, and this breed of magic can be unstable," Cathal warned. "Your delicate plans will easily shatter with even a minor falter. The wraiths might take you instead. They are pretty temperamental. You do not disturb the Otherworld lightly."

Koll stalked toward them, his black robes flowing. "I understand the power of high magic. I command it, it does not command me. We will control the wraith guardians. The nine gates of Otherworld will open, and Ashur's soul will return to this realm. I have studied this ritual well. I have spent my life hunting for ancient magic from that lost Bloodstone era. With it, one day I shall find the lost tomb of Obsydia, the Bloodstone Queen."

"You are mad, Koll, to desire Obsydia," Cathal said in a grim voice. "She once made our world a well of violent sacrifice for her father, Ahridum, the god of darkness and chaos. Do you crave to live in such a world?"

Koll smiled and spoke gently, as though he spoke of a heart's first love. "Yes. She was a true goddess of the world. What do you know of gods, Cathal? Nothing!"

"I could debate that," Cathal replied.

"This numinous endeavor will take a long time of mystical labor," Koll said. "When the wraiths enter this world and take you and your friends in Ashur's place, it will be worth it. We know the price; and have the coin."

"You do enjoy playing with death, Koll," Cathal said. "Be careful, it might want to play with *you*."

"Silence, fools!" Naloia wailed. She turned to her daughter, bitter tears flowing down her face. "Panthara, bring him back to me! The Gate of Souls holds my beloved prisoner. Release him!"

"Yes, Mother," Panthara said calmly. She pointed to the prisoners. "Chain them in a circle on the altar around the crystal," she commanded.

The guards pushed them up on the altar and proceeded to chain each one of them to the iron spikes placed around the red crystal. They then gagged them to keep them silent.

Panthara mounted the altar. Koll followed her, a shadow of wickedness. He handed her the scroll. She accepted it, holding it in pale hands. Azmadu sat at her feet.

"Do not falter now, Panthara," Koll whispered.

Naloia rose from her prayers to Ashur and in passing, took a handful of Panthara's hair and yanked her head back. "Do not fail me, daughter," she hissed. She let go, then descended the altar to take her place next to Azrul.

The old priest, Azrul, was anxious for the unholy rite. A man who spent years sacrificing to the god of war was accustomed to blood and carnage. This mystical sacrifice would be a true treat for Azrul's shriveled soul.

The spectators, even the Rashurkeen, knelt in mute witness of the resurrection of Ashur.

"Let the ritual begin!" Koll commanded and rapped his staff on the stone floor three times.

Panthara raised her arms. "I am Sorcerer born! I invoke the power of Necromancy, ancient as time's beginning, to unbar the gates that separate this world from the Otherworld. I call upon the Wraith Guardians to release Ashur's soul, so he may take new life in this body we have resurrected and keep the memories of his past life."

Koll picked up the first staff and laid it at the base of the red crystal.

A mystical spark burned Azmadu's scales. He inhaled the first flash of mysterious power warming the air. He stepped back, afraid, but a sharp glance from Xabral stopped him.

Panthara continued to raise her arms to the unseen heaven. "I summon the Wraith Guardians by their true names. I command you! Come to this world."

"Come to this world," Koll repeated, and circled the red crystal.

Panthara bowed her head. "I invoke the true and forbidden name of the Alzghoul, Guardian of the First Gate. I call the First Keeper of the Gate of Souls, to deliver Ashur to this realm."

With each summons, Koll laid a sorcerer's staff upon the altar around the crystal. With each knock upon mystical doors, they called immortal demons from their eternal watch to do their bidding.

The crystal began to pulsate with crimson light.

CHAPTER 24

Koll planted many wards," Sirah confirmed, kneeling in the sand. Her palms were up and her eyes closed. She would have been very vulnerable, if it were not for Arial, her large white wolf familiar, at her side.

Darcus and Jadon squatted next to her, swords ready, but kept a respectful distance as she sensed the area.

"It's difficult to detect them without using a spell," Arial explained.

"And if we use magic to attempt to break into the cave, we will instantly alert the Rashurkeen—and Koll," Sirah said with her eyes still closed. "We need to be beyond Koll's rim of wards before we could even attempt magic without sounding off the alarms. There are too many assassins teeming about."

They managed to use rock cover to sneak close to the cave entrance but kept clear of the many guards that patrolled the entrance.

Arial, sat on her haunches and sniffed. "You are right, Sirah. The wards are powerful too," Arial confirmed.

"Can you determine where they begin and end?" Darcus asked.

"I can," Arial offered, but I must go alone if we are to venture deeper into enemy territory. Sirah will remain here, to protect you."

"It's too dangerous, Arial," Sirah said, standing. "Perhaps you should not go into the cave."

"We need to gather as much information as possible before we attack," Arial countered. "Plus, I can also determine if they have even begun the ritual yet."

Darcus shook his head. "I would not have you risk it," he whispered.

"It is not a risk," Arial said. The wolf stepped back, then faded from view.

"She's invisible!" Jadon whispered excitedly.

"Not quite," the unseen Arial said.

"Where did Arial go?" Darcus asked.

"It's magical camouflage ability," Sirah replied with pride. "She is quite stealthy. She blends with the landscape."

"I can't see her," Jadon remarked.

"You won't be able to, but I can," Sirah commented.

Arial reappeared. "As you can see, I have an advantage."

"Very well, Arial, go investigate, but be careful," Sirah said.

"I hope this works," Jadon said. "I'm at a loss to figure out how we will distract the Rashurkeen from the cave if this plan doesn't work."

Sirah gave them a wicked smile. "I could dance naked in the desert. That might get their attention. After all, my dancing once captivated the heart of an Emperor."

"Sirah!" Jadon gasped.

"I'm only teasing, but you must admit, it would make an amusing story to tell my grandchildren. All men have the same weaknesses, after all."

Darcus laughed. "Lady, that would surely turn their bones to butter," he said with appreciation.

"Runa's idea is chancy, but it has merit," Jadon said. "We may not have any other options."

Darcus agreed. "Once we have drawn the enemy from the cave, it will not matter if the mages use their magic. Koll and Panthara are a threat, but they will be occupied with that ceremony. We will still have to fight our way in, but we will have more of an advantage."

Sirah turned to her familiar. "Arial, will your inborn ability alert the wards?"

"Not likely, Sirah," Arial replied. "I'm not doing a spell."

Sirah nodded. "Very well. Be careful, my lovely wolf."

"I always am, Sirah," Arial said. Then the wolf's image faded into the sandy, rocky landscape.

"Are you sure she will not alarm Koll's traps?" Darcus asked.

"She would have by now,' Sirah replied, "and she hasn't. Remember, Arial is using her inborn special magic. It was touchy to try it, but Koll's traps are not disturbed, as you see."

Jadon looked around and shivered. "This mountain is evil."

"You are right," Darcus said. "It is disturbing. I was here years ago, when we fought Ashur's forces and Cathal defeated him in that cave. Inside, is an old temple from the wicked era. It still reeks of blood sacrifice."

"The place is cursed," Sirah agreed. "In the ancient legends, it was in this mountain where the first blood offerings to Obsydia were made. The world fell into darkness."

Darcus looked around. "Speaking of which, we better take

cover until Arial returns. There are too many sentries about."

"He's right," Jadon agreed. "We can't chance exposure, yet."

"We can backtrack away from the wards," Sirah said. "Then I can cloak us from view."

"I'm disappointed," Darcus said in mock sorrow. "My sword arm was hoping for a little exercise."

"You'll get plenty of that later," Sirah promised.

~ * ~

Arial ran across the hot desert sands and passed the many guards who walked about. She stayed close to the rocky mountain, her talent for blending with the background shielding her. When she looked up at the sky, she noticed gryphons in the air flying patrols. It was getting late too. Soon it would be dusk. Arial looked out across the sands to the ridge in the distance where they had camped. It looked empty, and that was good. It was supposed to be, at least to the eyes of the enemy. Sirah's magic was strong.

Arial kept close to the rough stone walls, avoiding the Rashurkeen. The reek of human sweat, cooked food, and smoke permeated the area. The gryphons, corralled near the mountain, were restless. Their high-pitched cries gnawed at Arial's nerves. The shaggy kundra beasts whined, sensing the evil of the area. There were few horses, not adapted to this environment as well as the other animals. Horses in the desert were used for speed but were not practical.

Arial entered the long tunnel at the cave's mouth. Torches of dark blue light burned along the walls. The odors within were not comforting, and the aura of old magic and murder still lingered. Arial was already aware of the hidden wards around the cave, but inside the cavern there were none.

The sound of a woman's voice was all Arial heard from within the cave at first.

Panthara's voice.

Praying her talent would keep her concealed from enemy eyes, Arial advanced deeper into the cave.

The narrow passageway widened then opened up to a vast cavern. But despite the lights of torches, a terrible darkness prevailed.

The scarlet crystal burned on an altar. It was a translucent tomb. Within it lay a man.

The congregation around the crystal was rapt with mute worship.

Panthara was invoking the dark guardians. Near Panthara was a tall man with black hair and bone-pale skin.

Koll the Sorcerer.

Arial looked further, to see the sorcerers bound by manacles and magic bane around the giant crystal on the altar.

One of her pack, Myrsalian, was chained on the altar. She had to leave now, to warn her sorceress. Many emotions, from rage to anguish, flooded Arial's soul, so much she wanted to howl.

Arial fled the cave.

~ * ~

Arial appeared again at last, running toward to Sirah. She whined and buried her muzzle in Sirah's hands. "I entered the cave. They are doing the ritual! We might be too late!"

"Did you see them?" Sirah asked in a shaky voice.

"Yes, I did," Arial said. "As yet they are unharmed, but chained on a dark altar. There was a flaming crystal. The wickedness made my fur stand on end."

"Take heart, Arial and Sirah," Jadon said. "A ritual like that takes time, though we have no idea how long we have."

"Sirah, I saw your father, Myrsalian," Arial said. "He is being very brave. All the others are there too. And—"

"What is it Arial?" Darcus asked.

Arial was upset. "They are summoning the Wraith Guardians. It reeks of demonic magic. I also smelled blood, old blood in that cave. The blood of violence, not of the hunt or feeding the pack, but offerings to thirsty demons. It is an abomination. Our friends are chained on the altar as sacrifice to these horrific beings."

Darcus stroked the wolf's back. "We will save them. Let's get back. The sun is setting. We need to move now. I just hope this plan works."

Sirah hugged Arial, mute with emotion.

Arial looked back at the cave. "It is true, there are monsters in the dark."

~ * ~

More than a hundred Rashurkeen guarded the cave entrance. Many longed to be within the sacred cave and witness this rare magic, but duty decreed they guard against the enemy.

The assassins surveyed the open desert with a calm, almost

bored vigilance until the sounds of warriors' cries in the distance made them look up at the sky. The sky, cloudless and empty even of the smallest carrion bird since they arrived, now darkened with malicious threat.

A cavalry of Raven Wing warriors flew over the mountains in the distance.

"By Rygon!" one of the assassins shouted. "There must be a thousand warriors flying toward us on cursed perytons!"

"We are under attack!" another said, rushing to mount a gryphon.

Battle cries issued from excited throats. Sun-browned fingers twitched with desire to cut flesh and bone. Eyes glittered with hunger for battle. They ran to their gryphons and horses to fight.

The eager assassins hated missing bloodshed, but some were commanded to stay at the cave's mouth to defend it.

So some stayed, scimitars ready, at the cave's entrance.

They were an obedient, if violent, sect.

~ * ~

Shielded just outside the edge where Koll's wards burned, Runa and her friends watched many of the Rashurkeen fly away. It did not eliminate the threat but helped to even out the odds.

"It's working!" Runa said with excitement.

"That was a clever idea, Runa," Belwyn said. "You made them leave the area without tripping Koll's wards. Good work Sirah!"

"Sirah's not listening," Dabiro grunted. "She's still wrapped up in the spell you are praising."

"Wake her up," Belwyn retorted. "We have a remote opportunity here before they double back. We need to be inside that cave before they realize they have been tricked."

"They are going to be very embarrassed when they start slicing at illusions," Jasper the tiger hare snorted, sitting on Hinkleburr's shoulder.

"Not to mention that they will be cranky," Mellypip added nervously from his satchel where Runa had tucked him.

"Sirah, come out of it!" Runa begged.

"Mother, wake up," Opaline cried, shaking her.

Sirah's eyes opened and she jumped to her feet. She took a deep breath. "Did it work?" she asked.

"Brilliantly," Belwyn complimented her. "Now move your—"

"Belwyn!" Runa scolded. "We don't have time!" She slung her

satchel over her shoulder, with Mellypip safely tucked inside. "Come on, everyone. We have an evil ritual to crash." She mounted Rono. "Fly!" she shouted.

"Yes, Runa! I fly!" The gryphon took off, joyous for any reason to fly, even a short distance.

Mellypip poked his head out of the satchel. "But Runa, I can't do battle in here!"

"That's right," Runa said. "You'll be safe. Don't argue. Be a good wampu." Runa excitedly kicked her heels against Rono's side. "Faster, Rono!" The black gryphon soared higher and faster.

Sirah flew up alongside. The wind whipped her flaming red hair, and her face was flushed with excitement. Ryen led his Raven Wing. They landed at the cave's mouth to fight the remaining enemy who barred their way. Darcus rode Redstorm, gritty and determined. Even Hinkleburr and his aides, Broda and Talwyn, looked fierce.

The remaining Rashurkeen at the cave entrance ran toward them, wielding their scimitars. The perytons were battle-trained and wasted no time butting the mercenaries with their powerful antlers and kicking with strong hooves.

Belwyn led the familiars, eager to fight for their sorcerer's lives.

Sanura, in her normal small feline size for the ride, leapt from a peryton's back and in midair shifted to her large panther form. A shocked Rashurkeen had little time to react when her claws gripped his throat.

One of the mercenaries charged toward Darcus, bellowing, "Die! Die!"

Darcus thrust the hilt of his sword into the man's veiled face. Mellypip winced at the sound of crunching bone. When he opened his eyes, the assassin was sprawled on the sand.

No longer concerned about alarming the enemy with magic, Sirah and Runa spun about and raised their staves. The wards screeched their warning as they sprayed magic at the soldiers charging them. The mystical wood glowed hotly from the heavy magic it emitted. Sirah's bright orange magic contrasted with Runa's blue-white. The spell Sirah had woven into their staves stunned their victims with only sleep, but it was potent.

Runa and Sirah also took care to shower the gryphons and horses with this sorcery, so it would put them to sleep, and keep them from harm as well as preventing them from attacking.

The kundra beasts were stampeding across the desert away from the chaos. The large, heavy animals were quite fast when provoked.

The sorcery formed a hazy cloud which entangled their adversaries; many of the mercenaries crumbled to their knees; unconscious. Some evaded the sorcerous jet, diving behind boulders or into the cave's mouth.

The perytons quickly steered clear of the stream of magic. It would be embarrassing to fall asleep in the middle of battle. Redstorm had to nudge a scared Rono out of the way. Sirah and Runa dropped many with their sorcery, though several avoided the vapors of sleep. Then the sound of clashing metal and battle cries filled air as the rangers and dwarves fought against the assassins.

Felisia and Belwyn flew through the night air, attacking with their talons.

Dabiro was in his element as he led the ground attack of the familiars, charging and ripping any enemy that dared to cross him.

Little Rosepetal rolled into a ball and shot her quills; though not deadly, it caused the enemy some grief and a loss of concentration.

Sanura, a deadly feline in her panther shape, prowled for prey.

Jasper helped too, deflecting the assassin's attentions by nipping at their feet and crying out warnings.

Buzzy the sloth used magical speed, which also confused the mercenaries as he managed to trip several by running around their feet.

"They know the attacking army is an illusion. They have turned back," Darcus shouted, pointing at the sky.

"Mother!" Opaline cried. "I think we need you."

"Coming dear!" Sirah replied. "The assassins distracted me."

"I'll watch your back, Mother," Opaline cried, her delicate hands clutching a fighting staff.

"Sirah! Where's the spell! We need it now!" Belwyn cried, seeing the Rashurkeen flying closer toward them like a swarm of mad wasps.

But Sirah was already conjuring her sorcery, and pointed her staff high as she whispered her spell. A stream of golden and red magic showered the air. The colors were brilliant and sparkled against the night sky like diamonds.

Arial remained near her sorceress, guarding her against harm should any dare venture too close.

A Rashurkeen jumped a distracted Runa from above, knocking her down. Mellypip was thrown across the sands as she struggled against the assassin. The assassin whipped out a dagger. Mellypip jumped at the attacker, biting his arm. The mercenary tried to shake him off, but a flash of black feathers and talons startled him.

"Get away from Runa!" a strange voice commanded.

Mellypip looked up to see a black eagle diving toward them.

The assassin dropped Mellypip as the strange bird clawed at the man's face with his talons. The black eagle raked at the Rashurkeen, his high-pitched cries sharp. His talons finished their grim work, and with bloody claws, he flew off his victim and landed on a rock next to them.

Runa scooted back and grabbed Mellypip protectively. "Who are you?" she said with a gasp.

"I am Urvuz," the black eagle answered.

"Ashur's familiar!" Runa cried.

~ * ~

Koll was aware when his wards were trespassed by illicit magic. His head snapped up, and he turned to gaze down the dark, rocky tunnel. A flood of images appeared, floating in the air like gossamer paintings. A visual warning from the mystical wards he cast showed the image of Runa and her friends fighting outside the cave! Where are the rest of the Rashurkeen? It raised his anger, but he remained calm. He did not wish to disturb Panthara's concentration.

Why can't anyone kill that girl? Xabral complained.

I must do that myself, but right now I do not have the time. We must watch over Panthara as she summons the Wraith Guardians. Are you enjoying the ritual?

I prefer a bloodbath, but the night's young, Xabral replied.

Be patient. The ritual has only begun. More than blood shall flow.

Koll looked at the altar of chained sorcerers. They too saw the images of Runa and her miserable alliance of good. The look of hope in their eyes, particularly Cathal's, made Koll seethe with fury.

Koll stepped away from the altar. "We have guests outside," he whispered to Azrul

Azrul summoned several of the Rashurkeen observing the ceremony. Hasty words were whispered. Then the assassins quietly bowed, drew their scimitars, and left in reverent silence.

Hopefully to murder the intruders.

Koll noticed Panthara's personal imperial guards that she brought with her were not sent, but then they were not reliable when it came to such things.

Panthara paused, and glanced at Koll with a tinge of fear when she saw Runa's image dancing in the air before Koll's magic made it vanish. He smiled confidently, hoping to calm her. "Continue, Panthara," he commanded.

~ * ~

The sudden appearance of the black eagle stunned everyone. Most of them knew who it was. Urvuz, familiar to Ashur.

Then two white ravens flew to his side. One of them shimmered into Iona.

Belwyn flew to Urvuz and gazed sadly at the eagle. "Old friend, I have missed you."

"And I you," Urvuz said. "But I am here to prevent an evil act, Belwyn. Ashur cannot be raised." Sad eyes glanced at Runa. "It warms my heart to see you, Runa, though I know you do not share that feeling."

Runa looked away. "I'm sorry. I don't know what to say or feel."

"This had better work," Belwyn warned, "or the results won't be pretty."

The cavalry of Rashurkeen riding the gryphons back to the cave came dangerously close.

"Belwyn, please shut up," Opaline said. "Go attack something!"

Sirah's shimmering dome formed, covering the immediate perimeter of the cave mouth. The charging Rashurkeen who swarmed around the magical barrier bounced off. Angry, the sound of their curses penetrated the shield, but they could not pass through her blockade of magic.

Sirah ran to Iona and embraced her. "I've been worried about you!"

"I would not let you face this alone," Iona said.

"More soldiers coming from the cave!" Felisia cried.

Sirah and Runa aimed their staves, washing them down with waves of magic that stunned them into sleep. Many fell in unwilling slumber as the streams touched them. But one of the assassins, untouched by the sleep spell, attacked. He leapt toward Hinkleburr, who was closest. Mellypip cried out.

Talwyn jumped in front of Hinkleburr to block the blow. His brave heart was no match for the strength and size of the assassin. He cried out when the blade pierced him. Gravely wounded, Talwyn fell into Hinkleburr's arms.

The assassin's brutal laugh angered Mellypip. He cried out and ran to help his friends. Darcus quickly scooped him up in his rough, calloused hand. The assassin attempted to strike Hinkleburr with the bloody scimitar. Sure of his conquest, the brute did not see Talwyn's brother, Broda, charge him from the side. With his short blade he managed to thrust it into the Rashurkeen's gut. Darcus finished off the mercenary with swift skill. Mellypip covered his eyes when the blood gushed.

Runa ran to them, and Darcus gently handed Mellypip to her.

"Poor Talwyn," Hinkleburr wept, carrying the bleeding young man to the rocky wall. "Don't die, my lad. Hold on! Please!"

Talwyn's side was bleeding. He was barely conscious and Broda tried to keep him awake. Hinkleburr's hands were red from putting pressure on the wound. Opaline rushed to their side, ripping her skirt into shreds for a makeshift bandage to stop the bleeding. Runa, pale and scared, fought back tears, and stroked Talwyn's head with a cool cloth she manifested through magic.

"Quickly, let me see!" Sirah said. She examined the wound. "I don't think any vitals were cut, but I will close the wound with magic. It will stop the bleeding. It's only temporary but will suffice for now." She held her hand over the gash in Talwyn's side, and a shimmering shell appeared over it. The bleeding stopped.

The earth began to shake.

Runa shivered. "Something is happening."

"We must act now," Urvuz said. "They are shattering the doorways between worlds."

"Go on!" Hinkleburr cried. "Broda and I will stay with Talwyn. Go! Go!"

"Let me shield you!" Sirah said, and her sorcery cloaked the dwarves from enemy eyes.

Another rumble of earth tossed them across the sands. The magical dome that held back the swarming Rashurkeen above them sparked with each assault by the determined mercenaries.

"We must hurry!" Urvuz flew inside the cave alone.

Runa scrambled to her feet, scooped Mellypip up in one hand and her staff in the other. "Let's go! We have an evil ritual to crash," she shouted then followed the eagle into the darkness.

"Damn it! Wait for me!" Belwyn called after them, pursuing them into the darkness.

"Runa!" Darcus shouted after her. "Now I know why Belwyn

complains!" he grumbled.

They all followed and ran down a long winding corridor lined with blue flame torches. The mystical energy was thick in the air. Runa shivered from it. Mellypip never felt so terrified. The whole cave throbbed with magic; it charred the air. The torches lost their flames.

Darkness descended in the cavern.

They stumbled several times. It was so silent! Mellypip could feel the magic literally crisping the air. A sudden wind inside the cave whipped their bodies. A flash of brilliant light stunned them all. Knocked down by its power, Runa pulled herself up, and continued to stumble toward a crimson light that now shimmered in the distance.

They entered the main cave, a mammoth cavern thousands of feet high and just as wide. Many were prostrated on the stony floor in terror, even the Rashurkeen.

Mellypip saw the reason for their fear. Upon an altar that hovered in the air, a red chrysalis blazed with black fire. Within that terrible flame, an ethereal illumination of a man with flowing black hair and dark blue eyes took shape. Panthara knelt before the apparition.

"What is that?" Sirah asked.

"The soul of Ashur," Urvuz said with sorrow.

"Oh no," Runa sobbed, falling to her knees. "We're too late!"

CHAPTER 25

Ashur's soul hovered above the glowing crystal where his mortal body lay, awaiting him to take possession. Runa's heart thundered with fear as she looked at the circle of Sorcerers chained around Ashur. Mellypip saw Cathal and Caliste, and others he had never had a chance to meet but knew them from the descriptions he had heard.

Dabiro's sorcerer, Liat, with his long dark hair and angular features. Buzzy's nervous and thin Riva, and Jasper's fierce Jiana with her tawny hair. Rosepetal's Ulan, skin black as night, exuding both power and grace, and Felisia's red-haired Myrsalian. Their faces blanched with fear and hatred as they gazed upon Ashur's ghostly shape.

Oh Melly, that's Ashur, just like in my dreams, Runa wept. *I hate him. I never thought I would ever hate, but I do!*

Mellypip perched upon Runa's shoulder, terrified not only by the apparition of Ashur, but the very essence of evil in this place. The walls had wicked carvings of demonic beasts. The smoky altar their sorcerers were chained to was made of bloodstone, and it hovered above the sandy floor mysteriously.

Iona turned to them. "The ritual is not complete," she whispered. "Cathal and the others are not bound in crystal for the wraiths."

"Koll! Panthara! Stop this now!" Runa shouted.

Koll turned and glared at Runa with black eyes. "You are too late," he said impatiently.

Koll's followers jumped to their feet and drew their scimitars. "No!" Koll commanded. "Do not touch them. It is fitting they witness this. Runa, you can do nothing now, except watch the wraiths rip their souls out."

Ashur shimmered on the altar. "Who summons me from the Eternal Lands?" Ashur demanded.

"I called you, Father!" Panthara cried with triumph. Arms outstretched with joy as she knelt before Ashur's spirit. "I am Panthara, your devoted daughter! I brought you back from the Otherside. I hold your enemies as an offering to the Wraith Guardians in exchange for your soul! Take your place once again to rule the world you once so nearly conquered!"

The circle of sorcerers chained to the floating bloodstone altar looked upon the spirit of Ashur with hatred.

"They are not bound by a crystal prison for the wraiths," Runa said in a hushed voice.

"Runa, something is off," Belwyn said quietly. "The ritual isn't complete for some reason. That can be very good…or very bad."

"Ashur doesn't look happy to be here, either!" Mellypip said quickly.

Runa broke away from her friends and marched toward the altar of shadow. The Rashurkeen stepped aside at Koll's nod. She leapt to the altar unafraid.

"Damn it girl, wait for me!" Belwyn scolded her as he winged over her head to land on Cathal's shoulder. The other familiars followed, each reuniting with their own sorcerers.

The Raven Wing formed a barrier around the altar, weapons drawn in case the temporary truce gave way. The tension between them and the Rashurkeen was thick. Darcus, Opaline, and Sirah followed Runa to the altar. Only Urvuz remained at the back of the cave, a lonely figure of sorrow.

Runa dropped to her knees to hug Cathal. "I told you I would come," she said. They held each for a heartbeat. "I won't let this happen!"

Azrul mounted the altar. "Get back, foolish girl! We are victorious." His bitter dark eyes were like stones as he laughed at her. "All you can do is watch your loved ones perish. Then we shall cut your throats in sacrifice to celebrate! I am Azrul, Rygon's Supreme High Priest, but I serve Obsydia, the Bloodstone Queen, above all others. Koll is Obsydia's High Priest, and this day is a reckoning. Now that Ashur has returned to us, we can find Her lost tomb. With Obsydia's return a new age of blood will arise."

"All this was to find Obsydia's lost tomb?" Cathal exclaimed. "Are you mad?"

"I'd just say stupid," Belwyn added mockingly.

The cavern shook with violence. The spectators were tossed to the ground and covered their heads as rocks fell around them. Even the cruel Rashurkeen looked afraid.

"The Wraith Guardians are coming!" Koll said with elation.

"Koll!" Panthara cried with panic. "The prisoners…they are not coffined in red crystal the way the ritual stated they would be," Panthara said fearfully. "Something is wrong!"

"They finally noticed," Iona said.

Koll's dark features then twisted with anger and confusion. "But the wraiths will arrive soon! It should have happened by now!"

"See what happens when you gloat," Cathal said.

Xabral slithered toward Azmadu. "What did you do wrong, little lizard? Did I not warn of bad consequences?"

Azmadu hid behind Panthara's robes, quaking. "I did nothing bad! I kept Panthara from being distracted, just like you said," he whined.

Koll ripped the scroll from the Panthara's hands. "What could have gone wrong?" he shouted. If they are not bound by crystal—"

"Then *all* of us are up for grabs when the Wraith Guardians arrive!" Cathal laughed ironically. He tugged at his sorcerer lock. "I think you made a huge mistake, Koll. This sorcerer bane you so diligently bolted around our necks has prevented the scroll's magic from directly affecting us. The ritual may be from the darkest powers, but certain rules still apply. You managed to summon Ashur's spirit, but when the wraiths come, they will take us all unless we get out of here." He turned to Runa. "And that said, get out of here, Runa. Now!"

"Not a chance," Runa said defiantly. "I won't give up."

"Stubborn, isn't she?" Belwyn said affectionately. "We all leave together, Cathal," he added.

"This is ritual is from the Bloodstone Age!" Koll raved. "Obsydia's own priests composed these ancient conjurations! They involve the power of an Eternal, not just magic!"

Cathal shook his head. "You and Panthara aren't Eternals, Koll. Neither are we. You don't have that kind of power to wield, though I am sure you are vain enough to believe it. The sorcery I used to defeat Ashur was similar, but he was not wearing sorcerer bane. You are a dolt, Koll. We all need to leave or we're all a feast for the Guardians of the Gates!" Cathal said as another tremor shook the cave. "I would relish you being taken, Koll, but I have my family and friends to consider."

The weeping of Ashur's soul continued. Cathal looked up at him. "Ashur, why do you weep?"

"Why am I called from Paradise?" Ashur asked. The spirit turned its face toward Runa. "Is that Runa? My daughter? Rualla and I agreed if we were blessed with a daughter, we would name her Runa. Has so much time passed since I entered the gentle gardens of

Paradise? Runa, you have your mother's lovely eyes. Cathal, where is Rualla, my wife?"

Cathal gave him a blistering look. "You killed Rualla, and my wife, Yllia. And a thousand more innocent people, Ashur. How could you be in Paradise?"

Ashur's soul wept louder.

"Panthara, release the prisoners before the wraiths come!" Iona said bluntly. "We all face death if you do not!"

"Father, hurry!" Panthara pleaded. "Take possession of the body we resurrected for you! There is no time!"

"No," Ashur replied in a booming voice.

Koll shoved Panthara out of the way. "Ashur, tell me where Obsydia's ancient temple palace is hidden! You said you discovered it before you died! How do I breach the magic that hides it? Tell me!"

Ashur stopped weeping and gazed at Koll with hatred.

A veiled woman with bronze-colored eyes pushed her way through the crowd of Rashurkeen and climbed the altar. "Beloved husband, come back. I shall be your devoted handmaiden. Our unworthy daughter, Panthara, has summoned you back so you may live again!"

Ashur looked upon her with pity. "Poor Naloia, I am sorry for the pain I caused you. I was anguished when I learned we had a child and stayed away only to protect Panthara. Forgive me. But Rualla was my one and only love." He looked down on Cathal and Runa, "I did not kill them, Cathal. I did not even live to see Runa born." Ashur spun around to Koll. "Koll is behind this tragedy! I had only just learned of Rualla's pregnancy and sent Urvuz home ahead of me to tell Rualla I would be there soon. There was a task I needed to do alone. I wanted to at least see my daughter, Panthara, once—though I could never claim her. On the way there, I met Koll, who told me he found an ancient relic I would be interested in studying. He said he knew of my reputation as a scholar and relic hunter. This unusual relic was in Mowad, he told me, and since it was on the way, I decided to investigate such a rare find. He brought me to this cave, where I found a sarcophagus from the Bloodstone Age upon this wicked altar; concealed for centuries. An earthquake had only recently exposed the entrance again. Its dark beauty fascinated me. When I opened it, the essence of a powerful demon took over my body. I died in that moment and my soul crossed over to the Otherworld. It was not I who did those terrible things. The demon used my body as a host. The creature that did these terrible things was one of Obsydia's demons. Perhaps Koll thought my soul was trapped along with the demon, and I would still hold that knowledge. Well, I don't. And even if I did, I would do nothing to help you, Koll."

Runa dropped to her knees, stunned by the news. "Then—you did not kill my mother or grandmother! You never did any of those evil things!"

"No, my beloved child, I did not kill anyone. I grieve that the demon possessed by body and caused this horror. But my life is done. Release me!"

Runa glared at Koll. "You are the reason for all this suffering, from the beginning!"

Azrul turned away from Ashur. "All this planning and conspiracy was for nothing! This spirit knows nothing. Send it back to Oblivion," he said in disgust.

Panthara stared up at Ashur with confused, tear-washed eyes. "Daddy?" Panthara whispered in a small, childlike voice.

Iona's resonant voice filled the cave. "Panthara, let him return to the Otherside. If you do not, you risk his soul being trapped forever in a limbo between worlds!"

"It's over, Mother," Panthara whispered in a defeated voice. "He doesn't want to stay. Guards," she commanded. "Release the prisoners. Now!"

The Mowad guards obeyed Panthara, unlocking the manacles and freeing the sorcerers. Another quake shook the cave, more violently. Rocks fell all around, and the entrance filled with broken stones, blocking the way out.

"That's not good," Belwyn hooted.

Naloia grabbed Panthara by the throat. "Bring Ashur back, or I will send you to join him!"

Darcus pulled Naloia off Panthara and pushed her off the altar.

Urvuz, Ashur's black eagle familiar, wept harsh tears in the shadows. Cathal's visage of hatred had softened to pity and sorrow. The sorcerers no longer looked upon Ashur with hate, but instead with fresh grief for a lost friend.

"Urvuz, beloved familiar!" Ashur cried when he saw his long lost familiar. "Come to me! Let me say goodbye."

Urvuz, the magnificent black eagle, spread his powerful wings and flew toward Ashur's spirit. But before he reached Ashur, Koll cast a wave of hot sorcery at Urvuz. It struck Urvuz in midair. He plummeted to the ground, his jet feathers smoldering and stained with blood.

"Damn you, Koll!" Ashur cried with anger.

"Why?" Runa cried.

"I do nothing for Ashur's pleasure now," Koll said. "Everything is ruined. All these years of planning, for nothing!"

Runa jumped from the altar and knelt by the wounded bird. Sobbing, she cradled the dying eagle in her arms. "Oh, Urvuz, I am so sorry I never knew you."

"I'm glad I finally saw you, at least once, Runa," Urvuz whispered faintly. He looked up at Ashur's soul. "Take me with you. I have grieved too long, thinking you had become evil. I have been so alone. I missed you."

Ashur spoke with gentle compassion. "We shall journey together, Urvuz. On the Otherside, no sorrow shall live in your heart. Over lakes of silver and green woods we shall soar until we are called into this world again to be reborn."

Urvuz closed his eyes and died in Runa's arms. Tenderly, she carried him to the altar and laid him at the base of the crystal. Her remorse and anger unraveled as she faced Koll, and her staff flared with power. Koll laughed, but before she could react another tremor shook the cave, more violent than the last. Koll was thrown off the altar, and stones covered his body.

"Koll!" Xabral slithered toward his sorcerer. "Koll!"

"Smash the crystal, Runa! Free me!" Ashur begged her passionately. "Know that I will always love you!"

"Yes, Father," Runa said, tears in her eyes. She swung the staff with all her might against the long scarlet crystal. The crystal shattered into a thousand blood red fragments, and the body within it withered to bone and ash. Ashur's soul smiled down upon her with love.

Then she gasped with joy as she saw Urvuz's spirit reunited with Ashur at last, perched upon his arm with pride. Together they floated upon mysterious ether back to the Otherworld.

"Goodbye," she whispered. "I am sorry. I could have loved your memory, instead of hating it. But I will love you now," she promised. "Both of you."

Another violent tremor shook the cavern, interrupting the tender moment of heartbreak. The air erupted with white hot sparks. Red mist swirled around them. The cave tunnels, disrupted by supernatural forces, began to collapse. Rock and sand filled the exits, blocking escape.

Naloia beat Panthara with her own staff. "You ungrateful wretch, I should have destroyed you in my own womb!" Azmadu snapped at Naloia's heels. Iona dragged Naloia off Panthara and struck her with her fist.

The air charged with power. Vortexes began to open above them on the hellish shrine.

"We're too late!" Iona cried. "The Wraith Guardians are here!"

Mesmerized with fear, they watched ethereal gray phantoms with eyes of black flame burst through fiery portals. They darted through the air, angry and hungry for their souls. Cathal and Darcus grabbed Runa and Mellypip, leapt off the altar, and ran toward the blocked exit. The other sorcerers followed on their heels, holding their familiars close.

Ryen led his rangers to form a circle of protection around the sorcerers.

"I'll try to blast through the rocks," Sirah said breathlessly, pulling a frightened Opaline along. "Help me, daughter. This might be a good time for your chaotic sorcery."

The Rashurkeen and Mowad soldiers wailed like children as the wraiths swept down upon them. Their blood-chilling screams reverberated through the ancient cavern. Demons lifted bodies high into the air, wrenching out their souls; what they dropped were little more than withered, broken husks. A few of the Mowad soldiers managed to elude the wraiths, and seeking refuge with the rangers; prostrated themselves and begged for protection. Azrul cowered behind a rock, whimpering. Suddenly, a wraith wrapped around him like a dark cloak, drawing out his life force with savage power before it released him to fall dead upon the rocky floor.

Another demon sped toward Caliste. She stumbled and fell. The wraith whipped around her. Sanura roared at the demon.

"Stay away from her!" Runa shouted, and her sorcery burst forth, sending a stream of light that shocked the wraith attacking Caliste. It backed away, turning its burning eyes toward Runa.

Naloia raged; dancing about like a mad woman. Panthara tried to pull her mother away just as a wraith took hold. The wraith's form brushed against Panthara's arm, and its force threw her across the cavern floor. The wraith cocooned Naloia with vicious speed. A final cry issued from her throat; cut short by death's brutal embrace.

Runa and Cathal huddled near the blocked entrance. Mellypip sucked his paw in terror, and Belwyn sheltered him with his wings. Opaline and Sirah cast sharp waves of magic to break through the blockade of stones.

"The whole tunnel must be buried," Sirah said in frustration.

Iona ran toward Panthara, trying in vain to lift her. One of the rangers rushed to assist her, carrying the dazed Panthara back to their group and laying her down. Panthara stared as Azmadu, huddled next to her, whining pitifully.

A wraith darted through the searing air toward Cathal.

"No!" Runa cried. "You can't have him!" Her hands flared with bright light again, pushing back the specter from its victim.

"Runa, your light!" Mellypip said. "It doesn't like your light!"

"It's true," Cathal gasped. "They find it painful! Quick, Runa, summon a shield with your light. It might give us time!"

Mellypip clung to her shoulder. "Stay close, Melly," Runa whispered, "and, hold on." She struck her staff into the ground by her side and lifted her arms. She called her light, a power which so astonished the Rowan; a fusion of Sorcerer and Drusai. Mellypip felt heartened as the illumination flowed from Runa, casting a shield of brilliant light that enveloped the group. Yet, he worried that, because many were still bound by sorcerer bane, it would not protect them. But, since Runa cast it above and around them, it shielded them from danger.

Runa became a blinding force of radiance as she summoned every ounce of her magical strength. The wraiths buzzed with fury about the created sphere, attacking her shield, but none could breach her dome of light. They howled when they touched her pure, bright essence and, at last, withdrew a short distance.

Sirah, Opaline and Iona worked to bore a hole through the rocks with their magic. Mellypip, inside her mind with the bonding, helped Runa focus, struggling to sustain her waning strength.

"I can't do much more," Runa cried. "I'm so tired."

"She needs help!" Mellypip shouted.

Suddenly, Jadon took Runa's hand. Mellypip sensed his warmth and power bond with Runa's. "I am Drusai, Runa," he whispered. "Take my light. Add it to your strength."

Iona took Runa's other hand, channeling her own light to aid Runa. Then, Sirah took Iona's hand. Opaline and Ryen followed. The combination of Sorcerer and Drusai light essence swelled, and bolstered Runa's unique blended magic. The shield held…grew stronger. Waves of white light expanded throughout the cavern, pushing back the wraiths. Runa's entire body, infused with brightness, became like a star shimmering in defiance against the darkness.

Runa, just a little bit longer, they are leaving, Mellypip said with relief. *The portals are opening up again and the wraiths are going away!*

Swirls of light radiated from her body, feeding the circle of protection that grew wider and wider. The black fires and red smoke dimmed, and the last of the wraiths slipped through the mysterious gates and vanished. The gruesome creatures had returned to their own Otherworld realm.

Drained of strength and bathed in sweat, Runa's brilliant light faded as she collapsed into Cathal's waiting arms.

They had survived.

The cavern fell silent. Only the harsh breathing and sobs of those fortunate few, who looked upon their own death and survived, echoed through the cavern.

EPILOGUE

Mellypip curled up against Runa beneath the tent, counting her every breath. Cathal dipped a cloth in a bowl of water and dabbed her brow. Runa stirred and opened her eyes.

"Grandpa Cathal, she's waking up!" Mellypip chirped happily. He licked her cheeks with his pink tongue.

Runa giggled and gathered him in her arms. She sat up and hugged Cathal. "Oh goodness, how long have I been asleep?"

Belwyn hopped over to her. "Seventeen hours, Missy. About time you woke up!"

"I think fighting Otherworldly demons must be very exhausting," Mellypip said.

Cathal laughed. "We are all safe and sound, thanks to you. But we need to have a long discussion about obedience to one's elders. Gallivanting all over the continent is just not fitting for a girl of your age. Thirsty?"

"Yes, please," Runa said.

He poured a tall cup of water and a chilly burst of magic frosted the glass. She sipped it and grinned. "You added ice!"

Belwyn chuckled. "He just can't stop using magic since they got those damned collars off."

"I have something for you," Cathal said. He took her silver locket from his tunic.

Runa gasped. "Oh, Grandfather, I hoped they hadn't taken it from you!"

He fastened it around her neck. "I never let go of it," Cathal said. "I was keeping it for you."

"Thank you," Runa said softly. "I will wear it always."

Hinkleburr poked his head in the tent. "How's the lovely Runa this morning?"

"Better," Runa said. "How is Talwyn?"

"I will be much better when I figure out how to explain to my King why I am quitting my post as Ambassador in the Ivory Kingdoms, but other than that I am feeling quite plucky."

Opaline entered the tent too, smiling and sunburned. Runa and Opaline embraced warmly. "You look rested," Opaline remarked.

"Yes, now that I actually got some sleep, I do feel better," Runa said. "But I despise all this sand. I feel like I will never be able to wash it off."

"Any dreams?" Cathal inquired.

Runa shook her head. "No…at least none for now. I think I have had enough of them. The Rowan did say I should return to Ilyrra so my abilities could be examined more thoroughly."

"That we will do," Cathal said. "But after we take Koll to Thill and turn him over to the authorities, I think we could all use a much-needed rest at home."

"Home sounds like heaven," Runa agreed wholeheartedly.

"I miss our tree," Belwyn lamented.

"A few of the Raven Wing are going to escort us home," Cathal said.

"I think Jadon is one of the chosen," Opaline whispered to Runa.

Runa blushed and Cathal raised an eyebrow. "What was that little conspiracy about?"

"Why Cathal, it is only girl talk," Opaline replied innocently. "But you must stay with us for a few days at least in Aybarr. It should take that long to get the sand out of our ears. You need to rest up after being a sacrifice. It must be quite tiring. Mother is an excellent cook, too. And you can meet my brother, Taran."

"That is a lovely offer, Opaline," Cathal said. "We would be happy to. Thank you."

Caliste joined them. "We are ready, Cathal. Runa, we thought we would honor them with a proper burial. We were not sure when you were going to wake, or if you wanted to join us."

Cathal stroked Runa's hair. "We planned a ceremony for Ashur and Urvuz while you slept, but if you are not up to it—"

"Yes, I am up to it," Runa said firmly. "My father, Ashur, needs to be honored, as does Urvuz. Ashur has been hated for too long."

Cathal helped her to her feet, and they stepped into the blazing hot sun. The ominous presence of Salomm Mountain would forever be a place of terror and sorrow to all of them, but it was also the place where Ashur's name was cleared.

Runa shielded her eyes against the bright light. She frowned when she saw Koll, though he was chained and bound by sorcerer bane. He was imprisoned in one of the tall metal cages that had confined the sorcerers. Glum and alone, he sat in the wagon.

"I find it insulting the Wraith Guardians missed Koll," Belwyn said.

"Has anyone found Xabral yet?" Runa asked.

"No, the slimy snake was not among the dead in the cave," Belwyn said.

"Don't worry, Runa," Cathal assured her. "We will find him. In the meantime, Koll is going to be transported to Thill, where the council on war criminals will be very anxious to punish him."

The other sorcerers gathered around Runa joyfully. Their family was reunited at last, and despite the heat and dust, they were all smiles. Even Dabiro was docile. Hugs and kisses were exchanged.

They stopped by another tent where Iona and Amun sat with Panthara. Mellypip kept a safe distance from Azmadu, the ornery crill lizard, but could not help but pity him too. A few Mowad guards stood by their fallen queen. Panthara, her blue eyes staring blankly, unresponsive to the gentle ministrations of Iona. Azmadu pawed at her forlornly. "Wake up, my Panthara. Please wake up."

"There's been no change?" Cathal asked softly.

"No," Iona lamented. "She has retreated from the world. The touch of death is hard to bear. I will take Panthara home with me to Thill. I will care for her, and call her daughter," she said gently.

"You have a habit of caring for the wounded and the lost," Cathal said.

"Why do Panthara's soldiers stay?" Runa whispered.

"She was our Queen," one of them replied. "Despite every-thing, she is sacred to our people. She has been good to us, unlike her mad mother, Princess Naloia. When we return to Tuenis, our capital city, we shall say the gods, loving her too much to leave her among mortals, called her to the Otherworld. That is where her spirit is now."

Azmadu pouted. "Don't wanna go to Thill. Cold there. Want my hot rock!"

Amun, Iona's white raven familiar, clacked his beak. "You will go, and learn manners too, young one."

"And we will make you a heated stone to rest upon in the winter," Iona assured Azmadu.

"Good luck to you, Iona," Cathal said sincerely.

"Thank you, Cathal," she replied. "Is it time?"

"Yes," Cathal said. "Perhaps Panthara should remain."

"I believe you are right," Iona nodded. "Captain, please watch over her. I will be gone only a few minutes."

"Yes, Necromancer." The soldier bowed.

"It's so strange," Runa whispered. "I still cannot believe Panthara is my half-sister. But I feel only sorrow for her now. She wanted her father back. Koll was the one who had more ambitious motives."

"Families are often filled with strange relations," Belwyn hooted. They left the tent.

Darcus walked toward them. "We are ready now," he said.

"Thank you, Darcus," Cathal said. The two men shook hands, and then embraced.

"Thank you for taking care of my Runa," Cathal said.

"I will always protect her," Darcus said. "I look upon Runa as a sister."

"That is easy to do," Opaline said, and the two girls squeezed hands.

"This journey led me to a new path in my life," Darcus said. "For that I will always be grateful."

All the sorcerers and their familiars gathered in a circle at the base of the mountain. A new grave, with a large boulder at the head, where the remains of Ashur and Urvuz were laid to rest together. They joined hands in silent prayer. Even Hinkleburr and his aides paid their respects.

The rangers bowed their heads when Runa and Cathal walked hand in hand to the grave.

After a moment, Runa knelt at the grave of her father and Urvuz. "Today we bury Ashur, my father. With him is his familiar, Urvuz. They were good souls. Let the entire world know of Ashur's innocence. Let their souls be at peace in Paradise." Cathal handed Runa her staff and her magic charged its tip as she wrote upon the plain boulder with sorcery. When she was done, this was the epitaph she carved into the stone:

> Here Lies Ashur, Beloved Father and Friend
> And Urvuz, most noble of eagles
> Souls lost to us for so long
> Hidden by darkness
> Your Light now restored
> With Love, we say farewell

Then Runa waved her hand over the grave, and a bed of desert flowers, bright and scrubby, bloomed before their eyes.

"I like the flowers," Mellypip said. "It will keep them protected."

Cathal put his arm around Runa. "Ashur and Urvuz would be proud."

Runa wiped her eyes. "I hope so."

"We have a long journey ahead of us," Cathal said. "Let's go home."

~ * ~

Obsydia stirred in her burning slumber. For a thousand years she slept in a prison of light. Dreams of the dark sorcerer woke her. He would be her salvation from this agony. Odd, for she had exterminated so many mages in her reign of blood and fire. A sigh escaped her red lips.

Soon, he would come to free her.

MEET THE AUTHOR

Avid lover of fantasy, science fiction, and all things joyous and geeky, Verna McKinnon crafts fantasy where heroines take the lead. Her newest release, *Bastard Sorceress*, follows Sabine Fable, a bastard and society outcast surviving in a world where magic is currency. In *The Bardess of Rhulon*, we follow Rose Greenleaf, a Dwarven Bard who flees an arranged marriage only to find danger in a strange new land. The Familiar's Tale series (*Gate of Souls*, Book 1 & *Tree of Bones*, Book 2) focuses on the bond of Runa the sorceress and her familiar, Mellypip, as they battle dark powers to save their world from Obsydia the Bloodstone Queen and Koll the Sorcerer.

The author of several published short stories and many planned novels, she writes obsessively and drinks lots of coffee. More fantasy tales brimming with heroines and magic are coming soon.

Visit http://www.vernamckinnon.com/news.html for updates on Verna and the heroines who shape her magical world.

More Books from WolfSinger Publications

The Seven Exalted Orders – Deby Fredericks

Arkanost has Seven Exalted Orders. No more, no less. When a magus goes renegade in a far-off province, the Mage Lords demand that something be done.

Ryamon is bitter and frustrated. He longs to be a Fire magus; as a Stone magus, he's miserable. If he can bring the rogue back, he has a chance—his last chance—to fulfill his dream.

It's a great plan—until he actually meets Valdira.

Tails from the Front Lines 2: The Thin Blue Line
– edited by Carol Hightshoe

Come meet some of the four-legged members of Law Enforcement who also serve and protect.

Here our authors will introduce you to the brave K9 officers who serve alongside their human partners. They are their eyes, ears, noses and sometimes when necessary they are their shield, protecting others.

Proceeds from this anthology will be donated to the El Paso County (Colorado) Sheriff's Office K9 program in memory of K9 Jinx who was killed in the line of duty on April 11, 2022.

Ring of Fire – edited by Dana Bell

Enter the Ring of Fire, as unpredictable as the land masses shaking a city and volcanoes erupting covering the landscape. Could there be other reasons for these events? Or could these rings be more than a geological location.

They may be dragons playing tricks
or magic portals opened to mysterious realms
or sacrificing the best work of a lifetime.
Perhaps a rescue during a forest fire
or an attempt to raise the dead
or even while attending a high school reunion.

Journeys are taken to far off lands, another world, and through caves, each with their own unique twist.

Each tale presents a new idea on what the Ring of Fire could be. It is more than what many have been led to believe. Pull up a chair and warm yourself by our fires—just don't let yourself get burned.

Coyote – Charles Combee

While camping in a remote canyon in Utah Jim accidently sees an ancient rite taking place with a coyote like creature presiding over it. Now this creature wants Jim dead.

Audrey and her family go hiking in Utah and are attacked by this creature. Audrey is the only survivor, but she is pulled into a strange world of darkness and glass. She is 'rescued' by Jim, but is still linked to the creature, whose hold on her will end in her death unless Jim can find a way to break that link.

In his dreams, or are they ancient memories, Jim begins to learn more about Coyote as well as the magics that previously bound him. But those dreams end without teaching him the full magics. Can he find a way to free Audrey and stop Coyote from once again terrorizing humankind?

Believing is Seeing – Joanna Michal Hoyt

What we believe shapes what we see. Sometimes the stories we tell free us. Sometimes they trap us.

Some people see things their neighbors can't or won't see. Are they inspired? Delusional? Who decides?

As the faithful people of her village cry out for their god's help in disaster, a young peasant woman faces the terrifying possibility that she may be that god.

A time-traveling Jewish refugee visits 21st-century churches and confronts almost unrecognizable versions of himself.

Three troubled people make the dangerous visit to The Library where the maddening stories lodged inside them can be removed— on certain demanding conditions.

Having been warned away from the vacant lot which is said to house a portal to Hell, the new girl in town naturally goes to investigate.

Early in the grid collapse—or apocalypse?—a Christian lesbian farm couple paint "WELCOME" on their barn and await visitors.

An old man in the Terran diaspora enlists in a crusade to save humanity and belatedly wonders if he's on the wrong side.

Step inside these stories and see what you believe—but don't believe everything you see.

Out of the Darkness – edited by Carol Hightshoe

Mental Health issues have long been stigmatized, with those facing them pushed into the shadows, often unable to deal with the darkness they find themselves trapped in.

In this collection, stories explore many types of darkness—Suicidal Ideation, Death from Suicide, Survivor's Guilt, PTSD, Chronic Pain, Chronic Illness, Depression, Death of a Loved One, Secrets, Bullying, and other forms of darkness are explored. Some related to mental health issues and some not, but all of them offer very human perspectives. As in real life, some stories have happy endings and sadly others don't.

We offer these stories of darkness without judgement, but with hope and compassion. Some roads should never have to be traveled—but we understand that for many they are being traveled alone.

Proceeds from sales of Out of the Darkness will be donated to the American Foundation for Suicide Prevention—or more information on AFSP please visit their website at: afsp.org

Never Cheat a Witch – edited by Carol Hightshoe

Magical curses. Arcane revenge. Being transformed into a frog. Things evil witches do to mere mortals who cross their path. But, what if there is more to the story...

Deals made with a witch are magically binding and can bring dire consequences to those who even think about breaking them.

Whether they are seeking revenge for wrongs done to them, helping others or simply trying to live their lives—it is NEVER wise to try and cheat a witch.

Open your spell book and join our authors as they relate tales of witches and mortals. From classic fantasy witches to modern day witches and even the legendary Baba Yaga. Good and Evil as well as every shade of gray in between. And, yes—there is a prince who is turned into a frog.

Blood Bride – Belle Blukat

Dr. Bertram Hoel had ignored all women he'd met until being introduced to Cira Landon at his first Science Fiction convention. Knowing he should ignore the attraction, he still takes the dangerous step to begin a relationship, aware that by doing so he is placing her life in peril.

Cira Landon wrote tales of vampire lovers unaware the handsome scientist she'd just met actually was one. Drawn to him, she finds her life threatened by an old enemy who would do anything to exact his revenge, including kidnapping her and selling her on the black market for rare blood types.

With no other options, Dr. Hoel is forced to appeal to the Elders for assistance, hoping rescue does not come too late for Cira and knowing if she is found, there is but one ancient tradition that may save her life.

Return of the Black Witch – M.R. Williamson

One should not expect to slap the hand of an old crone and expect to walk away without at least a limp. The old witch Ethrel Ibenus is up to her tricks again and this time they've turned deadly. But where did her spirit go after Professor Martin shot her with his wee pistol?

Now, all are looking for the crone's familiar, Seleene. But the big timber wolf cannot be found. The search for the spirit of Ibenus now begins in earnest. Will Entwhistle and her Dwarves be able to help? Perhaps the Green Witch Pereen will be able to use a crystal derived from one of the Witch's own spells will do the trick. Fearing failure, Entwhistle improvises a plan 'C', the use of a mythical creature once thought to be long dead.

Time Capsules – edited by Carol Hightshoe

Time Capsules—history and mystery—a gift or a message from the past to the future.

Messages that can easily be misunderstood.

What were the reasons for passing along a pair of pink, fuzzy handcuffs?

A glass vial containing a perfect dandelion puff?

A Japanese Katana?

A red and blue scarf?

A wooden spoon?

What magic do these items contain? What stories do they tell?

From the past to the future. Mysteries and meanings abound within these pages, as well as reminders of the things people find precious. What will you find?

US/THEM – edited by Carol Hightshoe

US/THEM – THEM/US

Fear of the Other breeds hatred of the Other

They aren't like us—so they must be bad…inferior… dangerous…

Humans are by nature social animals, but we tend to bond with other humans with whom we have something in common: beliefs, experiences, likes and dislikes, etc.

With the expansion of humans across the planet, it seems that, even as our numbers grow, we find ways to whittle our groups into ever narrower, specialized, and exclusive blocks. We target the Other for the most minor differences and interpret everything from THEM as an insult or an attack.

Within these pages you will witness hatred, intolerance and fanaticism as well as love, understanding and acceptance. Most of all, I, and the authors, hope you discover stories that will cause you to pause and think before condemning someone as being THEM and not US.

Crunchy with Ketchup – edited by Carol Hightshoe

It has been said that one should never meddle in the affairs of dragons—for you are crunchy and taste good with ketchup.

Come enter the dragon's lair.

Take your chances with other would-be heroes and heroines who decide to face off against one of the biggest, baddest predators ever.

Witness a dragon civil war.

Hear the true story of the Battle of New Orleans.

Find out what it's like in the belly of a dragon.

Discover why cats can spell disaster when stealing a dragon's egg.

Meet a group of dragon riders who protect us from nuclear devastation.

Follow legends of modern dragons, only to find something very unexpected.

And more…

So enter in **BUT** tread carefully—remember you are crunchy and taste good with ketchup.

Crunchy with Chocolate - edited by Carol Hightshoe

It has been said that one should never meddle in the affairs of dragons—for you are crunchy and taste good with chocolate.

Come enter the dragon's lair and roll the dice. Within these pages you will still meet some of the biggest, baddest predators ever—but if you are lucky, you will also discover some that have a sweeter side.

Meet a dragon with a soft spot for hard luck cases and another who is a hopeless romantic.

Enjoy a musical battle between a dragon and the specter of one of the greatest guitarists to ever play.

Meet a dragon in trouble with other magical creatures because he enjoys hanging out with human children.

Join a mother and daughter and their teams of dragons on a dangerous cross-country race.

Reconnect with an imaginary friend—who is not so imaginary and escape the isolation of the pandemic.

And more…

So enter in **BUT** tread carefully—remember you are crunchy and taste good with chocolate.

Time Out – Jamie Mason

After the war, Chris's family fled to Earth. Chris grew up believing he was human. But his parents' unique cruelties soon awaken him to the truth: he and his family are Chronox, alien beings capable of time travel, now hidden among humans.

Dissatisfied with refugee life, Chris's father decides to break the Chronox pact and use time travel to gain dominion over their human hosts. Chris resists, sabotaging his father's efforts to create a working time machine for the military. In punishment, Chris is placed in the ultimate "time out" by being flung back and imprisoned within the pre-digital past of the 1960s. There he experiences a glimmer of acceptance among Laura, Theodore and Yogi Joe, whose friendship inspires him to awaken his repressed Chronox powers and return to the future to set things right.

The battle-lines are drawn. On one side, Chris. On the other, an implacable alliance between time-traveling aliens and the U.S. military. A frightened, shattered boy who has never known love must begin a desperate race through time to stop a global genocide.

Bast's Chosen Ones and Other Stories – Dana Bell

Long ago in the land of the flooding Nile and sweeping sands, Bast created warriors called the Chosen Ones. They are her warriors. To them has been given the responsibility of protecting cats, whether on Earth or other worlds. Not always an easy task since often an ancient evil lurks, ready to pounce.

Not all felines walk in the goddess's domain. Some live in the far reaches of space, battling beside their humans or walk in lands long thought legend. Others tell their own version of human stories, walk as envoys of the creator, or appear as ghosts.

These cats walk where others dare not and do not prefer the comfort of cuddly lap warmers. Rather, they wish adventure, in present day, the past, or the far future.

Beyond Big-G City – S.D. Matley

The year is 2025 and Hermes is on the Olympus, Inc., hot seat. He has two short years to halt climate change before the irretrievable tipping point is reached, an existential threat to mortals and immortals alike.

David Bernstein embarks on a quest to learn about his unnamed mortal father. Assisted by would-be girlfriend, Cleo Petra, David scours the Middle East for clues that lead him to Rome, Italy, and points beyond.

Jim Smith observes unsettling changes in Stella, his mental health client, and fears an evil force, The Power, has secretly escaped its prison to terrorize the City of Mount Olympus once more.

And what of Seattle? Clifford Essex leads a desperate race to solve the riddle of an unstable seawall, poised to crumble and take a major transit tunnel with it.

From Mount Olympus to the Underworld, from Petra, Jordan, to Seattle, Washington-much is afoot Beyond Big-G City!

And more – check out our books at www.wolfsingerpubs.com

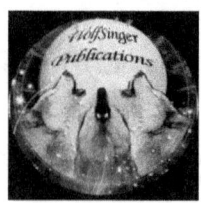